KILLER HEART

A Vermont Mystery

Other novels from the
Maverick Hearts collection
by Carolyn Haley

Wild Heart
An Equestrian Romance

Cosmic Heart
A Paranormal Romantic Suspense

KILLER HEART

A Vermont Mystery

Carolyn Haley

Borealis Books

This is a work of fiction. Names, characters, places, and incidents are either the product of the author's imagination or are used fictitiously, and any resemblance to actual persons living or dead, business establishments, events, or locales, is coincidental.

First U.S. print edition published by Borealis Books
East Wallingford, Vermont, USA
www.carolynhaley.wordpress.com
ISBN 978-0-9887191-5-6

Cover design:
Leslie Noyes Creative Consulting, Inc.
Bennington, Vermont, USA
www.lmncreative.com

Cover image:
Oleh Slobodeniuk (iStockphoto)

Published in the United States of America

Dedication

To the Green Mountain Goddesses and supporting team

"Some people were born unsupplied with a human conscience and those people needed killing."

—from *News of the World*, Paulette Jiles (2016)

"The earth was wonderful and life was good,
but everywhere...there had always been and always
would be weak, greedy, and evil men.
Perhaps they balanced life.
Anyway, they had to be met and killed."

—from *The Arizona Clan*, Zane Grey (1958)

CHAPTER 1

Over the years of our friendship, Luce has been searching for the proper term to describe what ails me, so she can help fix it.

She favored "agoraphobia" after I reversed from being a girl happy to travel solo around the world to someone who only goes out when necessary and feels compelled to have an escape route from every location.

When she realized my malaise was more about people than places, she decided I must have "anthromopophobia," and I really needed to get out of the city. She had already pushed me out of office work, but that wasn't doing the trick.

My loss of joie de vivre and ambition led her to think "clinical depression"; then she figured "premature menopause" when my desire for sex and romance disappeared, too.

I poo-poohed them all when I found the right word: "weltschmerz," which my dictionary defines as "mental depression or apathy caused by comparison of the actual state of the world with an ideal state." I did not tell Luce that my weltschmerz had curdled into misanthropy—"a hatred or distrust of humankind"—because by then it was turning dangerous.

Yet I resisted her urgings to get professional help. My state comes from disillusionment, not a chemical imbalance or psychic trauma. Disillusionment can't be fixed by drugs, therapy, or religion, unless you want to numb yourself to living, or replace disillusionment with delusion.

No, the only cure for weltschmerz is to keep on keeping on. That's my choice of recovery program, based on the maxim "Where there's life, there's hope." You don't have to feel hope to recognize that you'll never feel it again if you close the door to possibility. I'd slammed shut just about every door when dumb luck proved that the impossible can sometimes happen, which reignited hope in my broken heart.

That's why I'm now the astonished owner of a little house in a Vermont hilltown—found for me by Luce. My new life contains just me, my furry children, and my writing, with Luce and my editor, and a few remaining cyber-friends, my only links to the outside world. I've jettisoned everything known to trigger my demons, and created a refuge where I can salvage what goodness is left in myself and life.

Unfortunately, doing this results in an isolation most people consider anti-social and abnormal—particularly exuberant extroverts like Luce. But she refuses to give up hope on me, and I hope to not let her down.

* * *

I stopped writing, clicked off the kitchen light, and put my slippered feet up on the table with a contented sigh. Outside, the third consecutive day of rain battered the roof; inside, the first official day of my new life promised twenty-four hours of rest. Everything vital was finally done, delivered, installed, and connected. The only thing missing was cell-phone service, which didn't exist in these hills so I could consider it crossed off the list. I was ahead of schedule for resuming work tomorrow on the latest Katy Fox novel, so today I could unpack nonessentials at leisure, or just kick back with a good book written by somebody else.

I decided to split the difference—read in the morning, unpack in the afternoon—and rose to refill my coffee. Its aroma didn't quite mask the eau de fresh paint throughout the house. I had cracked open most of the windows when I'd gotten up, but now more chill was coming in than odor going out. I did a circuit to close the windows, assigning priority to cartons and piles as I passed them.

Back in the kitchen, I looked through the rain-streaked window beside my chair. For the first time since moving in, I could see across the side yard. Somewhere beyond the weeping clouds out there lay a mountain vista, which I might see tomorrow if the forecaster was right. That small hope brought a smile as I settled back into my padded chair with fresh coffee and a halfway-read book.

But I couldn't stick with it, distracted by the sounds of silence. Instead of honking horns, farting buses, thumping bass notes of rap and rock music, wailing sirens, and arguing neighbors, I heard the rain changing tempo and the refrigerator starting and stopping. My chair creaked when I shifted and my mug thumped when I put it down between sips. I even heard tires hissing on the road out front, so intermittent that each car drew attention. I could tell what direction it came from and track its approach, passage, and departure. In its wake rain and refrigerator noises settled in again until the next vehicle came along, five, ten, twenty minutes later, and tugged my hearing outside.

After half a dozen of these passings, I found myself tense and waiting. I could have eliminated the suspense by booting up my sound system or setting up audio or video streaming on my computer—radio and television having long ago been abandoned; instead, I considered moving to the armchair by a front window so I could see what went by.

I didn't have time for the switch before a car entered hearing range from the kitchen side. Unlike its predecessors, this one slowed then thump-splashed onto Rock Maple Road. That dead-end dirt lane formed the side border of my twenty acres. I pivoted to look through the kitchen window and saw a flashing yellow light atop a black squarish blur go by. Ah, the mailman's Jeep.

I relaxed and went back to my book. Just as I got absorbed into the story, the Jeep growled and whined back into hearing range. A moment later it bucked by the kitchen window at twice the rate it had passed the first time despite hub-deep muck caused by late-melting snowpack saturated with April rains. But then, instead of pushing for refuge at the paved intersection, it cut the corner across my front lawn!

I yelped and scooted to the front window. The Jeep gouged ruts into the grass and jerked to a halt across my walkway. The driver, bug-eyed, sprang out and pounded on my storm door.

"Please—I've got to make an emergency phone call!" he yelled through the glass.

I heard him even through the inner wood door, where I moved to peer at him through the peephole. Shocked into muteness, I switched off the alarm system and unlocked, despite all social programming against opening to strangers. If I hadn't known about the cell reception problem, I wouldn't have done it. But he had little choice but me if he needed help fast.

At least I knew this stranger by reference, and understood that something dire had happened. That put me into emergency mode, shutting down all emotions even though my mind sparked and sizzled with questions.

I pointed him toward the kitchen. He crossed the living room in three strides, adding muddy footprints and puddles to what the movers had left behind. When he spotted my wall phone just outside the kitchen doorframe, he grabbed the handset and punched 9-1-1 with a shaking finger.

I pushed past him to start a new pot of coffee, unsure what else to do. I gave him space but not privacy, for whatever his drama was, it had abruptly become mine. Resentment flamed, but I throttled it back to retrieve and nurse later. Curiosity, I allowed to flow.

He was saying into the phone, "Yes, I want to report a murder."

What!

I clunked the coffee pot onto the counter lest I drop it. Between the muted gobble on the line and the mailman's responses, I caught the key words: *Ned Cavendish, gunshot, Jake Baldwin, Rock Maple Road.*

The mailman closed with, "Okay, I'll wait here," and hung up.

At that, I opened a cupboard and reached for the bottle of top-shelf whiskey my editor had given me as a housewarming present. I plopped a glug into my mug then poured a full shot for the mailman to jolt his spinning eyes back into focus. It was bad enough that the type of mess I had sought to escape had penetrated my sanctuary; I couldn't handle that plus a stranger who might ramp up into hysterics. Even odds for it to be him or me.

He threw the shot down in one gulp then gasped, "Thanks." Almost instantly, color returned to his cheeks and intelligence into his eyes. I sensed his adrenaline ebbing as he began to register his surroundings. It changed him from an intrusion into a man.

I pulled up short and looked at him, seeing a male of my own physiotype: forty-ish, plainly pleasant-looking, brown haired, brown eyed. Average height-weight-mass, apparent good health. Both of us wore workaday clothes, neither flashy nor grubby, and still stood with our drink vessels in hand.

He came conscious of himself under my regard and flashed a sheepish smile. Passing his glass into his left hand to extend his right, he said, "Hi, uh, I'm Ned Cavendish. Sorry to bust in on you like this, but you're the closest phone..."

"I know. It's okay." I held out my hand in response. "I'm Jane Brown."

"I know. I've got your mail outside."

We shook. His hand was dry, which surprised me given his initial distress and soggy clothes. The strength and thickness of his hand surprised me on another level that shook ghosts loose, but I shoved them back, too.

I pulled my fingers away and thumped into my seat at the kitchen table. "What happened?"

He placed his glass on the counter and shook his head. "Guy down the road got shot. I just found him. Corpse lying there with a hole in his chest."

I made a noise and drained my mug. The whiskey bit going down but shuddered me back to attention.

Ned snapped off his ballcap and started pacing. "Looks like Jake opened the door and got blasted point-blank. That's what caught my eye—the door wide open. In the rain. That old bastard would never let the heat out or anybody in. But his truck was still in the dooryard yet nobody around. I looked around and shouted. Finally I went up to the front door and found him on his back in the hallway."

He gulped and looked away, letting me fill in the blanks. *Gunshot to the chest at point-blank...?* I felt my breakfast turn over inside.

The whiskey bracer on top of coffee didn't help in the nausea department, but it had steadied both of our nerves. We needed comfort food to go the next step, something that went down easy, like toast and scrambled eggs.

Ned was still dripping and looking white around the eyes, so I said, "Here, put your jacket on that hook and have a seat."

I gestured back toward the door then forward to the table still hosting my breakfast dishes and book. Also my recovery journal. Even though the notebook was closed and unlabeled, I slid it under a paper pile then snatched up the dishes and put them into the sink.

He obeyed like a robot, his mind still out of sync with his body. When he pulled out the second chair at the table, Tommy the Tiger, my brown tabby with white paws, leaped off the seat cushion and shot out of the kitchen.

Ned startled then laughed. His face suddenly cohered, fitting the smile lines etched into it. His eyes gained an amber spark.

"Thank you, Miss Brown, though I was hoping to meet you some other way. Let me get your mail. Oh crap, I've got to call my supervisor—I'm off the route till the cops get here. Might be all day so I need someone to cover. Can I use your phone again?"

"Of course."

While he called, I tidied up and pulled out bread and butter. My actions were automatic while I recalculated my plans. It required another harsh stamping down on what I was truly feeling, and accepting that my schedule could absorb one more day of disruption. Once rationality retook the reins, I acknowledged that if I was going to succeed in my transformation, I needed to practice easing another person's troubles. Wise people through history had counseled that the best way to spiritual peace was to look outward and give. I'd been turned inward for so long that I'd forgotten how to help anyone else. Here was my opportunity to start learning.

Ned hung up the phone and turned to me. "All set. Thank you. Do you want me to wait in the car?"

Yes.

No. Although I deserved the privacy I'd worked so hard to attain, he didn't deserve banishment into the weather just because he'd found a dead body on his route. His needs trumped mine by a mile this morning, and I was touched by his awareness of how a strange man imposing on a strange woman alone in a house in the boonies might be received.

"Stay here, that's fine," I said, on the fence between truth and falsehood. "I'm just unpacking. Do you want something to eat or drink?"

He tried to decline, but I made him some toast anyway. All the while I visualized what he must have found and speculated as to how he'd felt, wondering how I'd react in the same situation. Wondering how a character in a novel would react, first in my adventure series for teenage girls, then in a romance, then in a mystery. *What if...*

Ned snarfed down the toast and fresh coffee then switched back to business. "Thank you, Miss Brown. That did the job. I'm thinking I should block the road with my Jeep or something—at least get it out of your yard."

Before I could reply, a new vehicle announced itself outside the windows.

Ned jumped up to look. I peered over his shoulder. It was the first installment of the crime-processing team. Ned identified each party as it headed down Rock Maple Road. The local rescue squad, sans lights and siren. Next a Vermont State Police car. I expected the trooper to stop here first to interview the guy who found the body, but instead he churned down the road to verify that a body was really there.

The trooper must have radioed his boss, because while we debated whether Ned should follow or stay put, or go outside and flag someone down, a second VSP vehicle lunged around the corner. Also no lights or siren, and wipers slapping across the windshield at a speed the driver tried to match. Instead, he decelerated abruptly in a mud patch, then bulled his way through spewing a rooster tail of wet glop as the vehicle wallowed. When he reached the drier upslope, he accelerated with a roar.

"Crap," Ned muttered. "I was worried about what tracks I might destroy, but these guys will obliterate them."

I hadn't thought of that. There was only one way in and out from the murder scene, with evidence already compromised by the weather.

I had settled enough for my brain to start whirring. It was visualizing a corpse with a bloody hole in its chest, lying in his hallway till he decomposed, save for the luck of Ned's curiosity and concern. That impressed me, because I wouldn't have checked on the open door.

I turned to him. "How long do you think…the guy's been there?"

Ned kept his face to the glass. "I last saw him Friday morning."

I shivered. It being Monday, that meant a weekend window wherein the killer must have driven past my house. I could have seen him, except I didn't. That's assuming he'd not walked in through the forest. Regardless, the rain had done a number on his tracks, making the killer either very lucky or a good planner.

Ned and I peered out the windows as an SUV labeled "Marble County Sheriff" joined the crowd. When it came back from the dead end and parked across the entrance to Rock Maple Road with all lights on, Ned returned his ballcap to his head and said, "I think that's my cue."

He yanked on his jacket and marched outside. I followed, stuffing my arms into a hooded slicker and feet into rubber shoes. Crossing his tire ruts reminded me that leaping out of my chair when he drove in had torqued my bum knee, and what had been a twinge at the time was working into a throb. I ignored it and pressed on.

I caught up to find Ned already talking into the officer's open window. Ned straightened at my arrival, tilting his head toward the house to signal, *About-face, you won't get any information here and it won't look good to try.*

The officer said, "Please wait inside, ma'am. A detective will talk with you shortly."

It was more longly than shortly, but investigators did eventually come. During the wait I asked Ned, "Who is Jake Baldwin, and why would anyone shoot him?"

Ned hesitated as we watched the county deputy reposition his SUV to admit a second State Police trooper in an unmarked green sedan. "Town creep, you might call him," Ned finally said. "Not known for anything good. Probably has a long list of enemies, though why anyone waited this long to take him out is a good question. And those guys"—he gestured out the window at a passing unmarked sedan in darker green—"are the ones who get to find out."

He straightened and guessed aloud, "They'll be coming back for us."

"Us?" I froze.

"Well, me. But you, too, since you're here and could've seen something."

"But I didn't."

"They'll need to know that."

I scowled, again feeling angry resistance rise. None of this was my business. There should be no official interest in me. I'd exhausted all my resources to close the world out, yet here it was, following me, shoving its ugliness in my face.

I wanted to shove it back—hard—and slam and bolt the door on it. I would have done so if a nice guy who had the bigger problem for the day wasn't stuck with me in my house. While he stayed at the window, watching officialdom organize itself to investigate a murder, I paused behind him, inhaled to the bottom of my lungs, and chanted silently, *Save it for the journal.* That's what it was for. Every day. Ten times a day if necessary.

So I kept my mouth shut and joined Ned in spectating. He was impressively calm for a man who might be arrested. I knew from reading that the person discovering a body was always a suspect. I should be worrying about that—had I just let a murderer into my house?—or else feeling sympathy for Ned, who'd had to face the gory results. I was nothing more than an innocent bystander, moving in on the wrong day. I should be caring about the person who lost his life, and feeling sympathy for the living people who had to sort it all out in the rain and muck.

The next wave arrived, a crime-scene unit with the fancy gear and experts needed to process the site and corpse. They lumbered past and barely made it up the hill to where Rock Maple Road snaked out of sight.

At that point, the substitute postman arrived in a white Subaru wagon with its own blinking yellow light on top. Ned went out to hand off his envelopes and parcels. The officer on duty at the intersection prevented any lingering, so the Subaru driver went off to spread the news.

Ned returned inside, taking off his jacket and hat after plopping my first mail to the new address on my table inside the door. On top lay what might be a letter from Jim, with funny paper and foreign postage. I ignored it for later.

Ned toed off his shoes before rejoining me at the kitchen window. "We have to keep sitting tight until the State Police talk to us."

I muttered an obscenity under my breath, then we resumed vigil at the window. The rain still hammered down.

The medical examiner and funeral home van took their turns down Rock Maple Road. Out on the pavement, a few passers-by hovered in their cars, with some getting out to talk to the county officer, whom they'd probably known since kindergarten.

A media van came along and tried to gain access, but the road guard shooed them away. Then shooed them more forcefully after the van pretended to move on then parked on the shoulder just past my place, and reporters headed back for my door. I wondered, had someone called them with a heads-up, or did they sit listening to police scanners and run out when cackling words told them something had happened worth investigating? Ned surmised a combination of both.

The first State Police car to return, the dark-green unmarked, slithered up to the intersection and paused for the county cop to move. Ned sucked air through his teeth and said, "Here we go."

The car hooked a right onto the pavement and a second right into my little stub of a driveway. At that I hissed through my own teeth, suddenly recognizing that I was a stranger in town to be interviewed by the police about a murder in my figurative backyard, within camera range of reporters. There went my dreams of living in quiet obscurity. The knot that had been forming in my stomach turned into a fist.

As the unmarked's doors slammed, I conquered the urge to hide with the cats and instead unbolted the inner front door again. No need to deactivate the alarm since I hadn't turned it back on after first admitting Ned. He hung behind me as I opened to a pair of men standing shoulder to shoulder under my front rooflet, wearing rain coats over weary suits with mud splattered up to their knees.

"Good morning, ma'am, I'm Detective Lieutenant Johnson of the Vermont State Police, and this is Detective Sergeant Greene."

He pulled ID from an inner pocket and held it up for me to peer at through the glass. It looked real enough; how would I know? I believed him without it. No pretend-cop criminal could arrange the scene we'd been watching. I unlocked the storm door and stepped aside for them to enter.

They stopped right inside the door on the runner I'd put down for the movers. Their presence felt ominous but not threatening.

"As you know," said Detective Lieutenant Johnson, "there's been an incident down the road, and we'd like to ask a few questions. Ma'am, are you the homeowner here?"

"Yes. I'm Jane Brown."

"May I see some ID, please."

I rummaged for my purse and then inside it. Detective Greene watched me; to make sure I didn't pull a weapon, I supposed.

Detective Johnson turned to Ned. "And you, sir, I understand, discovered the body?"

"Yes."

He knew not to reach for the wallet in his back pocket until Johnson nodded.

"We'd like to take your statements, please. Ms. Brown, do you have a second room here."

Not a question. They could see for themselves without moving, but I understood they were giving me the choice of which room with a closed door to use for private talking. I chose my office, which, though still a mess, was immediately to hand, as well as my stronghold. The Detective Sergeant entered with me while the Detective Lieutenant kept Ned in the living room.

Detective Greene and I remained standing. He took out a notebook and opened, "I gather you just moved in."

"Yes, sir."

Did I have to say *sir*? Would I seem impudent if I didn't?

"And when did you arrive?"

"For good? Saturday morning."

"Just yourself."

An assumption he wanted clarified. I said, "No partner, if that's what you mean."

He waited. I added, "I've been here many times since the closing a month ago to check on renovations, but Saturday is when the moving guys brought my big stuff and I finally took occupancy." Jeesh, I sounded like the Realtor.

He jotted then looked up. "Where did you move from, Ms. Brown?"

"New York."

Did I have to specify city or state? He didn't seem to care; it was far enough to be the moon.

"And do you have any connections with North Allenburg that led you to move here?"

I shrugged. "I used to ski around here, so I know the area and like it."

True, but the real reason was more complicated. Luce, who owned a second home in Orton, the next town over, had spent months scouring the area for a simple, reasonably priced sanctuary for me and three cats within easy driving distance of her part-time availability. I'd based at her Orton condo when my lease in the city had expired weeks before I could move into my new place. I didn't think the cops needed to know that, so I stuck to the minimal response.

Detective Greene finished jotting down my statement. "Did you see or hear any vehicles entering or leaving the road since you arrived?"

"Sorry, no. Between the rain and all I had to do, I would have missed a parade."

His lip twitched in a hastily repressed smile. I did same, feeling duty bound to remain somber.

To help him out, I added, "I hear background traffic on the main road, but this morning was the first time I've heard any vehicle turn in." I thumbed over my shoulder toward Ned on the other side of the door.

"So you've not seen any of your neighbors on Rock Maple Road."

"Not yet. Just…"

Oh hell. I'd have to tell him. "Just the guy I think was Jake Baldwin, last fall, when I was first checking out the neighborhood. He came out into his yard when I was turning around at the dead end, and I waved, but he waved back with a shotgun."

"Did he fire it?"

"No. I took it as a 'keep off' gesture and got out of there."

Nod, followed by jotting. "Did you ever encounter him again?"

"No."

"Do you know anyone who might want to hurt him?"

Yeah, the whole town—according to what Ned had insinuated. But I knew nothing for a fact, so shook my head. When Detective Greene looked up at me, I verbalized, "No."

He held my eye. "But you still moved here after being threatened by a neighbor. Why is that?"

I stifled a jerk. Good lord, did he see me as a potential suspect? No, no, he was just doing his job.

Trying to sound reasonable instead of tart, I said, "I come from the city, Detective, where neighbor means same building, or maybe the one next door, not a mile away. A hermit with a shotgun, along with lack of cell service, did give me pause about buying here. But since the house suits my needs, I figured a mile was enough distance from a creep if we both minded our own business. Being chased off gave me the impression he wanted to mind his own, and minding mine was the whole point of coming here."

Detective Greene allowed himself a sniff. "Did you happen to hear any sounds like gunfire?"

"No, just the rain."

The unrelenting rain. I was starting to wish I'd cranked up the stereo to drown it out. I sure didn't want to explain to a policeman why I'd opted for a quiet house. Besides, could I really be expected to hear a gunshot a mile away when I was indoors with the windows closed, in a drilling downpour?

More relevant was the actuality of guns. It hit me at that moment, with a cold sizzle in my diaphragm, that I hadn't yet dealt with the guns in my possession. They were still deeply packed, and I hope-hope-hoped the detective wouldn't ask about weapons. It seemed a logical question, in the circumstance, and I didn't know whether to lie or tell the truth if he asked if I owned any firearms.

To my relief, either Detective Greene didn't think me having firearms was germane or he considered me beyond suspicion. He wrote a final note then asked, "Are you in residence full-time now?"

At my nod he said, "Please provide your contact information."

Since we were in my office, I was able to turn and put my hand on a box of business cards. Detective Greene arched one eyebrow when he read the one I gave him.

"So you work at home."

"Yes."

"And you're a professional writer?"

That's what the card said, but he needed it confirmed. Anyone could print business cards calling themselves anything. For all he knew, I could be running scams through my computer. He was wise not to take me at face value, considering what I knew about myself and what he probably knew about people. I expected he would research me online later.

I told him, "I write series fiction for a New York publisher. Under a different name."

He looked at the card again. "Jane Brown a.k.a. Susan Silver."

"Yes."

He nodded and inserted my card into his notebook upon flipping it closed. "Thank you, that's all for now."

He gestured for me to precede him back into the living room, just as Detective Johnson finished with Ned. Johnson said, "Please call us if you remember, see, or hear anything that might help, no matter how unimportant it may seem."

"Of course," Ned and I chorused. Ned followed with, "Are we clear to go?"

"Yes. We'll contact you if we need you."

The detectives nodded and headed for the door. Before departing into the rain, now just a spatter, Johnson paused. "Thank you for your time, and sorry for this welcome into our state, Ms. Brown. But both of you, think about keeping your doors locked."

We murmured thanks and assurances, then I closed the storm door behind them. Through it I saw the media van still parked on the shoulder, while some of the lookers had gone home.

I closed them out of sight with the inner door and locked it by reflex, even though Ned would be leaving soon. The sooner the better, as my control was slipping and I didn't want him to see my volcano erupt.

Unaware that anything was brewing beyond our front-row seats at a murder mystery, Ned again donned his jacket and ballcap, then turned to me. "I'm going to attempt getting home. Lead those reporters away from you, if nothing else." He smiled.

I smiled back, warmed by his considerateness. Perhaps I should say cooled by his considerateness, as the surprise of it dropped my internal boil to a simmer.

I knew people who'd be thrilled by proximity to scandal or drama, and would volunteer to be quoted in the newspaper or interviewed on TV. Ned not only showed no desire for such attention, but also seemed to sense my aversion to it and was offering to deflect it. Wow—that was downright gentlemanly, especially given his awkward position. Or was I reading him wrong, and he wanted the spotlight for himself?

No. I looked again into his eyes and saw kindness, not ego. In appreciation, I expanded my smile to a full-tooth grin. Normally I held my lips partway closed to hide the two front fakes, the originals having been knocked out in a skiing accident that also ruined my knee. The dental work was good enough to pass muster with all but the most observant critics, but I still felt self-conscious about it.

Dropping that self-consciousness was something I could give back to him. I expanded it to a sincere, "Thank you."

He nodded, still holding my gaze, and touched the bill of his cap. "I'll come back in a day or so to resod those ruts."

"You don't have to—"

"Yes, I do. I'll see you then. That is"—he paused with his hand on the door—"if I'm not arrested."

When my mouth fell open, he added with a wink, "Thanks for the tea and sympathy, Jane. And, um, welcome to North Allenburg."

He unlocked the door and popped out to his Jeep, entering it from the passenger side because it was one of those right-hand-drive versions used by mail carriers. As he drove off, the house closed around me in sudden quiet. My safe haven, when I relocked the doors, felt more like a cell.

CHAPTER 2

Is it paradox or irony that everything I worked so hard at removing from my life broke back into it as soon as I got away?

Arrrgggghhhhhh!

I had to hit the dictionary again to make sure I got the right word. Turned out to be irony: "a state of affairs or events that is the reverse of what was, or of what was to be expected: a result opposite to and as if in mockery of the appropriate result."

I feel very mocked right now.

Other people might blame the irony on God, gods, or karma. Maybe they're right. All I know is, twenty-four hours ago, I was queen of my cocoon. Now I see how stupid I was to think the world can be shut out by the click of a lock and pull of the blinds.

I've known that all along from working on the Internet, but there I have control of the on/off button. Likewise the TV. Not true with reality.

My first step in recovery was to banish the garbage that comes in through the media. I'm convinced that half the world's problems come from the that source. What used to be news reportage and entertainment has turned into propaganda, fear-mongering, and misinformation. Millions, maybe billions, of people guide their lives according to that flow.

It works both ways: Righteous causes can be promoted, just as flames of hatred can be fanned. Fascinating and useful information can be had instantly at one's fingertips. The problem is it's too easy to get information. You used to have to work for it, learn how to do it, and the people who provided it had to meet standards of capability, education, and performance. Communication, too, used to be challenging. Now anybody can say anything and spread it like a sneeze around the world with a few keystrokes or finger swipes. And of course, since sensationalism always wins out over facts, the juicy stuff gets turned into "truth."

The reporters who knocked on the door after Ned and the cops left yesterday couldn't understand why I refused to open.

What really kept me cowering, though, was the memory of how I'd once planned a hit on someone awfully close to what happened to Jake Baldwin down the road.

My target back then was the guy down the hall in my apartment building, years ago in Philadelphia. I was earning enough as a technical writer to escape the low-rent part of town, but this mid-rent neighborhood was still sketchy, and we had some dubious characters in the building, the worst on my floor.

I'd thought gentrification would catch up with the neighborhood but it didn't during my tenure. The streets remained tainted by bums and junkies on porches or just slouching in the shadows; sometimes they menaced women who hurried by. What could have been decent buildings were boarded up or decayed. I wanted to move but was saving up for a house in the suburbs, and also needed to replace my car, so I was stuck running the gantlet every time I came or went.

The period was one of the few times I lived alone, and I missed having a boyfriend or roommate every time that asshole down the hall cranked up his ugly music loud enough to register on the Richter scale, or slapped up his chain of girlfriends until they screamed, or he pissed in the stairwell, or opened the door to his drug buddies and released a toxic cloud into the hall. He intimidated me twice in the basement laundry room, and once, I swear but couldn't prove, he keyed the side of my car.

I looked him up online and found through news sources and arrest reports that he'd been a loser all his life. From what I saw or heard daily in the building, he would remain a loser until somebody knocked him off. I began to fantasize about doing the job myself. By then Cal had given me a pistol and taught me how to shoot it. (Got to admire Cal's ego, in that it never crossed his mind I might shoot him when he dumped me for someone else.)

I also had the little purse revolver my brother, Jim, had given me when I went off to college. Unlike Dad, a white-collar office guy, Jim understood that the streets between office buildings could be dangerous, and women could be victims whether they acted provocatively or not. By then Mom was long in her grave and couldn't warn me constantly of danger. Thanks to Jim's practical gift, that guy down the hall would be a cinch for me to dispatch if I could figure out how to do it without getting caught.

I never came up with a foolproof plan, but the frustration sure gave me plots for future novels! I got one halfway written before other forces intervened. The fact that I genuinely wanted to kill someone was a different and haunting problem. It goes a hundred percent against everything I've been taught, everything I believe, and what everyone I know considers acceptable. I don't want to be a person who others hold in contempt, so I put extra energy into hiding my feelings. That suppression just makes them more intense.

Thankfully, my education has indoctrinated me with the slogan, "If you can't do the time, don't do the crime," so I've been able keep thought and action separate. The line between them is mighty thin on some days, though.

No one will ever know my secret hatred if I keep my mouth shut.

* * *

I took the extra step of locking my journal away.

To make up for the time lost in response to the murder, I typhooned through the tasks I'd originally planned and got them done by dinnertime. Working at double pace kept me from backsliding into acrimony; and being set up to write this morning held my attention forward instead of replaying the day in my head and spiraling back down into a black hole. The energy needed to suppress and push simultaneously for so many hours, however, left me too drained to eat.

The moment I melted onto the futon couch, Twinkie, my yellow tabby, came out from where she'd been hiding and sprang into my lap. I petted her absently, assuring her there would be no more strange men thudding around the house. I had performed my civic duty and the police should be done with me. I was merely one of the stones they would not leave unturned as they pursued the murderer and put him away.

That was my last thought before conking out. I blinked awake to discover I'd slept through to morning. Aside from a stiff neck, I felt limp and released, as if I'd escaped an ogre by crawling through a tunnel into a brighter world. Indeed, the rooms glowed with more light than they'd held since my arrival. I still felt pain in my heart but that's because Tommy the Tiger was standing on my sternum, meowing, "Feed me! Feed me! Feed me right now!"

Twinkie was right behind him, purring innocently while she leaned all her weight into her forelegs on my bladder.

Their tactics forced me up, only to stumble over fluffy old Tessa on my way to the bathroom. All three cats laced between my ankles until I was properly herded into the kitchen. They bobbed up and down mewing then lined up in established order when I placed down their bowls. I took the lineup to mean they had accepted their new residence. Which meant that I had, too, though acceptance hadn't drifted to frontal consciousness yet.

I spread the kitchen curtains open to inspect the day—and gasped. Sunshine lit the landscape into vivid green springtime, as if in apology for the deluge. I could finally see the mountains, which farther south would be turning reddish as the forest swelled into bud, but here they still wore blue-gray cloaks around their shoulders. The rain had removed the last of their snowcaps, and left behind sparkling droplets on the grasses and shrubs near the house.

I reopened the windows, and the air that whooshed in was damp and cool and lush with aromas my nose didn't know how to separate and identify. I'd last encountered this mass fragrance when I'd camped in New York State's Adirondack Mountains, more years ago than I could recall before coffee. If asked what I was inhaling this morning, I could only answer *green.*

The lungful also filled one of the holes in my tattered soul with…gratitude. This view, this corner of place, was mine, and it could be mine for the rest of my life if I stuck with my commitment to heal. Nobody would punish me if I failed; I would just slide back into that dark pit of loathing that turned existence into hell. I didn't ever want to go there again, though I still couldn't see a clear path away from the edge of the pit.

I took another step in the right direction by stoking my body with food and caffeine, cleansing it with a shower, and adorning it with fresh clothes. The sequence reconnected my mind with my body and readied both to go back to work. I liked my new office, which some previous owner had created by moving the wall between a cramped dining room and living room to create a smaller private space and larger living area. Two of the office walls were devoted to bookshelves, which left just enough room for my desk, chair, and filing cabinets, plus skinny wall space around a front and side window to hang art.

I booted up the computer and three monitors and settled at the desk with Twinkie on my lap and Tommy atop a filing cabinet looking out the streetside window. Before my system finished loading its software and joined me in awakeness, a vehicle rumbled into the driveway, followed by a knock on the door.

I went rigid as both cats shot away. All the gratitude I'd inhaled earlier steamed out both nostrils in a hard sigh. Curiosity managed to prevail, despite yesterday's overdose of human interaction. I rose and peeked out the window Tommy had vacated, to see Ned's Jeep in the driveway and himself waiting on the front stoop.

Okay, this intrusion might be worth opening the door to.

I hadn't expected to see Ned again beyond watching his daily vehicle passage. He must have meant it when he said he'd come back to fix the lawn. Wow. Maybe I'd had the bad luck to walk into a murder scenario, but it had been countered by the good luck of meeting what seemed to be a genuinely nice guy. A hundred personality types could have been the one who found Jake Baldwin's body. I could have been stuck half the day with one of them, and vowed to never open my door again.

When I opened both doors again to Ned, he smiled and tipped his brim, then handed me a folded newspaper stuffed with envelopes.

"Good morning, Miss Brown," he said in flirty formality. "Here's today's missives. I wasn't sure if you get the paper, so I slipped one in."

"Uh, er, no, I don't. Thanks."

I slid him a look, uncertain how to react to his tone, then took the bundle and stepped aside for him to enter. He hesitated, adding, "You might want to check it out."

"Oh?" I lifted a brow as he scraped his shoes on the mat. Then he followed me into the kitchen, his Jeep still running outside. Taking that cue, I didn't offer him coffee. Instead, I unfolded the paper on the table and flinched upon reading the front-page headline:

Murder in the Mountains!
North Allenburg Man Shot Dead on His Own Doorstep!

An expletive escaped me as I scanned.

While most folks try to do something exciting on weekend nights, 72-year-old Jake Baldwin was quietly watching TV at home.

"How do they know he was watching TV?" I asked Ned. "Was it still on when you got there?"

"If it was, I didn't notice, being, ah, preoccupied with what was on the floor."

I grimaced and read on, a rime of ice creeping back around my heart.

But sometime late, a mysterious visitor came calling, and shot him point-blank when he opened the door. The bullet that authorities found in the wall was a .45 caliber.

Other than that, the killer left behind nothing more than a smeared mud track on the front step; any other signs of his presence on the dead-end dirt road were erased by the steady rain that fell between time of the killing and discovery of the body on Monday morning by postal deliveryman Ned Cavendish.

There followed quotes from Ned about finding the body. Then:

Police investigation is being hampered by the absence of both witnesses and evidence. All the neighboring homes are seasonal and closed up, save for the corner house that became occupied on the day of the murder by popular youth novelist Jane Brown, better known as Susan Silver.

Oh crap. Somebody had done their homework. I'd known it might happen but had been hoping to escape mention. Reading on, I relaxed a bit to see that my presence hadn't been blown out of proportion.

> There is no reason to think Ms. Brown has any more role in the murder than being a person arriving into the neighborhood at the wrong time, but certain locals are already wondering what connection she may have with Baldwin that brought her to town.
>
> Other residents laugh at the thought, wondering how the State Police will sort through the dozens of people with motives to hate Baldwin as well as the means and opportunity to kill him.

Jeesh. What a pathetic legacy. That guy must have been a monster! I rued being associated with him in any context, but at least the article left me behind.

It segued into a screed against too-liberal Vermont gun laws and too-few police to patrol the outlying areas that dominated the state. I remembered the shock I'd felt when looking into moving and learning that Vermont had a population of just over six hundred thousand, compared to the multiple millions in each of the metro areas where I'd lived. And if I recalled correctly (I would have to look it up again), the ratio of police to citizens was something like one to five thousand.

I looked up at Ned, who had been watching me read. His scrutiny, now that I'd come aware of it, made me squirm.

"I take it," he said, "you talked to the reporters yesterday."

I shook my head and turned away from the *Marble Valley Tribune.* "They dug me out on their own and jumped to their own conclusions. But they've given my books a bit of free publicity, so I can't justify complaining."

I gave a weak smile. He didn't return it, just said, "My nieces read them" and held my eye.

"Really? That's good to know."

Since he didn't respond, just kept looking at me, I got nervous and said the first thing that came to mind. "Tell them…there'll be another one in time for Christmas, and I'll be happy to sign it."

"They'd love that. Thanks. I'd like to chat more, but gotta go." He turned for the door, reciting, "Neither rain, nor sleet, nor gloom of night stays these couriers from the swift completion of their appointed rounds…"

I smiled with a nod, recognizing the unofficial postal service motto, and thumbed back over my shoulder. "And I've got a deadline to meet. Thanks, and see you later." I hoped. Then chastised myself for hoping.

He waved and strode back to his car. I called after him, "May your route go without excitement today!"

He half smiled then halted and turned back to face me, sober. "You know…what bugs me about yesterday…is the similarity between me finding Jake, and the widow lady in February."

That jolted me back into fear. "This is your second body?"

"No, the oil deliveryman found the first one." He gestured toward a nearby hill. "Up on Bear Pond Road. Much more remote than here. Fiona Cobb. She lived with her son—a total loser, but he was confirmed to be elsewhere during the time she died. Looks like she came out to get the mail in a coat over her nightgown, but must've slipped and fallen down the steps. They found her at the bottom with a dent in her head that could have been made by a stair edge. It also could have been made with a long blunt object." He stopped to let the implication sink in, then shook his head and concluded, "The fall didn't kill her, but she froze to death overnight. Must've been twenty-five below."

I shuddered. "Do you think…the two deaths are connected?"

"Don't see how. The victims were the same age, nothing more." He paused for thought. "But they grew up in this town together, and their families go way back. You never know."

"A coincidence, then?"

"Yeah, except we haven't had a murder around here for decades. And it seems like both bodies were left to be found."

We looked at each other and I felt a zing of connection. I wasn't sure what it meant, but I recognized that I'd come across a peer intelligence, the same way I had instantly connected with the few people who had become my friends and lovers over the years.

I wanted another friend, having alienated or abandoned too many; but I definitely did not want another lover. I had nothing left to give in intimacy, and no belief that enough of my better self would ever come back. Yet I hungered for the resonance of like minds and tastes in a way not shared with Luce. Her heart was big enough to hold the world, and she had acted over fifteen years as my mentor, surrogate mother, big sister, silly companion, shoulder to cry on, protector, defender, and mirror to reflect my best and worst. I would be eternally grateful for all she had done for me, but we didn't connect at the most basic level. I wrote novels; she never read anything beyond business documents and the newspaper. She had no comprehension of the challenges involved in crafting a story or imagining other people and worlds. Often when I spoke, on the most mundane topics, she did not know the meaning of the words I used.

Ned, I suspected, had a vocabulary that would allow balanced communication. I wanted to blurt "antidisestablishmentarianism" at him to see what he'd do.

This was not the moment for such an experiment, for he flicked his gaze away and turned again for his car. "Let me know," he said, "if you want me to keep delivering to the house, or slip the mail inside the storm door, or leave it at the post office. For that you'll have to pay for a P.O. box, though."

He cocked his head toward the roadblock on Rock Maple Road. I hadn't registered it when I'd looked outside. The police were gone; in their place, they'd erected barriers. My mailbox stood on the wrong side of them, despite the fact my proper address was on the main road. Long ago someone had planted my box on a pole under an apple tree just before the intersection, so the carrier would not have to stop on the main road's crumbling shoulder. The only way around the barrier to my box was across my lawn.

Ned, seeming to read my mind, said, "I'm thinking Saturday to repair those ruts. Will you be around?"

"I expect to be here most of the time."

He smiled suddenly. "Right. Books don't write themselves, I suppose."

"You suppose that right." I returned his smile, thinking he was a classic case of somebody's smile transforming their appearance and compelling others to reciprocate. I'd smiled more since I'd met him than I had in years.

"And mail doesn't get delivered when one is standing around, so as much as I enjoy talking with you, Miss Jane Brown, I've got to keep rolling. See you later."

He tipped his ballcap and departed. I locked up after him, feeling the same disquiet as when he'd left yesterday. Did this mean I was lonely, or afraid, or sexually attracted? Maybe nothing more than disoriented from surprise. Instead of tranquil solitude following move-in, I had murder on one hand and an appealing mailman on the other. Neither was something I could make go away unless I harshly shut it out and started a fresh domino chain of alienating people.

No, that would defeat the recovery plan. Somehow, I would have to cope—especially since, having failed to tell Ned that I would get a P.O. box, I could reasonably expect him to swing by again with tomorrow's mail.

Jake's murder, meanwhile, would hang like a miasma over the community until it was solved.

Please, I sent through the ether to Detectives Johnson and Greene, *find that killer fast!*

For now, I double-checked the locks, closed the curtains, and got back to work.

CHAPTER 3

Loneliness is something I suffer in a crowd. When alone, I'm happy and relaxed and productive—that is, when I can avoid thinking about all the things about reality that sicken me with rage. Those things drag me back toward the pit, seething over the injustices done by people to other people, and nations to other nations, and humans to other life forms, or to the Earth itself. All my life I've seen it every day in things like litter, rudeness, ignorance, waste, cruelty, neglect—and relentlessly through the media, which seems to have become an international enterprise of highlighting the worst that people can do to each other and the world.

The news corporations and TV networks make money making drama where there isn't any, or else ramping up anything real that happens into a surreal calamity. It seems against some invisible rules to report good news beyond token feel-good moments. Instead the media revel in bad news with phony sobriety, which hardly masks their glee from talking about murder and mayhem, corruption and disaster. Any time I think of it, I accelerate back toward the pit.

Living in the city, where you can't move without bumping shoulders with people, or competing with them for parking spaces and subway seats, opportunities and attention, or just places in line—and you can never, ever stop seeing or hearing them—I not only boiled internally but boiled over. I ab-so-lute-ly had to get away from that pressure or go mad.

I'm not completely blind and obsessed. I've always recognized that individuals can be, and more often than not are, wonderful human beings. I couldn't function without those people, and owe everything good in my life to them. I want to be like them, but I've lost hope because of the powers amassed against us all.

By "all" I mean us ordinary folk, who are suckered into buying stuff we don't need by soul-less corporations, most of which don't give a hoot about the consequences of their industry. We're chained by government officials who care more about getting reelected than doing right by the country, so they can keep lining their pockets with lobbyist dollars. So many jobs have been robbed of their dignity and opportunity that for a huge segment of the population "employment" has become a synonym for "indentured servitude." That's assuming you can get a job, with a living wage.

It all makes me sick, sick, sick.

The saying "Only the good die young" can be amended to "Only the good pay for the bad." Also: "One bad apple spoils the whole bunch." The bad people in the world have a chokehold on the good and keep preventing them, era after era, from fulfilling their positive potential, or else keep undoing what the good ones have achieved. This trend is not a hundred percent but it has dominated across time. Any student of history will recognize it.

I'm convinced our species will eventually self-destruct, and ruin the environment as well, because it's infinitely easier to destroy than create, and a single act of destruction can abruptly affect much more than an act of creation does. The exception is procreation, which humans do unchecked and in such abundance we will ultimately be crushed under the weight of our own numbers and drown in our own waste.

In the face of this, it remains unclear to me how you're supposed to get through the day—or why you should even bother trying to get through a life. I can't imagine how hard it must be if you live in a place that's been devastated by war, natural disaster, or overpopulation.

Here in the privileged USA, the idealists claim all you need is love. That's fine if you can find it, and give it (assuming you have food in your belly and a roof over your head). The twelve-step folks are more pragmatic, counseling one step at a time, one day at a time. The success gurus declare, "Act confident until you are confident." In other words, stride forward in a state of bullshitting yourself and others.

Of these, the twelve-steppers seem the most realistic, which is why I've modeled my own recovery program on some of their ideas. The other guiding adage I've adopted is, "Do unto others as you would have them do unto you—and mean it." That seems the best way to attract what positivity remains in the world. If I can get more of that back in my life, I might be able to care again.

* * *

I've been practicing caring on the cats; it's a lot easier to do with animals than people. Animals live in the now, and are direct and honest with their needs and feelings. Attending to them, protecting them, sharing their company has allowed me to reach outside myself and feel love. While I can't save every polar bear and frog and bird and insect needing rescue, I can at least save the critters whose paths I cross. Giving a home to Twinkie, Tommy the Tiger, and Contessa is probably the most genuinely altruistic thing I've done.

In the worst of times, I still loved my animals, as well as all nonhuman species trying to survive in this hostile world. That might not have gotten me any closer to loving my own species, but it proved I wasn't a total sociopath. When you're climbing out of a pit and keep slipping back from the edge, that plus-point counts.

I knew I wasn't the only single person to live companionably with cats or dogs or horses or birds, which also was comforting. I wouldn't mind living with only animals, but there's no getting around the fact I needed humans to earn the income that would feed and shelter me and my furry family.

Among them, Twinkie was living sunshine and always brought a smile. That spring morning she trotted into my office, mewing in her high squeaky voice, as soon as I settled at the computer. Although a tabby, her stripes were almost invisible, so her tawny gold set off a white bib and belly that reminded me of the cream filling in the spongy bad-for-you snack she was named after. I had acquired her from a shelter after I stopped traveling and could take care of pets. She was half of an inseparable odd couple, the other half being Tessa—short for Contessa—a regal black long-hair, twice Twinkie's age and opposite her sunny nature.

Not long afterward, I'd rescued Tommy the Tiger from the street. He'd been a ragged mess that good vet care, patience, and neutering had rendered lovable. The trio had lived with me in four apartments or shared houses in three states, and now showed their resilience by accepting our new digs with new speed.

Plucking Twinkie from atop the keyboard and parking her on my lap, I checked my e-mail and found the incoming I'd been waiting for from Luce.

Yesterday she'd flown home from vacation half a world away, so she'd been incommunicado for most of the day. I, between interruptions and emotional backslide and unexpected sleep, had been likewise incommunicado.

"OMG!" she shrieked onscreen. "First thing I hear on landing is somebody finally nailed that old scumbag Jake Baldwin! Good riddance to bad rubbish. I'm sorry they waited until you were there. Hope move-in day went well, despite it all. I'll check in when we finally stagger to a halt. Look for me at your door by weekend."

I flopped back in my chair in relief. More than ever did I need her support. I felt held together by twine and paper clips, and needed a dose of her practical zest to help regain perspective and keep on track.

We'd known for months that her trip would conflict with my relocation; her cruise had been booked in January, she'd found my house in February, I'd closed on it in March, and couldn't move in until the repairs and painting were finished in April. She'd let me use her condo as a staging area until she flew away two weeks ago, at which point I'd become a house sitter until I locked up and transferred to here.

Sighing yet again, I returned to the keyboard and tunneled my attention into *Katy Fox and the Calamity*. In that world, I could remember the starry-eyed child I used to be and channel her into something that engaged and inspired other girls. That these stories transformed into books you could hold in your hand, which people paid their hard-earned money to read, proved that ideas could become manifest, and the healthiest thing I could do was keep generating the ideas and banging away on my keyboard. On this I based my recovery.

I was halfway to my daily word count when a rapping came at the door, startling me half out of my chair. Twinkie launched like a rocket under the desk. I cursed and saved my file before peering out the window.

My office was on the street side of the house so I kept the café curtains closed, but looking over them let me see the front entry at an angle if I pressed close to the glass. That gave a better view than through the front door peephole. Out in the driveway stood a cubelike red SUV, and its driver, my real estate agent, waited on the stoop in a red coat with her hair frisking in the breeze. She was looking around with her hands in her pockets, as if assessing what had changed since she'd been here last.

"Hi, Jane!" she greeted when I unlocked to her. "Just stopping by to see how it's going."

"Good, thanks," I replied as she passed inside. This time she was empty handed, unlike at my closing, when she'd gifted me with a jug of locally harvested maple syrup as a Welcome to Vermont gift.

When I stepped up beside her, she was scanning my living room. She couldn't avoid noticing the changes, since the house had been empty when she showed it to me. My unopened boxes and stuff-draped furniture advertised the difference.

"Oh my—all this color has revived the place! I love it. Wish I was as brave—my entire house is done in eggshell and ivory."

That came as a surprise, given her car and coat. Underneath the unzipped coat I saw a red-dominant patterned blouse over black pants.

"Thanks," I said. "Can I get you a coffee, or you just passing through?"

"I'll take a quick one, thanks. And I'm dying to see what you've done to the kitchen."

There went another hour from my writing time. I served up coffee, and she sipped it while wandering around with a running commentary.

As with Ned and the cops, I was furious about the intrusion but knew I needed to take the opportunity to practice being a friendlier and more caring human. *Act confident until you are confident.* Its corollary: *Act nice until you are nice.* Hopefully that day would come.

In the meantime, Tammy asked what contractors had worked on the house, how I'd liked them, and oh by the way, how had those big ruts gotten into the lawn?

Her tone was a little too casual on that last question, cueing me to her curiosity about the murder. I gave her the abbreviated witness report, watching her face turn hard. Her voice matched it when she said, "It's about time somebody took out that bastard."

I cringed but she didn't notice, as her commercial instincts kicked in.

"Maybe now I can finally sell that ski house."

I ran a mental tally of the dwellings along Rock Maple Road and remembered an A-frame set back amid the trees. "I thought that one was occupied during the winter."

"Yes, but only by low-budget renters. Jake used to complain to the constable about them all the time."

"Huh? How could they bother him? They're out of sight from his place."

Jake's closest neighbor was a hunting camp, sited in the woods between him and the offending renters. Between them and me were only three other properties, spread out of sight from each other: a rarely used summer cabin, a three-season modular owned by a retired couple who wintered in Florida, and a farm where an enterprising couple raised children, alpacas, and a market garden. Their farm was the logical place for Ned to have stopped for a telephone after he found Jake's body—except that their only access on Rock Maple Road was a gated two-rut for tractors. A car had to go back to the main road and turn to reach their driveway a half mile later, passing my place on the way.

Tammy sniffed. "Out of sight didn't matter. I think he drove back and forth by them just to have something to gripe about. Called them druggies and silver-spooners and queers—whoever he had a grudge against that week. Said the young ones kept him up all night with their loud music and loud cars, and they blocked the road when they couldn't get in their own driveway because they were too stupid to buy snow tires."

She shook her head, which made her frosted curls jiggle. "He was such a pain that I couldn't sell the ski house to anyone local because they all know about him and didn't want to be anywhere near him. And out-of-staters always want a nicer place."

She darted a look at me, the brand-new out-of-stater who had ignored her attempt to sell me that dark, damp ski house. From her pause, I knew she recalled not mentioning the downsides and hoped I wasn't noticing her gaffe.

She threw on a grin. "You know what I mean." She looked around. "This place is so much better. I just knew it was perfect for you, and I'm glad nobody grabbed it before you came along." She spread her arms. "Was I right, or what?"

I returned her smile, because I had to agree. Then I asked, “What about Jake Baldwin’s place? Do you think it will get sold, or is there some family who’ll take it over?”

She shrugged. “There’s an ex-wife but I doubt she’ll want to come back here. She’ll probably try to sell, though it’s such a dump it won’t move. A convenient fire might make the land marketable, though…”

I looked at her in surprise. She glanced at me with a glint in her eye that reminded me of the introduction to an old radio program: *Who knows what evil lurks in the hearts of men? The Shadow knows…*

For a moment I thought I was looking into a mirror. Tammy had failed to fully mask her hatred and desire to destroy an obstacle in her way. Did those emotions live in us all, and I was stupidly hypersensitive to demean myself because I felt them, too? Or was I “normal,” like she seemed to be until that moment, and as long as neither of us acted on our harsh emotions, we were absolved from the taint of them? Or did the act of feeling them condemn us?

I would probably never know, and couldn’t take the mental time to examine the question while she was standing before me.

Tammy tossed her curls, put on her Realtor smile, and glanced at a tiny wristwatch. It had a skinny vinyl band the same flaming red of her coat. “Gotta go,” she said brightly, not looking at me. “Walk-through in town and just enough time to get there.”

She strode to the door. “Thanks for the tour, Jane, and I’m so happy to see how well you fit the place and how nice you’ve made it. I’m still hoping to sell that ski house, so let me know if you have any friends who want to follow you into the area!”

I promised vaguely, not admitting that I had no friends left other than Luce. Her voice and image in my mind prompted me to trail Tammy outside and wave after her from the stoop. *Act nice until you are nice.* Tammy returned a *ta-ta* wiggle of the fingers then drove away.

As I turned back to the house, my eye was drawn by the ruts carved into the lawn. I made a note to examine them more closely during my next writing break, as well as to scope out the overgrown gardens around the house to see if any bulbs were poking up. I didn’t want to think about anything more complicated.

No person or thing interrupted for the rest of the day, so I managed to meet my quota. It was actually the weekend's quota, as I'd composed a few thousand words verbally into a recorder while driving back and forth before the move, then in fits and starts while unpacking. I had to transfer that data onto my computer and set it up properly into files, then review the text before incorporating it into the working manuscript so I could continue from it in the next writing session.

Completing the task left me feeling virtuous by suppertime, and relaxed from the creative surge. When that energy was pent up, it made me jittery and bitter; when released, I felt healthy and looked forward to the next day.

I contemplated tomorrow's to-do list over a drink on the back porch—a rickety but roofed and screened-in appendage to the original house, which was one of those Sears catalogue kit homes from the 1930s modified higgledy-piggledy over generations. The porch overlooked my chunk of field and forest, and the sunset-washed hills in the distance.

Not only did I love that view, along with the house's space and layout, and the fact it had been in serviceable condition for a reasonable price, but also it came with an ideal solution for indoor cats. Some previous owner with dogs had attached a kennel to the back. I could open a door into a utility room with a lockable pet door that swung into a covered run. The fence links were too small for cats to squeeze through and the roof prevented climbing out, so the run provided a safe playground for them to enjoy the outdoors.

They'd never had that luxury before, aside from Tommy the Tiger's city-streets hardships. I didn't dare let the cats run free in the countryside, even though urban logic said that was the ideal environment for them. I knew enough about woods and fields to understand that coyotes, bobcats, fishers, and owls lived out there and could snack on kitties for breakfast. Just because I hadn't seen or heard any wildlife yet didn't mean they weren't skulking nearby. Even closer was the main road, adding mechanical hazard to my pets' freedom.

It worked in reverse, too: Cats were responsible for appalling losses to the songbird population. I wanted to attract birds to my yard with feeders. Not fair to sucker them into a trap. My predatory trio would have to make do with keeping mice out of the house, and chasing whatever crawled, fluttered, or slithered in the kennel run. They could sit outside all day and night if they wanted, watching and sniffing—a major upgrade from viewing life from a windowsill.

Since the day had warmed enough for me to leave the interior door open, the cats could start exploring the porch. Tommy the Tiger came first, creeping out, belly low, sniffing the perimeter and the furniture. As he passed underneath my chair, I asked him, "What should I do about the guns?"

He looked at me with green eyes like exclamation points, then set off after a fly.

I sighed, wishing I had someone to talk with about guns. Luce was the only person I could confide in, but she—goddess of peace—didn't know I owned any firearms, and I intended to never tell her. I wouldn't be thinking about guns now if the police hadn't been here and a killer wasn't lurking among the community. What if the killer feared I had seen him and came back to make sure I never talked? I could hardly credit the possibility, but, remembering my own thoughts about the creep down the hall, I knew better than to assume my safety.

During the nadir of my black period, I had managed to keep the guns put away, always aware of the consequences should I give in and shoot myself or somebody else. Other people, however, were farther around the bend than I had ever peeked during my craziest. Although I could limit my exposure to other crazies, I could not forget they existed.

Nor could my brother or my former honey Cal. Both had gifted me with pistols, worried about the neighborhoods where I lived. So thanks to Jim and Cal and what I inherited from my father, I owned a small unregistered arsenal. I kept the fact private, because some folks might look upon that unfavorably—a shunning I didn't want or need—and also because it gave me an element of surprise should the situation ever warrant it.

I knew how to shoot from taking a beginner's course at a private range. I'd also taken courses in basic self-defense, evasive driving, and wilderness first aid. All those skills needed practice to master, and I'd had neither the place nor opportunity to follow up. Now I owned private acreage where

I could shoot safely and unobserved, heard only from a distance. It would be an error to start practicing now, when gunshots hadn't been heard on the road before the murder. I would just draw attention to myself and maybe agitate the neighbors. Besides, how stupid would it be to introduce the chance that someone might discover I owned a .45-caliber pistol, just like the killer?

That was the most dangerous point. By happenstance, I had two of the classic three qualifications for a suspect: means and opportunity. No motive, but I was in trouble if anyone could believe I'd slosh down the road in the middle of the night to take out a guy I didn't know, or move here with the objective of doing so. In a world filled with nut cases, though, someone who didn't know me might find me as good a suspect as any. Likewise, anyone could take a shot at me for no other reason than I existed. Ergo, for me to publicly introduce guns into the equation was a Very Bad Idea.

Again sighing, I returned inside to deal with the problem while it was on my mind.

All of my guns were secure in their cases and secreted in chests and drawers. I'd kept them there because the previous states I'd lived in had strict laws, plus I needed barriers to any urge to use one. That had all changed in a day. Now I wanted a weapon easy to hand. Just because I'd installed an alarm system in the house didn't mean it would shield me in every circumstance.

I didn't need Dad's sniper rifle from his Vietnam days, unless I planned on taking up big-game hunting or human assassination. His skeet-shooting shotgun was fancy and expensive and I should probably just sell it. Maybe I'd do so after the murder had been solved.

Dad also had an all-purpose pump shotgun—perfect for home defense. I wanted that in reach of the front or back door, but out of sight.

For handguns I had my grandfather's WWII .45-caliber service pistol plus the modern .22-caliber semiautomatic from Cal and the .38-caliber mini revolver from my brother designed for concealed carry. The service pistol I put in the drawer of the table inside the front entry; the semi I placed atop the refrigerator; the revolver I put in the drawer of my bedside table.

Walking through the rooms pondering options brought my thoughts back to the Jake Baldwin murder weapon. A .45 could be a rifle or pistol; most likely a handgun—a freaking hand cannon, like granddad's semiautomatic from the war. There were probably lots of them floating around the countryside that had been similarly inherited.

It still amazed me that the killer had just walked up to Jake Baldwin's front door and blown him away. Had they really driven right by my house? Or was there another access?

My novelist's mind went to work on how it could have happened. The hilly woodlands behind Baldwin's place were surely riddled with wildlife paths and hunting trails. A rainy night would hide a person's passage equally well in the woods as on the road, though it would be a lot easier to see where you're going using car headlights. A flashlight or headlamp in the woods would be risky. If you didn't turn it off soon enough, the victim might spot your bobbing light where one didn't belong if he glanced out a window. With the trees not yet in leaf, a light could travel far. You'd have to park a vehicle somewhere, which might be noticed and have to be explained. Better to use a muddy pickup or old Subaru—both ubiquitous in Vermont and anonymous in rainy darkness. Just drive in, shoot, and drive home, barely getting wet.

Same with that lady on Bear Pond Road, Fiona Cobb and her staircase. A little shove, and you were done, and never seen. What might tie those two victims together?

What if, what if...

Oh damn, I felt a story coming on. I had to throttle the urge, because such a story was inappropriate for the girls who kept me in paychecks. They wanted my wholesome heroine, Katy Fox—but someday that well would run dry. If I was serious about writing professionally for the rest of my life, I ought to have a drawer full of plot outlines and character sketches for other genres. If I just carried ideas in my head, I would lose them.

"No time like the present!" my mother used to say, so I ditched the gun problem in favor of a dig through my archives.

It took a while to find, but eventually I unearthed the notebook containing my half-written novel based on dispatching my previous nasty neighbor. I created a new file folder for it in my active drawer, then tore out the coverage on Jake from the newspaper and put it in its own folder, and set up alerts on my computer to follow the investigation. I made a mental note to research Fiona Cobb's death, along with past killings in Vermont, toward the idea of creating a new mystery novel.

While at it, I jotted down a related idea that I'd toyed with for years, a science fiction/fantasy tale in a society where everyone was allowed one legal kill during their lifetime, and the permutations of that. Between that and real-world crime novels, I stayed up too late capturing thoughts before they vaporized.

By the time I fell into bed, my mind was relaxed and empty, and let me sleep.

CHAPTER 4

I should answer my brother's letter, but can't bring myself to do it. What can I say: I've run away to the mountains to shut out the world, and failed?

He doesn't know yet that I've moved; his envelope is stamped with forwarding information. Last he heard, I was thinking about leaving the city but hadn't picked another place. We've communicated once since Dad died, and I last saw Jimmy at the funeral. He looked awful, gaunt and leathery, but glowing in the eyes like a zealot. That's appropriate, since he's a man with a mission.

Sometime during college, he found God, who has since led him around the world doing good deeds for the impoverished and devastated. Look for any natural disaster or wartime ruination outside our country, and you'll find Jim.

I'll give him credit: He's doing good works from the goodness of his own heart, and has never tried to convert me. That's allowed us to remain civil, albeit estranged. He's ten years older—we've never known which one of us was the surprise baby—so we had nothing in common to begin with. Add his extroverted idealism against my introverted cynicism, and you get two siblings as alien as beef jerky and puff pastry.

The only thing I've ever done that he approves of is write Katy Fox novels. Without including a syllable about religion, I've managed to capture moral virtues and hope through realistic, knock-down-and-get-back-up tales. If people knew how much it bled me to do that, they'd be amazed. I don't plan to explain it, since conceiving Katy is what saved me. Dad's money just provided the means to a new end. The causes and effects are too private to be anyone else's business. And I did all the work myself, no deity intervention required. Just because I'm not done yet doesn't mean I'm defeated.

* * *

By day four of my new life, I knew what time to expect mail delivery, so I kept my ear tuned for Ned's vehicle over the keyboard clatter of my day's work. I'd risen early, loaded with ideas, though none for my future crime novel, and was already one-third of the way through my daily quota for *Katy Fox and the Calamity* when Ned's Jeep pulled in.

I met him at the door with "Good morning," which he returned while handing over the folded newspaper enclosing my bills. He tapped it with a forefinger, saying, "We've been relegated to page two already."

I dropped the bundle onto the side table, since my morning e-mail alert had already led me to the online source of what Ned was referring to. I wondered what he would think if he knew a pistol lay a few inches below the mail pile.

"Nothing new on the investigation yet," he added, "though it's 'in process' and they're talking to 'persons of interest' and all that folderol."

Folderol. That brought me up short. I'd never heard it spoken, only read it in cultured or satirical novels.

He caught my blink and tweaked his lips in a one-sided smile. "Well, if I'm going to talk with a writer lady, I might as well whip out my best vocabulary."

"That's certainly a good one."

"I'll give you another one tomorrow. You want me to keep going with hand delivery?"

"Yes. It makes me feel like a princess. But"—I pointed out the door, where my old mail basket from a previous apartment now hung beside the exterior door frame—"you can leave it here if I'm not around."

"Okay. By the way, my nieces want to meet you."

"Oh! Well. I suppose so. But…not right away. I really need to get my feet under me."

He nodded. "No hurry. But you'll definitely have to autograph the next volumes I give them."

I smiled, warmed by the novelty of the request. "That I can do."

"Good enough. See you later."

He hopped back into the Jeep and continued on his appointed rounds. I stayed outside for a while, savoring sun on my face and my hair lifting in a mild breeze, noting that the near vista had gained green and the far vista's hills had caught up to southern New England and turned purplish from dormant maples budding out. Ah, spring at last! I decided to do the yard circuit right then to inspect my flower beds. Being ahead of quota gave flexibility to my day.

Having purchased the house when snow was down, I didn't know what to expect from my dooryard. Well, I did to a certain extent: neglect, because the house had been unoccupied for over a year, and the previous owner had been a retired plumber (said Tammy) who wanted nothing to do with plants. Which was why lilacs and cedars pressed up against the siding, the apple trees at the yard's four corners had broken limbs and peeling bark, and I had to scuff through dead overgrowth to find edges around pocket gardens. Within them I saw daffodils emerging, and remnants of gone-by crocuses. Too early yet to spot peonies or other hardy perennials, though some daylilies and irises had broken through.

The backyard had a weird raised rectangle in the center, which Tammy had said was a filled-in swimming pool. Somebody had once planted a vegetable garden on top then bordered it with forsythia on the corners and rambling roses down the sides. All had morphed into a vicious tangle I wasn't ready to breach.

Around the whole backyard ran a chain-link fence to contain dogs let loose from the kennel. I wanted to mesh that fence for guaranteed cat containment, but that would be a wasted effort and expense because the cats would climb right out unless I covered the whole half acre with overhead screening, like some big chicken yards I'd seen. I would have to settle for staked-out space, and the furry children would have to settle for the covered run. Maybe someday I'd have the time and wherewithal to enclose the yard.

For today, where the backyard fence ended and the unfenced front yard began was where Ned had cut the corner. Those gouges were deep enough to contain standing water, and the edges were mushy, so I walked along them to press them down. Nevertheless, dirt and grass seed would need to be added. I hoped the weather would hold through Saturday so he would come back and stay for longer than the daily front-door exchange. I was starting to like his company.

That realization stalled me in my tracks.

I wasn't supposed to be liking company. Or wanting it. My plan was to live as a hermit, sticking out tentative feelers now and then after I'd been cloistered long enough to notice. Ned had brought the ugly world back to my doorstep before I'd even escaped it, and kept handing me print reminders of what I had invested so much in to reject. Yet, after a little friendliness, I was already letting my guard down after vowing to make it impenetrable.

Was that a good sign—healing faster than imagined—or a bad sign: I was more screwed-up than I thought?

I couldn't tell, and no one to ask. So I could either wander around the house bemoaning my fate, or get away from myself by leaving the house and exploring a new world, or reimmerse in Katy Fox's world, where the rules were clear and problems were solvable. Easy choice.

Intense concentration brought me to writing quota by lunchtime. Meeting each day's minimum output ensured that dollars would eventually land in my pocket. If I failed to deliver a manuscript on time, I would not only run afoul of contract and face penalties, but also begin delays that would cascade through editing and production and sales and royalties. The luxury of working alone at home didn't mean I lived without employment pressures.

With my head down, I didn't notice that the outdoor temperature had risen almost twenty degrees since sunup. It became obvious while I was preparing a meal, so I opened windows to let in the spring. I also unlatched the swing door into the kennel run and placed bowls of cat kibble beyond it. Tommy the Tiger found the aperture immediately, and by the time I finished lunch, Twinkie had followed him out. Tessa was still cowering, but she had graduated from under the bed to atop a stack of boxes in the storage room. I felt I could safely leave them all, so departed for the town library.

My hamlet of North Allenburg was a higher-altitude adjunct of Allenburg proper, named after Vermont's Revolutionary War hero Ethan Allen, who'd led the Green Mountain Boys. Or so I'd been told by the librarian during one of my reconnaissance missions last month. Ethan Allen had no direct association with the town—it was more like the "George Washington slept here" mythos—although Allen's descendants one step removed ran a dairy farm in the highlands next town over.

It was a fifteen-minute drive downhill from our hamlet to the bustling town center. The drop put the town two weeks ahead of us on the hill, so its daffodils were in full bloom, along with tulips and hyacinths, and trees were leafing out. One man was already mowing his lawn.

A private reason I had moved to the community was to have Allenburg's library. It was a wonder of native marble construction, built by a marble baron in the 1880s and gifted to his hometown. Vermont marble was white and gray, in infinite combinations. That gave the building a stout, planted, historical look that made me feel at home.

The librarian looked up from her desk when I entered, and bloomed into a smile. "Hello! Nice to see you again. Are you here to stay?"

"Yes, finally. I moved in on Saturday."

"Just in time for our murder, I hear." Her smile turned into a frown. It didn't quite work with her soft pink cheeks, soft white hair, soft blue eyes, and soft gray sweater dress.

"That was an unfortunate coincidence," I replied.

"But without it, I wouldn't have read the article that informed me you're the author of one of our most popular youth series."

I couldn't help but smile. It was hard to claim credit for books when you wrote under a pen name. My publisher had insisted on pseudonyms to protect our privacy and allow multiple authors to work on one series. So far I was the only author of the Katy Fox series, but if I bailed out or got kicked out or couldn't produce fast enough, someone else could step in.

"Guess I've been outed," I said, half proud, half bashful, then hastily added, "Not that it's a problem."

"I'm hoping the opposite. Will you do a talk for us once you've settled in?"

My back tightened. In one day I'd gone from nonentity to two command performances! I didn't know how to respond. *Can't my books just sell on their own?* They'd been doing so without me up to this point. Random milliseconds of fame was one thing; hours of direct interaction with strangers was another.

I had to say something. "I, uh, sure, thank you. But not for a while yet."

When she smiled blandly and nodded, I added, "Keeping pace with my contract schedule means little off time. But I get ahead sometimes, so I'll let you know when I see an opening."

"That would be lovely. For now, should I call you Jane or Susan?"

"Jane, please. Thanks for asking."

"I'm Helen LaCroix." She extended her hand across the desk. I shook it, not surprised to find it as soft and warm as the rest of her.

"Is there anything I can help you with?" she asked.

"Yes. I'm looking for some history on Allenburg, and recommendations for good mystery series."

She focused like a bird dog. "What kind of mystery? Police procedural? Cozy? Closed-room puzzle? Classic British whodunit? Wilderness noir?"

"Um…not too noir, not too violent. I'm particularly interested in creative ways to kill people, to start getting ideas for my own someday-book."

Helen dropped an eyebrow and looked at me intently. "Well…in that case, try Charlotte MacLeod, who also writes as Alisa Craig. And Agatha Christie. Maybe Nevada Barr, though those can get intense. They're all shelved by author; we don't have separate genre sections beyond fiction and nonfiction. And one for youth," she added, smiling again.

I consulted the card catalogue—yes, they still had one, no barcode system yet, thank heavens for small-town, small-state budgets—while Helen checked out books for the man who had come in behind me. I couldn't avoid hearing their conversation, because the high-ceilinged space with wood and marble floors enhanced sound like an auditorium. In the metropolitan libraries of my past, noise was dampened by acoustical tile and wall-to-wall carpet, and people were chided if they spoke above a whisper.

I managed to tune them out, and half an hour later returned to the desk with laden arms, after a pass through the youth section to see all of my publisher's series for girls lined up on a dedicated shelf. Several volumes were missing, presumably out on loan rather than stolen.

"All set?" Helen asked with her kindly smile. Then she patted a three-book stack beside her on the counter. "I've found some local history for you. One of these has to stay here, but you can have the others for a month, and renew them if you're not done."

I plunked down my books and quickly fanned through the history volumes. "I'll take these two and look through the other one next time I'm in."

After checkout I gave her my business card then returned to my sanctuary. Despite the fact my first outing had been successful, I still felt tension drain so fast that my knees went gummy and head got light when the door closed me back inside home.

Food and liquid restored my fortitude, so I went looking for the cats. All three were out in the kennel run, staring through the fence at passing birds and bugs while twitching nostrils in the breeze. I promised them I would provide benches and climbing trees tomorrow, and returned to my computer. Another thousand words poured through my fingers, putting me ahead of quota for the next day.

That day dawned sunny again, and my productivity marathon continued. By the time Ned arrived with the mail, I was a full day ahead.

He handed me two books from the Katy Fox series, volumes one and two. "My nieces want your autograph," he opened. "One of them gets the odd-numbered books and the other gets even, then they swap. So you can address them to both."

I blinked a few times, delighted but befuddled. "You gave me the impression I'd be signing the new ones."

"Yep, but they don't know I'm planning to give them those, so they'd be thrilled by you signing ones they already own."

"Thrilled?"

He smiled. "You're a star. Didn't you know?"

"Um, no." My royalty statements didn't reflect that status. But if I could be a star to some youngster—heck, even two!—then my commitment to this work was validated.

Flushing, and hoping Ned didn't notice, I invited him in to wait while I signed the books. His Jeep idled in the driveway, signaling no intent to loiter. While I wrote, he said matter-of-factly, "Jeroboam."

I looked up. "What?"

"Jeroboam. That's my word for the day. Know what it means?"

"Yes, it's a really big wine bottle. I don't recall exactly how much it holds."

"Three liters, if you speak metric."

"I try not to."

He smirked. "It's also the name of an old king of Israel."

I handed him the books with a smile. "Did you actually know that, or did you look it up this morning?"

He grinned. "Half and half."

"I'm starting to feel challenged. Maybe I'll have a word for you tomorrow."

"How about tonight? Do you have any dinner plans?"

I stiffened then slumped with a sigh. Such pleasant, harmless banter, making me feel welcome and normal; suddenly a male thrust I had to parry. Ten years ago I might have been titillated, but now I was just ticked off, wanting nothing more than the simple pleasure of a few minutes with a platonic word-nerd friend whose nieces were appreciative readers.

Keeping the corners of my mouth turned up in a pseudosmile, I tried to balance politeness and frost. "Yes, I have dinner plans every night."

He caught the frost. "I take it that means you're not interested."

"I'm interested in going out to dinner, but not going on a date."

"Friends go out to dinner together all the time."

"And if you were a woman, I wouldn't blink."

"But because I'm a man, you won't go?"

"Not without knowing you better."

He shrugged. "Fair enough. Though I might need you to put up a billboard when you've decided you know me well enough so I can ask at the right time. I've always considered a relaxed meal in a nice place to be a good start on getting to know someone better. If you think that's hot pursuit, then I don't have a clue how to proceed."

I looked away and hesitated long, feeling him study my profile.

"No need to proceed," I said finally, then turned back to him. "But I'm not against being friendly acquaintances."

He grinned again. "We can be that."

"And I hope we will. We already are." I gave a little smile to show no resentment. In actuality, I was flattered and utterly nonplussed.

"How about a cup of coffee here on Saturday?" he temporized. "I'm coming to do your lawn, anyway. The dinner idea was just, well…thanks to circumstances neither of us could foresee, you've already served me booze and breakfast. So we've sort of skipped a step. I want to offer something back as a gesture of appreciation. If coffee on the stoop is good enough, then let me know what kind you like and I'll bring it with me."

I gave him points for a good save. When my expression didn't change, he added a flourish: "After all, you saw me with my psychological pants down. Give me a chance to be a suave, totally-in-control gentleman."

"Well…"

I was going to say, *Let me think about it*, but then he knocked me off balance by saying, "Think about it. I've gotta get going." He touched the brim of his ballcap. "Have a nice day"—then scampered out to his waiting Jeep.

I stood staring at the space he'd vacated, grateful that I'd met my writing quota for the day. I couldn't go back to that innocent adventure story with a jibbering mind and off-kilter heart.

He'd struck me like a lightning bolt, or a car accident, or any of those things that stop your life in its tracks when you least expect it. In all my planning for a new reality, I had not factored a man into my equation—any more than I had expected a murder!—beyond male hired help and affable townspeople, and Luce's husband, Peter. Maybe in the foggiest corner of my hopes, I'd envisioned possibly meeting someone to love or lust for, a long, long way down the road when everything else was right again…if it ever could be. Only by hoping it might be, someday, could I continue getting up in the morning.

I could try to write off Ned as an affable townsman, but his eye had held a familiar glint. Disclaim as he might, I knew his invitation had been for a date; he was testing the waters, making a move. I'd not be able to relax around him again.

When my eyes resumed focus and I began to turn indoors, I spotted his signed books atop the entry table that contained my granddad's service pistol. The juxtaposition unnerved me anew. I retreated to my office, wondering if Ned had planted the books for an excuse to step inside again when he next delivered the mail, or if he'd been as jangled as I was and put the books down reflexively. I tried to replay our conversation in my head but couldn't recall when the books had left his hands.

I put a book into my own hands, the first one in the library stack I blindly reached for, and tried to read it, but that didn't push him from my mind. Nor did researching on the Internet, or working on delayed unpacking. I should have written in my journal, but my thoughts were an incoherent mix of Mexican jumping beans and Turkish taffy. What normally comforted and centered me seemed too much effort.

I cooked dinner but couldn't finish it; rounded up the cats and fed them, too; then took a long shower to force muscles to relax. Instead, nakedness made me body conscious and awoke memories of past lovers. That brought sex to mind, which brought Ned back to mind, which put sleep out of the question, as my body hungered like it hadn't for years.

Nevertheless, I went to bed for lack of a better plan, and lay staring out the window at the stars. Last night I'd been grateful to see them again after so many years living in urban lightwash, and had promised myself to learn the constellations; tonight I regretted the effort and expense I'd squandered to get here. Not even a week had passed and I was backsliding into the turmoil I'd sought to escape. Solitude eluded attainment, and the security I'd expected in these underpopulated mountains had been violated by a murder just down the road. On top of that, after years of rejecting men because I believed they were all alike, an interesting one had come along who might be different.

The poet Robert Burns had it right when he wrote about the best-laid schemes of mice and men oft going awry!

CHAPTER 5

There's a lot to be said for celibacy. I can see why some religions demand it of their priests. It eliminates the deeper complexities of intimate human interaction, and if the person can get past the pain of repressing sexual urges, celibacy can open the way for higher levels of compassion and thought.

For someone like me, whose dark side overwhelmed the light, disconnecting from intimacy is imperative for survival. Maybe when the light side regains control I can think about sex again. Before then I need to grow impermeable psychic boundaries to avoid leaking poison onto another person when they are most physically and emotionally vulnerable—and vice versa. Sex wouldn't be a problem if I could enjoy it recreationally; in today's slang, have a "friend with benefits."

The latter is what I suspect Ned is after. For me, though, a friend with benefits amounts to marriage, else you just have lovers, and everyone else as platonic pals. You can't go on indefinitely with someone through the intimacy of daily life if you aren't friends, and the intimacy of sex needs that kind of solid foundation to go on for just as long. Lust never lasts forever, so if you give in to it and marry, ending up with someone for decades, you need to really like them and enjoy their company when the physical fire fizzles out. Else divorce or perpetual misery is inevitable.

Ned, I'll bet, is probably one of the few who can stay friends with someone he once slept with. Or maybe he still sleeps with them, on and off, while everyone gets on with their lives. I didn't see a ring on his finger, or the shadow of one, so I'm assuming he's not married. Yeah, a guy like him as a pal with "benefits" would be nice, but it's not what I want. A half dozen lovers have proven that I don't need bondage based on lust that fizzles out.

* * *

At 9:30 the next morning, my front storm door again banged with insistent knocking. There stood Ned with my mail in hand.

"Triskaidekaphobia," he greeted.

I stared like a slack-jawed owl, still half asleep after a bad night. Finally I mustered, "English, please."

"Triskaidekaphobia. Surely you know that one."

My half-caffeinated brain scrambled to retrieve the word from foggy depths. Yes, I knew it, but, but—tip of my tongue—

"Ah. Fear of the number thirteen. Jeepers, did somebody actually use that in conversation?" I finally said, my brain flickering on.

"Yep. My uncle."

"You must have an interesting family." I stepped back, leaving the inner door open, since the morning was awash in sunshine. His Jeep, as usual, was idling in the driveway.

He followed me in and stayed on the entry mat. "Yes, we're a wordy bunch." He turned right away to the signed books he'd left on side table and swapped them for my mail pile. Then he paused, looked at me squarely, and said, "Listen, I'm sorry I offended you yesterday. It wasn't my intent."

He waited for me to reply. I had no idea what to say. His eyes were clear and keen, so I believed him.

"I wasn't offended, Ned." *Thrown for a loop? Yes! But offended? No.* "Even so, apology accepted."

"So…are we still friendly acquaintances?"

"Yes. Yes, of course."

"Good. In that case, I come with a non-date invitation. Two, actually."

"Oh lord, I'm not awake yet." But I managed a smile.

"You don't have to answer now, just factor them in. The first is months down the road: Join my clan in one of our Scrabble parties. The other is for tomorrow: the community supper the grange hosts for local charities. This is the first of six, through October. Our donations help the volunteer fire department, old-folks home, historical society, and their ilk."

"Ilk. You really must be a Scrabble player."

"We like Jeopardy and Trivial Pursuit, too. Anyway, the dinner starts at five and everybody goes. Ten bucks a head, covers costs with the rest to the charity du jour. You can come and go on your own; not a date, though if we coordinate we can sit at the same table and you'll get to make some other friendly acquaintances while at least knowing one person. Sort of."

"Tomorrow? Luce will be here by then."

"And I'm sure she'll attend."

"I, uh—you know her?"

"Sure, who doesn't? She and Pete are the closest we've got to big philanthropists in the area. You mean, you don't know that?"

"Well, I do in a general way. But I don't know everyone she knows."

He shrugged. "We don't really know each other but are aware who the other is. And that," he concluded, grinning, "makes two people you'll be acquainted with at the dinner."

"Well…" I scraped hair back from my forehead, suddenly realizing it was the same gesture he used between taking off and putting on his ballcap. Which he wasn't wearing today. Which I appreciated, since I thought they made every wearer look stupid. Yeah, I understood the ballcap's technical value—sun protection, adjustable fit, cheap yet indestructible, option to feature one's alliance through a logo, and for the older guys, covering bald spots—but aesthetically I found them a big ick. People who wore ballcaps backward turned me off from a hundred paces. Thankfully, Ned didn't wear his that way, though he might during the bulk of the time when I didn't see him. I discovered that I wanted to know that.

"I guess I can go…" *Act friendly until you are friendly.* "Where is it?"

He rattled off directions, then scooted back to his Jeep.

After he'd driven away, I took another mug of coffee out onto the screened porch and savored it and the view as, one by one, my mental cylinders resumed firing. It struck me anew as ironic how after living amid thousands or millions of people most of my life, this tiny community was pressing against my borderlines so much more swiftly and insistently. I'd expected that my only social contact here would be Luce—at least for the first few months. She had made it clear during the lead-up to my move that she was going to browbeat me into meeting people until I had a happy and healthy social life.

I didn't want that. I didn't need that. Even so, I was managing to have a social life without lifting a finger, whether I wanted it or not.

I finished my coffee and sat at the computer. All this people-practice was diverting too much time from what I came here for—to write. Rereading the last paragraph I'd written before Ned stopped by, to remember where I'd left off, I elbowed real people from my mind and replaced them with the more fascinating imaginary ones. Then started tapping keys.

Apparently the tension relief afforded by Ned's changed tactics unclogged some channels, for I not only continued my productivity run but turned almost breathless with inspiration. My fingers couldn't type fast enough to keep up with ideas. Scenes flowed, characters blossomed. Normally I took a break every hour or so, but this time I pounded the keyboard until midafternoon. I ignored e-mail and chores and cats, who were fine with that, having discovered the joys of the flap door and kennel run. By the time I ran out of gas, I had exceeded my record word count for a day and drafted perhaps the best story of my Katy Fox series so far.

I poured myself a celebratory drink and toasted my new home and literary achievement.

The glow lasted until I checked my e-mail. A day-old message from Luce informed me she was en route to Vermont and would connect with me in person…today. Uh-oh—time to scramble! I needed to tidy up before she blew back into my life. With tomorrow scheduled, too, it was a good thing I'd gotten ahead in my writing.

I dashed off an e mail to my editor, informing her that our little library had all our publisher's series in stock, and I was already signing books for the locals. I mentioned, too, that the new book was moving briskly along. Everyone else—friendly acquaintances I'd acquired in my travels and from previous jobs, cyber-pals from writing forums—none of whom I'd ever meet, or meet again—could wait until a more leisurely moment.

A check out the windows before stepping into the shower revealed that sometime between Ned's visit and wrapping up my day's work, the town road grader had smoothed the worst of the ruts on Rock Maple Road and somebody had removed the "Road Closed" signs and blockade. If I'd missed all that in broad daylight, then no mystery how I could have missed a murderer coming and going on a rainy night!

Likewise I'd failed to notice if anyone had taken advantage of the reopened passage. I should be more vigilant, I chided myself, but knew I wouldn't be, because that would inhibit my creative focus. I couldn't let traffic rule my attention. Let the cops set up a camera if they wanted to know who used the road.

I could hear approachers well enough when attuned, which is how I knew Luce had arrived late afternoon. As her vehicle swung into the driveway, I popped outside to greet her.

She sprang out of the car like a floral jack-in-the-box. I always had to fight the urge to step back after not seeing her for a while, because she carried so much energy and flashed it around through big eyes, big gestures, and a big-toothed smile. Tonight she was browned and sun streaked from a tour of the Aegean islands, and had garbed her buxom frame in the splashy flower prints she favored, her clothing flapping around me like curtains when she swooped forward to embrace.

"Janey! So good to see you! So happy you're here for good, at last!"

I squeezed back, unable to resist smiling in response to her effusive warmth. "Good to see you, too. Welcome back!"

We detached and she followed me into my dwelling, so dull and shabby on the outside compared to her. Once inside, she flung her arms out and spun, whooping. "You've done exactly what I wouldn't, and it's gorgeous! Can I look?"

"Of course."

She scurried through the house. I chuckled in her wake, marveling at our contrasts. As a plain girl, I decorated in vivid colors, eclectic objects, and abundant art and photography. As a flamboyant girl, she decorated in classic styles and muted tones, with very select objects placed in just the right spots.

"I'm glad to see you updated those dreadful appliances," she concluded, plunking onto my futon couch and accepting the wineglass I handed her. She was referring to the appliance colors—avocado green and harvest gold, popular in the 1970s, along with the brick-pattern linoleum I'd also replaced—but in fact I'd upgraded the appliances for energy efficiency while opportunity allowed, doubting I'd have those thousands of dollars in another five, ten, twenty years, when the original appliances likely would conk out. The replacements were in brushed stainless steel atop a mottled-color soft-linoleum flooring that disguised dirt and was easy to clean and comfortable to stand on.

I settled opposite Luce in a grandaddy-size armchair I had hauled to every place I'd lived. Twinkie appeared from wherever and leaped into her lap, instantly purring. Luce stroked her with a hand loaded with rings. "In fact," she said, "you look totally settled in."

"Not quite"—I gestured at still-unpacked cartons and mostly pictureless walls—"but I'm getting there."

"Hard to do with a murder right on your doorstep!"

I shrugged. "It was a one-day wonder for me. Not for the town, though—and, of course, the guy it happened to and his family."

"Everybody around here is talking about it, I'm sure. Most exciting thing to happen in decades."

I frowned. "Tomorrow at the community dinner it will probably be topic number one."

"You're going?" Luce's contoured eyebrows arched higher. "I thought I'd have to roll you into a rug and kidnap you to do anything social."

I shrugged. "Ned talked me into it. I figured I'd give it a try."

"Ned, eh? Watch out, girl—he's one of those knight-in-shining-armor types, rescuing damsels in distress."

"Then why's he coming on to me?" I blurted without thinking.

She hesitated then said, "Probably because you vibrate with a Woman Hurt aura from a hundred paces."

"What?"

Luce had never said such a thing to me before, and it made me wonder how much else she perceived that I hadn't confessed to her.

Unperturbed, she added, "It's probably something he can sniff out."

I rolled my eyes. "Jeesh. I don't want to be rescued." The familiar hot lump of resentment began to rise inside me.

Luce had to think about a response. During her pause, a thought came to me. "If he's such a rescuer, why is he still single?"

She shrugged. "That's one of the local mysteries. He's got a laundry list of desirable qualities, and he's worked his way through half the ladies in the community, but none of them has stuck. Most of them end up marrying other guys and living happily ever after. Which is why I say 'buyer beware.' There must be something off about him to have so much opportunity with no result."

She turned an eye on me. "Kind of like you, now that I think of it."

I sniffed. "Not everyone needs to be married at twenty. How many who did, still are?"

"Enough that it's weird to find two forty-somethings still unattached."

"I'm only thirty-nine."

"And still unattached."

"At any rate, I don't want or need some guy with a hero complex."

"He's who we get our maple syrup from, by the way," Luce tossed out in one of her normal non sequiturs.

"Right now he's just delivering my mail. We met rather abruptly because he came here for the phone after he found the body."

I gave her the details she hadn't heard yet.

Luce nodded, intently following my eyes as I talked. At the end, she shook her head and drained her wineglass. "It's sad, really. I never heard anyone say a single nice thing about Jake. He was a pig to everybody, whether just being an aggressive rube or beating his wife and starving his dog."

"He must've had some redeeming quality." I didn't believe that but was trying to train myself to think charitably. "How did he make a living?"

Luce blinked at me, sensing a change she couldn't quite identify, then leaned back and stretched her arms along the back of the couch. "I'm not sure. I think…he worked at the lumber mill until it burned down, then survived on a pension and Social Security, supplemented by meat that he poached."

"You mean…"

"Deer and turkey, moose and bear when he could get them. In and out of season. You know, jacklighting and setting bait then picking the animals off when they came in to feed."

I winced. Luce continued, "He might have done some trapping and sold the furs. I really don't know. I do know he wasn't enterprising enough to run syrup or cut wood or any of those seasonal labors off the land that so many people do to get by. I'm not surprised that someone finally killed him. I'm sure he had vendettas or old grudges that infuriated someone enough to blow him away."

I sipped my wine, ruminating. The word pathetic came back to mind. Jake reminded me of the guy down the hall I'd wanted to zap from the face of the earth, unable to see the value he offered to anyone. What had ultimately stopped me from acting on my judgment of his worthlessness was realizing that somebody, somewhere might think that about me. You had to have a stark black-and-white value system to make such judgment and defend yourself against others' judgment. I waffled helplessly in a world of shifting grays, able to see many points of view at the same time and being unable to decide which of them, if any, was the correct one.

This didn't change the fact that the world was full of despicable human beings. Why would one warrant murdering while the rest just got away with sucking off society and earning contempt? There must have been some specific hurt Jake had committed that made someone take the trouble—and risk—to kill him. Someone clever enough to cover their tracks in a simple manner, leaving an open field of suspects. I felt sorry for the police, who would have to comb through all the possibilities.

Yet I had to admit…if I wanted to eliminate a person I despised, what Jake's murderer had done was an effective way to go about it. After Luce left, I would add to my notes for the someday-novel.

She stayed for another two hours, during which we caught up on each other's news and made plans for future gadabouts and get-togethers. The first would be the next night, when she picked me up for the community dinner. That arrangement resolved any anxiety I had about going alone, and left no opening for Ned to volunteer as chauffeur. No way, then, that either of us could consider it a date.

After Luce swooped away, I tidied up, ate a sandwich, then donned a jacket and sat out on the porch again to listen to the spring peepers in nearby invisible ponds. Their screech masked the intermittent thrum of a passing car on the main road, and gave the illusion I had finally gotten away from it all.

But as dusk descended, I acknowledged the truism that you can't get away from yourself no matter how far and fast you run.

CHAPTER 6

I had meant to retreat into blessed solitude by moving here, yet look at me: Mere days after arrival I'm going to a community dinner filled with strangers! Is it because I can't hold up against social pressure from a seemingly nice guy and my one remaining friend, or because deep down I want to have friends again? Or just want to see if a small community is any better than a big one? I can't sort out my feelings and thoughts.

Luce thinks interaction with others is healthy, and I'm sure Ned does, too, given that both of them are people-persons. To me, there's nothing healthy about being stressed half out of your mind. Luce can label me agoraphobic or whatever, but what she doesn't know—nobody does—is I'm just a human version of geologic forces.

In the same way as the weight and movement of the earth crush rock to a molten state, I am ground and compressed by reality. I have to exert enormous energy to suppress loathing and rage and fear, which creates an internal magma that pushes ever toward the surface, seeking cracks and weak points it can seep or blow through to relieve unbearable pressure. I cannot allow that release, because to survive, I must interact socially and professionally with people, and I know well that sour, vicious, negative, scene-making people draw the same back to themselves. I don't want those folks in my life, and I don't want to be one of them.

That means I have to lie—a lot—in order to share civilized company. I'm afraid to show people my dark side lest I scare them away. Which is why attending things like community dinners is fraught with danger. I can't chance having some well-meaning person flip my switch with the wrong word at the wrong time. By backing out of the dinner, however, I'll draw both Luce's and Ned's more-pointed attention. Much as I want their attention because both are so relaxed and upbeat, I'm certain that neither of them can understand the depth of my neurosis, and I don't want them to see it. I don't want anyone to see it, ever.

I still get cold sweats when remembering how close I came to exploding.

God knows what I would have done; probably something that would have made national news. Like so many of the emotional-exploders out there, I was ticking down like a time bomb. My timer stopped one second before detonation because of astounding good fortune: A six-figure check came into my hand.

My father died suddenly—unlike Mom, who'd deteriorated slowly during my teens—and I'd had no idea he'd socked away such assets. Even though he split his estate evenly between me and Jimmy, my half was enough to clear all debt, replace my car, buy a house far from a city, freshen it up, and sock the leftover into the bank. All after taxes.

The shock of the gift created a new kind of explosion: golden visions blooming in my mind like a fireworks show. For the first time in decades I could consider possibilities, disinter dead dreams. I even dared think I could change my toxic mindset and start healing the black hole in my soul.

All of which led me to here. Which leads me now to a choice I never expected to have to make. Do I stick to my life-saving intentions and avoid everything known to inflame my internal hellfire, or do I reach out and follow two sunny people into a possibly brighter, healthier light?

"Act friendly until you are friendly." That seemed at first to be a recipe for hypocrisy, but I see now it's the only path I can take.

* * *

Saturday morning, I was still in my jammies again when Ned arrived at the door. This time, no mail; he was geared up to repair the front lawn.

"Somebody else does the route on weekends," he explained. "So I don't know when you'll get your mail."

"Doesn't matter," I said. He hovered for a moment, waiting for me to say something else, while I waited for him to say something else. The moment extended to discomfort, so he turned abruptly and said, "Guess I'll get started, then."

He returned outside to maneuver his pickup truck full of dirt, with a wheelbarrow perched upside down on atop the pile and a shovel sticking out the side. I hastily dressed and decided to monitor his progress while puttering around the yard.

It was a gorgeous day so I didn't mind being outside and active at such an early hour. Having overshot my work quota thanks to the recent creative energy burst, I could afford a day of R&R. Well, it was neither restful nor relaxing—raking, carrying totes of scruff to a compost pile, resetting stone and brick borders that had sunk into the ground—but I enjoyed the exercise as well as a sense of my little domain coming into tidiness after long neglect.

Ned, meanwhile, worked with the easy vigor that comes from a lifetime of labor and consequent physical fitness. Though he wasn't beefy with muscle, I could see his strength in the sinews of his arms and hands, and movement of his back under his shirt. He hefted tools and materials as adroitly as I handled pen and keyboard, always returning to upright posture between tasks, moving fluidly and economically. I couldn't help admiring the effect.

In seemingly no time he had filled the gouges, flattened their edges, raked them smooth, and sowed grass seed. Then he spread straw over the area and called it quits.

Done before I was, he watched me in turn through mirrored sunglasses. I felt awkward under scrutiny but didn't really mind. It had been a long time since a man had looked at me for more than two seconds.

Finally I joined him on the stoop to review our accomplishments.

"Looks good," I said sincerely.

He nodded. "I don't suppose you have anything to drink…"

The water bottle beside him was empty. Only then did I realize he hadn't brought coffee like he'd originally offered. I'd never answered his request for what I might prefer, which might account for it. Did his non-action mean I'd successfully discouraged him, or he was waiting to see how I'd react after he backed off? We'd left it that I would "think about it."

Apparently the back of my mind had been mulling while the front of my mind was distracted. I offered, "How about some iced coffee?"

"That would be great." He smiled.

I nipped inside and poured from a jar I had prepared yesterday and parked in the fridge. I popped my head out to ask about milk and sweetener, then tailored our respective glasses and was back before he could get restless.

"Thanks." He glugged, reminding me of the way he'd thrown back the whiskey shot that first morning in my kitchen. I sipped more demurely, wondering what to say.

He saved me the trouble. "The whole yard looks better than it's been in a long time."

I nodded, pleased. "I gather from Tammy—my Realtor—that this place was empty for a long time, and the previous owner was a plumber. That's probably why my kitchen, bathroom, and heating system are good, and the rest was, well, a mess."

"Did she tell you he was my uncle?"

"No. Was he the uncle with the big vocabulary?"

"No, that one's still around."

"It sounds like you have a lot of relatives."

"That I do. Frankly, I've lost count. Yeah, plumber uncle died about two years ago. And this house was actually owned by another uncle, the one who runs the dairy farm"—he gestured toward the out-of-sight village, beyond which the oldest family in the community owned umpteen hundred acres—"and he let plumber uncle live in it. I don't know what the deal was, but we have a lot of properties scattered around the area, with various relatives and farm hands and hangers-on living in them. I'm in one of those, myself."

"Where?"

Another gesture. "Up on Tamarack Hill. I've got a leaning house and the remains of a hill farm."

I wanted to ask about direct family, like ex-wife and children, but Luce's remark about knight in shining armor who rescued damsels in distress still lingered in my ears. I concentrated on not projecting a Woman Hurt aura.

"So why'd your family sell this house?" I hoped there wasn't some hidden liability I would learn about the hard way.

"Needed cash for the farm. Lots of. Always. Since nobody was hot to take over the place, we decided to unload it."

"Well, I'm glad you did."

"Would you mind if I went in and looked around? I'm curious about what it looks like now. I haven't been inside in decades."

Surprised and pleased, I said, "Sure." I stood up to lead him in, suddenly nervous. My home said a lot about me, and I couldn't anticipate what he might read into it. Neither of us needed to say he'd been oblivious to his surroundings the first time we'd met, so this viewing would be his actual first.

He tugged off his work boots and left them on the inside mat, then ambled through the six rooms—all but my bedroom, which I shut off while he checked out the bath—with hands in pockets, scanning and making "hmm" noises.

"Sure looks different!—and much nicer," he decreed. "Women really do make better nests than guys do." At my warning eye flash, he smiled. "Sorry about the stereotype, but I'm sure you've noticed it's true."

"In general, yes," I conceded.

I braced myself for his remarks to become more personal, but that didn't happen. Not until he reached the photos in the living room, which I'd been putting up in odd moments and finally finished. I had devoted each wall to a different subject, with my travel shots comprising the largest group. The Rockies, the Alps, European cities, tropical islands, American national parks, a few corners of Asia, ski and metro areas of Canada, and New England from coast to interior hills, all four seasons.

Ned examined each one then glanced at me over his shoulder. "Looks like you get around to some interesting places."

"Got around," I corrected. "I'm pretty much done with that now."

"Retired already?" He pivoted and looked at me fully. "You sure don't look sixty-five."

His eyes were full of questions I didn't intend to answer. Instead I just quirked up a corner of my lips in a sardonic half smile. He returned a full one, then moved to the next display showing family and old friends, all mixed around so the ex-boyfriends didn't stand out. I'd put them in a mélange to remind myself that I'd had a rich life filled with good people. While the downsides of those relationships, compiled, had fueled much of my degeneration, I needed to be daily, visually reminded of what had been good so I could open my mind to the chance it might come around again.

I could hear the questions Ned wanted to ask hanging in the air, but he restrained himself. As he studied the photos, I studied him, liking his straightforward masculinity and relaxed confidence, and respect for my privacy.

After puffing a breath through puckered lips and shaking his head, he headed toward the door then bent for his boots. Halfway down he straightened again and looked at me. “I don’t get it, Jane. From what I see, you’re a worldly woman. But it seems like you’ve chosen to hide in the backwoods of Vermont. So I can’t help but wonder…what happened.”

“And you’re too much of a gentleman to push, right?”

He gave me his own version of the one-cornered smile. “Right. But I’m mighty curious.”

“I’m sure you’ve heard that curiosity killed the cat.”

He blinked at me then bent again to put on his shoes while I reflected on the echo of my words. Had curiosity killed Jake Baldwin? Would Ned’s curiosity provoke me into rejecting or even killing him? He stood inches away from my pistol in hiding. If I strode forward to extract it from the drawer, I would surprise him so much he’d probably freeze long enough for me to fire.

No—both those ideas were too radical to entertain, except in novels.

I expelled them and said stiffly, striving to be polite, “I’m flattered by your curiosity but I came here to mind my own business so am not interested in sharing my personal history.”

His gaze fixed on me and stilled as he went through a decision about me. I couldn’t tell if it was determination to write me off as an unavailable woman immune to his charms, or to find a way around my defenses and do his knightly rescue thing. Either way, something subliminal passed between us, and I knew he wouldn’t mess with me. Perhaps he recognized and respected the obvious: that I was a woman alone in a strange world, with the right to harbor my own secrets and open or close the door to whomever I liked.

He broke our staredown by relaxing and saying mildly, “I understand.”

“Good.” My face thawed and I lightened my voice to parody a haughty lady of the manor. “In that case, Mr. Cavendish, thank you for fixing the yard. It looks wonderful.”

“No problem, Miss Brown. Might there be any other manly chores I can do for you while I’m here?”

He'd adopted the tone of an English butler with twinkling eyes.

A little giddy with relief, I said, "Not today, thank you kind sir, but I may need some assistance in the future."

He switched to an elegant courtier. "Then might I still hope you'll favor us with your presence at tonight's banquet, milady?"

"Yes. Lady Lucinda is fetching me in her gilded chariot."

"Thank you, milady. If you'll graciously meet us outside the hall at around five thirty for the second seating, we can all share a table."

"Sounds divine. I'll see you at the appointed hour."

He gave a careless salute and departed, shaking his head in bemusement. I closed up behind him, half chuckling and half shaking in my shoes.

CHAPTER 7

Katy Fox came to me at the nadir of my depression. I don't recall what prompted her into being; it wasn't anything as obvious as looking in the mirror and seeing what a bitter hag I'd become, or receiving a verbal slap from anyone who had watched me slide downhill. She just coalesced in my mind when I was doing something mundane, the way creative ideas often do, and I adopted her as my mascot, my icon, my inspiration—my reminder that once I'd been young and fervent, and believed it was possible to save the world. Somewhere inside me those qualities survive, though I still don't know how to bring them back to the surface in real life.

Katy stewed in the back of my mind until a door of opportunity opened to actualize her. I had enough wits left to recognize that opportunity when it came, and enough energy left to pounce. Thus I ended up with the contract to write about her: the first step that led me to here.

Up until then, I'd been struggling with my kill-the-neighbor crime novel. I'd thought it would be a healthy purge of my demons, but instead it kept poison flowing in my veins. That book had to go if I intended to write upbeat novels for teenagers. I should have burned or shredded the pages instead of consigning them to a drawer where I could get at them again. Keeping the manuscript worked like my guns, echoing in my subconscious like a siren challenging my will and skill to prevent crashing on the rocks. I often wonder if alcoholics keep a bottle in the closet to test themselves the same way.

Then Dad died and my inheritance gave me the means to write full-time instead of as a second job jammed in the spaces around whatever paid the bills. Those jobs ranged from corporate media positions to waiting tables, and they withered in importance as writing bloomed. I had written four volumes of the Katy Fox series by the time Luce found my house, and I was earning adequate advances and royalties to maintain a simple life if I cleared all debt and incurred no major expenses. The pieces came together and shifted my mindset from believing there was no hope to thinking there were three kinds of luck: the luck you make, the luck you take, and dumb luck. When it comes to the publishing contract keeping me going, all three apply and I'd best not forget that.

* * *

I worked off the jitters Ned had left me with by overexerting myself in the yard for the rest of the day. My morning raking had barely made a dent in what needed to be done, so I tackled the next step. As well, the cats needed something to climb on and hide under in the kennel run. I gathered some old benches and side tables I'd kept for the purpose and piled them into a kitty gymnasium.

The problem I couldn't solve was the kennel run's underfoot environment. Half eroded concrete and half packed dirt, it would ultimately be taken over by grass unless I acquired a midget lawnmower, a power trimmer, or manually clipped enough square footage to sprain my hand. The prospect reminded me that I needed a serious lawnmower for the yard, something I should get advice about from—I sighed—probably Ned. Perhaps I could ask him at the dinner.

While showering off the day's grunge, I pondered what to wear for the evening. Assuming a community meal at a grange hall was essentially the same as a church supper, I opted for plain but clean, with a touch of pretty. That meant a pastel striped blouse with tan slacks, comfortable flats, my hair contained by a silver barrette. I added a dash of makeup and my favorite silver earrings. Since I wasn't driving I didn't need my wallet, so I tucked the dinner fare and my cell phone (for whatever that was worth in these parts) into the pockets of a vest that tied my colors together and protected from evening chill.

Luce arrived in her golden chariot—a champagne-bronze deluxe SUV—and surprised me with her own outfit, an exaggerated version of my own in the same color scheme. "Hello, hello, hello! Hey, it looks like you got some sun today. I didn't know writers actually went outdoors during daylight!"

Another smothering hug, as if I hadn't seen her in months. Then she bundled me off for the ten-minute ride to the grange hall, a white rectangular box with peeling paint and warped windows, outside of which trailed a line of people. Cars were parked anywhere they'd fit along the road, including the edge of front lawns across the street. Luce parallel-parked her chariot between a rusty Subaru and a modern pod-on-wheels I couldn't identify. I had to get out into a drainage ditch.

The happy roar from within the hall could be heard from where we parked, which boded well for the food quality. Half the line outside comprised Ned's clan, or so I deduced from the way a bunch of people who seemed to know each other clustered around him. He was tall enough to see over much of the crowd and found my eye almost immediately. I tensed; he smiled; and I relaxed, glad that our earlier encounter had not set us back.

Several people came out, and the line advanced. Luce chatted with the folks in front of and behind us, introducing me, pulling me into benign chat with kindly and mostly wrinkled faces about the glorious weather. It bathed us in slanted gold rays and gentle breezes. The vintage homes crowding around us all had mowed emerald lawns and spring perennials in full flower.

Inside the hall was a fug of heat and aromas. I sniffed roasted meat, buttered vegetables, overcooked coffee, and fresh-baked pies. People consumed it all from tight seating at trestle tables, two across and eight rows on both sides of an aisle where servers scurried up and down. As we hovered inside the door, waiting for a block of seating to open, I spotted pies on their own table, against the end wall where we clustered around the entry, single slices on paper plates in at least six varieties. Beyond the pie table in a side wall, a pass-through counter into a kitchen showed sweating men transferring dishes back and forth to servers.

Scattered through the hall were people I recognized—the postmistress, the guy who installed my generator, the painter who turned my kitchen from blood maroon to sunshine yellow, one of the women I hired to scrub the whole house floor to ceiling before I moved in, Tammy the Realtor—all of whom nodded or waved as we were led to our table. We went through an awkward stage of pulling out chairs back to back with the too-close adjacent table and squeezing into our places.

At that point I got separated from Luce, who ended up at the far end of the table with me at the other. A white-haired woman sat on my left, and a middle-aged couple took seats across from me. Ned sat about halfway down the other side, bookended by his nieces, whom I'd been introduced to outside. He and Luce conveyed more introductions, which identified my companions as his aunt on my left and his brother and sister-in-law opposite.

While we waited for food, Aunt Mary turned to me with a smile. "So… I understand you're a novelist."

I decided that frank curiosity ran in the family and responded with my standard line. "Yes, I write an inspirational adventure series for teenage girls."

"Katy Fox!" cried Ned's eleven-year-old niece Alicia, whose book I had autographed. She hadn't stopped looking at me since we'd met in line.

I smiled. "Yes. Katy's the heroine of the series I'm working on."

"When's the next one coming out?" Alicia interjected, holding a fork in her fist, tines up.

"Not sure. A few months."

"But I could read one a month!" she declared.

I laughed. "I'd write you one a month if I could!"

Aunt Mary asked, "How long does it take to write one?"

"About three months to draft it, but then there's editing and production, so we can only put out so many a year. That is, per writer. We're up to six writers now, each on their own series. The grand design is to ultimately have a dozen core authors and select freelancers, all working on different series under a collective pen name so nobody burns out on their own line. Same multi-author model as the old Nancy Drew and Hardy Boys series, updated for twenty-first-century girls."

Conversation stopped as food arrived and steaming dishes were passed up, down, and across the table. The reaching arms and scraping spoons and bumping elbows reminded me of long-ago Thanksgiving dinners, when I still had both parents and a herd of relatives, who lived close enough to get together. All that, so long gone.

Tonight's meal was roast pork with potatoes and carrots accompanied by bread, cole slaw, and applesauce. As we tucked in, roving pitcher-bearers stopped at either end of the table to ask, "Juice or water?" and "Regular or decaf?"

When things settled down to contented eating, Aunt Mary resumed her gentle interrogation. I appreciated her interest, as writing was the one thing I could talk about comfortably with anyone willing to listen. Normally I did it online through writers' forums; nice to have flesh-and-flood conversations on the subject.

Most people at the table listened in as Mary and I talked.

She prodded, "How did you get into such an unusual occupation?"

I sliced my meat, not looking at Ned, whose eyes I could feel upon me. "A friend told me about a request for proposals from a new publisher—Boudica Books, named for a Celtic warrior-queen—which wanted stories about strong women who would appeal to teen and preteen girls. They had selected six themes, projecting a dozen books for each series. I pitched for three themes and got Animal Adventures."

"What were the others?" she asked between mouthfuls.

"Well, they're all about careers in some form. Katy Fox wants to be a veterinarian, so her adventures have something to do with animals. So far, she has helped with broken raptor wings, pets hit by cars, retired greyhounds and racehorses destined for slaughter, abused livestock, and now she's involved in post-natural-disaster rescue operations."

"What's it called?" Alicia called down the table.

"*Katy Fox and the Calamity.*"

I turned back to Aunt Mary. "The Sport Adventures series is for girls who want to be professional athletes. The Domestic Adventures series is for girls who want to be wives and mothers. Science Adventures is for tech-y types who want to be astronauts or inventors or doctors, whatever, and Arts Adventures is for dancers, singers, et cetera. Oh yeah, there's Outdoor Adventures for future environmentalists, wildlife researchers, explorers, and so forth."

Aunt Mary beamed. "I'll have to read them."

"The library has the complete series, I'm happy to say."

Which reminded me: I'd espied Helen the librarian across the room when we'd entered, and had hoped we'd land at her table. Nope: She was on the other side of the aisle, halfway to the front of the hall while our party filled a table at the back. When I looked over to find her again, she was already waiting to catch my eye. She nodded with a slight smile. I nodded and smiled back.

Mary and I paused for more eating, while people talked around us. Nobody at our table was discussing the murder, but I heard snatches of discussion about it around the room. To keep it at bay, I volunteered more information to my eager listener.

"The managing editor has asked us for proposals for more series lines. I've pitched for National Parks, and one of my colleagues has proposed World Travel."

"Oooh! I want to read those!" interjected Alicia. Her older sister, Nicole, hadn't said a word, but she'd been keenly following our conversation. I wondered if these girls would like the series I hadn't proposed yet: Girls in History. That included Sybil Luddington, who'd done a Paul Revere–type ride during the Revolutionary War; Mary Jemison, who'd been captured and raised by Indians…

One of the uncles also had been tracking the conversation. I guessed he'd been listening to murder talk behind him at the adjacent table, as well, for when he craned to see me around Aunt Mary, he asked, "So what might police and firemen—firewomen—fall under?"

"And armed services?" interjected a grizzled old fellow, who I'd bet my dessert was a veteran.

"We haven't figured that out yet," I told them. "The 'Helping Services' just doesn't sound right. Any suggestions?"

"Altruism Adventures?" offered Ned.

"Rescue Adventures?" said Ned's brother—Bud?—across from me. He was a taller, handsomer, older, and quieter version of his sibling. This was the first time he'd spoken since the meal had begun. The silent Nicole must be his daughter.

Other suggestions flowed as the table brainstormed. Delighted, I scribbled the ideas on a napkin, promising to forward them to the managing editor.

"I can't imagine why anyone would want to be a policeman or fireman, or EMT," said Bud's wife, whose name I couldn't remember. "I mean, we need them, and I certainly appreciate them with all my heart, but I don't think I could deal with the gore and risk and heartbreak."

"It's pretty awful," agreed our server, who had tuned in while removing empty dishes and replacing them with full. I recalled that this night's dinner was benefiting the Allenburg Volunteer Fire and Rescue Squad. "But the satisfaction you get from helping people, sometimes even saving their lives, can't be beat."

Inevitably, this line segued into talk of the murder, with anyone who hadn't heard the story asking Ned to describe finding the body. I finished my meal without speaking, relieved to be out of the limelight on that topic. He acknowledged my kindness that day—everyone at the table turned to look at me then—but they switched their attention back as his story continued, then they talked around me. As I expected, they kept repeating the same theme.

Jake Baldwin had been a monster, everyone agreed. Not a living soul cared about him, save for his buddies, who only hung out with him because they were losers, too. He'd once had a wife, whom he'd abused until she fled decades ago. Thank goodness he'd never had kids. He contributed nothing to society; took more than his share of anything he could grab. The killer had done the world a favor. Good luck to the cops to figure it out! Many people hoped they wouldn't.

I couldn't help but wonder what Jake had felt upon opening his door to the Grim Reaper. It brought to mind my own dark fantasies, which caused a mental click like two and two adding up to four and five simultaneously. *What if the killer is a woman?*

Everyone assumed it was a man. But if Jake had been as hostile and suspicious as people said, he wouldn't let an enemy or stranger approach his house. So either his killer had been a buddy, or he'd heard a noise and gone out to investigate and been ambushed—both options I assumed the police were considering—or the caller was so unexpected and harmless-seeming that he didn't hesitate to open up. Bang! Done. And nobody the wiser.

I liked that idea for a crime-novel premise. It would certainly solve some of the plot problems bogging down my manuscript in the drawer.

How could I find out about women in Jake's life who might want to avenge a careless or intentional hurt, without drawing attention to myself?

As I contemplated this, several people proposed Jake's ex-wife as the likeliest suspect. Others felt that was too obvious. For my purposes it didn't matter. The whole situation was so rife with possibilities, I itched to write them down while the flood was in spate.

It triggered internal conflict that spurred a need to flee. *Okay, Luce: Time to go*, I telegraphed in her direction.

But she was yakking with Ned's grandma, a hunched but still sprightly chickadee who'd packed away more food than any of her descendants. She got jostled by someone from the next table wedging himself between chair backs en route to the pie table. Already folks were returning with two or three flavors.

I was tempted but, after double helpings of the meal, I wanted to limit my calories. Couldn't ignore the fact I sat at a desk all day and wasn't getting any thinner.

Then Ned stood up and wriggled past, saying, "Anything I can get you?"

"Thanks, but I'm not sure yet."

I tapped my foot, trying to catch Luce's eye to signal, *Let's go*, until Ned returned with a yummy-looking berry pie in one hand and a chocolate cream in the other. *Oh, calories be damned!* When was the last time I'd had—or the next time I'd ever have—homemade pie?

I popped up to get my share while the getting was good.

Among the people circling the pie table peering at the selections, I met Helen. "Hello!" she said cheerily, looking at me with eyes like Ned's, sharp with intelligence and a knowing that went unsaid. It was a familiar gaze, one I'd used all my life to identify people I wanted to know, or at least thought would be safe and friendly. I'd only been wrong about that once, with a disastrous boyfriend who now lived on the other side of the continent, thankyougod.

"What looks good to you?" Helen said.

"Mmmm…I may have to close my eyes and just grab one."

She went for lemon meringue. I got a better look at her than times previous, and hoped I would be as trim and kindly when I reached her age. She waited for me to make my choice, so I went for chocolate. As she seemed in no hurry to get back to her table, I straightened for a moment of chitchat.

"I'm still hoping you'll do a talk for us sometime," she said. "The Friends of the Library do their own fundraisers—nothing on this scale, we're more the bake sale and book sale type—and I'm sure if you came in for a signing or presentation, we'd get a good turnout."

"But I'm not a big-name best seller. Who would care?"

"Well…two groups. Those for whom writing has a mystique, so they're interested in meeting a real published author; also, the young people who know your books. I would love to promote your publisher's series. I think it's a great idea, and we have a lot of children's programs."

I thought of Alicia and Nicole, who had so eagerly requested my autograph. Heck, they had asked me to write one book a month! I had been squelching my reaction to that, unwilling to face what it meant. But what it meant was…hope again. Somebody was hearing what I was saying and wanted more.

Paychecks had proven that truth for a while now, but it hadn't really sunk in until suddenly faces were attached to it. Helen's and the girls' enthusiasm, technically, made me a celebrity—a hard concept to wrap my mind around. I associated fame with headlines and flashing cameras, crowded attention I didn't want, even though I recognized it sold books.

But this? Having my work important to someone I might meet face to face? It was yet another surprise, but this time one I could appreciate and be thankful for.

Tension I didn't know I'd been holding suddenly eased. "Sure, I'll do something," I said to Helen in a brighter tone. "What would work best?"

The way she eyed me suggested she'd sensed my internal shift, but she kept on topic. "How about a short talk about the whole series, where the idea came from, its diversity, and so forth, then autograph whichever of your titles people bring in?"

"I could do that. But…not quite yet. I've…gotten a bit knocked off stride by the move, so I still need some weeks to wrap up what I'm working on."

Helen seemed sympathetic, and I let her maneuver me into a tentative date in early June. After nods and smiles, both of us falling shy of a handshake, we returned to our respective chairs and consumed our respective pies.

The hall was half empty when Luce finally wound down and conceded to drive me home. Ned had left before us to shuttle home his grandmother. He'd shot me a look before departing, which I couldn't interpret, leaving me relieved to not have to talk with him again. That was a bad sign, I thought. I shouldn't give a damn.

The next day, Sunday, was a true day of rest. I slept late and well, and, owing to the return of April showers, spent the day reading one of the mystery novels I'd acquired from the library. In breaks I browsed through the rest of the stack, and augmented my crime-novel file with a separate folder on creative ways to dispatch somebody.

I'd given up trying to ignore the urge to write a mystery. The urge might have dissolved on its own if I hadn't stepped straight into an actual murder case. Secretly I had hoped to learn something new about the Jake Baldwin case at the dinner, but everyone had just repeated the few known facts, colored with speculation. That started my own speculation, which niggled Writer Me into wanting to create something from it. Maybe I could do it differently this time, without toxifying my soul.

Among the crime novels I browsed, I found several imaginative murder weapons. An eight-inch vintage hatpin; unexpected allergies (aspirin in one, nicotine in another); a huge icicle—strong enough to serve as a lance—and then the evidence melted; postage stamps tainted with drugs that enslaved the population that licked them. I was mighty glad the USPS had switched to self-adhesive stamps.

Seeking more novels to study, I searched the Internet. That unearthed two series involving older ladies. One was a sleuth who, owing to her innocuous, harmless appearance, served as a courier and spy for a secret crime-solving agency; the other was a down-on-her-luck former society woman who still had access to private affairs that slick upper-class criminals frequented. She simply carried a pistol in her purse, shot the culprit, and walked out during the subsequent confusion. Nobody ever looked twice at her, aging and unimportant, motiveless, above suspicion.

The combination supported my growing feeling that Jake Baldwin's killer was female. No muscle needed, just surprise, isolation, and the cover of weather. If I tried to directly research the prospective suspects, like, by asking questions of the locals, I would expose myself to too much interest; but as things stood I had good ideas to base my future novel around, and I could tie in the story Ned had told me about Fiona Cobb freezing to death at the bottom of her stairs. Who could know if she'd been going out for the mail or responding to a hail from outside, and just received a push that knocked her out? Mother Nature would do the rest. Again, surprise, isolation, and weather.

When my neck and eyes started complaining about overuse, I parked my notes in the file drawer, donned a sweatshirt, and sat out on the covered porch to wind down by watching the weather. This day's rain was gentle, greening up the world almost as I watched, with the distant hills turning vaguely maroon against gray background, and veiled by shreds of cloud and fog that lifted and sank as the day progressed. Quite different from the deluge that had accompanied my arrival. Whereas then I'd felt alienated and disoriented, now I was starting to feel settled, and cautiously optimistic.

The cats signaled their approval by accepting the altered environment I'd provided, and resumed sleeping all night on my bed. That made rolling over hard, but it was the normal arrangement for us, and I welcomed its return.

CHAPTER 8

How long has it been since I've slept with a man? Two years, I guess, more or less. The last one was Dave, a one-nighter for old times' sake after Dad's funeral, when we both needed to reaffirm life. Our previous relationship added a level of safety to the encounter: We already knew it wouldn't be going anywhere come morning.

Dave is the only one of my boyfriends to ever interact with my father, during the interval between college and settling into a career. Dave was the most easygoing of them all, and the most straightforward. I attribute this to his love of nature, a deep study of which—coupled with much time spent in the wilderness—gives him a different slant on life from the rest of us caught up in the rat race.

He ended up loving mountains more than people, and has devoted his life to climbing and protecting them. I still admire his passion and vision although I think it's futile. Maybe time will prove him right and me wrong. I hope so. I would be up there with him if he'd been able to love me as much.

* * *

Monday, I got back to work. I'd used up all the gain from last week so returned to daily quota, building Katy's adventures from a mix of notes, some research online and in reference books, then letting my imagination run to fill in the blanks.

I expected no interruptions. Luce had things to do, and there was no longer a reason for Ned to stop in; Rock Maple Road was open and all he had to do was pop whatever mail into my roadside box and move on. When I heard his Jeep turn in, I stayed at my desk lest he see me peer out at him. Unexpectedly, he continued down Rock Maple Road. I wondered why, since Jake had been the only full-time resident beyond me. Perhaps the retirees were home from the south, and he was delivering to their place.

Hmm. That gave me opportunity to intercept him at my box on his way back. I wanted to; I was ready for a break and still feeling good, and would enjoy a few moments of friendly banter. I couldn't risk it, though, because he could too easily misinterpret my motives. Probably would. Better to play it safe and stayed ensconced.

Nevertheless, he tooted his horn at the house after slapping my mailbox closed, then zoomed away.

Outside it was wet again, a hanging mist rather than actual raindrops. I didn't bother suiting up against it when I went outside to retrieve the day's offerings. Whoopee—three bills and some junk mail. Also, a folded note. I didn't see it until a white square slipped from among the envelopes and landed in a puddle. I snatched it up, and although splotched it was still readable.

> Sesquipedalian. If you don't know this one, I'll eat your junk mail for a week!
>
> —N.

I laughed. Of course I knew that word! "Having many syllables," I answered aloud. The dictionary confirmed: "given to or characterized by the use of long words."

The exchange gave me a silly glow. He had picked the perfect way for us to platonically flirt, which is all I wanted. I amused myself composing a suitable reply to put out tomorrow morning, then went back to work.

After lunch, when the skies were starting to clear, I heard a vehicle rumble into the driveway. I peeked out to see a dark-green pickup truck, high-mileage looking but not as workaday as Ned's, and a petite woman in a cowboy hat and sunglasses waiting on the stoop.

Who…?

Recalling my speculations about armed women surprising people at their doors, I only opened the inner door and greeted her through the storm-door glass. "Hello, may I help you?"

"Hi. I'm Anna Rawson. Are you Jane Brown?"

"Yes. And…"

"I'm here to ask permission to park on your land to hunt turkey. Previous owner always let me—there's a pull-in down the road, and a nice area around back your hill where I've had good luck. The shot won't come anywhere near your house, and I'm usually in and out early."

"I, uh, well, I don't know, I guess so. Um, when will this take place?"

I unlocked the storm door and held it open with my arm.

Anna stepped back instead of coming in. "Season starts next week and runs all month. But I'd like to do a little scouting first."

"Okay, sure. I'm sorry, I've never had to deal with this before, and I don't really understand what you do and what it means."

"Well, you're not the first. Better decide quick if you want hunters… you'll have to post the land if not. I'm hoping you'll stay open. Really, most of us are okay. There's a second turkey season in the fall, but I skip that one. You'll get a lot of deer guys, though." She paused and cocked a hip. "At least you won't have to deal with poaching anymore, now that Jake's gone."

I didn't know how to respond to that. "I guess I'd better learn what the hunting seasons are," was my best attempt, meanwhile thinking: *Good grief, more death!* The whole month of May, with another to come in the fall.

My magma started to bubble again. Here I'd thought I could buy myself some privacy, only to learn that my land was considered public unless I fenced people out. Posting signs wouldn't be enough: too easy to ignore or tear down, too vulnerable to weather. I would have to spend a fortune to fence twenty acres, or hire someone to patrol, or just give in.

I turned away and sighed while Anna waited. At least she'd been polite enough to ask.

Really, how could I refuse her? I owned acreage that could give people food. Just because I came from a sanitized world where meat arrived in plastic-sealed foam trays didn't mean everyone else did, or was required to. Plenty of rural folks obtained meat from the wild, just as they raised livestock or grew vegetables. I was already contributing passively to the local food economy by having a nearby farmer cut my upper fields in exchange for the hay he fed his cows. That deal had come with the house, thanks to Ned's uncle, who had also allowed hunters to share his bounty.

The other thing I had to consider was my own hypocrisy. How could I think about killing people for emotional reasons then deny someone killing animals for food?

I turned back to Anna and said, "Yes," even though I felt my face get hot and tight from rising blood pressure. "Please feel free. And thank you for asking. But I would appreciate it if you let me know when you're going to be around. Hold on a sec."

I nipped into my office, grabbed a business card, and handed it to her. "Just call or e-mail on days you plan to come, and when you're done for the season. I wander around sometimes and don't want to get into your line of fire."

She pocketed the card and grinned. "Wear orange, I guess. Or those jingle bells some hikers wear. Don't worry, I'm careful—won't shoot anywhere near the house. Well, anyway, thanks. I'll let you know."

She took herself off, leaving me staring after her.

I paused in thought, then locked up, realizing as I did so that the gesture was silly. Anyone who wanted to break in could waltz right in the back, at least while I was home.

I'd taken to leaving windows and curtains open, doors unlocked, on all sides except the front, where road frontage made me feel too exposed. The difference between front and back amounted to only a few yards and angles, but closing the front gave an illusion of privacy and security. I'd lived with that illusion most of my life, as too many people too close together tried to shut each other out. The open back, in contrast, made me feel free. I ended up locking the back door before I resumed work, having been reminded by this train of thought that a killer was still on the loose.

I forgot about it through immersion into writing, and didn't resurface to reality until dinnertime. After eating I retired to the screened-in porch to nurse a drink, bundled up against a sharp drop in temperature and rising wind. Tessa on my lap listened with me to a woodcock doing his strange mating cry and flying ritual, and then owls hooting mournfully. The sky had fully cleared and no light competed with the stars beyond what I generated inside the house.

Thank you, Daddy, I sent into the ether. He had been a dedicated city man but understood that some people needed quiet and space. He and I had never been close, but he had always done right by me, and I hoped he somehow knew that his departure from life had given life back to me through his material gifts. We'd had a disconnected sort of love, but love it was in the end. I'd never gotten it from my mother because she had died too early, taken out by cancer when she was thirty-eight and I was eleven; and my brother had been gone from the house before I could get to know him. He'd been on the other side of the world for enough years that I'd lost track.

Suddenly fatigued, I prepped for bed, thinking about love of all sorts, and wondering if I'd ever have another lover. I had sworn off sex but sometimes missed it; what I really missed was lying against a warm body, and having someone to kiss. Ned, I was sure, would volunteer in a heartbeat if I gave him the right sign, but I didn't want to deal with him trying to rescue me, or whatever woman issue he had. Everybody had issues—sexual or otherwise—which was why I didn't want a lover. My own issues were more than enough, thankyouverymuch, and it was impossible to add another person to the equation without adding more issues.

Ned did seem willing to engage mind to mind. Was it possible with him to have a semi-regular, light, noncommittal interaction without sending the wrong message? Or should I cut him off now and stick with my plan to stay safe in the sanctuary I'd worked so hard to create?

The answer didn't come before sleep…a rich, deep sleep that was hard to dredge myself out of in the morning. A glance out the window woke me up faster than coffee: The landscape was white! Three inches of snow! What the heck! Last week of April!

Well, mea culpa. I hadn't checked the forecast, and this was the Green Mountains. I'd skied here with Luce in May some years back; and any year the weather cooperated, the big ski areas stayed open until June.

My furry kids didn't know this, though. In fact, they had never experienced snow. I let them out in the kennel run to discover the new medium where it had blown in, and tossed a few slushy snowballs for them to chase or leap back from while I tracked around the yard inspecting daffodils shoots still green and forsythia screaming yellow in contrast to the white coating. Then, hands frozen, I slopped across the lawn to put my note to Ned in the mailbox:

You won't have to eat the junk mail, at least this week. Sesquipedalian means "having many syllables." Here's one at the opposite end of the spectrum: foy. Bet you've never heard that in conversation!

I certainly hadn't. I'd encountered the word in a book and had to look it up ("a farewell feast or gift"). I couldn't figure out how to work it into a young-adult manuscript, so I moved on to writing in simpler terms, saving the fun of finding another word for Ned for when I took a break.

Midmorning, I again heard his Jeep turn in; again, he tooted his horn on his way back out. The gesture warmed me enough to ponder introducing a romantic element into young Katy's adventures. She was only twelve but heck, I'd been younger than that when I'd had my first crush. For adolescent romance, however, I would have to consult my editor. These novels were supposed to be chaste and focused outward, loading girls with inspiring education and experience. Our job as series writers was to make the stories interesting and emotionally compelling without getting heavy. First crush, first love, was heavy-duty stuff.

Doing my job right absorbed me until the phone rang in the early afternoon. The shrillness startled me into a gasp, then I stalled, deciding whether to let the machine pick up. Only a handful of people had my number, and I wasn't sure I wanted to talk with any of them. I was ready for a break, though, and curious to know who wanted to speak with me enough to call, so I got up and checked Caller ID then answered on the kitchen wall phone.

"Janey! Have you heard?" cried Luce.

That cued me to sit down. "What?"

"There's been another murder!"

"No!"

"Yes, last night! They're thinking it's the same killer!"

"You mean, another front-door point-blank shot?"

"No, another mysterious killing, in the middle of bad weather."

A guilty thrill ran through me. There really was a case building up worthy of a murder mystery!

I asked Luce to hold while I swapped the wall phone for the cordless in the kitchen and sat at the table, pulling a notepad and pen to the ready. "What happened? Who was killed?"

"Len Gustave, one of the town zoning commissioners. They found him half a mile from his house on the roadside next to his truck, with his head bashed in."

"Yikes! Does he have a family?" If so, my heart wrenched for them. Unless he had been a stinker like Jake Baldwin, in which case they were probably relieved. In which case the cops would have to look at the wife.

"Yeah, a wife, an ex-wife, and a pair of kids from each of them."

"Oh, jeezus. Who found him?"

"Town road crew, plowing and sanding before dawn. They got heavier snow up there and found him partially covered."

I was jotting notes while she spoke, so only said, "Uh-huh."

"They figured he was on his way home from the monthly zoning meeting, but why he stopped and got out of the truck, nobody knows."

"Uh-huh."

I bet I knew the answer to that one: a damsel in distress. In the snow, in the dark…some lady pulled over with flashers on and hood up…

I didn't verbalize these thoughts. The police would probably figure out the scenario, as was their business, while mine was fiction. I didn't want to think about the victim as a person so I could make up my own means, motive, and opportunity, and address emotion later.

Still, I was curious. "Who was this guy? I haven't heard of him."

"You're probably better off. He was another rotter."

Oh-ho. Another. I wasn't the only one thinking there's a pattern. "So do we have a twisted Robin Hood on the loose? Instead of robbing from the rich and giving to the poor, he's killing the bad guys for the sake of the good guys?"

"Maybe." I could almost see her shrug. "If so, we're all in trouble. What if somebody out there is playing God and deciding who is worthy to live and die? That's what we've got laws for, so people won't run around doing that to each other."

"Guess that will motivate everyone to be extra nice so they're not the next victim."

"Meanwhile locking their doors and turning hostile to strangers, mistrusting their friends and neighbors, packing guns everywhere they go..."

Not a pretty picture, I agreed, but also not so far from what was going on elsewhere in the world. Why should Vermont be immune?

I felt heat and pressure in my head from remembering that the social deterioration I'd tried to escape had followed me. Then I shuddered, remembering my own thoughts about turning vigilante. More and more I was convinced someone had reached that point and believed they were performing a social service.

"So...what was so bad about Gustave?"

Luce sighed. "He was a developer and general contractor, and took every opportunity to screw people. That's why when you asked me for local referrals I didn't give his name. He's faked perk tests on land he's sold, forced illegal rights-of-way, swapped maps out of the town hall records and replaced them with bogus ones; and, as a zoning official, he's denied permits to people who needed them, and given them to people who bent the rules. Especially himself. All while promoting himself as a devout Christian and smiling to your face while stabbing you in the back. But there's some sort of good-old-boy network that protects him, so he's been able to get away with it."

"In that case, I'm wondering why the killer didn't stab him in the back."

"No, they just coshed him on the head. Tried to make it look like the hood of his own truck came down on the back of his skull, but the cops weren't fooled."

"How do you know all this?"

"A lot of it was in the online local news. Which I assume you didn't read."

"Not yet." I wondered whether a certain someone was going to leave the relevant print edition of the paper in my mailbox tomorrow.

"Then on the TV news," Luce added, "which I assume you didn't watch."

Nope. I would check as soon as I got off the phone.

"Also," Luce added, "I have a few pals who have other pals, and information got unofficially passed along."

"Helps to be connected," I said, while wondering how I could connect with the community well enough, and subtly enough, to learn more about local women's stories without being conspicuous.

"How old was this guy?" I asked after a pause.

"I don't know, maybe fifty-something."

Drats, there went my theory that the killer and victims had been in school together. Jake had been seventy-two, and that Fiona Cobb who "fell" down the stairs—didn't Ned say she was similar age? Still, those two were parental generation for Gustave. Maybe there was a vendetta that went way back. If the cops didn't connect the dots right, they might miss a hatred that had begun decades ago.

"Was Gustave a native?" I asked.

"Not sure. I can find out." Luce paused. "You sound like you have an idea."

I laughed with false casualness. "I always have ideas. That's what they pay me for."

"Well, why don't you come over tonight for dinner and tell me more about them."

I stiffened, quashed the reflex, and said, "That sounds great. What's cooking?"

"I don't know—Peter's on duty tonight."

I hadn't seen Peter since before my move, and missed talking with him. Also, he was an imaginative chef. So I accepted the invitation and, unlike months earlier when I hated going anywhere with anyone, began to look forward to the get-together.

After some repeating of what we'd already said, Luce and I signed off.

I shifted to my desk and looked up online news reports. They said essentially what Luce had conveyed, with the additional info that the crime had taken place about five miles away from me as the crow flies, but nowhere near in terms of topography. Between my location and the road where Gustave had died stood a ridge whose serrated top touched over three thousand feet and divided the regional watershed into easterly and westerly flows. It also carried the state's primary hiking route, the Long Trail, which in this section shared a track with the Appalachian Trail. It would take ten or more miles of roadway to connect the sites. *Not in my backyard this time*.

While online, I checked my e-mail for the first time since morning. The external world engaged me for a few minutes, then I logged off and got back to work. By then, the snow had already melted away.

CHAPTER 9

Skiing with Luce long ago, we rode up the lift together then took different trails down the mountain. Our skill levels were comparable, but she liked moguls while I liked long swishy runs. Each trip we warmed up on the same slopes then drifted apart, skiing solo and meeting at the bottom if just the two of us, or traversing the mountain with other folks if we'd come with a bus group. The company we worked for was so huge it owned a ski house in Orton for employees to use, and ran one day trip and one weekend trip per month every winter.

On that bluebird-sky day of perfect snow, I stood at the top and soaked up the scenery. I should have gloried in its beauty—Adirondack Mountains on the western horizon, White Mountains to the east, the Green Mountains undulating brown and white in between—but instead I saw the rape of the land and realized what it meant. Everything my eyes beheld had once been aboriginal lands and habitat for wildlife, destroyed for later people's travel and recreation or their food and shelter so they could survive and reproduce. And reproduce. And reproduce, which they will do until nothing is left. Two world wars and umpteen regional ones in the last century have killed millions of people around the globe yet the population keeps growing into the billions. There's nothing to stop it. We will fight and kill and consume until Earth can't support us anymore. It's happening so fast now, on such an enormous, cancerous scale, led by so many stupendously stupid and greedy people, that I can't imagine humanity lasting another century.

That day on the mountain, guilt consumed me—for existing, for the privilege of standing on the mountaintop, for needing the resources that had gotten me there, and which fueled my life and everyone else's and directly or indirectly consumed the land without giving anything back. I was helpless to change a thing. The only possible long-term outcome was downhill.

The enormity of it drove me to plant my ski poles and shove away, leaping downhill literally with hair-streaming speed. I skied so perfectly that run, I could have won an Olympic medal—until one ski tip caught roughage at the edge of the trail and wobbled my balance. While I flailed to keep it, a reckless snowboarder whooshed up from behind and cut across my skis, nailing my shoulder with a flying hand and sending me tumbling while he—she? I never saw—disappeared beyond the snow plume I plowed up with my face.

I recall little after that, just broken images and fireworks of pain as the ski patrol sledded me off the mountain. I came to fully in the hospital, where Luce waited to take me home. That was the end of our skiing together, and the beginning of my slide down a different slope to another crash.

* * *

My skiing wipe-out had occurred not far from the door of the slopeside condo now owned by Luce and Peter at Fall Line Resort. They'd bought their unit well after my mishap but before the real estate boom turned Vermont's surviving ski areas into four-season resorts, and they would eventually reap a big profit from it. For the time being it was their home away from home in Connecticut.

These days, Luce spent half her time here while Pete stayed downcountry bringing in the bacon. During my perch in their condo while suspended between New York apartment and new Vermont home, they'd both been mostly in Connecticut then on their vacation cruise.

In prep for the evening, I leisurely showered and leisurely dressed, followed by a leisurely drive to Orton. My almost-new Subaru Forester lumbered up their twisty driveway, and I tucked it at the end of the lineup on the condo's parking pad: Peter's black BMW sedan, Luce's gold SUV, and somebody unknown's brand-new white Lexus.

That somebody proved to be Fall Line's owner; or, rather, one-half of the owning couple, Bobbie Banella. I had met her in passing years ago, although I barely remembered her and was sure she'd forgotten me. Luce had known Bobbie since college. Both had been superachievers at one of the Seven Sisters colleges that churned out movers and shakers. Bobbie was short and compact, solid of body but soft of face, a package made attractive by smile folds and a touch of pink lipstick. I could scarcely keep my eyes off her haircut, a masterpiece of scissorwork that kept a straight chin-length bob in perfect place no matter how she moved her head.

Peter popped out from the kitchen to say hello then retreated into a cloud of intriguing aromas. He remained in view, a tall, dark, square-jointed figure in an apron, with a bald spot sticking out amid rugged curls like a peak above the treeline. He danced back and forth between the granite countertop framing the cook area and island that divided the kitchen from the lounge, coordinating vegetables and cookware.

Once Luce had given me a wineglass and I placed myself on one of the tight-fabric armchairs flanking the couch Bobbie sat in the middle of, they resumed their conversation about Len Gustave.

"I used to hire him for our developments," Bobbie said, jangling silver bracelets as she waved a dismissive hand, "but he either screwed up everything or padded his bills. Then, when I booted him, he threatened to sue. Not that he had a leg to stand on, so I laughed him off. He's been bad-mouthing us ever since."

"You didn't kill him, I presume," I said, evoking a double eyebrow arch from Luce.

Bobbie laughed and drained her glass. "No, but I admit to the temptation. I'm trying to figure out what to tell the police when they catch up to me."

"Call Frank," came Peter's voice. I gathered he meant *call your lawyer.*

"Pete, honey, show Jane the updated story," Luce directed.

He picked up a tablet computer from the counter where he was working, tapped it a few times, then slid it across the countertop between rooms. I rose to take it, then stayed standing to read about the murder as the headline story on the *Marble Valley Tribune's* website:

Vermont's Own Serial Killer?

Leading Allenburg citizen 57-year-old Len Gustave was slain last night less than a mile from his home on Settlement Hill. The body was found at 5:30 this morning by the Allenburg plow crew, who noticed Gustave's truck parked on the shoulder and a suspicious lump in front of it under the snow. Gustave was wearing the clothing, coat, and hat he was last seen in when leaving the zoning commission meeting at the Allenburg Town Hall on Monday night.

But the hat wasn't enough to protect his head from a vicious assault from behind. State Police are searching for the murder weapon, which may have been a metal tool from Gustave's truck or the assailant's vehicle. An autopsy is planned, which will narrow down the possibilities.

There was no apparent reason for Gustave to have stopped on the roadside. His truck appears to be running perfectly. If he was flagged down by another motorist or he intentionally met someone will never be known, as any tracks were obliterated by the late-season snowfall, and no passing drivers have been located who might have seen anyone on that dark stretch of road between houses on Settlement Hill.

This is the second homicide in a week involving Allenburg citizens. Jake Baldwin, 72, of North Allenburg, was shot dead in his home, also on a night with weather that erased any sign of a person or vehicle.

Police have not found a link between the victims. They are confident one will emerge to explain this pair of astonishing murders.

The article went on to recount Vermont's lack of serial murders over time, and listed a number to call if readers had any pertinent information. It closed with a singing of Gustave's praises. I would have believed them if I hadn't been informed of his real nature. Instead I wondered what cultural imperative had started the practice of not speaking ill of the dead, to the point of turning everyone into a saint after they passed away. Disgusted, I slid the tablet back across the counter and to my seat.

"So, do you think it's a serial killer or a coincidence?" Bobbie asked the room while raising her empty glass. Luce lifted a bottle from the side table and tipped the rest of it into Bobbie's goblet.

"Serial killer," said Peter.

"I concur," said Luce.

I abstained from opining by sipping from my still half-filled glass and turning my attention to Bobbie. "How long did you know Gustave?"

Bobbie shrugged. "Since high school. He was a loser then, and a loser now. A total phony. I'm not surprised someone killed him."

I slung a look at Luce, projecting, *This is getting to be a popular refrain.*

"Did you know him?" I asked her.

Luce shook her head. "Only to say hello to."

I turned back to Bobbie. "So is he from Orton, or did you grow up in Allenburg?"

"I'm born and bred two miles from where we're sitting. Thought I'd gotten out of here for good when I went to college, but family business brought me back. Lenny-boy's family has been here longer than mine, which is what gave him an in with local enterprise. Which of course he milked for all it was worth."

I could see how that might happen. Orton was a "gold town," meaning, it had higher taxes owing to its prosperity. Skiing was a dominant industry in Vermont, despite its shrinkage over decades, and many well-heeled out-of-staters vacationed at the resort year round now that it offered golf and mountain biking and rock climbing and zip-lining. The town kept growing to accommodate visitor demand. The resultant cost-of-everything differential was one reason I lived on the other side of the hill, outside a town whose industries had died off with the advent of the internal combustion engine.

The differential made me wonder anew what Jake Baldwin, barely solvent in Allenburg, and Len Gustave, a successful if unscrupulous builder in Ortonbut resident in Allenburg, had in common. Yet…the towns were only twelve miles apart, so no reason there couldn't be a history. A deal gone bad. A person. A woman. But who, and how?

"Janey has some ideas about Lenny," Luce prompted.

I shook my head. "Not really. I'm only playing around with ideas because the situation might make a good plot for a novel."

"Well, you've got yourself a nice little murder mystery," said Bobbie. "I can think of at least ten people who'd be happy to kill him. I don't envy the cops their job."

"Do you know of any connection between him and Jake Baldwin?"

"Other than being bastards?" Bobbie shook her head, her liquid bronze helmet flipping tidily then falling back into place when she stopped.

"There are a lot of bastards around," Luce said, swirling the wine in her glass. "I wonder how many are going to get knocked off before the killer gets caught."

"The bigger problem," said Peter, entering the room and wiping his hands on a towel, "is who the killer thinks is a bastard. I keep worrying about who we might have insulted without realizing it."

"You're safe, lamb," Luce said, smiling at him. "I don't think you've insulted anyone in your life."

He smiled back. "You'd be surprised."

I would be, too. Peter was the nicest guy I knew. It still surprised me every time I met him to recall that he was the chief financial officer of a megacorporation. I expected someone in that role to be more aggressive and dynamic than this relaxed and quiet man. Then again, I shouldn't be surprised, having only interacted with him on his off time, in his home, where he puttered and read and cooked and supported local interests. Maybe he was a tiger at the office, and didn't bring his work home. He must be a tiger in bed to still have a warm and often frisky relationship with Luce after so many years. First marriage for both of them, having met at first job out of college.

He called us to table and served a tasty mixed-ethnicity meal. After we'd praised him about the food, and fallen silent for minutes to tuck into it, he continued the conversation topic as if uninterrupted.

"What troubles me about these killings is they've left the bodies around."

We all paused and stared at him, forks halfway to our mouths.

"Look at it this way. Vermont is the land of backwoods and backhoes. Anywhere in the north woods, or the remote west, for that matter, is so sparsely populated and underpoliced that people can just kill whoever they want and bury them where they'll never be found. That is, if the killer is careful. This one must want be caught, because he's not bothering to hide the bodies. Yes, there's a delay before finding them, but in essence it's immediate—compared to the time it might take for anyone to find missing people in the backcountry."

"Years," Bobbie said, then resumed eating more slowly, with a scowl. "Or never."

"Maybe," Luce said, "the killer is too weak to move the bodies. Neither of the victims is small, especially Jake. I sure wouldn't want to lug his dead weight around, and I'm no delicate flower!"

I chuckled privately then suggested, "It could go the other way: Maybe the killer is an obvious candidate for burying people with backhoes, so he's doing something opposite to throw the cops off the scent."

Something about the backhoe put me off my food. While the others gabbled in agreement or disagreement, I felt my consciousness receding into vision of an industrial-size backhoe, an excavator, one of those ugly yellow machines with arms and claws…hearing the deep flatulence of its diesel starting up and belching black smoke from a pipe with a rattling top…the creak and rumble of treads as a faceless operator swiveled the cab and extended the arm to pick up the body and trundle it off into the forest, or started attacking the earth to dig a grave…

The cold-bloodedness of it all transformed the intriguing idea of killing someone into a gory reality. There would be blood. And stench. And heavy, lifeless limbs, perhaps gaping eyes. Somebody would never get home to feed the dog, or turn the lights on, and other somebodies would wonder where they had gone. Or maybe not, which was worse. Still other somebodies would have to search for them, and deal with their possessions and property, or have their heart broken and their routines forever disrupted, with an abyss occupying the dead person's place.

My angry fantasies about doing away with evil people had never included aftermath. Or, more accurately, the only aftermath I had considered was the relief, maybe even joy, that came from the problem person being removed. I hadn't thought about the problem person losing their life. I'd never cared. But suddenly I was sad that such unlovable, cruel, useless people had been denied their four-score-and-ten. Why should they? Why shouldn't they? Whose job was it to decide who lived and died if there wasn't a deity to do it?

Looking around the table, I marveled that my companions, whom I believed to be practicing Christians, had not yet expressed dismay that two of God's children had been robbed of their existence. Neither had the media reporters. Had the victims really been so awful that these god-fearing, generous people applauded their demise? Or was everyone a moral phony, like me?

A desire to talk about this with Ned seized me. I promptly smothered it.

Looking to a man to echo and justify my feelings was number-one stupid on my list of Things Not To Do In Your New Life, Jane. But I wasn't comfortable talking at the next level of intimacy and complexity with my friends at the table. Something about Ned had suggested to my subconscious that maybe I could talk about such things with him. Should I heed my gut reaction or dismiss it?

I never knew which to pay attention to: my rational self or the intuitive other. There seemed to be a right time to do either/both, but in four decades I'd not gained the sense of which to do when. Part of my subconscious was waving yellow warning flags. Were they about Ned, or my desire to use the in-my-backyard murder mystery as a plot for my own novel?

My desire to know how it was going to play out was interfering with my visions of how it might do so. Curiosity could get me into trouble if I started nosing around. I felt my curiosity rising to discomfort level as talk about Jake Baldwin and Len Gustave continued around me. I needed to either change the subject, mentally withdraw for a while, or leave the room and do something else.

I withdrew from the conversation to think about murder mysteries. I had enough information about the real killings to invent a fictional scenario, an exercise that would serve as personal therapy. Unlike imagining killing my apartment neighbor, which was driven by hostility, using the murders of Jake Baldwin and Len Gustave—total strangers, nothing to do with me—would pull me outside myself. I could apply my intellect and harness unresolved feelings into drawing authentic characters. That would reduce the daily battle between my better self who wrote Katy Fox novels and the ugly self I had to keep stuffing back into a fireproof box.

All this was way too personal to discuss over dinner at Luce and Peter's. They and Bobbie had worn out the subject of Len Gustave's murder by the time I surfaced from my thoughts, so I initiated a change of subject.

When Luce, Bobbie, and Peter paused in their discussion to clean their plates, I inserted, "And now for a complete non sequitur."

They looked at me. Into the silence I said, "Can any of you recommend a lawn service?"

They blinked but accepted the shift. To help them help me, I elaborated. "I need to either get a push mower, which will be hard on my knee, or a lawn tractor, which will be hard on my wallet and something I don't want to take care of and store year round. My yard isn't much—I could do it with a push mower—and the big fields are going to be taken care of by a local farmer, but there's an area in between I don't want to go completely wild, and I'll need a riding mower for that. It's growing so fast, I swear, two inches since this morning, even with the snow! If I buy a riding mower, I'll need a truck and trailer to get it home or pay extra for delivery. So I'd like to get numbers for mowing services and compare against buying."

Peter nodded. Luce offered, "We use Green Mountain Maintenance."

"But they're in Orton, not Allenburg," Bobbie said, "and will charge her extra for travel."

"True," said Pete, then turned to Luce. "How about Ned?"

Luce looked at me in wide-eyed innocence. "Great idea. Lawn-care is his gig when he's not doing post office."

I fought to keep my own eyes from widening. The idea surprised, appealed to, and bothered me at the same time. I was sorry to have set myself up for this because now I'd have to concoct a reason to reject the suggestion. Or else accept it, and be glad.

"I didn't realize he had his own business," I said blandly, wondering when he had the time around a regular job.

"Sure," said Pete. "He's got several. Mowing, sugaring, plowing, some handyman, on top of backup farm chores and animal care for his clan. That combination used to be how he made his living. Then he got the rural delivery route, and a nice steady paycheck. But it doesn't take all his time, so he's kept up with his other business interests, just backed them down a notch."

Pete didn't quite shake his head in amazement, but I knew from previous conversations that he held the seasonally and self-employed folks of the north country to be bewilderingly heroic. He'd suckled the teat of white-collar security all his life, and now earned a salary the envy of most Vermonters—nay, the majority of northern New Englanders. Positions like his didn't exist in the region; there were no businesses of that scale.

The same held true for Luce—and me, for intermittent chapters of my career. She and I had met at the corporate headquarters of an insurance company in Connecticut, where she managed the division and I wrote policy text and collateral documents. I had loathed the job but been good at it; she loved running the show in any context, and because she was happy, she looked outward instead of inward, and had seen my throttled discontent. She'd set me on a new course by telling me during an annual performance review: "My cousin works for *Women on the Move* and they're looking for reporters and reviewers. You ought to check it out; might be a better channel for your skills."

Three months later, I was jetting around the world on somebody else's dime and discovering that the rigors of international travel outweighed the thrill of writing about it. Still, it was the longest job I'd held until my current one as a series writer, and I compiled a terrific portfolio while visiting cathedrals and skyscrapers and exotic island resorts, ancient aqueducts and tunnels, museums and spectacular ruins.

While seeing the world in all its wonderfulness was exhilarating, seeing all the people who populated it had the opposite effect. Each subpopulation was utterly alien compared to one another, making it impossible for me to conceive how we could all live in peace together. They formed a wonderful mélange of cultures and potential but en masse remained the same in their petty concerns and turf wars, and their endless use of resources. I started to recognize just how many people there were in the world; and that number was as psychologically crushing to me as it was physically crushing to the planet.

Upon return to my own city where so many people were concentrated, and multiplying that number by the cities everywhere, I found it impossible to believe that we wouldn't consume everything there was. How could Earth possibly support so many who used so much, every single minute of every single day? And that didn't count the war-torn and impoverished poisoned areas—which, thankfully, I had managed to avoid.

The upside was, wherever I went I found a percentage of people to be kind and friendly, and a similar percentage to be brilliant and industrious. But they were outnumbered by the lemmings and overpowered by the manipulators behind the scenes. On a globe-hopping scale, I became more aware of and appalled by the numbers, the sheer numbers, of people trampling the environment and doing horrible things to each other. The day I saw news footage of a tsunami devouring a coastal city in Japan, I recognized the parallel between humans devouring themselves and their home.

It made me sick enough to back out of the travel journalist job as soon as I could. Bartending and waitressing, even bagging groceries, seemed a better plan. Dealing with folks on a local level made it easier to cope than when I viewed humanity on the global scale.

I couldn't regret the travel experience because it had led, eventually and indirectly, to writing novels for a living—a business Peter found as morbidly fascinating as logging and farming. We never sat in the same room without him asking me, "How's it going?" and really wanting to know.

At his inquiry tonight, I answered, "I'm mostly through the current manuscript, due in about a month. I don't have to do heavy research for this one so am able to mostly bang away at word count. Next week I'll probably get the galleys back for proofreading the previous book, which will be a fall release timed for holiday purchase."

"How many per year are you under contract to do? Sorry, I forgot."

"Three, but it might be four next year. Or I might switch to another series. That's all up in the air."

"And you're paid royalties, what, quarterly? And get an advance for each book?"

"Yes. It doesn't add up to much for an annual income, but now that I've paid off all my debt and bought both the house and car clear, I can live off a pretty slim paycheck."

I didn't have to explain to him that the big money had come from an inheritance, since he already knew. I'd also previously told him how the job worked, but his asking the same questions showed he'd not been listening before. Now I had his full attention, probably because I had actually pulled off my relocation and, as far as he knew, was making it work.

He moved on to the practical side. "Do you have an accountant up here yet?"

"No. Can you recommend anyone?"

He recited three names. I dug a notepad from my purse and wrote them down. Then I thought for the umpteenth time how grateful I was to have a steady writing job so I didn't need an agent to place my work and do contract service for me. That would consume twenty percent of my meager earnings.

"My goal," I told Peter, "is not only to keep this up indefinitely, but also to win a prize. Like, the Newbery Medal, which is top honors for children's literature. I'm not sure a volume in a contracted series will ever get it, or is even eligible, but that's the kind of brass ring I'm aiming for."

He nodded understanding and went back to his food and drink, while I privately moved on to envision other prizes. I could never win a Pulitzer but there were some juicy awards available to be won with a good debut mystery or a stellar romance.

I was contemplating how, or whether, to raise the subject of our local killings again to shore up my murder-mystery ideas when Luce broke out of her conversation with Bobbie and said, "You joining us for Green Up Day, Jane?"

Her voice contained an edge I recognized as a directive phrased as a suggestion. I resisted it by answering, "If I'm caught up on work, then sure. Which day is it again?"

"It's always first Saturday in May—this Saturday. Four days from now, so pay attention to your calendar. We meet at the library at 8:00 to get our special green trash bags and road assignments."

"Yeah, I guess so. I'll let you know on Friday."

I planned to go but played hard-to-get to remind her she wasn't my boss anymore. Yeah, I owed her favor payback, but that didn't mean she could run me. This friction arose between us now and then, and had since we were employer and employee. We'd managed to keep it from flaring into dominance wars, using it instead to keep each other's feet on the ground.

Even when we were in friction mode, I appreciated her caring intention to integrate me into the community. Back when I'd been house hunting, she had said of the villagers: "You'll stay in their good graces if you volunteer in local activities as well as use their professional services. You want those graces, because if the natives like and care about you, then they'll look out for you. As a woman alone, that's important."

I conceded the point, knowing I wasn't one of those female dynamos who could wield chainsaws and repair furnaces, or had a black belt in a martial art. I had built up my castle with every preventive and safety I could think of, which put me in a secure position, but I also knew that life always tossed in wildcards, and security could not be taken for granted. I needed other people, whether I liked it or not.

That's why I would help pick up roadside litter on Green Up Day and bring a dish to the potluck lunch in the park afterward. And probably go on the river cleanup a few weeks later, which Luce was already discussing with Bobbie.

CHAPTER 10

By the time I got home from Luce and Peter's, I knew I'd been lying to myself again. I did okay all evening, balancing emotion and rationalization, until the Green Up Day pressure at the end. The thought of cleaning up other people's trash, just because it's the right thing to do, bunted me back over the lip into my dark pit.

I can't stop wondering: Where's the line between being a responsible and compassionate human being and letting other people dump their responsibilities on you? So often—too often—people just get away with doing things, be it litter or murder, and other folks have to clean up after them. The do-badders rely without guilt on the do-gooders to compensate for them, while folks like me feel guilty because we resent or even abhor the do-badders. I feel guilty because I was raised in a society I didn't make or voluntarily join whose mores I'm supposed to adhere to. These include a lot of "shoulds," like taking responsibility for the irresponsible; and one mega "should not": I should not feel the bad things I feel and think the angry things I think, else I'm either selfish, sick, or immoral.

The fact anyone causes problems for others, by intention or from inconsideration or idiocy, creates an agonizing schism between my head and heart. Intellectually, I believe that the do-badders outnumber and outpower the do-gooders and nothing I do will matter in the end. Nothing anybody does really matters if you think on a universal scale. The meaning of life is: There isn't one. Humans are just biological organisms following their genetic imperatives, just like every other living thing on the planet. The fact our species can't accept that, thinks it's a higher order and better than everything else, makes our doom inevitable.

But then there's my heart. Actually, what I think is in my heart lies within my genes. I've inherited the biologic imperative to survive, which is what has kept me from picking up one of my guns and blowing my brains out, or doing same to anyone else. Something so deeply internal I can neither identify nor fight it compels me to hang in and see if there's a good reason for living despite evidence to the contrary. Humans have found a word for that: hope.

I'm starting to suspect that hope is a chemical rather than an abstract concept. There's none of it in my head or heart today, but my body thrusts forward as if hope is right there in sight on the horizon. The season change burgeoning all around me screams a message of revitalization, of rebirth—of hope—that I can't deny.

Maybe that's the silent force behind twelve-step programs, and pop-psych variations like "Act confident until you are confident," "The longest journey begins with the first step," and all that. The body knows what the mind might not accept, providing an inherent faith that simply continuing will take you to where you need to go, whether you feel like it or not. It might be the same mechanism that allows injuries and illness to heal.

If that's the case, if I allow myself to be the physical organism I am underneath all the thoughts and feelings that are by-products of being human, then maybe I can reconcile disillusionment with reality. After all, sheer panicked instincts led me to where better is possible, and my brain interprets that as hope.

* * *

The next morning I was so divorced from emotion, trying to fit words, sentences, and punctuation together into coherent Katy Fox scenes, that I didn't hear Ned's Jeep pass in either direction. When I surfaced for a break and went out to the mailbox, I found yesterday's newspaper folded around the bills and junk mail, along with a note.

> You've probably heard all about it from Luce, but here's a souvenir copy of the official story.
>
> As for "foy," the closest I've come to hearing that word in conversation is my aunt talking about her Roy the Froy toys from the 1960s.
>
> Am enjoying our persiflage.
>
> See you at Green Up?
>
> —N

I smiled and tucked the note into the back of my journal. *Persiflage*. He hadn't stumped me yet: I knew it meant "frivolous bantering talk" and "light raillery." Again I checked the dictionary to be sure. I would have to come up with something good to respond with. Hmm. Non sequitur?

Cheered by Ned's wordplay, I settled back to work. Sentences flowed better until hunger distracted me to break for lunch. I took a sandwich and book out onto the screened porch, and in the attention pauses while turning pages, I monitored the cats exploring the kennel run and sniffing the spring air. I shared their sense of confined freedom; the porch let me enjoy nature without having to go hiking and camping to find it. I could feel safe, holding the fantasy that life was good and could continue without threat.

After dallying for too long, I couldn't resist dallying for another moment longer to compose my response to Ned.

> I actually heard this used in a conversation once: "bandersnatch." Can you identify the source? Meanwhile, I hear you do lawns. Interested in another customer? If so, let me know when you can stop by to discuss.

I placed the note in my mailbox, then did an assessing circuit of the yard to see what next needed doing. Perennials could use more housekeeping, and there were bare spots where I could tuck in some colorful annuals. I calculated that the lawn would need cutting sooner rather than later, and there were piles and thickets that should be addressed.

I attended to none of it, not having blocked out the time, as well as not having a clear plan. I was working up a plan when I heard gunshots, so sprinted back inside before realizing I had reacted.

It took a moment for my heartbeat to stabilize, then to start berating myself. Silly to be startled; the shots came from so far away they couldn't possibly hurt me. I couldn't tell from which direction, though, because the surrounding hills bounced the sound around like in a bowl. I could tell only that they were muted but sharp, lacking any resonating boom. So it wasn't something of big caliber.

Bang-bang-bang; pause; *bang*, another *bang*; another pause; another few bangs, then silence.

I wondered: a hunter practicing for turkey season? Maybe Anna Rawson? I should have asked where she lived, might be right around the hill or other place nearby, which could account for what I'd just heard.

If not a hunter, then maybe somebody just target shooting. Then again, those shots might mean the killer wasn't satisfied with picking off one victim at a time and had moved on mowing down groups in some gathering place. Should I call the cops? Or trust that other people, closer to the source, would be able to tell the difference and call in anything abnormal?

Normal, abnormal—how was I supposed to know? Where I came from, gunfire might make national news. Here, it seemed, people could just fire away whenever they felt like it. The thought flashed me back to when Detective Greene had asked if I'd heard any gunfire over the rain. Hah. I'd wondered at the time, and again now, how far the sound would travel. Maybe Ned would know.

I wasn't going to ask. This experience underscored my decision to *not* target practice on my own land while a murder investigation was under way. Somebody might notice, care, and act.

Another series of bangs sent me to the floor to comfort the kitties. They were taking it better than I was, their heads popping up or whipping around at each muffled shot then their ears swiveling and twitching between reports. The fact they didn't dive under the furniture told me danger wasn't imminent. Nevertheless, they wouldn't play with toys or touch catnip until the gunfire stopped.

Okay, fine, I told myself. Welcome to rural Vermont. Another thing to cope with.

Coping itself would take some practice, I realized when I found myself unable to get back to work. An amorphous agitation preyed upon me. I knew I should channel that energy into another great work session, but an atavistic need to run was electrifying my nerves.

Find a way to spin it, Jane.

I decided to call it "spring fever." It was spring; I was in a fever. Even before the gunshots, I'd been itching to move, without exertion and focus; itching to explore my new realm and start defining the new me. So that's what I would do, braving the world where people fired guns whenever they felt like it.

I'd crossed off enough items on my to-do list that I could afford time for a drive-about. I gave it purpose by starting at the place I always felt comfortable—a library—then I would swing into Mapleton via the scenic route to restock my larder and maybe pick up some plants.

I grabbed my fabric grocery bags, a local map, and the library books I'd already read, and motored down the hill to Allenburg. At the library I walked in on two women at the desk gossiping with Helen about Len Gustave. She turned away from them to greet me and look at the mystery novels I was returning.

She met my eye with a smile. "Get anything out of them?"

"Yes and no. Enjoyment of the stories and the clever murder techniques, but nothing I can use for my own book."

I winced as soon as the words left my mouth. *Not* a good idea to advertise I was writing a mystery, as well as reading them, when there was a killer in town! The fact the book was years from fruition, if it ever happened, was irrelevant to the patron who looked at me over the top of her glasses. I wanted to smack myself upside the head.

Instead I said to Helen, "I'm not sure I'll stick with any of these series, so I'm going to browse for a while."

Which I promptly did, sailing out of the ladies' sight.

The library was tiny compared to others of my experience, but I still had a long way to go before I could say I'd sampled all its offerings. Within moments I was absorbed in pulling books and scanning their jackets and opening pages. The women resumed their conversation, probably assuming I was out of hearing range.

"Mellie is devastated," one woman said. I presumed she meant Gustave's wife.

"But maybe not surprised?" said the other. "I heard he was stepping out on her."

The first lady snorted. "Nothing new there."

"But who? They found him close to his house, but nobody else lives near there."

"He was on his way home," Helen said. "If he'd had an assignation, it was over by then."

"Have they figured out when he died yet?" lady number two asked. "Was there enough time after the meeting for him to have gone somewhere else?"

"I don't know. And if the police know, they're keeping it under their hat."

"Hell of a way to go," number one said. I envisioned her shaking her head.

"But who could've done it?" number two persisted. "If he had a, um, lady friend, then probably his wife did it. Or maybe his paramour did it because he wouldn't leave his wife."

"You've been reading too many novels," number one chided.

"Could be on the business side," Helen offered. "I've heard about more than one dirty deal."

I could understand how she might hear things, if people talked this freely at normal conversation volume with this place's acoustics. The ladies chorused agreement on the subject of dirty deals and launched into alternating recitations of stories they'd heard. Helen remained quiet. I moved between aisles and cleared my throat once or twice to remind them of my presence, but it didn't disturb them.

"Oh, I hope we don't have a serial killer running loose!"

"Don't worry, they always use the same method. That's how the cops catch them—their signature."

"Still, it's strange to have two killings so close together, and so close by! I knew they had a drug problem growing in Mapleton, but there's been no sign of it here."

"Maybe this is the first sign."

"I sure hope not! It's always been so peaceful here."

"Not anymore," Helen inserted.

I agreed with a sour snuffle.

Lady number one said, "I can't imagine that Len would be dealing drugs."

"Maybe some druggie was trying to rob him. He's pretty rich, you know, and it's awful isolated up there."

"Perfect place for an ambush."

"That's why I..."

I wearied of eavesdropping and moved to the reading nook where unborrowable materials were housed. A few moments of poking around unearthed the local history Helen had referred me to on my previous visit, so I parked in a chair and thumbed through it. I was surprised to learn how many enterprises had once packed the area, all of which had disappeared with the coming of first the train and then the automobile. What I was really hoping to find wasn't there: stories of local murders. Or scandals. This history was too old; I needed something a few generations more recent, like newspaper archives, and local school yearbooks that could supplement names and dates—which took up more storage space than Allenburg's little library could offer. Unless it had a really big basement...?

I didn't dare bring attention to myself by asking Helen. Besides, my purpose in moving was to mind my own business, right? There would be plenty of time during the long, dark winter to do that sort of research. By then the murders would be stale if not solved.

More patrons came and went. Finally the library was empty save for myself and Helen, so I brought the novels I'd selected to the desk for checkout.

She beamed and said, "All set?" as I presented my library card. She popped it into the slot of the kind of date stamper I hadn't seen since I was a kid. Then she pulled paper cards from their pockets in the back of the books and punched them into the stamper with an old, familiar clunk that had been replaced most everywhere else by barcode scanners.

As she tucked the cards back into the books, she looked up. "You'll be interested to know there's been quite an uptick in loans for your novels."

I smiled. "I guess that means people know I've moved into town." I waited a beat then added, "I appreciate the interest, but it would serve me better if they bought them."

"Ah, but maybe introducing them through the library will lead more people to buy more volumes in the series."

"That's what we hope." *We* meaning myself and everyone at my publishing house.

Helen turned brusque. "The traffic in your books suggests that people will turn out if you do a talk and a signing. Have you decided on a date yet?"

"Ah…no. I'm still sorting things out."

Helen's face crinkled then smoothed as she contained her annoyance. "While you're sorting, here's a Swedish crime writer you might enjoy." She withdrew a volume from under the counter. "It's a little dark, but the murder weapon is unusual. I find all the Swedish writers dark…perhaps because of their long winters. I always thought we had long, dark ones here, but then I remember all those high-latitude lands—Scandinavia, the British Isles, Russia, and Canada…even our own Alaska…"

Her usually rosy glow seemed to fade as her gaze turned inward. Something had taken her back into a private darkness, making me wonder what grief she held in her heart. I glanced at her hand and saw no wedding ring. Did that mean she'd never married, or her husband was dead or otherwise gone? Or was that irrelevant, and she was like me, yanked in opposite directions by conflicting heart and mind?

What you really need to mind, Jane, is your own business.

I gathered my books and hustled off to do my grocery shopping. All the way to Mapleton, I fretted over the possible connection I'd left behind. Something potent but fleeting had passed between me and Helen. I couldn't guess its nature, but it left me hungry to find out. By walking away I had missed a chance to learn something, and now had stuck myself in the frustration of Mapleton's rush hour.

Commuter traffic here was laughable compared to metro areas. Nevertheless, it got thick enough to be aggravating as people funneled through the town's big-box strip. I could have been anywhere in suburban America if I ignored the Green Mountains skyline, and the congestion drew me back into old fantasies about having a cannon mounted on the car's hood. I defused my temper by reminding myself how lucky I was to be able to shop whenever I felt like it. That was a luxury nine-to-fivers couldn't know, and it made me feel liberated.

At the same time, in the back of my heart I felt a fluttering of…not homesickness, but familiarity, which made me feel less adrift on an alien sea.

Still, the dense, erratic car flow and uncoordinated stoplights reduced me to cursing. There was no route around the strip except one that looped ten miles out of my way—the scenic route I'd decided not to take after I'd spent so much time at the library.

Luce and others had warned me that Vermont was short on roads, which map study had confirmed. There were few alternate ways to get anywhere—a liability proven several years back when a tropical storm had drifted too far inland and washed out main arteries as well as byways, and brought the state to a halt. Although everything had been put back together, nothing new had been added.

A high percentage of the state's roads were dirt or gravel and dead ends. I'd discovered this while house hunting, which had motivated me to select a place on a paved main road that took me in one direction to Allenburg and the other to Mapleton, by way of the only other paved main road in the quadrant.

Mapleton was an island of commerce surrounded by hilltowns and villages. People flowed into it like streams downhill. I followed the flow, zipped through the supermarket, and caught the traffic light sequence just right getting back out of town. I couldn't wait to get home and put my feet up on the screened porch.

En route I pondered Ned, the maybe-positive side of the surprises that had popped up on my doorstep. The question I couldn't answer was, should I shut him down or cultivate his interest?

I'd learned that platonic relationships with men were impossible if there was the tiniest spark of sexual attraction. I hadn't felt that spark in years and wished it wasn't flaring now. I wanted a friend, not a lover, yet my recurring interest in Ned was hard to explain without admitting to a spark. I was pretty sure he would try another approach toward me, since I hadn't shut him down hard enough. Could I keep him contained—did I want to?—and enjoy his friendship on platonic terms, or would he do something that made it a black or white choice?

No answer by the time I reached my sanctuary. Well, maybe the answer was the disappointment I felt upon not finding him waiting on the stoop.

CHAPTER 11

When Ned had perused my photo collage, I went tight in fear that he would see through my camouflage and spot my ex-lovers who are spaced throughout the display. Since they're intermixed among friends, family, and strangers, their presence isn't obvious, and Ned apparently wasn't looking for clues about my romantic past.

Last night I stared at the collection when I couldn't sleep. There they all were, spread across twenty years: Dave building a fire at a campsite in the Adirondacks. Eric posed on a Swiss Alps cornice against cerulean sky in a jazzy ski outfit and mirrored sunglasses. Cal leaning against the fender of a cool car back in Philadelphia. Phil looking stiff and stupid in a tux for our senior prom. Kent, my one-night stand, clamping a hand atop his cowboy hat and gripping the other hand on the strap around a bucking horse in Montana. JJ, the one who really mattered, who came and went over many years and places.

They were all wonderful, unique, good while it lasted, and we parted amicably enough (save for that disastrous boyfriend whose name shall not be honored with a mention; and, since technically he never became a lover, he doesn't count). I'm out of touch with all of them now, though I did locate each except JJ through Internet searching.

Whether JJ's invisibility means he's dead or just someone who eschews connectivity, I can't determine. No obituary has turned up for him, which is a good sign. I long ago set an online alert for his name in all its forms, but he, like me, has a super-common name: Robert James Jones, who had jazzed it up to JJ by the time I met him in between high school and college. Any combination of his names draws a zillion false positives. So far, adding place of birth, last known address, and birth date haven't narrowed the possibilities down to a clue. I could pay for a search service but refuse to accept I'm that desperate. What would I do if I found him? I may have loved him most of all, but so many years later it's irrational to think we might pick up where we left off, or start something new. I just want to learn what became of him, without cost.

I have to blame Ned for making me think about past lovers. I really don't want another one. I'm too old, too tired, too damaged to try again.

* * *

At sunrise I booted up my computer and typed "Ned Cavendish" into a search engine. Instantly dozens came up, including some of Ned's ancestors back to the 1700s. I found his address, a listing but not a website for his lawn service, and town newsletter mentions of his participation in local events. His full name was Edward Lowell Cavendish, born in North Allenburg, Vermont, forty-one years ago, graduated from—*whoa*, this explained a few things!—Harvard University with a bachelor's in History and Literature, and another degree from Cornell in agricultural engineering.

Interesting combination. Since details were not available without paying for them, I settled for the basic profile: well educated, no arrest record, no marriage record, nor any social media presence or technical forum participation.

I had to leave it there; work deadlines were pressing. It was the last day of the month, my manuscript was due in another month, and I still hadn't completed the draft and needed weeks to polish it. The proof copies of my previous book were slated to arrive soon, and I had to review those, too.

Since I needed time more than human interaction and Doing the Right Thing, I decided to forgo Green Up Day. My run of good writing days had led to storyline snags I had to work around. Those required more than a finger snap to fix. So I sent my apologies to Luce then applied myself to what I was being paid for.

I got through a whole day without interruption, but that was all I was going to get. In the Friday morning mail came Ned's response to my note:

> Will stop by end of day. Hope you like Chinese. Bandersnatch is a fast, nasty creature invented by Lewis Carroll in "Through the Looking Glass."

I sighed upon reading this, tore it in thirds. Writer Me was intrigued—had he recognized the literary reference from being well read, or had he cheated and looked it up?—while Woman Me was flattered by his continuing interest, and Rage-Recovery Me was annoyed by his misinterpretation of the request. My "Let me know when you can stop by to discuss" had not been an invitation to arrive whenever he felt like it. I had expected a response like, "I can come on Friday around X o'clock; would that work for you?"

And what was he going to do if I didn't like Chinese food?

And, since this was supposed to be a business meeting, did he expect to split the cost?

Clearly, the writer and the Harvard graduate had a communication problem, along with a different sense of proprieties. Not a good sign.

Then there were the below-the-surface discomforts. If I cheerily sat down to sup with him, he could interpret my business proposition as an excuse to see him socially. Then again, it would be enjoyable to sit on the porch chatting the evening away over tasty food nobody had to cook. I would be a lot more enthused about that prospect if I understood what I was getting into.

It kept me at a low cauldron-bubble all day, unable to wholly concentrate on work. I'd planned to spend the day and evening in the stained slouch clothes I usually wore for desk riding, but now I had to decide whether to clean up and play hostess or show disdain for him by not bothering. Or would that just reflect badly on myself?

In the end, I decided to be glad I hadn't regressed fully into volcano mode, and to take this development at face value. I had no idea what a man of Ned's occupations considered "end of day" so I ended mine early and took a shower and put on clean clothes, so he wouldn't surprise me at some inopportune moment. That was the right plan, for his pickup truck grumbled into the driveway a little after 5:00. He arrived at the door toting two plastic bags supporting paper bags that emanated spicy smells.

"Hungry?" he greeted as I steered him to the back porch, grabbing plates and utensils on the way by. I had worried about that detail, too: If I'd laid out everything in anticipation, I'd belie any attempt to appear casual. The whole thing made me feel too nervy, but I pulled myself together and faked it with a smile.

"Ravenous."

"I don't suppose you have any beer," he hinted.

"Actually, I do."

I always stocked beer, wine, spirits—a habit left over from house-sharing days. Much easier to have on hand what was needed for any occasion than to have to run out and get it if something unexpected came up. Like lawn-service men inviting themselves to dinner. Or mailmen finding bodies and needing a stiff belt of whiskey a few hours after sunup.

I sent him back to the kitchen to fetch his own beverage while I shoveled out a buffet's worth of food. He returned with two open beer bottles, handed me one, and settled at the table to tuck in with vigor, using chopsticks from the takeout place instead of the fork and spoon I'd provided. I watched him for a moment, registering that he'd come bareheaded instead of wearing his ballcap, revealing soft dark-chocolate waves. The other times I'd seen him hatless, his hair had been flattened and needing a wash. It pleased me that he'd cleaned up for our meeting, having expected him to come over right after work, in whatever shape he'd been in at the end of the day.

I had to say something to open conversation. I also needed to cover my disconcertion over him having selected my drink without asking. What was I supposed to make of that?

Squirming, I ventured, "Where's this restaurant?"

He eyed me between glances down at his plate. "You've been into Mapleton, I assume."

"Yes, a few times. But I haven't spotted any oriental food places."

"You have to look hard; this one's tucked into a corner of the shopping plaza on the far side of town." He chewed and swallowed. "Chow Ling's Chow, believe it or not."

I laughed. We noshed for a few minutes while two of the cats, having recovered from the scariness of a strange man's feet clomping around and voice resonating through the normally quiet house, slinked into the room, keeping to the edges to investigate the smells.

"Hey, puss-puss." Ned made kissing noises. Twinkie stared at him. Tommy disappeared under my chair.

"That's two," said Ned. "Any more?"

"One, who you will probably never see."

"Ah, one of those. So I take it you're not a dog person. We figured whoever bought this place would be, because of the kennel. Never thought about cats."

"It was a big sell point."

"Hah, who'da thunk?" He grinned and ate more. When I added no further conversation, he wiped his lips with the paper napkin I'd provided and said, "You ought to think about getting a dog anyway."

"Hm. The cats might disagree with you."

"I'm sure they can work something out. Seriously. It's good security for a woman alone."

Ugh, I was getting sick of that theme. "You'll notice I chose a place right on the main road instead of in the woods."

He shook his head. "Useless. Someone could pull in and blow you away just like Jake. Even if a passer-by saw the bad guy's car, small chance it could be identified. Maybe my truck would, 'cause so many people know it, but a stranger? In the dark?" He blew a raspberry. "Forget it. Unless you're being attacked in the front yard in broad daylight when someone happens to drive by and cares to do something about it, being in full view isn't very helpful."

"Thanks for making me feel better."

"You're welcome. I'm trying to find out if you understand what you've bought into. So many people move to calendar Vermont thinking they'll never have to lock their doors again, and their children will grow up in happy concert with nature. That's still true in a lot of places, even here until the murders. But it's always been risky for women alone."

He was making me squirm. To hide that, I rose to clear the dishes whether he was done or not.

"The idea," I said tartly, "was to live where there are fewer scumbags per square mile."

"And you've got that." He followed me into the kitchen and put his empty beer bottle on the counter. "But don't let it seduce you into a false sense of security. You may be vaulted in like a bank here with your security system, but a dog can go with you out and about, and give you warning when someone's approaching the house, so you can decide whether to let them in. If I were a bad guy, knowing there was no barking dog or motion-activated outdoor lights here, I could park down Rock Maple Road after dark and creep in with no one the wiser. Remember, having no neighbors means no one can hear you scream."

I stared at him, my gut going hot and cold at the same time. A jolt of raw fear sang through me when he stepped to the refrigerator and plucked my semiautomatic from atop it.

"Then there's this."

He kept the barrel pointed upward and his finger off the trigger. Still, I froze, my heart pounding three thousand beats per second.

"If I was a bad guy, you'd be dead, Jane. I can see by your clothes you're not carrying concealed, though maybe there's a little gun strapped to your ankle. Even so, I've got the drop on you."

All I could do was pretend he hadn't shocked me. I turned to the sink and began rinsing whatever was in it.

Not fooled, he kept talking. "I saw this the minute I walked in, because I'm taller than you. You positioned it too close to the edge and right in my line of sight—easier for me to reach than you."

He returned the gun to the top of the refrigerator, now a few inches out of my reach. I unwound a smidge, until he said, "Having been duly warned, I kept my eyes peeled when we went out the back door to the porch. So I spotted the shotgun behind the umbrella stand."

Thankfully, he did not move to retrieve it. Instead, he put his hands in his pockets. "Given those two, I can only assume you've got something at the front door, and probably one in your bedroom and in the car. Purse, too?"

I couldn't trust myself to answer. Best I could do was wipe my hands and get into a chair before my legs betrayed me. Ned took the opposite chair at the kitchen table, putting us back to where we'd started that rainy morning ten days ago. This time I was the one who needed a shot of whiskey.

I stayed put, careful to not show my hands shaking, careful to keep my voice level. "Since you haven't killed me yet, I assume you're not going to, and this is a…lesson."

"Correct." He flashed a genial smile. "I'm not the kind of guy who likes to toy with his victims."

I was not reassured, but my pulse began to stabilize. Still, I wished I really did have an ankle holster and could pull a derringer and march him out the door with his hands up. While I recognized the importance of what he was saying, he'd made me look a fool and I didn't appreciate that at all.

"So your point is I've been merrily deluding myself," I sneered despite an effort to neutralize my tone.

"Not quite. My point is, your strategy is fine but you need some improvement in your tactics. If you're going to do your solo woman thing, then get it right."

That stung but I put it aside. Cal and Jimmy had similarly bullied me into facing a reality I'd wanted to ignore, so I took Ned's abrasive directness to indicate he cared about my safety. Like the two other men, he instinctively wanted to take care of the little woman but had been culturally conditioned to respect our feminine need to take care of ourselves.

Leavening my voice to stay intellectual, I said, "Strategy and tactics. Sounds a tad military. Have you been in the service or something?"

"No, I'm just a savvy citizen who also lives alone. What I really want to know is, do you know how to shoot, or do you just own those weapons? How many do you have, anyway?"

I hesitated and glared at him. "Which question do you want answered?"

"First, how many."

"Six."

"Jeesh. You don't kid around."

"I try to avoid lying, too, but that's much harder."

He sniffed a chuckle. "Okay, then let's get practical. Do you know how to shoot at all, never mind the differences between all six of them?"

An easy one to answer, and I relaxed another notch. "I was taught, but haven't had opportunity to practice in years."

"No problem there. I've got a range, and my uncle set up a nice one out there in your back forty. You found it yet?"

My eyebrows went up. "No. But I haven't fully explored."

"Well, when you do, take me or somebody else along. Not only is there a killer on the loose, but if you get into trouble out there, then your screams will go even more unheard."

I frowned. "I should be safe on my own property."

"Yeah, well, that's a dangerous of assumption. Accidents happen anytime, anywhere, to anybody. That's why I'm pushing you on this, Jane. You can create your own problems if you aren't fully educated, and coming from where you do—or where I think you do—it's common for people to *over*estimate their ability and *under*estimate the potential for getting into trouble."

Unable to argue that, I didn't try. Neither of us spoke for a minute in parallel rumination. Finally Ned probed, "So give me a frame of reference. Do you have six guns spread around the house because you lived in the city and it scared the crap out of you? Or did something specific happen that no way, no how, you're going to let happen again?"

I sucked in a breath but held it instead of retorting, recognizing genuine curiosity and concern. That deserved an honest answer.

"Nothing specific. I'm not a victim of violent crime or anything."

That was true, but not wholly honest; I still wasn't going to tell him the rest because I didn't want to explain or excuse myself. In the culture I'd been formed by—WASP heritage, Montessori preschool, Catholic grade school, liberal secular high school, a Seven Sisters college, establishment employment—the rule was simple: You did not own weapons. Doing so implied either mental illness or some explicable paranoia, such as a trauma of victimhood you hadn't gotten over yet. Lacking that, it was unthinkable to own a gun, because it implied a wish to harm others. Killing was only acceptable in self-defense or in righteous purpose, à la World War II against the Nazis. I could claim neither justification.

I could claim, however, a secret empowerment. Anyone who might consider me a victim would be mightily surprised. The guns that had come to me unrequested gave me not only psychic security against someone's aggression, but also internal strength, from the fact that I resisted using them despite my murderous fantasies and suicidal depressions. *Put that in your pipe and smoke it!* I said to the psychologists and other judgmentalists of the day.

My guns also gave me courage to face the broader enemy. Evil was out there, even if not in my living room on any particular day; and I knew that the only way to get rid of evil was to destroy it whenever it emerged. If the time came that I had to face it directly, I wanted the tools that would give me a chance to blow it away.

The rest of the time I worked hard to avoid evil, even knowing that we the people would never be free of it. History had shown that humans were unwilling to control themselves to the extent they could breed evil out of the population. I would be long dead before such a movement might ever occur. That left me to face the prospect of having to face evil at some point during my lifetime. What kind of fool was I to assume I could avoid it forever?

I could not admit such thoughts to my peers. Among them, knowledge of evil—the cruelties and exploitations perpetrated on other living beings or against the planet as a whole—wasn't just cause for homicidal outrage, unless you stood up and did something about it. In other words, if I didn't walk my talk, I was just a whiney privileged white bitch. Doing something meant hands-on good works or financial support for those performing the good works; something visible and measurable, like I should do for Green Up Day. Acts that were intangible and unreligiously spiritual, like creating role models for girls through storytelling, didn't count.

These thoughts raced through my head while Ned waited for me to enlarge upon my answer to his question. I yearned to tell him everything, but couldn't take the chance. I barely knew him. One wrong word could result in months or years of consequence. Life and death were not topics I wanted to discuss with people I might misjudge.

So I said, "It's more like, the city and my travels scared the crap out of the men in my life, who bought or bequeathed the weapons to me since they couldn't run around protecting me themselves."

Ned twisted his lips while raising his eyebrows. "Nice. Six guns represent a hefty chunk of change."

I smiled grimly. "A fact I appreciate."

"Would you have bought them on your own?"

"No. Never felt threatened enough to go through the paperwork and training. I've always lived where that was a big, conspicuous deal. Instead,

I went for prudence in line with my lifestyle. You know, pepper spray and wasp spray, and self-defense classes. Still have all the sprays, but the guns sort of trumped them. The threats I really feel a need to protect myself from are things I can't do anything about."

That was the closest I'd ever come to telling anyone the whole truth. Ned eyed me closely but stopped asking questions.

"Okay. Then let's work on the tangibles. How about some target practice?"

"Well..."

"Think of it as free school, and a basic survival skill for life in rural Vermont."

Considering Anna Rawson, I asked, "Do you hunt?"

"Yep. And that needs practice. I do sessions about once a month off season, then weekly then daily as hunting season comes around, so you might as well join me."

"Uh...okay. What do you hunt, deer?"

He nodded. "Hoping to fill my freezer."

I still couldn't get past the idea of killing my own food, so I shifted to a new topic. Actually, an old one: shooting people.

"If you weren't in the service, were you ever a cop? That strategy-and-tactics remark still sounds professional."

"No, I just grew up with guns. There are a lot of us around."

"Maybe that's why the cops don't suspect you of the murders."

His brows arched. "Why would they?"

"Because you're the most obvious. Not only did you find the first body, but also you have guns—including a .45, I'll bet—and use tools, so you could have shot Jake then walloped Len Gustave. You've lived here all your life and know everyone, and probably all their dirty laundry, and with your legitimate reasons to gallivant around the backroads, your presence isn't suspicious anywhere. I'll bet you have no real alibi for any of the murder times. Including that lady who froze to death at the bottom of her stairs."

He shook his head and half laughed. "Nah, you've got it backward. I have an alibi for all of them. Believe me, they checked."

"Good to know, since I took you at face value and let you into the house."

He slouched back in his chair. "I hope I've proved I've got your best interests at heart."

"I suppose you do, unless you really like to toy with your victims and are cruelly setting me up." I showed my attempt at jesting with a tweak of a smile.

He sighed. "I guess that's possible."

I sighed, too. "How am I to know?"

We looked at each other, not needing to say there was no way to foretell. We had to go forward on a mix of instinct and reason, and hope for the best.

He broke the tension by digging into the food bags he'd brought and withdrawing the fortune cookies, tossing me one without watching to see if I caught it, and ripping open the plastic on his own.

With exaggerated solemnity, he cracked the cookie in half and pulled out its little paper treasure. "You will meet a stranger who will change your life."

He looked at me with high-arched brows.

I dodged his eye and broke open my own cookie. "A cynic is only a frustrated optimist."

Silence for a beat while we considered each other. Then I said, "First time I've had two fortune cookies tell the truth."

CHAPTER 12

It's starting to settle on me that this move to the country was the right idea. Despite all the shocks, I'm feeling better on average than I have in years—in under two weeks. Just goes to show how simplifying one's life can be beneficial. I have more energy and brainpower available now that there are fewer things to deal with. My magma isn't getting activated as often, nor as severely, even though some of the surprises have come out of left field and cut way too close to the bone. I'm recovering much faster from emotional shock than I used to.

What really matters is that my writing has taken off. Being able to work longer and more intensely creates a self-perpetuating loop. Energy breeds energy; ideas breed ideas. I feel, for the first time, that I'm truly a writer rather than a faking-it hack. It's amazing how time expands and slows when you're not being pecked half to death by external forces. I get more done during four hours now than I ever did in ten.

Maybe a Newbery Medal for Katy Fox isn't so far-fetched a dream.

* * *

The sun had set, and Ned was still in my kitchen. He hadn't made any motion to leave, and I remained unbalanced enough to withhold any obvious gestures to move him along. I needed to learn whether he was what he seemed to be. The only way to determine that was to keep talking with him.

We'd graduated from beer to cognac, though in keeping with the meal and the circumstances, we should have been sipping Chinese tea. Sometime during the interval I'd shifted into writer mode and was thinking about my future mystery novel.

This motivated me to ask him, "I was hoping you'd know some common denominator between the victims."

He sipped his cognac. "Other than the fact everyone hated them? No, 'fraid I don't. Wish I did."

"They never worked together? School together? Somebody's ex was somebody else's ex, or messed with a sister or brother?"

He cocked an eyebrow. "Where you going with this?"

"Nowhere in particular. I just keep thinking there's got to be some commonality. Otherwise, if the killer's motive is getting rid of local bad people, why not just wait until half the town is in one place and blow it up, or bust in and gun everybody down? I'm sure there are plenty of hated people in the community. There always are."

"True, but it's hard to slaughter a crowd and not be caught. This person looks like they're at least trying to remain anonymous."

"Lot of people worried that they'll be next."

"As am I, having made a lot of not-friends over a lifetime here. You're probably the safest one in town."

"Unless the killer thinks I saw him, or just doesn't like strangers."

He paused to think about that. "But you're not really a stranger."

"But I am. I only ever came up here to ski or visit with Luce—in Orton, or a dozen other ski towns. Never put a toe in Allenburg until shopping for real estate."

"Making you not a stranger. How many people worked on this house, over how many months, before you actually moved in?"

I didn't bother answering. He'd made his point. People didn't know me, but they knew who I was, well before I took residence. Even Jake Baldwin must have known. If he'd bothered to ask around town who that woman was who'd been snooping down Rock Maple Road, probably six people would have told him.

Why this bothered me, I wasn't sure; maybe it was because I was a city person, used to the anonymity afforded by crowds. For whatever reason, my inner magma started to boil. I sidestepped it by rising to put the leftovers into the fridge.

"Okay, so I'm a not-stranger in town and a woman alone. That combination is why I asked you over in the first place."

He cocked a brow while processing my words, slouching back in the kitchen chair with his legs extended and ankles crossed. Then he connected

A and B and said with a composed smile, "Cavendish Lawn and Landscaping at your service, madam."

"Okay. Good. Thank you." I rejoined him at the table and leaned toward him on my elbows, asking earnestly, "How much does lawn service cost? I'm trying to decide whether it's more economical to buy a mower or just pay somebody to keep the grass below knee height during growing season. Timewise, it makes sense to hire out, but I need to understand the economic equation."

He pulled his legs in, sat up, and shrugged. "It's the same decision as plowing in the winter. Do you want to shovel yourself out, pay somebody to do it, or get a snow blower, or a truck with a plow? A plow truck would be a little extreme for the size of your driveway, but the idea is the same."

"I figured to shovel, and if I couldn't deal with it, then get one of those electric blowers."

"Okay, then for grass you could probably do your lawn with a push mower if you like exercise."

"Liking it's one thing; having a bad knee is another."

"What's wrong with your knee?"

"Skiing accident." He nodded, needing no other explanation. Me, I still had to stifle nausea at the memory of how fast the fall had come, the paralyzing shock, the sickening sound of my ligaments tearing, the slam of my face onto hardpacked snow. Whoever said that the body doesn't remember pain was full of baloney.

"Then it's a riding mower for you," Ned said. "Or you hire me. For a yard this size, and the fact I have to drive by it all the time to get to my other customers, I can do you for low enough that it would be hard to justify buying your own mower. Unless you're also going to do the fields?"

I explained my deal with the inherited farmer who would continue haying the upper field and once a year brush-hog the lower one so it didn't revert to forest. I was surprised Ned didn't know about that, given his relatives. Maybe he did, and just wanted to see how I framed it.

All he did was nod again. "Okay, so, simple lawn. No problem. Earliest I can get to it is Monday—Green Up tomorrow, then other stuff on Sunday.

I do my mowing after I finish the mail run, and I have somebody lined up for that afternoon, but I'll be passing here and can take a zip around your lawn on the way back. Will that do?"

"Yes, that would be great. Would you bill me monthly, or do I pay each time?"

"However you want to do it."

"In that case, per mow for this first year. Check, cash, or credit card?"

"How about you take me to dinner?"

Jeesh! There was his next move, I knew it was coming! The zap in my chest could have been thrill or fury. I couldn't tell the difference.

I denied it by saying, "No, let's keep this business."

"Bartering is perfectly legitimate business." He smiled.

I didn't. "So…check, cash, or card?" I drummed my fingers on the tabletop.

"Oh darn, I was hoping that would work." He gave me an exaggerated Cheshire Cat grin then straightened his face. "No card, you choose which kind of paper. Just don't stiff me, and we'll be good."

I nodded and inhaled to respond.

He beat me to it with a "But"—then waited for me to give him the hairy eyeball, which I resisted, placidly waiting for him to finish—"if you want to be businesslike, you can pay me back for dinner tonight by taking me out for dinner next Friday."

I had to give the guy credit for persistence. "How about nice, straightforward cash?"

"Nah, I'll just add it to your bill and deduct the expense as marketing."

He grinned and stood and pushed off toward the door. I followed him to it, saying matter-of-factly through a suppressed grin, "You're a wolf, Ned."

"We try harder." He went to tip the bill of his ballcap, only to remember it wasn't there. As I stood holding the edge of the door, signaling intention to close it after him—if not in his face—he said, "So, see you tomorrow at Green Up?"

"No, I have to work."

"Aw c'mon, it's Saturday."

I huffed. "You're self-employed, you know the drill."

"Yeah, make hay while the sun shines."

"In my case, it's make hay twelve days out of every fourteen. And I've already used up my allotment for this fortnight."

"Fortnight! You must read British novels."

"Lots of them." I didn't mention two in the past week, which is what had refreshed the word in my vocabulary. Instead I said coyly, "Oh darn, now I can't use that one for my mailbox notes."

"So what's the next one down the list?"

"I was thinking *petrichor*, but I've never actually heard someone use that in conversation."

"Well, we can change the rules. But, just so you know, *petrichor* is that lovely smell you get after a summer rain when it's been dry."

I gaped at him. "Damn, this is going to be harder than I thought."

"Well, somebody's got to keep you on your toes."

I slid a sideways look at him. "It seems you've assigned yourself the duty. Like Luce, determined to make me into a social animal."

"She'll be pissed that you're copping out tomorrow."

"I promised her I'd do the river cleanup instead." Which I dreaded, but fair's fair. I had to make up for a cop-out if I really meant to honor my recovery plan.

"But yes," I continued, "I really do have to work all weekend. I'm not a celebrity writer who makes millions per year."

"You'll break people's hearts when they learn that." He tweaked a smile again.

"So who's going to tell them?" I gave him a one-eyed dubious look under a slanted eyebrow.

"You know what I mean. In those months between when you bid for the house then moved in, you drove people wild."

"Really?" My hand slackened and fell from its ready position on the door. "What on earth do you mean?"

"Well, people speculate you must be rich because you bought this house in cash."

"Jeesh, who let that out?"

"It's a small town. But then you confused people by choosing a simple, scruffy little house and neither tore it down nor remodeled it, just freshened it, meanwhile installing a whole-house emergency generator—which costs a small fortune—and is usually only put in by part-timers to cover things when they're not here. The logic is, if you have that kind of money, why are you here all the time, and drive a regular car that's actually sensible for the climate? That doesn't fit the typical flatlander image. Likewise you didn't complain about costs to the contractors and paid on time. Luce told them you're a 'famous writer' so we expected someone either artsy and unreliable but basically lower income, or a high earner equivalent to James Patterson and Stephen King. But nobody'd heard of you, though once the paper let it out you have a pen name, things made more sense."

A proper response eluded me. Didn't matter, for he was still explaining the community response to my existence.

"They're wondering if you're a widow or a divorcée, with some worried that you're going to prey on our very limited single-male population—like *moi*—and others are worried that you're gay so will be going for the females. The rest are worried about you living here alone. Last winter was so cold they couldn't decide whether you were smart or dumb-lucky that you picked a place with a good well and plumbing so the pipes never freeze, even though water hardly ran all season between owners."

"Good lord! I never imagined I'd be so fascinating to strangers."

"And I'll bet you that at least three people have driven by here this evening and recognized my truck. So don't be surprised if somebody asks when we're getting married."

"I'll…keep that in mind."

"The plus side is, the village is starting to see you as under my protection. Which will make them less inclined to mess with you. Keep up being friendly, and you should be okay."

"I…I…"

…didn't know what to say. I was touched and irritated at the same time. Being under someone's protection was both comforting and patronizing.

Being of such interest and discussion among folks I didn't know was both flattering and intrusive. Having my intent to live solo in peace thwarted by multiple people's involvement lit fuses I was struggling to keep wet and dormant so nothing would ignite and explode. The push-pull of it all stalled me in my shoes, struggling to master the conflicts while Ned watched me with too-curious eyes.

If he hadn't been there, I think I would have settled. Instead, under the pressure of his waiting for my response, I collapsed internally against the rise of temper.

"It looks like I'll have to move to the Yukon Territory to mind my own business."

Instead of flinching against my tone, he shrugged. "Maybe, but up there might be worse. They've got less than one person per square mile, so the population would be even more keenly interested in its neighbors."

He was right, so I couldn't retort. I'd researched demographics before moving and learned that Vermont packed sixty-something people per square mile, compared to Los Angeles at ten times that number. I'd never lived in LA, having found the East Coast metroplex dense enough; but in that moment I missed the city, any city, where so many different types and weirdos coexisted in such close proximity that we all developed a mental callus—the ability to ignore each other. Here it was proving impossible to be invisible.

Ned's lack of reaction to my temper flare made it worse. I knew I was being irrational but the demon had awoken, and the best I could do was restrain from shouting or booting him out the door and slamming it in his face.

"So you're saying I'm fine as long as I hang on Luce's coattails and hide under your arm. Unless, of course, the killer doesn't decide you're next, and takes me out just to hurt both of you."

"Hm. Hadn't thought of that." Again, he took my words at face value rather than responding to my attitude. "If you want, I'll spread word that you're a pistol-packin' mama."

"I'd—rather keep that as a surprise." What I really wanted to do was run around shooting everyone who crossed my path.

"Well, you surprised *me*." He flashed his wolf grin then sobered. "But if you don't want that to get around, and you're unwilling to get a dog, then we can let it be known that you've got a damn good security system."

He'd stopped me in my tracks again. No use flinging anger at someone impervious to it. I felt suddenly weak and depressed as adrenaline-fueled rage ebbed. I had to struggle to recall what we were talking about.

"I would've thought the guys who installed my system would have blabbed that by now," I managed.

"Unless one of them's the killer and knows how to get around it."

I shuddered at the thought. Ned noticed and added, "Which is another reason why I think you should get a dog."

"Nice idea until you remember they can be taken out with a poisoned chop or a bullet."

"Hm. Got me there. Well, if you won't buy me dinner, and you're dumping Green Up Day, then I guess I'll see you Monday. Have a good weekend."

He departed before I could answer, leaving me unnerved and fuming.

CHAPTER 13

The aftermath of rage is always depression. The emotion surge is exhausting, and followed by self-flagellation. I should have done/said/thought/felt X instead of Y. I'm a bad person to have such feelings. Et cetera, ad nauseam. I hate being this way and want to stop it. I try. I keep trying. But then I have to deal with people, who come at me from directions I don't anticipate, and I don't know how to behave, and I react the wrong way, and the cycle starts anew.

Ned is particularly maddening because he fits no pattern I've encountered before. Why does he keep giving me come-ons, and ignoring my inappropriate responses? Is that knight-in-shining-armor rescue thing Luce warned me about some neurosis of his own, in which case I should avoid him, or is it some sort of compassion and self-confidence so rare that people like me have no idea how to recognize or react to it, in which case I should open the door and let him in emotionally as well as literally? Or is he just a cocksure asshole?

I can't tell the difference.

* * *

Green Up Day was Gray Down Day at my house. My mood matched the weather—glum and cold and weepy—and despite best intentions, I barely got two pages of work done before I gave up the pretense of writing and snuggled in my comfy chair with a book, and Contessa on my lap.

The warm purring cat might have soothed me, but I kept listening to the rain. It reminded me of move-in weekend, when I still believed I was starting a clean new life. Instead, already, here I was, back in my pit. Outside, nice people like Luce and Ned were slogging around in the wet performing a community service, and probably cracking jokes with their teammates about the discomfort, while I hunkered inside wanting to think I was smart to have avoided the physical misery, only to embed myself in misery because I was copping out not only on social altruism but also my excuse for doing so.

In other words, I felt like a heel, then angry at myself for having such feelings, and at a loss for what to do about it. That made it a good time to wash dishes, do laundry, read a book—anything but contemplate why I was in here and they were out there.

Not long into the day, I heard muted voices outside and peeked around the front curtains to see the subject of my thoughts in person. A troop of Green Up workers in rain suits was sloshing along the berm, toting green trash bags, bending and plucking and stowing as the sky spilled down on them. I didn't recognize anyone, though that was moot through the blur. None seemed to pay attention to my house, which let me watch their passage rather than duck back behind the curtain. Their heads were down except when they tossed remarks at one another, their teeth flashing as they laughed.

How easy it would be to pick one off with a rifle, I mused. The very next thought was, *Why don't I put on a rain coat and run out there to join them?*

I still owned weather gear that had kept me warm and dry in the wilderness. For a few hours here on the civilized fringe of the Green Mountains, the garb would more than suffice. And surely the workers would not reject help, however belated.

But I feared appearing pathetic so stayed in place. I tried to expand my first, nasty thought into a murder mystery, but couldn't figure out how a killer shooting out the window of their own house at sitting ducks might get away with it. So I abandoned plot conniving along with good intentions, but stayed at the window watching until they wandered out of sight. There went any chance to *Act nice until you are nice.*

It came to me then that someone would have to pick them up; they couldn't be expected to walk the length of every local road. There must be some relay system involving pickups and drop-offs. If nothing else, they had left full bags behind them at roadside for another party to gather. I could have been that driver.

Too late now. I closed the curtain and withdrew to my chair.

Tessa was still in the room, so I hoisted her back onto my lap and spent a long while cuddling her, then petting the others, dangling strings for them, doling out catnip treats, and reminding all of us that I had done one very good thing in my life: saved them from certain early death, after a miserable existence. They now had warmth and love and food and safety, and would for as long as I existed. I decided that my epitaph should be, "She did care about something."

That restored me enough to resume caring about Katy Fox and the animals she rescued, in this volume from flooding after a devastating storm on like Hurricane Katrina. I returned to my desk and banged away at her story for a few hours. That regained lost ground and restored some self-respect.

My ups and downs had squashed my appetite so I forgot about lunch—hard not to, when the gray light didn't change all day, making it seem like dawn and dusk at the same time for all waking hours—but by late afternoon, clock time, I was relaxed and hungry. I saved the session's work and reheated Chinese leftovers for an early supper. That was a mistake, because it brought my thoughts back to Ned.

I diverted from those by stacking my Allenburg library books on the kitchen table and fanning through them while I ate, identifying each murder mystery's killing technique. After that, I went through the mystery titles in my personal library and added to my list. When done I had good fodder for future projects. I expanded on my notes with some Internet searching, then sat back with a cognac and drew a conclusion.

All those murder methods were ingenious and credible but too complicated for our local killer. She (I was still convinced) was being careful to employ the simplest methods for her madness. Push down stairs. Shoot point-blank. Smash on head. All where no one can see you. Done and go home.

I suspected that she lived alone so didn't have to explain her comings and goings to anyone. As well, those who interacted with her knew her car and her routines, so she would have to conceal her dastardly deeds during her normal schedule or when no one would be out and about—like nighttime downpours and blizzards, and subzero cold.

The thoughts sent me back to my computer to search for news stories about deaths in Allenburg in February. That turned up a few obituaries then an archived report about Fiona Cobb, who had been found midmorning of a scheduled oil-delivery day, frozen solid at the base of her front steps. Her position was consistent with a slip that had skidded her backward to crack her head on the nose of a stair tread. She had been in rickety health, rumored to drink, and was wearing smooth-bottomed slippers. Her walk path and driveway, said the deliveryman, were "hard as a bobsled run. I fell about three times while wrassling the hose up to the house."

With no foul play suspected, and no surface to capture footprints or tire tracks, nobody looked for clues of a malice-minded visitor. The signs wouldn't have been there, anyway. The road was plowed and sanded over iron-ice ruts, the porch and stairs cleared just enough to allow feet to pass, with streaks of ice filling cracks in the unfinished planks, well exposed between embedded scatterings of woodstove ash. No trace of an arriving killer then, and nothing left now after months and a season change. The good-for-nothing son got the house (did he still live there? did it matter?) and another cranky old lady passed out of life.

Further search brought up Fiona's obituary, which revealed that she had graduated from Allenburg Consolidated High School in the early '60s, married and divorced, had two children, one who died young. I switched to the obituary I'd already filed for Jake Baldwin. He, too, had attended Allenburg Consolidated in the same time frame. But Len Gustave didn't overlap anywhere.

Exhausted and none the wiser, I retired for the night. The phone rang just before I turned off the light, but I let the machine pick up. Luce's voice rang through the rooms: "We missed you today, and envied you at the same time. We got soaked! I hope you got a lot of work done. Our turnout was still pretty good—you wouldn't believe the stuff we picked up. Ned said to tell you some of it would make great targets. Peter's heading home tomorrow so let's do lunch next week. Call me."

Her caring knocked drowsiness away. Damn it, she was so nice; she didn't have to act it, the quality was built in. I couldn't remember the last time I'd done anything nice for her, yet she continued being nice to me. How did she do it? What gesture could I return that might warm her heart?

Well, I could do what she asked, and lunch with her next week. Unlike me, she was uncomfortable being alone. On my bad days I wanted to fling diagnostic words back at her—*monophobia* being the zinger ("dread of being alone")—but when mellow I understood that for folks who didn't like flying solo, even my cranky company would be a favor.

I sent her an e-mail asking what day she'd prefer, then headed for bed.

Even then I couldn't escape my mood see-saw. After falling easily to sleep, I woke up at 2:00 in the morning, resonating with a revelation: My efforts to punish the world by rejecting it made no difference to anyone but myself. While I truly was as impotent as I believed—nothing wrong with my brain—turning away friendship, fun, and love just because I was furious at the world was, well, stupid. The problem lay in my heart, not my mind.

This realization didn't solve the question of how to become an authentic, honest person who wholly and joyously embraced life, but it released me to genuinely be nice sometimes while I was acting out the role. More, it opened the door to good things while still locking out what I hated, and allowed me stay angry, which my conscience demanded.

In other words, I could live in a contradictory state without going mad, if I gave myself permission to do so. The only change this made in my daily norm was a reduction of the pressure that comes with trying to make oneself into something one is not. That shift was an important step forward that let me to fall back to sleep.

In the morning, rested, I nonetheless felt rebellious. Acknowledging this contradictory state, I decided to use the day to prove my independence. As a woman alone, I owned twenty acres free and clear, which I'd not yet taken the time or responsibility to explore. Today I would deal with that.

Back in the winter, when I'd purchased the place, I had refused to close until the boundaries were confirmed and the acreage matched the numbers I was paying for. At that time there was a three-foot snow cover and daytime temps hadn't gone above freezing for weeks. Tammy the Realtor had earned her commission by arranging for two snowmobiles to take us to the far corner marker. Three of the four markers were along my two road frontages, but that last one was uphill in the woods. Owing to my knee, I couldn't trek there on snowshoes.

Since then, I hadn't ventured farther than my dooryard. Now, with the weather at spring peak, there was no excuse for Anna Rawson and Ned Cavendish to know my land better than I did. I would hike around until I found my own shooting range, maybe even practice a bit once I found it so I had a chance of hitting one of the "great targets" Ned surely would bring along at first opportunity. I didn't care anymore if anyone heard me. I had total legal right on my own land to practice using legal weapons. If somebody wanted to make a big deal of that, let me at 'em.

Over coffee, I dug out my homestead file and extracted property maps, an aerial photo, and a vintage topographic map of the quadrant containing my parcel. As soon as I spread out the papers, all three cats hopped onto the table, putting their paws everywhere I wanted to look. Though helpful details were marked on the property map, like location of my septic tank and two wells, there was no big X labeled "Shooting Range Here!" on any of the documents. I spotted a likely location by comparing the property map to the topo map, and confirming it with the aerial view and a quick check of Google Earth.

A shooting range would have to be an open area backed by a hill or in a sand pit. One candidate site about in the middle of my acreage, where forest and fields converged, was almost reached by a lane along a fenceline accessible from Rock Maple Road.

That would make an easy hike that my knee would accept, so after breakfast I donned my neoprene brace and appropriate clothing, sprayed repellent from ankles to hairline since I'd probably get into tick territory, unearthed my walking stick, and loaded a teardrop backpack with handy miscellaneous—including my little revolver, ammo, and ear plugs—and took off into a bright and blustery May day.

I struck out along Rock Maple Road, briefly considering walking all the way down to Jake Baldwin's place, maybe meeting the returned retired couple along the way, but no, I wanted to keep the day to myself.

I found the lane easily enough; it opened off the pull-in that Anna Rawson had said she would use for parking on her turkey days, halfway up the first hill on Rock Maple Road. Some rain-blurred tire tracks showed where she had left the truck at least once; indeed, I had seen her drive out a few mornings ago, though I had not heard any gunshots correlating with her presence. The shot series that had spooked me had occurred in the afternoon, and no vehicles had come or gone on Rock Maple Road during that period.

It bugged me that Anna had not bothered to advise me when she was going to be around, as I had asked. I didn't see what I could do about it except dig out her phone number or address and ream her out. But what would that serve? I could barely balance my positive relationships against my issues, so it made no sense to initiate negative relationships on top of that. What I should do was watch out the windows more conscientiously and try to get outside fast enough to wave her down next time I saw her, and have a grown-up chat. Or maybe spend the money and post the property against hunters. Yep, that would really help integrate me into the community.

At the moment all I could do was hope she didn't use a different access on different days and wasn't now stalking nearby with her shotgun. I should have worn something brighter, or tied bear bells to my stick to announce my presence.

The sunshine made me feel lucky, so I strode onward through grass brushing my knees, studded with poplar and crabapple saplings planted by birds. The lane would need to be brush-hogged like the swampy former cow pasture that lay between it and my house. The lane tracked levelly across a narrow plateau against the hillside, following a mostly busted post-and-wire fence that had once confined cows. Uphill stood mixed deciduous and evergreen forest bounding my upper field, out of sight beyond it; downhill lay the swampy pasture. Onward lay a recovering clearcut at the foot of another wooded hill.

A stand of sumac closed around the lane and blocked my view of the house and distant mountains. I soon came upon a cul-de-sac that could only be the range. Gravel and more grass and saplings filled a half bowl whose curved slope sprouted brush and stumps, and falls of dirt and sand. Near the slope I found broken bottles, bullet-punctured cans and sap-collection buckets, and wheel rims. Stones that took two hands to lift had fallen or been displaced from a stack among the debris. I hoisted a few into a rough pile, mounted two cans atop it, and missed them both with ten rounds from my revolver. Finally hit a sap bucket after another cylinder's worth of tries.

Satisfied, I headed back. My knee was tired but still steady in its wrap. As long as I walked squarely I could go up, down, and level as if never injured. The joint was only troubled by twists and jerks.

Back in the open on the lane, I surveyed my queendom. The view could have been a Vermont scenic calendar page if my house had been a red barn. A straight line to it, half the distance of the road route, would take me down the pasture slope, across a stream, and up a more scraggly slope to my backyard. From my height I discerned a stone wall I hadn't seen before, which divided the swampy pasture in half. A stream twisted through a collapsed area of the wall. I saw no gate to the pasture anywhere, save for the decrepit skinny one that accessed my backyard. So where could a tractor enter to brush-hog the pasture? The farmer who'd be haying had done it before, but I couldn't see how. Clearly, the pasture and slopes hadn't been mowed in a long time.

I decided to inspect the conditions by way of the straight line home. Poking ahead with my stick, and probing beneath the grass with my feet, I found the downslope tussocky but consistent, the rocks long ago picked to build the walls. Not a dozen steps down, however, my left foot found the edge of a hole and rolled, just as I put weight on it. That's all I had time to think before I pitched downhill while a hot poker stabbed through my ankle. I landed on one shoulder and whiplashed my head against the ground.

How long I lay on the slope, dazed, I couldn't tell. Probably just a minute, for when my head cleared enough to take stock, the light and temperature hadn't changed. I found grass poking into my nostrils and dirt clinging to my lips while my ankle throbbed in cold/hot pulses. This was better than waking up in the hospital after a face plant on a ski slope—I still had my teeth and my knee wasn't screaming—but more complicated because now I had to deal with getting myself up and out. No ski patrol was going to sled me home.

I sat up woozily. My shoulder ached but moved, my neck muscles were locked, and the sharp bruise along my ribs proved to be from the walking stick I'd landed on. My ankle was the bad news, already the size of a grapefruit and heading for watermelon. I had worn stout walking shoes instead of hiking boots so there'd been no ankle support against the twisting fall. Both knees felt gummy but unharmed, though without the ankle's cooperation I couldn't test them by standing. Three attempts at getting upright proved that returning the few hundred yards back to the house would be like climbing the Himalayas. Any pressure against the ankle returned pain so intense I nearly vomited and left me shaking in cold sweats.

I wriggled out of my pack's arm straps and eased onto my back, staring at the sky beyond the swaying grass tips. Clouds were forming from yesterday's moisture rising as a new air mass swept in. In fact, I discovered, the ground was wet beneath me. Not sopping, but damp enough to penetrate my clothes. I hoped like mad there were no ticks discovering me.

That was a minor worry compared to the stark fact that I was in trouble, real woman-alone trouble. The question of how a tractor could enter my pasture was nothing compared to how I was going to get myself out of it.

As Ned had mentioned so bluntly, nobody could hear me scream. Nor could anyone see me, unless I managed to stand and wave at any car that drove by on the main road, directly perpendicular to my position so there was little chance my speck of neutral color and desperate waving against a background of windblown grass could be spotted from the corner of anyone's eye. Rock Maple Road was closer, but so few people traveled it that only with the wildest luck would anyone come along and see me. Of course I wasn't carrying a cell phone, since there was no service in the area.

What could I do? How long before anyone noticed me gone?

Best hope was Ned, a day and a half away.

Oh god. Here I was, doomed to die of exposure in my own back pasture. Why worry about murderers when you could kill yourself with a careless step? More galling was realizing that those who had warned me about venturing out alone had been right.

The desire to prove them wrong saved me. After allowing myself a few minutes to sob—nobody around to see, why be stoic—I propped myself up again and started to think. First, test the screaming theory. I inhaled as deeply as I could, moved my foot to ramp up the pain, and blasted it out with the volume and intensity of a jet engine right next to your ear on an airfield. The atmosphere absorbed the sound so thoroughly that none of the nearby hills echoed it back.

Fuck!

Okay, that's why people carried emergency whistles. I withdrew mine from my pack and blew three shrill blasts at even intervals in standard S.O.S. style. The breeze swallowed that sound, too, making me feel like an ant in a lifeboat in the middle of the sea. I wanted to S.O.S. with my revolver but had used all the ammunition I'd brought. Besides, who, how far away, would figure out that someone was signaling instead of practicing? Distant gunshots were a common occurrence around here, often in even sequences. My own practice session had probably been dismissed by whoever might have heard it. Too bad I couldn't just set the pasture on fire. That would bring help in a hurry!

Since my wilderness survival kit had gone into storage after my knee injury—no chance of hiking into the mountains anymore—I didn't have on me the tools I would need to send up a signal flare or camp in place until help came along. Old habits remained, though, so I did have some things to work with: a half-full water bottle, one energy bar, a nylon wind/rain shell, a bandana, a pocket camera, and a multi-tool, plus the walking stick, whistle, gun, sunglasses, and a broad-brimmed hat.

I was about to drink from the water bottle when I realized it was still cool to the touch. Cool by definition was halfway to cold; my ankle needed ice desperately; I soaked the bandana and bound the ballooning joint. While recovering from the pain of that exercise, I eyeballed the stream below: the nice, numbing-cold stream halfway between me and the house. Maybe I could roll down there, freeze my foot, then crawl up the other side to safety.

That idea went down the tubes as soon as I shifted weight and realized just how bad it would hurt to crawl. Or roll. But was trying to walk any better? If I turned my hiking stick into a splint or a crutch, I would be unstable as well as in agony and risk another fall. No, no. Did Not Want That.

To reach either the stream or the lane, I had to go down or up a nobbly slope. Up was starting to look better, because it would raise my visibility by putting me eventually on Rock Maple Road. There somebody *might* pass, which was better than never being seen either here or at the bottom of the pasture. I had to go with might, even though it meant more distance, and

I would first have to crawl up to the lane. There I could rest on the flat and jerry-rig a crutch.

If all else failed, I could walk the whole way on both feet—if I could bear it. I knew desperate people could endure darn near anything, and many who had been hurt worse than I was had extracted themselves from more horrifying situations. Like that guy in the news a few years ago who'd cut off his own arm after getting pinned by a boulder in the wilderness. Compared to that, my problem was peanuts. I hated the thought of double-damaging my injury, but the sooner I started, the sooner the ordeal would be over.

Just suck it up, Jane—get up and walk!

Before I could wimp out, I repacked my bag, slung it around me, and started shimmying backward up the slope on my butt. It worked if I pushed with the good foot and held the bad one off the ground. Still, every wobble, every touch or thump made me swear, cry, gag, or shriek, and those few yards were hell in slow motion.

But I made it!—and flopped sideways onto the flat of the lane, sweating and shivering. The grass still reached over my head but it was much thinner and drier. I kept the bad leg crooked and balanced across the good one to hold my foot off the ground while I panted and indulged in another round of weeping.

Then, a long rest later, I rigged a forearm crutch by combining the walking stick's wrist strap, my camera strap, the backpack's waist straps, the lanyard from my emergency whistle, and the nylon shell. It let me lean hard and hoist myself all the way up, almost falling, but a toe-touch—*AAIIIEEEEE!*—gave me a tripod.

Once balanced, I limp-hobbled the quarter mile to sanctuary, whimpering all the way.

I burst into full tears again when I finally made it indoors. The cats swarmed me on the kitchen floor, wondering what was happening and trying to help. As soon as I'd recovered enough to reach the phone, I called Luce and almost fainted from relief when she picked up.

"Can you take me to the emergency room?" I gasped without a hello.

"What? Yes, of course—what happened! Janey, are you all right?"

"Yes and no."

I explained, and she was there in twenty minutes.

CHAPTER 14

Reluctantly, I have to face the woman-alone problem. There must be a way to live independently without having to worry about getting hurt or dying every time you turn around!

Now that the insecurity has been planted, I can't stop thinking about all the disasters that can possibly happen, from which I'd never be rescued. I thought I'd covered everything else in my plans. In a one-story house I don't have to worry about falling down the stairs, but the house is so secure, nobody can get in if I fall off a ladder while changing a lightbulb with the doors locked. Outdoors, as my hike proved, I could die in sight of home, had my injury been worse. And as Jake Baldwin, Len Gustave, and Fiona Cobb have proved, things can be plenty worse and only serendipity means your body will be discovered.

More worrisome, who will feed the cats if I disappear? How will anyone know if I collapse in the kitchen from a heart attack? My editor might notice my absence after a few weeks; Luce might notice after a few days, as would Ned. That thought comforts me, though it raises the question of what could happen to them, too, without being discovered. Luce's condo has plenty of stairs she could tumble down when Peter's not around, and I would never know it. Ned, I gather, lives alone on some sort of farm, and uses power tools—those are loaded with injury possibilities, and who would find him if he fell off a roof or cut off his arm?

Any of us could hit a deer on a lonely road and have it go through our windshield, or in avoiding it plunge off into a ravine like the steep and deep one on the road down to Allenburg, to be trapped in our car for long enough to starve or freeze before anyone notices.

Is the solution to change one's whole life and cohabit with others, just to stay safe?

No, because that won't protect us from every conceivable risk. You can live with someone full-time, yet if they go on a trip you could get into trouble five minutes after they leave and be just as stuck as you would be on your own. Even if they only go to work or the supermarket, or do a chore out of shouting range, or if you go on your own junket without telling them, or change your plan—if the right mishap occurs, you or they could as easily lie undiscovered, and leave the other with a terrible guilt trip, to boot.

* * *

"You really didn't have to work so hard to avoid me," Ned teased the next morning. "A simple 'no thanks' would have sufficed."

"Really? To the man who never takes no for an answer?" I teased back.

He twinkled. Luce looked between us with interest. She had stayed overnight to watch over me, as well as called Ned when we'd returned from the hospital and asked him to bring my mail to the door for the next few weeks. That was her rationalization, at least. I suspected a matchmaking motive.

I hadn't heard their initial conversation, being zonked out from exhaustion and painkillers, but from Ned's remark in the morning, I deduced she had filled him in.

"Hey, you gave me the idea," I continued teasing him. "I just wanted to find my own shooting range." Luce delivered a shocked look, reminding me I'd never told her I owned guns. Hastily I added, "It gave me a destination for a break from my desk."

"And here I thought you'd have your nose to the grindstone all weekend," Ned quipped.

"I did, save for that." I sighed. "I guess work is all I'll be able to do for the next while."

My ankle was badly sprained rather than broken, so the therapy trio of periodic icing, wrapping my foot in breathable stretch tape, and moving the joint without bearing weight on it would keep me chair or sofa bound most of the time, thumping around on crutches for the rest, until healed enough to put the foot down. Never had I been gladder that I'd bought a one-story house and an automatic-transmission car!

I was also glad for an excuse to not go anywhere for a while. But that did not mean being left to my introverted devices. Disablement made the interruption syndrome worse.

Luce started it by inviting Bobbie over for drinks late that afternoon, and we sat on the porch watching Ned mow my front, back, and side yards. While on one hand I appreciated the cheerful company and distraction from my pains, on the other hand watching the mowing depressed me into silence. The pretty purple violets and yellow dandelions in my yard, along with the bumblebees and early butterflies feeding upon them, were being shredded and spattered for the sake of uniform greenness.

I hadn't thought about grass before, having never owned a lawn, but it shamed me to be paying for cosmetic improvements that killed innocent plants and insects just trying to survive and which couldn't, to the best of my knowledge, hurt me or anyone else. Their slaughter reminded me of an article I'd read years before about fawns and other wildlife being ground up during harvesting of farm fields by the gigantic machines needed to process crop acreage. The machine operators couldn't see the animals until too late, if they saw them at all; or else didn't care. Bottom line was, what had to be done to feed a human population turned part of the animal kingdom into mush.

Worse, just days before, I'd found a dead bird outside the house, which had broken its neck from flying into my window. The reflection in the glass, just right that time of that day, made the bird think it could fly straightforward through the outdoors. So just existing in my dwelling, not doing anything predatory, I managed to kill a migrating songbird.

When I multiplied how often deaths like these happened, I fell back into lost hope that humankind and all other species would ever be able to coexist peacefully on Earth. Luce and Bobbie's background chitchat only aggravated my bile. Their concerns were so superficial, so human-centric and ultimately meaningless, that I gagged on my thoughts and feelings. Meanwhile, Ned motored around us, lost in the droning Zen of mowing while showcasing his sculpted arms, muscular back, wild hair, and loose, careless way of moving that expressed comfort in his male-mammal body.

He came in for a beer when done, and informed me exactly where the gate to the pasture was that I'd failed to observe yesterday. It was right where I'd expected it to be—center of the fenceline alongside Rock Maple Road—but so overgrown with wild vines and a bowing crabapple tree that you had to know it was there to see it. He volunteered to prune the growth back, which I evaded answering because I didn't trust myself to speak.

Then Luce invited both him and Bobbie to stay for dinner without asking me first. While I choked back resentment about that, at the same time surging with relief that I didn't have to provide a meal for myself or anyone else—getting all torqued up from so many contradictory emotions—we all drank more wine and beer, and she whipped up a tasty meal on the stovetop from what she found in my refrigerator.

It would have, should have been a merry evening among warm and caring friends, but by then I was not just emotionally eroding but also blurring out from a wine-plus-painkiller cocktail. The effort of hiding my feelings while behaving civilly drained my reserves. I escaped by falling asleep on the couch in the middle of a conversation. Thank you, body.

Luce woke me up to tell me they were all leaving, and to ensure I could handle getting myself to bed, then left me alone—at last—to wallow in guilt and gratitude. I caught Ned's eye on his way out the door, but couldn't read his expression.

The next day Helen stopped by on her way to the library, bearing a get well card and a stack of outdoor-wilds mysteries. She was tactful enough to not press me on particulars about the talk and signing, but I sensed her smothered impatience about the delay. In turn she sensed my smothered desire for privacy and honored it by keeping her visit brief. Thank you, Helen.

The next day Anna Rawson arrived holding a zip-lock bag containing a marinated half-breast of wild turkey. She couldn't have timed her arrival better, for by then I was burning to speak my mind.

"You're just the person I want to talk to," I declared upon swinging open the door. She hesitated on the stoop, not sure how to take either my words or my tone. I couldn't blame her, as I'd blurted them out without greeting in reaction to surprise tainted by the residue of frustration.

"Sorry—please come in," I amended, leaning aside. "I'm hoping you can help me work something out."

She passed me with a sideways look and deposited the baggie on my kitchen counter while I crutched into the living room. She joined me there, still wearing her cowboy hat, and stated with shaky bravado, "Betcha never had fresh meat before. Good for what ails ya."

She perched on the lip of the armchair resting her elbows on her thighs. Her denim-clad legs were half the diameter of mine.

"You're right, and thank you."

We nodded at each other. Then, after a pause, she said, "What's up?" in a tone that was casual though her face was taut with uncertainty.

I pretended to not notice. "Couple of things. First, the meat. Did you, um, get it here?"

"Uh, no, up on Bud Park's land. He's over the hill off the back of yours."

I nodded. "Second, I'm confused by your kindness"—I gestured toward the turkey in the kitchen—"and your rudeness in not calling or e-mailing me when you'd be around, like you said you would."

She looked away. "Sorry about that. You're the only one who's ever asked for it, and I forgot because I usually decide to go when it's too late or early to call the landowner. The deal is generally you get permission to hunt then go when you want, so I kinda forgot I'd said anything different to you. Sorry."

I waited, wondering whether to plunge into my main concern or give her more time for response. After a silent moment that almost went on too long, she said, "I'm not a computer or phone kind of person, anyway. Part of hunting is getting away from people and rules. Actually, that's sort of why I'm here…when I heard what happened to you, I put the shoe on the other foot and realized…anyway, it kind of shook me."

I twinged in surprise and warmth. "Thank you. But that's what I really want to talk with you about."

She looked back at me through cautious blue eyes. I continued, "I'm wondering what kind of grief people give you about going off alone into the woods."

Her face skewed then relaxed into a smile. "You had me going there for a minute. I thought you were gonna cancel my hunting permission."

I returned her smile. "No, I wish like crazy you'd been out there yesterday and heard me screaming! But while I was lying in the grass, I got to wondering how often hunters find themselves in trouble and nowhere near help.

Or hikers or whoever. And what they do about it. And why they get into that trouble by going out alone in the first place."

Anna shrugged. "You go because you don't want company. Anybody with a brain takes a cell phone or radio. But around here"—she twirled her finger—"obviously, no-go on the phone, and if you're alone, no point having a radio. So you just tell someone where you're going and when you think you'll be back. And carry a first-aid kit, of course."

"Of course." Standard protocol for wilderness ventures. Too bad I hadn't considered my back acres to be wilderness. "But that's part of my point. If what happened to me happened to you, and I'd known you were out there, I'd have thought to keep an eye out for you, and could call in the cavalry if your truck was still there after you should've been gone. Do you intentionally fly under the radar to challenge fate?"

She flinched. "Uh…no, I just want to hunt, and you need to be low-profile for that."

"So, how does your husband or mother or friends feel about you going off solo? Do they argue with you? Or not care?"

She looked at me like I'd asked some stupidly obviously weird question. I felt our cultural divide then, between a girl who'd grown up with freedom of the outdoors, and one who'd been raised on warnings about dangers around every corner.

"They're fine with it," Anna said. "Who do you think taught me? We all do it. Well, a bunch of us. Some people like to hunt or hike alone, others prefer a partner. I take my horse out on the trail by myself, and several of my friends take off on their ATVs or snowmobiles. As long as we do it responsibly, no one gives a hoot."

"So you don't think I'm reckless to have gone hiking on my own land by myself."

"No, but I get what you're saying. You didn't think to tell anyone you were going, and you're right that I should have told you when I did."

"Good. Then we understand each other."

Finally Anna cracked a wary smile. "I guess if we're both going to be wandering around out there within shooting range of each other, then yeah, we'll have to communicate. Not a problem for the rest of this season. I've already gotten my limit."

I took advantage of that moment to obtain her telephone number. If she wasn't going to contact me, I wanted the ability to contact her. Maybe... though this was a thought for the future...we could target practice together...

I didn't say anything about that, and while I was tucking away the scrap of paper I'd written her number on, her gaze fell to my bandaged foot. She said, "But to your question, my husband knows when I'm going out. For you, I guess if you're single and you didn't tell anyone, well, it sounds like you've got somebody squawking like an old hen about you as her chick."

"You're right. And I'm trying to figure out if I'm right."

"Well, you're a city slicker, and look what happened."

"Yeah, but what protects you from the same?"

Anna shrugged. "Nothing, really. Some skill, some luck. There's always a risk. But that's true for anybody who does anything. I know a logger who dropped a tree on himself in his own woodlot and had to crawl home through the snow half a mile with a crushed leg. And a farmer whose tractor rolled over on him while mowing a slope he'd mowed a hundred times before. A roofer who broke his neck sliding off his own roof while trying to clean his chimney, and a hunter who accidentally shot himself and died in the woods. All of them knew better. All of them had gotten hurt or had near misses before, when working with other people around."

"Yet you're still comfortable going out into the forest alone."

"Sure, why not?" Anna flipped a hand. "You never think it's going to be you. If you thought about that all the time, you'd never go anywhere or do anything. I'm careful to tell somebody my plans, and carry the phone for whenever there's reception. Been doing it most of my life and haven't needed saving yet."

"Lucky you. So my real question is: If you lived here—as in, right in this house with your own land—would you bother arranging for backup? Or think you were perfectly safe popping out when you felt like it, to no more than a mile from home?"

"Do you really mean, should you have called somebody and told them you were going for a walk?"

"Yes. It seemed like my right and privilege, but I got shocked into thinking I might have to be…more practical. I want to hear from somebody who actually does it, not from those afraid to."

She looked up at me from under her eyebrows, then smiled. My return smile was sheepish; I was still mortified that I had not anticipated everything—again—on top of a simmering fury that my intentions kept getting thwarted. I'd long understood that money couldn't buy happiness, but I'd believed it could buy private space and control over one's affairs.

Anna stood and paced with her hands in her pockets, gaze dancing around the room. "Maybe, since you're a computer type, just e-mail your mother hen when you go someplace people aren't likely to trip over you for a while. You know, 'Hey, I'm heading up to the back forty to pick some flowers, be back before supper, I'll shoot you a note.' You'll probably be well home before she even notices the message, and in case not, she'll know where to send the search party when she figures out you're gone." Anna pivoted on her boot heel and gave me a wink. "Or just take Ned-baby with you everywhere, I'm sure he'd like that."

"I'm sure he would."

I winked back, swallowing the urge to yelp, *Jeesh, does everyone think he's my lover already?* He'd been right about watchers, and people talking about me around town.

"The other thing you have to think about is who's going to find you if anything happens right here," Anna said. "I mean, indoors. You could be hobbling around on your sticks, a cat runs under your feet, and you take a header, crack your skull." She gestured toward the coffee table. "You're a goner unless you've got a date and somebody notices you missing. Or when you're healthy, you find out you're not by having a heart attack. Or somebody like that killer running loose comes for you next. Who's going to know?"

I shuddered, hearing my own thoughts reflected. Outwardly, I remained cool. "Everyone who lives alone has those concerns."

"Just as risky hiding in a hole as it is tromping around in the woods, wouldn't you say? And there's just plain driving. Jeezum crow! I've had more scares on the road than anywhere else. Speaking of, I've got to get going."

Instinctively I tried to get up, having been so distracted from the reason for this conversation that I forgot about its consequence. A shot of pain reminded me to move more slowly and, better yet, stay on the couch.

Anna took her leave after suggesting tasty ways to cook the turkey and advising me that fresh wild bird differed in flavor from the supermarket turkeys most people bought. I couldn't voice that the thought of eating one of the turkeys I'd heard gobbling in the distance a few mornings ago made me feel sick. Maybe by Thanksgiving I'd be able to deal with it. For today, I placed the package in the freezer and fixed a cheese and tomato sandwich for lunch.

Anna's visit lingered in my mind for the rest of the day. Ideas had already been forming on multiple planes; for starters, I now understood Pete's "backwoods and backhoes" comment from dinner. It had been hard to believe how our local killer could so easily get away until I'd found myself unfindable in sight of my own house. The mishap had also provided a good incident to use for my future mystery, and inspired my next Katy story: alone in the wilderness with a wounded animal. Once I developed the idea some, I would pitch it to my editor.

Said editor, meanwhile, had just sent virtual flowers along with the proof copy of *Katy Fox and the Also-Rans*. That story had been a heartbreaker to research, learning about the dogs and horses that made up the racing fields but never won, so were retired early, not retained for breeding, and disposed of in not-so-nice ways. My story had a happy ending, of course—Katy helped a bunch of people start an animal rescue and retirement farm—but getting there had been painful. I was in no mood to proofread it, but contract said I had to do so in five business days.

Regardless, the conga line of guests went on. Each day brought a door knock in addition to Ned's morning mail delivery and Luce's afternoon check-in. On Thursday I received Tammy, on her way back from showing the ski house on Rock Maple Road to an unpromising prospect. On Friday Pete came up for the weekend so he and Luce took me out for dinner since I was moving around solidly on the crutches and starting to hop around without them indoors. By then I had gotten over my snark and started to appreciate I had real friends, even some potential ones, and to wonder what I could do in exchange for their kindness and support. Being so out of practice, my ideas came up short.

On Saturday Ned returned and mowed the lane to the shooting range. By the time he was done, the air flowing in my windows was saturated with the aroma of cut grass. I offered him a towel and a beer when he came in for his pay, seeing that he was ruddy and shiny-sweaty from riding his machine over rough terrain. The combo made him appealingly sexy, though I did my best to stifle the thought.

After popping open a bottle for each of us and slipping my check into his back pocket, he headed for the living room instead of the front door, placing my beer on a coaster on the end table beside the futon couch. I hitched along on my crutches and sank gratefully onto the cushions.

"If you want," he said after a swig, "we can go up to the range and practice. Easy to drive in now, and I set up a bunch of targets while I was up there. You can use the folding chair I've got in the truck."

I shook my head. "Not ready, but thanks. Maybe later."

I took my own swig then replaced the bottle on the end table and slid down on the couch lengthwise, bending an arm over my eyes. I could feel Ned looking at me.

He probed, "You okay?"

"Yeah, just…" I wasn't sure what. Just depressed. A week's worth of coping had ground me down. What I really craved was a nap, but I couldn't ignore that healthily humming body sitting across the lounge space. He wouldn't let me ignore him, anyway.

"Next month you'll be cavorting around like this never happened," he said. "So let's make it a date to practice. Since I do it anyway, you can join me. We can alternate my range and yours."

"Strike the word 'date,'" I mumbled.

"Then let's call it training. One month from today, June…" He popped up, stuck his head in the kitchen to look at the wall calendar, then sat again. "Ninth. That's a Tuesday. I'll pick you up after my route."

I shook my head. "I'll be driving myself by then."

"Fine, we'll work it out. A few months of practice, and you'll be shooting well enough to scare people."

"I already scare people." I sighed, recalling my less-sane moments.

"Well…maybe some. But really, as long as you don't run around shooting your guns inappropriately, nobody around here will be scared of you. Maybe a bit put-off, 'cause you're new and different, but not scared."

With that judgment, he fell silent to nurse his beer. I lifted my arm and twisted around enough to reach my bottle, sliding a glance at him. Seeing his beady eye behind a bland expression, I knew he'd wiggled some bait and was waiting for me to rise to it.

I obliged. "What makes you think I won't run around shooting inappropriately? You don't know me at all, and you've made the point that I don't know what I'm doing with firearms."

He plunked down his beer. "If you were that cuckoo, you'd have shot me or somebody else already, I expect. Beyond that, there's not much you can do to hurt me, so I'm not afraid."

"I'm sure I could come up with some way to hurt you if I tried hard enough." I spoke in jest but underneath I was serious. He'd have reason for fear if he knew what went on in my head. I was glad I'd tucked my journal away so there was no chance he might espy it.

"I'm sure you could," he replied, unperturbed. "You're a novelist, after all. Most people in your line—most artists, really—channel their passions into their work rather than the real world. I'm sure there are cases where artists have killed someone, but I'm not aware of any. They seem more likely to kill themselves." He held my eye. "And you don't give off the vibe of a cuckoo artist ready to prove me wrong."

If you'd met me two years ago…

All I said, after a long pause, was, "I'm not sure whether to be flattered or insulted by your assessment."

"Oh, I mean to flatter. I don't usually pursue women as uninterested in me as you are."

"A pursuit, I confess, that bewilders me."

"Probably because it's too simple."

"What do you mean?" I half sat up.

"Man want woman. Woman not kill him yet. Ergo, green light."

I laughed. "You're the only caveman I know who speaks Latin."

"*Ergo* has long been absorbed into the English language."

"You know what I mean."

"Yes, and that's why I like you. I can speak caveman Latin, and you know what I mean."

Those statements flattered me, albeit from a sideways angle. I tried not to blush. "Fair enough. But you're seeing a green light where I'm giving yellow, at best. What makes you think I'm ever going to give in?"

"We're here having this conversation, aren't we?"

Hmmm, he had a point.

I twisted again to place my bottle back on the end table then stretched down the length of the couch. "Okay, let's say I give in. Then what?"

"Then we have fabulous sex and start seeing each other regularly."

His bluntness astounded me. It also made my nether regions tingle. I defied them and him by saying, "No way. I just invested everything I have, and ever will have, in moving into my perfect home for exactly the life I want. No way am I giving a molecule of myself or an inch of my space to another person again."

He hesitated then said, "Harsh."

"Yeah, well, I've earned the privilege of choice, and I don't care if anyone thinks I'm a selfish bitch."

"Did I call you that?"

"No, but most people think that a solitary life, and defending it harshly, are unhealthy and selfish."

"I'm not most people."

"I'm starting to catch on to that."

He shifted in his chair. "And I'm not talking about moving in with you. I guard my own turf pretty fiercely, too. Besides, I have a better view than you, which I'm not about to give up." He grinned. "So we can keep our toothbrushes in our own sinks."

"You just want a bed buddy, then."

"Absolutely. Don't you?"

"No."

He sighed. "Why not? Did somebody hurt you so bad you won't take another chance?"

"Simpler than that. They bored me."

His eyes popped open wider. *Ha ha*, I thought. *Surprised you back*.

After a long moment he said carefully: "I would have thought violence, or something more objectionable than boring, would make a woman swear off men."

"It's more than men—no housemates or daily companions of any kind. I would be a hermit if I didn't have to rely on others to live. I do wish to have a few precious friends, so I'm trying to learn how to be a friend in order to have some. But another lover?" I shook my head sharply enough to flap my hair. "Been there, done that, not going there again."

"That leaves a big hole in one's life."

"Not really. When sex and romance prove boring and lonely, when lovers want your body but not your heart, the whole thing loses appeal. There's plenty more in life to do besides have relationships. Celibates through history have proven that."

"Abstinence leaves an unhappy body, though. Most people our age still need and crave the energy of sex, unless there's a medical condition in the way. I'm assuming you're not sick."

"Physically, no."

He paused at my insinuation but let it pass. "And you're plumbed heterosexual."

"Yes."

"And have a normal libido."

"Not anymore."

"Hm." He stopped again for thought. "Maybe your psychology is stifling your physiology."

"Probably. That doesn't change the fact I don't want a bed buddy."

"No, but it makes things a little more hopeful for me. I'm up against something that isn't personal."

"Meaning…"

"You don't want a bed buddy, versus you don't want *me*."

"Amounts to the same thing."

"A fine shade of difference. I just have to figure out how to not bore you."

"You don't, so far. I'd rather keep it that way. Then we can stay friends. Which, as I told you, I want and need. Way more than another affair that goes nowhere."

"But then you'll never know if it's possible to have a non-boring lover. Who's also a friend."

"That's called a soul mate. I've completely abandoned hope of ever finding one of those."

"I haven't. That's why I press on."

I sat all the way up. "Are you seriously considering me as a soul mate?"

"I'm interested is all I can say. Plus, nothing ventured, nothing gained."

"But—if we venture, and it doesn't work, then there's loss, not gain. We can't be friends anymore."

"Why not?"

"I—"

I clapped my mouth shut, unable to answer the question. I could feel the answer burning in my heart, but I couldn't put words to it.

"I can't believe we're having this conversation," I finally blurted.

"I'm glad we are."

"Do you talk like this with all women you've just met who you want to sleep with?"

"No, it's usually not possible. With bed buddies, you don't need to, and with the rest, they mostly want to get married and have babies. Or else have me rescue them from whatever hole they dug themselves into, or life pitched them into. But I'm like most everyone, Jane: I want the right person for myself, and I'm still looking for her. In the absence of my soul mate, I'll settle for a compatible bed buddy."

"I...appreciate your honesty, but I don't know what to do with it."

"Then let's be friends, until I can persuade you to be my bed buddy."

"Or I can persuade you to stop trying. Might be tough, because it looks like you don't understand the word *no*."

"Oh, I understand it, and accept it when delivered with serious intensity. You haven't convinced me yet."

"How violent do I have to get?"

He chuckled. "Something less than bullets, thank you."

He paused to give me an opportunity to reject him with serious intensity. I failed.

"In which case," he continued, "I model my approach after Sir Edmund Hillary. If he took no for an answer, he wouldn't have climbed Mount Everest, would he?"

Ned finally stood. "And you, my dear, definitely require ice axes and crampons."

No smile this time. I couldn't argue, since his analogy was apt. I stayed with his mountain-climbing theme. "Tell me this. If you're so into challenges, what happens after you've planted your flag on the summit? Don't you get bored, too, and move on to the next challenge?"

"Depends."

"On what?"

"On whether you like the view from the top, and it was worth getting there, and the mountain lets you keep your perch."

I could relate to that. My progress to where I was as a writer had followed a similar course. There was a higher peak yet to ascend, and I planned to get there eventually because I wanted it and would not quit. So if I was the peak Ned wanted to climb, well, I couldn't condemn his determination even though it made me squirm. How simple all would be if I felt the same about him!

Seeing me lapse into thought, he headed for the door. I snapped alert and called after him, "If you want to get a foothold on that mountain, Ned, try saying something like, 'Great job you did getting your wounded self back from the wilderness, Jane. Pretty good for a pathetic city-slicker woman alone.'"

He rounded on me with a stare that put a sizzle into my belly. I added, "And since you're closer to the kitchen, would you be kind enough to grab me an ice pack?"

He paused a moment longer, still regarding me, then sidetracked to the refrigerator, pulled one of my packs from the freezer drawer, and tossed it across the living room. I caught it with one hand. He acknowledged adroitness with a nod but kept his face blank, saying, "Great job getting your wounded self back from the wilderness, Jane. When do you want to practice again?"

I trilled internally in triumph. "June ninth will be fine."

He gave a curt nod, still holding my eye. "If you're driving by then, let's do it at my range. If not, I'll meet you here. Meanwhile, see you tomorrow with the mail."

He sashayed out the door and revved his truck alive.

I wrapped the ice pack in the towel I kept on the sofa arm before applying it to my ankle. Then I lay back and thought about what had just occurred.

Putting aside the fact that was the strangest conversation I'd ever had with a suitor, I recognized that we both had scored points, with and against each other. I'd put him in his place; he'd bounced right back with an improvement. His willingness to do so earned big points in my book. Maybe he really was what he presented himself as being. Just because I'd never met someone like him before didn't mean such a person couldn't exist.

This thought opened new horizons. With Ned, I was starting from a clean slate; although I still couldn't fathom why he was attracted to me, it seemed that he was, so I must be showing something positive for a change, which drew this friendly and frank person's attention. I didn't want to think he was simply a horny dog. That didn't ring right. Problem was, I couldn't trust my antennae to discern a game-player from a genuinely honest and open person.

After this conversation, however, I felt I should take him more seriously. He had honored my request and given me credit for self-rescue. I really valued that. So maybe...maybe, after burning through a half dozen relationships before giving up, I should consider the chance there might be a lucky seven. Ned qualified as the most straightforward person I'd ever met. He had yet to tell me a thing about himself, but then, neither had I rattled off my own biography. We had jumped into a strange intimacy without any background, like strangers on a transoceanic ship. That alone was new and different.

I thought about him for the rest of the day. When my ice pack thawed, I hauled myself back to the kitchen to return it to the freezer, then poked around doing simple chores. The cats watched me clunk and thump, and exercised me by wanting to go out, come in, go out again, eat food. Work was a no-go, so I took a nap. That left me awake much of the night, willing my heart or my body to send up a signal flare telling me Ned was The One. Both remained silent.

By the next day, I had recovered enough equilibrium to resume work and push through to the last page of the draft. Ta-da! *Katy Fox and the Calamity* was done. On time, too!

It was a hollow achievement, having no one to crow about it to. Most everyone I knew was busy celebrating or being celebrated for Mother's Day. That holiday held no meaning for me except as a reminder of dead parents and the dead-end choices I'd made that had lured me away from my folks while they were alive.

Unusually, I wanted company, and of the acquaintances I'd made so far, the only realistic candidate was Luce. Since she was always willing to celebrate anything good, and I knew that by evening she'd be done with her family affairs and Peter would have left for his downstate business week, I invited her over for dinner. She accepted with alacrity and brought along Nan, a new acquaintance for me. Nan had recently lost her mother, and her children were spread around the world, so Luce was mother-henning her. Nan turned out to be interested in the arts and letters, as well as cats, so we had a fine time together and I retired for the night feeling all was well with the world.

Until the next morning, when I hobbled out to fetch the mail. There among the bills and fliers was a folded, one-word note:

Ennui.

I didn't have to look up that one, as I knew it by heart: "a lack of spirit, enthusiasm, or interest…a feeling of weariness and dissatisfaction."

Damn him!

It was creepy being seen through by someone I barely knew and didn't understand. I stood in the yard, not seeing anything, for a several minutes, then dragged myself back to my computer.

Before I could gather my wits to resume work, the phone rang. Luce started squawking as soon as I picked up.

"Janey! You won't believe it! There's been another murder!"

CHAPTER 15

Too much pressing in—too many people, too much reality. My magma has started boiling again; I need to step back before it blows.

What I need most is to take a month off and read. Bolt the doors and draw the shades, turn up the music, and just steep myself in other people's creative art. Break to watch movies, venture out to museums, then go back to books.

The working novelist's life might be a luxury I've struggled for and deserve, but the juice to sustain it has to come from somewhere; I am not a bottomless wellspring. To keep pumping out stories, I need fuel from other artists' energy and ideas. Not to steal them, but to assimilate and reprocess them into something new.

Of course, writers needs to live some real life, too, in order to have experiences to draw from and mix with ideas; but the ability to integrate reality and fantasy into story comes from reading and writing, then reading some more.

I can deduct writing-study time from my taxes, but reading for pleasure and inspiration and health is on my own time, and I have to take that time from something else.

I keep trying to take it from the outside world, but that world keeps taking it back.

* * *

The *Marble Valley Tribune* featured the latest murder on the home page of its website:

Tragedy in Roaring Gulf!

Late Sunday night, 21-year-old Franklin Nye was killed in a one-car crash on Roaring Gulf Road in Allenburg. His passenger, 19-year-old Darcie Boon, was injured and transported to Mapleton Hospital, where she remains in stable condition.

According to Boon, she and Nye were returning to his home after a party at a friend's house in Allenburg when an oncoming car swerved at them and blinded Nye with its headlights. He steered right to avoid collision and his car hit the end of the guard rail and plunged into the trees, then tumbled down a rocky embankment into the Roaring River, which runs alongside the road and originally carved the Gulf.

Nye, not wearing a seatbelt, was thrown from the car into the river. He was pronounced dead at the scene. Boon, who was belted in on the side of the car that landed upright, was rendered unconscious by the impact and her injuries, but awoke in the hospital to describe what had occurred.

Police are looking for a dark-colored vehicle whose driver was wearing a Stetson-type hat. Whether there was contact between the vehicles remains unknown.

Nye was driving a 1966 Pontiac GTO which he'd inherited from his father and restored. He and Boon had displayed it earlier that evening at the season's first Summer Fun Cruise-In. The vehicle has been totally destroyed.

Funeral arrangements...

"Jeesh," I muttered to myself, then sat back and thought.

Luce had called it another murder. The police weren't going that far, at least in print, but if someone had forced the kid off the road, that suggested intent. What could our local killer have against a car-happy youth? Certainly, his age blew my theory about a grudge-holding old lady. Unless Nye had perpetrated some crime against her in recent times? Or against someone she loved?

I sighed. More research, coming up.

Luce had reported that the kid was a widely disliked tough who probably sold drugs, and I was willing to bet his girlfriend had a reputation as a tramp. Those stereotypes tended to occur together. Gossip about both of them would be easy enough to stir up. Did I really want to? Each new development affirmed my intention to stay uninvolved. I could make up a murder mystery just fine without knowing the truth about the one going on in my backyard.

Yet I was visited the next day by Detective Greene.

Seeing him through the window moved me to present myself on crutches, even though I'd spent most of the day gimping around without them. His eyebrows rose when I swung open the door.

"Uh, good day, Ms. Brown. I'm…sorry to disturb you, but we're following up on new leads in the case and have a few questions."

"Please come in, Detective. But I'll have to sit down while we talk."

"Of course."

He followed me into my office, where he'd interviewed me before with both of us standing. This time I sat in my ridiculously expensive ergonomic chair and propped my crutches against the desk, while he stood in the doorframe and took out his notebook.

Nodding at my leg, he said, "Can you drive," without the upward voice inflection people normally used when asking questions.

"Not yet."

I was sure I could, given that one didn't need a left leg for an automatic transmission, but my ankle remained puffy and sore and I wasn't eager to bang it around in the car's footwell. I thanked it silently, for I now had a perfect reason to not be the person who ran Franklin Nye off the road Sunday night.

"What happened," Detective Greene stated.

I told him I had fallen while exploring my property, eliminating reference to the shooting range. Since my trip to the emergency room could be easily verified, he did not waste time probing for details.

Instead he asked, "Have you recently noticed any red pickups or dark-colored trucks, SUVs, or station wagons passing here regularly, or out of place on Rock Maple Road?"

"How recently?"

"Since, say, the last weekend in April and now."

The window when Len Gustave and Franklin Nye were killed.

"Sorry, no. There's almost no traffic on Rock Maple, and when I do see a vehicle, I usually know who it is. My real estate agent drives a red SUV, not a pickup, and almost everyone I see around drives something dark. White or bright cars are rare enough that they always catch my eye."

He scratched a note on his little pad. Without looking up, he said, "Have you seen anyone around wearing a cowboy hat?"

Yes, Anna Rawson. Who drives a dark-green pickup. Should I rat on her?

I couldn't believe Anna had anything to do with the killings, but if she did, I shouldn't obstruct justice. If she was innocent, she could take care of herself, well supported by a clan and cronies.

Either way, the question reignited my magma. I resented having my privacy disturbed yet again and needing to suppress anger yet again for something that just wasn't any of my business but put me in a compromising position. *Go away, go away!* I wanted to shriek.

Instead, in a slow and cold voice, I said, "Anna Rawson likes to wear one."

He gave no reaction, which irritated me more.

"Do you know where she was last night?"

"No, but I'm sure she'll tell you."

"Anyone else?"

I shook my head. This time after he scribbled a note, Detective Greene looked up and held my eye. "What about your blue Subaru. Has anyone else driven it recently besides yourself?"

Grrrrr! Now I had to defend my car that had been parked for nearly two weeks!

"No. Or not that I know of. But I doubt anyone could steal it and return it without me hearing the garage open and close. I'm here almost all the time."

"But not always."

"No." *Sigh.*

"Were you home last night?"

"Yes. I was entertaining friends." I gave him Luce's and Nan's names.

"Have you ever met Franklin Nye," he said when he finished writing.

"No. As with Len Gustave, I'd never heard of him until I read about his death. And Jake, as I told you before, I knew by reputation but never met him directly. You're barking up the wrong tree if you're thinking me as a suspect."

He gave me a steely look. "Routine checking, Ms. Brown. The more people we eliminate, the easier it is to find the ones we need to suspect."

"I understand." I almost added an apology, but that would be indigestibly submissive. He was doing his job, and I was defending my turf. That kept us at a stalemate.

Then he surprised me by saying, "Because you're a newcomer and someone who watches out windows, and lives close to where three murders have been committed in three weeks, the chance exists you might have seen something without recognizing its importance. We've found people like you can often be helpful. You're the first one we've had with a trained imagination."

One of his eyebrows lifted, while both of mine sprang almost off my face. He'd just delivered one of the weirdest compliments I'd ever received. *I think*. He could also be a spider luring me into his trap. With cops you could never be sure.

"I'd love to share my thoughts with you, Detective Greene, but only if you can assure me one hundred percent that I'm not a suspect."

He went motionless. "It's not in my authority to do that."

"Then I've said all I can." I swung the chair to give him my back.

He waited a few beats then stated, "We've confirmed your background; the timing of your move and presence inside the house the night of the first murder; have a witness that you were also in your house the night of the second one, and no tracks in the snow entering or leaving your premises to contradict that"—*Oh really? When was somebody skulking around looking?*—"and you've provided an alibi for the third that we can easily check, along with evidence"—he gestured with his chin at my foot—"making it highly unlikely you were driving at the relevant hour last night."

We eyed each other in mutual skepticism until I said, "I see." Meanwhile, my mind was going a million miles a minute. What did he want from me? And would telling him what I thought result in being arrested, or helping him with the case?

Carefully, I said, "Okay, if you want random ideas and oddly connected patterns, then I can give you those. Count me out for facts, though."

He nodded and waited.

"Um…do I need a lawyer?"

"Only if you have something to hide."

That was a tricky response. I had plenty to hide, but nothing from the law. My secret thoughts didn't count.

What really made me hesitate was how much I wanted to open up to him. Of all the people I knew, he more than all of them could find value in my experience and speculations; I yearned to express them without penalty. Yet he more than anyone could hit me with the worst consequences.

I didn't know what he knew and could easily put myself in jeopardy by saying the wrong thing. Just as easily, he could be at sea and desperate to find a lead anywhere. The results of opening up or clamming up were a fifty-fifty roll of the dice.

I inhaled and said, "First of all, you're assuming I see anything. Most of the time I have my head down and ears turned off because I'm concentrating on my work. That said, I do get around and shoot my mouth off, so you've probably picked up that I'm researching to write a murder mystery. Anyone who's overheard me at the library can attest to that. Having a real mystery under my nose has given me lots of ideas."

I paused. He waited. I bit back a snarl then unreeled my thoughts.

"You've got to understand the premise, Detective. I make my living by dreaming up stories from simple what-if questions. In this case, from the framework given by the media, salted with bits and pieces of gossip, when I ask myself *what if…?* I imagine someone getting back at people for hurts so old everyone else has forgotten them, and my gut feels it's a woman."

Detective Greene raised his eyebrow again.

I soldiered on. "Jake Baldwin, for example, could have done something awful to her or her family decades ago. Len Gustave could have ripped her off in some heinous way. Or one of them sexually assaulted her way back when. Franklin Nye could have done doughnuts in her lovingly cultivated front lawn with his hot rod, maybe run over her cat. That would be a lot worse."

Detective Greene continued to wait.

I shrugged. "That's all I can think of. I don't know the players, and there's only so much digging around I can do online. Especially for situations before the computer age. I'm betting that none of the original problems were ever reported, and the guys got away with whatever they did. Why else would be someone be seeking justice?"

At last he spoke. "You're thinking vigilante."

"Absolutely."

Then I dared to add, "It's what I would do myself. Vengeance is mine, sayeth the Lord, and revenge is a dish best served cold, sayeth I'm not sure who. Both would be especially true if I was diagnosed with a terminal disease and had nothing to lose."

Detective Greene hadn't stopped staring at me throughout my monologue, but the quality of his stare tightened in such a way that I felt he'd seized upon the idea.

"Please assure me," he said, "that you don't have a terminal disease."

I gave a dry laugh. "Not that I know of."

He closed his notebook and looked ready to leave.

That's when I took the biggest risk of my life, confiding: "The reason I'm sure it's a woman is because she's walking the path I'd mapped for myself before I turned off it onto another road."

He blinked. A long second stretched between us, until he prompted, "And what path was that?"

I sighed. "Despair."

He waited. Damn, he was good at that. Standard interview procedure: Keep silent until they're nervous enough to talk.

I talked, disregarding the fact he was a policeman, focusing instead on my need to be straightforward like Ned. This detective was not out to get me, right? If I was wrong, and the situation flipped upside down and put me in jail, then I would get a lawyer and extract myself from the mistake. What mattered now was to tell the important points to someone who might understand. I was pretty sure he wouldn't have knocked on my door if he couldn't.

"It was a few years ago," I told him. "I had one of those days when the world comes crashing down. Nothing specific happened; rather, many things added up and I realized like a bolt of lightning hit me that I was a nothing more than a meaningless amoeba among billions, my life was a complete waste, and both human civilization and the planet were so screwed up that apocalypse would probably happen within my lifetime. That threw me into deep despair. But not so deep that I couldn't face one fact. I had to decide whether to live or die, and if I was going to live, then I had to define what really, truly mattered to me and do it before I died."

I glanced at Detective Greene. He was still standing and had not reached for his notebook. *Off the record.* So I told him the rest.

"I literally ticked off options on my fingers. Option one: Don't bother. Just be done with it all and kill myself. Option two: Continue ignoring reality like most everyone else, and fumble through my days pretending there would always be a better tomorrow and other people would solve all the problems. Then get horribly surprised."

Looking down at my hands, I saw that I was counting on my fingers again. The detective remained watching my face.

"Three: Become a proactive superwoman. You know, marrying that expression 'If you're not part of the solution, then you're part of the problem.' That meant diving into politics and devoting my life to preventing escalation and injustice wherever possible, maybe even hitting on the one thing that might turn the lethal tide." I scoffed. "Yeah, right."

Detective Greene still did not react. I could just as well be dictating into a recorder while looking at a poster.

I pressed on: "Option four: Take the fatalist hedonist route. Meaning, surrender to what I could not change and savor each day as if it were my last, trashing financial security, love, and morality to indulge full-time in every pleasure, because life is too short even without pending doom, and it's the only life I'll ever have."

I hesitated before verbalizing the point that counted. "Five: Go radical and become a stealth problem solver—an assassin—traveling the world to find the evildoers who instigate mass pain and destruction, and knocking them off for everyone's benefit."

I splayed all five fingers and looked up. "That, sir, is what I think the killer is doing. Thinking globally but acting locally. It's too hard to pull off international assassination if you're just an ordinary person without special-forces-type skills and political or diplomatic connections. So why not help your own community by getting rid of the scumbags, especially if they've caused personal misery at some point in your life? Planning it would be fun. And if you don't care what happens to you, then it doesn't matter if the cops nab you. In the lead time you've built up, you've at least rid the world of a few vermin and done something good for other people, and can die satisfied."

Detective Greene kept his eyes on me, but they had gone flat as the gears behind them whirred.

When he'd collected his thoughts, he said, "Since you apparently haven't taken options one, three, or five, Ms. Brown, is your move here part of option two or four?"

"Actually, it's option six: withdrawal and immersion. Unlike most depressed people, I got a lucky break—winning my dream job, right at the pit of my despair. I couldn't write inspiring stories for girls while I was a bitter, seething, basket case, so I had to find a way back to mental health. The chance came when my father died and left me enough money to set myself up in just the right situation. The day it all came to fruition was when our invisible assassin struck. About when I was happily unpacking."

I held my breath while Detective Greene processed my words. I hoped he wouldn't find some way to twist them into a cover story for my guilt.

He stayed businesslike. "Do you have anyone in mind for this invisible assassin?"

I shook my head. "I only know about half a dozen women in the area, and only one of them well. None look like a candidate for my theory."

I thought of Bobbie Banella but said nothing.

"If any of them does, or someone new fits the profile, please contact me immediately."

I nodded, having run out of words.

He gathered himself to depart. "Thank you for your candor, Ms. Brown. It may prove helpful. Most helpful, however, would be restricting your theories to your writing, and leaving the investigating to us."

My cheeks went hot. "Of course."

He nodded curtly. "Don't get up, I'll see myself out."

I didn't get up, because I couldn't.

Many minutes passed before I limped to the front door and sealed up after him. My foot and head throbbed in asynchronous waves. I treated myself to a painkiller, resisting the temptation to swallow the remaining pills in the bottle as my reawakened despair begged me to do. *All that for nothing.* He didn't even react. Stupid, stupid to reveal myself to a policeman. Self-delusion again, thinking I'd moved past it, and my cock-eyed view of reality might actually solve a crime.

Then again, did this sudden willingness to talk mean I was getting better? Or was it a crack in my control that showed I was getting worse?

I still believed that other people did not need to know my secrets; it was part of the Golden Rule to not burden them with my neuroses if I didn't want to hear about and get involved in theirs.

Maybe the secrets I'd just let out were a test run, knowing that sooner or later I would break down and tell Ned, or Luce, or someone with whom I had a personal relationship. Maybe I needed to challenge fate with a dangerous risk. If the cops took me seriously, rather than interpret my story as a clever ploy to deflect suspicion away from myself and they came back to clap me in irons, I would be able to accept I was sane again, and worthy of being loved.

That idea sickened me. I should believe myself worthy. I should know I was sane. I should not imperil my freedom and privacy because I needed to come clean in my soul.

Digging deeper, I faced the fact I was sick of being chained by despair. I had to do something to break my fetters, and I might have just done it—only to trade them for a different kind of fetter. At least I'd be psychically free.

Meanwhile, the day was still young, and I had work to do. Until something happened to prevent moving forward, I was free to continue doing what I'd labored so hard to make possible. Option six.

That meant get up, stop feeling sorry for myself and worrying about what I couldn't control, and get back to work.

CHAPTER 16

Secrets, secrets. I'm starting to believe they're the curse of humankind, the origin of so many miseries. Secrets eat people from the inside out and drive them into craziness or desperation from the need to keep their secrets hidden. For killers, it makes sense to keep secrets to avoid getting arrested; for the rest of us, keeping secrets doesn't make sense, because the worst that can happen is humiliation, or perhaps getting fired from a job or socially ostracized.

It's possible to recover from those setbacks, whereas committing capital crimes has severe, long-term consequences. I've not committed a capital crime, but I've sure wanted to, and if I knew I could get away with it, I might take the chance. That's why I'm privately cheering the invisible assassin, even while trying to help the police find her. Having been drilled by family, school, and church that thoughts equal deeds, however, I have to hide my own dark thoughts and desires. The most courageous thing I've ever done is confess a portion of them to Detective Greene.

But what about Ned? I can't tell him why he's right about me. I truly am disillusioned, wallowing through ennui, with a heart already shattered by the time I realized the world was, too.

Thank JJ for the killing blow. JJ, my first love, my deepest love, the one who got away. Half my life ago, on a romantic-escape weekend, we smoked a little weed then rolled into bed. That night was magical; the boundaries between us dissolved during lovemaking and I felt more connected to another human being than I'd thought possible. This must be what it means, I'd thought, to connect with a soul mate. I was so happy and fulfilled I feared I would die of ecstasy. But as I rose toward climax, JJ thrust away from me. He sat up and blurted, "Oh my god, I'm too disembodied, I can't—"

And that was the end of the weekend. Shortly, the end of the affair. What the hell happened?

After months of mourning, all I could figure was that we'd gotten too intimate during intimacy. I didn't understand why someone wouldn't want to meld that closely with another, but he proved it possible; his rejection wasn't about me being the wrong woman—he didn't dump me for another, he just disappeared—but now I understand why one might want to close the door to other psyches, and barricade oneself against further soul-decimating hurt.

That night was the true start of my downward spiral.

* * *

My first month in North Allenburg ran to its close with no further drama than the leaves coming out and wildflowers starting to fill the fields and line the roadsides.

"Maybe the murderer is done," Luce postulated over the lunch. "He had a list, and has crossed off everyone on it."

"And maybe," I countered, "he's waiting for his next chance. All these killings seem to be opportunity driven."

"But how could the killer know just when Frankie Nye would be driving up that road, and identify him in the dark?"

"Because of the car."

Luce tilted her head.

I elaborated, "His 1966 Pontiac GTO. That's a giveaway. I looked it up online, and it has a unique headlight configuration: two stacked up-down on each corner, versus a side-by-side or single-lamp arrangement like most cars. Easy to identify from a distance, especially on that stretch."

"I don't really know where it happened."

"Between my house and the library. It's the only road, and the only long sight line, where you can pass. And see somebody coming for a while."

I'd studied that twisty, scary road in anticipation of winter driving. Somebody else had studied it for the right place to play chicken with someone and force them off the side into a rocky ravine. If I had the same intention, I'd do it in exactly the same place.

This thought made me squirm. The murders were looking too easy. Was that because I had the heart and mind of a killer, or because the real killer was following the K.I.S.S. principle: *Keep It Simple, Stupid*!

Luce shook her head. "Too crafty for me."

"Which is why you're not a murderer." My voice was teasing, but my smile grim.

"I suppose anyone with an Internet connection could figure out the headlight thing," she said. Then, after a moment's thought while she poked at her salad, she added, "But there can't be that many people with Internet who also have a grudge against those three guys, and knew when Franklin Nye would be driving that road on that particular night."

"That will help the police narrow it down. But even if they figure out who, they can't do doodly-squat without evidence. As far as I know, all they've got is a .45 bullet for Jake, and now a report of a silhouetted hat, from a girl with a head injury, who was sloshed during the incident."

No wonder Detective Greene was fishing for ideas!

I didn't tell Luce he had revisited me, and didn't intend to. Her mind was back where it started, anyway. She stated, "I just hope the killer is done," and changed the subject with a shudder.

Thereafter, my subconscious kept getting tickled by the *K.I.S.S.* principle I'd recalled during that luncheon. I'd seen the slogan somewhere since I'd moved, for the first time since high school. Not in any online searches, but in print. Where? I hadn't been too many places…but the location of the sign resisted mental prodding and wouldn't pop up.

What did surface was memory of another poster that used to hang in the break room of a long-ago office: *THIMK*. That still made me laugh, so I decided to either print both signs as reminders to myself and post them over my desk, or slip them into the mailbox for Ned.

No, that wouldn't work. If I teased Ned with *K.I.S.S.* and *THIMK*, he'd find a way to take them as an invitation. Granted, I was starting to think about things like what would happen if I kissed him, but that was not on the action agenda. Better if I hit him with this old chestnut: *Never assume. It makes an ASS out of U and ME.*

Heck, I ought to challenge him to an initialism contest. OMG. ROTFL. PIA. WTF. FWIW. And the like. Instead, I waited for his response to my response to his "ennui" note. I'd thought about some obscure words, like *marivaudage*—an "affected writing style," or, more appropriately, "banter, especially of a flirtatious nature"—but I doubted anyone used that one in normal conversation. So I chose a symbol instead, the Chinese yin/yang. It expressed what I wanted from him: a balance of male and female, positive and negative, dark and light, give and take, intimacy and independence.

Either he didn't get it, or he was stumped on how to reply. It seemed he wasn't blowing me off, for he gave me the friendly-acquaintance and business deal I'd asked for. He beep-beeped whenever he passed on his mail route, waving if I was in sight; and he arrived as arranged to mow my lawn and keep the upper lane open. We only exchanged pleasantries when face to face, such as when I paid him, and if not for a flare that stayed behind his eyes, I would have thought I'd mistaken his initial interest. This was enough to hold me back from asking whether Detective Greene had talked to him again, too.

Ned's note, when it did come, was an invitation to his family's Memorial Day barbecue. Luce confirmed that oodles of people would be there, including herself and Pete. She offered to give me a ride, both for company and to spare my foot from driving. While the foot was recovering nicely it was not fully healed, so I appreciated her offer. Nevertheless, I balked for a day to weigh it against how badly I wanted the freedom to arrive and leave at my own time.

Ultimately I remembered the purpose of my recovery program and replied "yes" to Luce directly, and same to Ned via mailbox.

The BBQ bash was slated for Monday of the holiday weekend, but first came Allenburg's Memorial Day parade on Saturday. Luce asked me to attend that with her, too. I accepted with enthusiasm, having not watched a parade since childhood, nor seen one on TV since that era, when my family gathered around the screen on Thanksgiving to watch the Macy's parade. The Allenburg version hardly compared to it, but our small-town zeal was the same as the big city's. Everyone lining the street waved flags and tossed confetti and hooted and honked horns and clapped for the fire department, the 4-H Club, the Boy and Girl Scouts, the town officials, antique cars and horse-drawn carts, veterans groups, and assorted others marching to the stumbling beat of the high school band. Watching the parade shoulder to shoulder with more people than I'd seen since leaving New York, I felt part of the community for the first time. Everyone I knew, I saw and exchanged pleasantries with. People I didn't know but vaguely recognized waved or said hello. The one person I didn't see was Ned.

Along Main Street, every telephone and light pole bore a fluttering American flag, and solemn ceremonies were conducted at various cemeteries. Some gravestones in them dated back to the 1700s. My own family's headstones dated from two hundred years later and were spread around the country, or didn't exist. Normally I didn't think about such things, but on this day I felt rootless and wanted to belong.

I couldn't help but wonder, though, whether among the happy faces lurked the killer, fooling us all and calculating how to nail the next victim.

Oblivious to human concerns, Mother Nature bestowed her best weather upon us the whole weekend. I missed most of it in between the parade and the barbecue, owing to desk time needed to compensate for the recreational time off. The concentration prevented me from getting anxious about seeing Ned socially while meeting a new batch of strangers.

I was in good shape by the time Luce and Pete picked me up, midafternoon on Monday, and conveyed us to the Cavendish family homestead. Cars already filled the driveway and lawn, with overspill lining the road. Luce dropped me and Peter off at the house while she sought parking. Pete gallantly loitered on the front lawn with me, until Ned emerged from the milling mob and crooked my arm in his.

"Welcome to the family manse," he greeted.

"Hi, and thanks." I was surprised to feel comfortable with him instead of nervous. Maybe because so many people were around, laughing and talking and cooking and eating, with kids romping among them and nobody paying us any mind.

"Is this where you grew up?" I asked, gesturing with my chin at the classic white-clapboard farmhouse. It sat grandly on a corner lot where two upland dirt roads intersected, backed by acres of yard and fenced fields and outbuildings then forest. The long-distance view was comparable to mine but not better, so I guessed this wasn't where he currently lived. Neither road was Tamarack Hill, anyway, which he'd said was his address.

"Yep. Me and Bud, and Louise and John and Perry, all born in this very house. Come around back, meet the clan."

Between his support on one side and my cane on the other, I walk-hitched into a group of more Cavendishes than I could keep sorted. They represented four generations, from the grandma I recognized from the community dinner to Ned's cousin's daughter's toddlers. Everyone I recognized from the dinner—Aunt Mary, Ned's brother Bud and his wife (who turned out to be Cindy), and their girls, Alicia and Nicole—was scurrying around with plates, dishes, drinks, and condiments. They acknowledged me cheerfully on the way by.

Ned left me in a rare vacant chair with a view of family members and a few strangers manning the grill and food tables, then moved off to mingle with other guests.

My cane and wrapped ankle gave people conversation openers, so I got a lot of mileage out of my embarrassing tale about being lost within sight of the house. Folks reciprocated with tales of similar episodes, some frightening, some funny, and some leading people to talk about the murders.

It had not escaped collective notice that the victims had all been killed at or quite close to their homes. How many people recognized that pattern from their own conclusions, and how many were led there by news reports, I could not determine. I wished somebody would cough up detail nuggets I could use to expand my theory. Maybe they'd all been interviewed by the cops and cautioned to keep their mouths shut.

I ended up monopolized by the handful of people interested in books. Ned's relatives who had quizzed me at the community dinner wanted to hear about my progress. They made a point to sit with me at a picnic table, offering to help me across the lawn to it though I could get there just fine by myself.

Then Helen, over cole slaw, finally cornered me into committing to a presentation at the library. Since I was wrapping up my current manuscript, had okayed the proofs for its predecessor, and was waiting for my editor to approve the proposal for the next volume, I had time to give. We settled on a date in the first week in June to augment an event the library was already planning.

Ned's niece Alicia, meanwhile, followed me at a distance for most of the afternoon. Then, as dusk settled in, she sidled up to me in a solo moment and offered ideas for more books in my series. Sensing an embryo writer, I encouraged her to capture her ideas in her own journal, maybe even compose complete stories herself, since there's no copyright on ideas and we could both write the same story from completely different angles in different styles. I invited her to share her efforts with me but didn't go so far as to offer to mentor her. I needed to see how she reacted to encouragement, first. If she really did write something and came back to me for more, I would take her under my wing. Why not? It was a sound pay-forward to the next generation by someone who would never have kids.

I kept scanning for Anna Rawson but didn't see her at the party. I would have liked a chance to find out if Detective Greene had approached her, and whether she was under suspicion for the murders because of her hat (a clone of which anyone could wear), maybe even help her if there was anything I could do. She might be avoiding groups to sidestep suspicion, however, for which I couldn't blame her.

I felt a twinge of guilt for even mentioning her to the detective. It felt like betrayal, because I kind of liked her, and had been wondering if maybe sometime after my ankle healed, she'd hike with me around my land and show me trails she surely knew about. What a bummer if she proved to be a murderer! How big a step was it, anyway, between killing animals and killing people?

Not a question I wanted answered tonight, though it kept poking at my subconscious. As with the parade, it was possible the real killer was mingling and laughing among us. That kept me on edge. If others were suffering the same unease, I didn't know them well enough to tell from their words and gestures.

Anna's absence, I hoped, could be explained by a headache, or her own holiday party with others. I had yet to learn the crisscrossed threads that connected people of the community. It seemed that everyone connected to the Cavendishes, and on this occasion their door was open to all Allenburg residents and their associates. I had been to neighborhood block parties in the city, but this party was broader in its invitation. If you lived within thirty miles and were linked to anyone who linked to the family, you were part of the family tonight, too.

Lacking anyone else I already knew to talk to—Luce was twirling around in social ecstasy, Ned was playing host, Helen had disappeared, and if Nan or Bobbie or Tammy came, I never saw them, nor did I see Peter after we arrived, he must've been inside having private conversations—I had to either hide in the shadows or wander around talking to whoever seemed friendly. Most people were, so I polished my rusty small-talk skills while stuffing myself with great summer barbecue fare.

Once it got dark enough for the patio torches and fireworks to come out, Ned drifted back into my orbit. We'd been keeping tabs on each other across the yard all afternoon, but neither of us had attempted conversation. When he finally zeroed in on me, he felt too close even though he stopped within a respectful distance. The darkness created intimacy even if not intended. That's when I realized I'd only seen him in full daylight before. In semi-silhouette he felt bigger and stronger, and, unexpectedly, smelled vaguely of aftershave.

He opened with a neutral, "You seem to be hobbling along pretty good these days."

"Yes, I can walk around in the house, but I wasn't sure what the conditions would be here so I brought along a prop."

"Empty chair over there." He swept his arm to illustrate.

"I've been cycling between them all day. But I'm starting to get restless, and want to either explore farther than I can realistically expect to move around the property, or just retire for the night."

"Exploring is better in daylight," he agreed. Then he shot me a grin that looked wolfish in the dark/light collage. "You can always stay here and look around in the morning. I can take you home after breakfast."

I caught his innuendo and resisted teasing, *Right, sleep at your parents' house when I just live a few miles away. Where are you gonna sleep, Romeo?*

"Thanks, but I need to feed my furry children. As soon as Luce is ready, she'll trundle me home."

That might be midnight, based on Luce's apparent comfort in a chair around the fire pit, nattering with everyone in earshot.

Ned followed my glance. "In that case, let me give you a lift."

I hesitated.

"I'll just tell Luce or Peter," he said before I could cut him off, "and we can be on our way."

"Thanks, but that's really not necessary…"

"Of course not. Do you *not* want me to take you?"

"I don't know what I want," I bleated.

That halted him. He looked at me like a curious bird, then smiled and plucked up my hand, carrying it to his lips for a kiss on my fingertips like the brush of a feather. Unwelcome tingles sang between my head and feet.

"I don't want to take advantage of you, Miss Jane, but that remark makes me think there's hope for me."

"I don't know," I repeated.

"Funny, I got the impression you were more definitive in your mind."

"I used to be." That definitiveness had crumbled since my session with Detective Greene. I'd let it all hang out for him, to no response or consequence, leaving me feeling more insecure than ever. Nothing for it but to keep plodding along, head down, reminding myself constantly: *Act confident until you become confident. Cross that bridge when you come to it.*

I seemed to be facing a bridge with Ned. Walk across, or stay safely on my side?

I sucked in air and said, "I'd like you to take me home, but I'm worried about what happens when we get there. I don't want to be a summit you plant your flag on."

He said softly, "Then what would you like to be?"

Instead I repeated the truth: "I don't know."

"Then let us climb partway up the mountain and see if we like the view."

I shrugged with a sigh. "That sounds too easy."

"No need to make things complicated."

"But they are. You keep giving me layers of complexity I've not had to deal with before and, well, I don't know how to deal with it."

"Ah—does that mean I don't bore you?"

"No, you just scare me."

He tsked. "Not what I had in mind at all."

"Too late. Try doing something to make me feel comfortable, and maybe we'll have something to talk about."

"How about this?"

He brushed my lips with his. It was delicious and I wanted more.

"Unfortunately, that does not make me feel comfortable."

"How about if I hold you tight all night in your own bed?"

I hesitated way too long before answering, and looked around desperately for an out.

Nearby, people were moving around, backlit by the flickering tiki torches and the fire, talking and laughing. Firecrackers popped and banged on the fringes of the property. I hoped that no one could overhear us; at least we were sort of out of sight, backed up against a stand of grand, ancient lilacs that emitted their fragrance so potently it felt like being stuck in an elevator with someone wearing too much cologne. They overpowered his aftershave except in errant tickles of breeze when he was too close.

Ned waited until I said, "I might consider that," while thinking, *Yes, yes, yes!*

His teeth flashed in the half light. "Well, consider that while I drive you home."

He headed for the fire pit to tell Luce we were leaving.

I stood in the lilac shadow, considering. If I went forward, it would be too hard to go back. If I was going to back out, I had to do it right now.

Heart pounding, I started to count reasons pro and con on my fingers but didn't get very far. I'd known him for what, five weeks, six? It hardly mattered; we seemed to have skipped all the preliminaries. Not that I required months of chaste courtship before I took a lover. Of my previous men, they'd ranged from one-nighters to multi-year live-ins, so I couldn't say that I operated on a rigid moral standard. It was just that…I felt the weight of consequence with Ned that I didn't think I could carry.

Still, I got into his truck, and we drove the bumpy dirt roads between homesteads in silence. In my driveway he cut the engine and said, "I propose a hot toddy. Or one of those top-shelf liqueurs in your cabinet. And then a massage of that sore foot."

Oh. What heaven that would be. My ankle was throbbing. I had planned to take a strong dose of either liquor or painkiller when I got home, but a massage would be worth a double dose of both.

"All right," I said meekly.

We entered the house; threw on the necessary lights; I fed the cats while he poured us two fingers each of my best whiskey, neat. By the time he brought the drinks out, I had reclined flat on the futon couch with my foot up on the armrest.

"That's no good," he said, handing me a glass. "Scootch back so I have room, then let me have that foot on my lap."

His lap. Danger zone. I didn't protest, though, when he sat sideways and took my foot across his thighs. I should have peeled off my sock and offered up a lotion to do the massage properly, but a barrier of fabric seemed important. He didn't question it, just started massaging my ankle as it was.

After the initial flinch against the pressure of his hands on the swelling, I welcomed the sensation. He kneaded the flesh in the gentle, steady way that aching parts crave, and it responded by relaxing. Pain faded into ease.

The house was silent around us. I hadn't bothered with anything like mood music, afraid to set up a mood. He didn't speak, just worked my ankle, then my whole foot—*ahhh*—then between my toes and up my calf. It felt so good I had to keep myself from moaning. I sipped my drink to give my mouth something to do.

"You know about reflexology," he finally said.

"Mm-hmm."

Yep, I knew about the theory that every nerve in the foot connected with somewhere else in the body, and that manipulating feet could heal illness and calm tension. It had been debunked by modern science. So what. It felt wonderful. I hadn't known my legs were as rigid as tree trunks. I hadn't been aware that my knees, especially the weak one, yearned for a kind touch. I massaged them myself routinely, often idly, but it was different when somebody else explored them and listened to their messages.

He shifted position then worked up my thighs. All touch was through my socks and jeans, but those fabrics might as well have dissolved. He bypassed my loins and worked up into my waist. Never tried to inch up my shirt, just massaged me through it, creeping steadily upward as my muscles melted and skin came alive.

He hesitated when he reached my breasts, then went around them. Up the sides of my torso. Into my armpits. Around my shoulders, down my arms, massaging my hands and fingers, never missing a beat. I sank into a stupor, aware of nothing but the golden glow of bodily happiness, which finally made my head shut up. He massaged my neck, the tense muscles of my jaw, my stiff face and scalp.

By then I really was moaning. I couldn't stop it. The moan became a surprised gasp when an orgasm, at first so slow and subtle I didn't recognize it building, abruptly rippled through me for long seconds, without him ever having touched a sexual part or inch of erogenous skin. He backed off when he felt it then bent forward to kiss me while I shuddered. I was too lost to respond, but not so far gone I didn't feel his lips and taste his tongue.

Then he sat up, leaving cool space between us. I ached to reach for him but was too limp to move.

"Next time," he whispered, and left me panting on the couch.

"No," I blurted. He stopped and looked at me. My voice fell back to husky as I invited, "This time," knowing we had to decide about each other, and the time was right.

He squeezed down beside me. I wrapped my arms around him and kissed him long and hard. Other than a hesitation from surprise, he returned the kiss with fire, and grew long and hard against my abdomen. Before long, we discovered the limitations of the futon couch, and he carried me to my bed.

CHAPTER 17

He was still in my bed when I awoke in the morning. For the first time in years, I was not in a position to write in my journal over coffee.

He was already half awake and stirred to tighten his arm around me when he felt me come conscious. I needed to pee but didn't want to send the wrong message by breaking away. All I could think upon feeling him was, *Glory hallelujah!*

Then: *This isn't what I planned.*

And: *What do I do now?*

Nothing, I realized. Absolutely nothing. My task was to accept what had happened and roll with it. Which wasn't an intimidating prospect, because I felt oddly whole. Oddly because I could scarcely recognize the sensation of wholeness. I felt like...myself, my old self, whom I had lost the ability to recognize until this moment. Good grief—did I only need to get laid to be healed?

That was a shaming thought, but I couldn't deny that my angst had vaporized. I felt so balanced, I could walk a fencetop without wobbling.

Is it because of Ned, or because something has changed inside me and any man would do?

No, it was Ned. He'd come into my life for whatever foreordained or random reason, designed to fit, and I couldn't undo that. I didn't want to. He had become a fact of my existence I wasn't going to challenge. One step at a time had led me here. Thank you, gods or luck.

My knee-jerk reaction to this bonus was mistrust, to curl into myself, or the reverse, to cut and run; but that was countered by relaxed muscles, relaxed mind, relaxed heart. These told me that I had made my second correct decision in life. The first was to buy this house, and the second was to embrace this man, even though I barely knew him. He seemed to have all that I lacked while overlapping or complementing my strengths. Usually when I hooked up with someone it was one or the other, leaving a big hole in between.

The kitties showed their approval by piling onto the bed. As I roused, I felt one at my feet, one between the headboard and my pillow, and one pinning the sheets over on Ned's side. He had drowsed off and was snoring lightly. I smiled and stroked his hair. He snuffled and snugged tighter against my side, deeper into the bedding. My heart did little skip-jumps.

Twinkie ventured hesitantly up my body to remind me it was past breakfast time. I wriggled my free arm out from under the sheets to pet her, wondering if I would wake Ned by extracting myself and if he would interpret that as rejection. I decided to chance it, because bladder plus kitties equaled Time To Get Up.

By the time I'd dealt with both and returned to the bedroom, Ned was awake and lying on his back, arms raised and crossed beneath his head, sheet pushed down to his waist to expose his chest.

"Mornin', sunshine," he greeted, his voice confident but smile tentative.

"Mornin', um…mister moonshine," I returned coyly, returning into position beside him, arms wrapped around.

He gave me a quick kiss then said, "I confess to surprise at finding ourselves here."

I smiled. "I'm with ya on that."

"But it's a good surprise."

"Yes. In fact, you hereby have permission to plant your flag on my summit."

"Why, thank you, ma'am." He grinned then made a fist and bobbed it, as if holding a pole and planting it in my head.

I said, "I guess I should rechristen myself Mount Everest."

"Hell no. Maybe Annapurna."

"That would make a good pen name."

"Anna Purna; nice ring to it." He nuzzled behind my ear.

"My previous high was Mount Fuji, so you're doing good." I nuzzled him back.

"Let's settle on K2, then, leave us somewhere to go."

I kissed him again to say, *Okay*. Who else could I jest with about the world's tallest mountains while lying skin to skin with our legs entwined?

Then he sobered. "But, I have to say: It seems a bit too easy. I was expecting to climb longer and harder and suffer more."

"Sorry to disappoint you."

My tone was flip, but anxiety had crept in. For me it had been hard to submit to being conquered, but I'd given in to get the rewards and wanted to embrace them. To embrace him.

He rumpled my hair. "No disappointment, just surprise. I've got to know, though. What changed your mind?"

"You."

"Okay, but…what about me?"

"Your bulldozer directness." I stroked his chest. "I decided to believe you. And I realized I need what you have."

"Which is…"

"Light."

"*Huh?*"

"You don't seem to have any darkness in your soul. No demons driving you, or that you're beating back with a sword. You seem to be like Luce, who just…lives, and enjoys it, and gives to others who have less."

"Well, uh, yeah, I guess that's true."

"What puzzles me is why. I thought everyone had demons."

"No…maybe a lot of people do, but not all of them."

"Aside from Luce, I've never known anyone without them."

"That would surely color your perspective."

He smoothed my hair back down. I pressed into his stroke, waiting, wanting more, afraid to move in case I lost what I had.

He inhaled hard then expelled, "I don't have demons, Jane, because I was born easygoing but also was raised by good people who take care of each other and laugh a lot and learn and are positive and helpful, and tackle problems early and straight on. Might be a different story if I'd landed somewhere else. Not sure where the line between nature and nurture lies."

"But you got the upside of both."

"Yeah, luck of the draw. I've always had what I need in life, except the right woman. While looking for her, I've avoided people with demons because most of them are so needy they suck you dry. Which might be why I've got energy to climb a Mount Everest like you."

"But I've got demons galore."

"Yeah, I caught on to that, and I want to know what they are."

"Why? That will only suck you dry, because demon people can't give back."

"Well, maybe I fancy myself a hero and can help you beat your demons with a sword."

"Dreamer." I sniffed in disdain, then wondered why I thought it was okay to share my demons with a detective but not with a lover.

"It's all a dream," he said, "until you give me something concrete to work with."

I stiffened and pulled away. "I can't."

He drew me back. "Maybe not today. But if I'm here in your bed, you'll ultimately have to tell me."

"Not if I banish you from my bed for evermore."

"Do you really want to do that?"

"No. But if you force me to, I will."

"So...okay, that's why you're willing to be my bed buddy. We don't need to know each other too well."

"Yes. And you said the view from your house is better than mine so there's no threat you'll want to move in with me, or other way around, so we can keep our toothbrushes in our own sinks. That makes me feel safe."

"I see."

We lay silent for a few minutes, thinking. The first one of us to speak again would set the tone for whatever followed.

He took the lead. "As much as I would love to ravish you for another round, and have an interesting argument about demons and the meaning of life, the fact of the matter is I am seriously late for work and would like to keep my job."

He rolled atop me and smothered whatever I might have said with a kiss. Then he sprang away in search of his clothes.

I lay back, pulsating from head to toe. He watched me while wrassling himself into shirt and pants and said casually, "How's the ankle?"

My body had been so flush with happy chemicals, and my mind so tangled with contradictory thoughts, that I'd forgotten about my injury. I wiggled my foot and got up to test my weight on it. "Stiff and sore but fine."

"How about the rest of you?" He stopped moving and waited with a serious expression while I slid into sweatpants and top.

I understood what he was asking and said honestly, "Body is on cloud nine. Heart is banging around like a bird caught in a house trying to get out through the windows. Head might explode within the next twenty-four hours."

"Hm. That's a whole lot better than I was expecting." He flashed a grin.

"How about you?" I said, wanting to know if we'd just done a hit-and-run or were poised at the beginning of something I couldn't imagine.

He smiled. "I'm a happy and lucky man."

He gave me a peck then dashed off to the post office without pausing for coffee or food. He had to help finish sorting the mail, then get on his route. By this time anyone who commuted to work or nipped into the village for coffee and paper would have passed the house and seen his truck in my driveway, which guaranteed his boss would learn the reason for his tardiness. As he drove off, I didn't care what the locals thought, and hoped he wouldn't face repercussions because of what they did think.

Indeed, my whole priority list had undergone an overnight tectonic shift.

Work still came first—a priority we shared—by necessity as well as purpose. With my hormones aflame, however, I couldn't get my day organized to do anything that paid the bills. Instead I puttered and frittered and played with the cats, waiting to hear his Jeep turn into Rock Maple Road—almost three hours later than usual. Part of his delay came from the buildup of mail after a holiday weekend, the other part from getting to work late; then a third reason revealed itself: He'd had to stop home to get some stuff.

On his return trip from the end of Rock Maple Road, instead of pausing at my mailbox, he passed it and swung into my driveway. That drew me to the window, through which I saw him hop out of his vehicle carrying a mop in one hand and bucket in the other.

Huh?

I scurried to the door and opened to his knock, smiling with question-mark eyebrows. His return smile seemed a little forced, but he said boldly,

"Good morning again. Somebody told me there might be a head explosion here today, so I came prepared."

He lifted his arms to explain the mop and bucket. I flung back my head and laughed, loud and free from the belly.

"As you can see," I said upon recovering, "the head is still intact, although a little whirly inside. Next week might be another story. Can you come in?"

"Not really, since I don't have to clean up after an emergency." He placed down the mop to reach into the bucket and pull out a handful of sunny white daisies, dripping from their ride in water but still cheerful and carrying the message he intended.

Thank you. I hope we can go forward in joy.

At least, that's the message I received. He might have meant something else but I didn't want to hear it. I just accepted the gift with girly noises of delight and hurried the daisies into a vase. He stepped inside but didn't follow me to the kitchen. When I returned I said a heartfelt "Thank you" back and sealed it with a kiss.

He drew the kiss out, assuring both of us that last night had not been a fluke. Then he muttered into my ear, "Someday when you least expect it, I'll have ten, maybe fifteen minutes free on my route, which will let us have a more interesting encounter."

"That would be…stimulating."

"Normally I'm only given slack at work for crises."

"Hmm, hormone overload not considered an emergency?"

"Ah, no."

We both remembered a real crisis—dead body—then pushed that occasion out of mind by kissing again, during which I cupped my hand between his legs in a promise of reruns to come. He tweaked me back, followed by a teasing bump-and-grind, then returned to his appointed rounds, smiling to himself.

"Later," he tossed back as a farewell. I acknowledged with a nod, appreciating both the assurance and the vagueness, then watched him head for the Jeep—only to stop and back up.

"I nearly forgot—I don't have your phone number."

"Oh. Ah. Of course. Do you want it written, or can you memorize it?"

"Recite, and it will be inscribed upon my heart."

I smiled and enunciated the digits, adding, "Do you have e-mail?"

"Nope. I've stayed out of the computer age. Here."

He handed me a business card for his landscaping enterprise, adding, "So...doing anything tonight?"

"I...don't know yet."

"How about calling me when you know, and we'll figure out a plan."

I didn't respond instantly, so he added, "That is, if you want the next step."

"I think so..."

"But..."

"That's all. I want to. But I need a pause to integrate. You've thrown me way off stride."

"Well, yeah."

"Please notice that I'm not slamming the door in your face."

"Well, yeah." He flashed his cocky grin.

"So, I'll call you when I know, and we'll figure out a plan."

"Okay. Have a good day."

He pivoted and left. I twinged, fearing that I'd hurt or insulted him, but unwilling to feel guilt about it. Until we truly knew each other and could anticipate outcomes, we had to negotiate each engagement.

Despite the twinge, I was still glowing from his affections, and withdrew to the porch to just think about him. How could I not? He had rocked my world. But having chosen to accept him, I now had to assimilate him. There was room in my daily affairs to accommodate his presence, but I didn't know how much my heart could give, how much it could absorb, how long I could hide my deepest ugliness from him. There was only one way to find out.

Another step forward.

The way to start, I decided, was to invite him into my work. I had to research exactly how Katy Fox might come across a wounded fawn in her next adventure, and how she could and should deal with it. Ned was a deer hunter who could help with verisimilitude.

Until I saw him again to pick his brain, I would have to visit the library if I wanted to keep moving on the book. Yeah, it would be nice to lie back and think sexy romantic thoughts all day, but deadlines ruled my reality. The library surely owned the two classic tear-jerker deer stories for youth—*Bambi* and *The Yearling*—which I should refamiliarize myself with before I advanced too far in plotting and drafting my own deer story. At least I could legitimately lie back with my feet up if I was reading for work.

By midafternoon I had isolated which facts I needed to chase down. I was intending to start on the chasing, but then the phone rang. I was hoping the caller was Ned but ID showed Luce. In the past I would have let the call go to the machine, but this time I felt the urge to acknowledge and talk with a friend.

"Hey," she greeted. "How'd it go last night?"

I could hear the *elbow-elbow, wink-wink* in her voice and silently cried, *Aaaiiiieeeee!*

When I balked at replying, she said in her manager tone, "Just checking to see if you got home okay. Last I saw, you were heading off into the night with a man you weren't certain about."

"It went fine," I assured her. "And what time did you get home?"

"Not too long after." She paused. "I've already heard that Mr. Cavendish didn't go back to his own place last night."

I sighed. "Well, yes, we spent some time getting…better acquainted."

"Oh, really?" she said with a few extra question marks in her voice.

I smiled. "Let's just say…he brought me home, he left in the morning."

That, at least, was technically true. Luce laughed. "I'm glad. He's a good man, and I hate the idea of you living alone forever. Not a good plan. Makes me crazy when Peter's not around."

"That doesn't mean I should shack up with the first nice guy I meet, does it?"

"No, of course not. But really, if you lived with someone responsible and affectionate like Ned, you wouldn't have gotten into that mess in the field."

I didn't see that as an *if A, then B* logic leap, but I didn't argue with her. She rushed on to say, "How's your foot, anyway?"

"Getting stronger, thank you. I'm still not up to driving, though, so if you'd be willing to haul me to town one more time, that would be great."

"Groceries?"

"Yes, and library. I need to talk to Helen about my presentation."

"I can take you to both tomorrow afternoon. Why not invite Helen to visit you?"

"She's already stopped by."

It dawned on me that Helen was a woman alone, too; perhaps I should invite her back. Offer dinner together, here or in a restaurant. Invite Luce and Nan and Bobbie along, form a Solo Women's Club. Nice idea. I wondered how many of the those women alone owned guns.

The thought brought me back to target practice. With Ned. Who had slept with me last night. And wanted to do it again tonight. I didn't feel up to it. Could he understand that? Should I call him, or play hard-to-get games and wait for him to call me?

No. No games.

The thing I liked—loved?—about him was his directness and (apparent) honesty. I wouldn't get anywhere with him if I messed with that. Nor would I continue on my personal recovery path if I exploited what he offered and acted like a selfish jerk.

"No reason not to invite her again," Luce was saying. I had to snap my head to get back on track.

"I'll sound her out," I promised, then we fixed a time for tomorrow's pickup and returned to our own affairs.

Hands shaking a few hours later, I dialed Ned's telephone number. Got his answering machine, which both relieved and annoyed me. I hadn't prepared a message, having expected him to be home at workday's end. The fact that he wasn't reminded me like a slap in the face that I didn't know enough about him and might be exposing myself as a fool.

Then I remembered his hands, his lips, his hot body, his whispered words. Even as he unnerved me, he sent something comforting into my soul—something I had to trust.

So I left an honest message: "Hi, my head hasn't exploded yet, but I think

I want to stay in this evening and sleep. Tomorrow I'll be working in the morning then running around with Luce in the afternoon. Let's connect later. Hope you're..."

Beyond that, I didn't know what to say.

By the time Luce picked me up the next day, I'd slept like a stone, gotten caught up in my journal, and wedged my professional feet back under me. My editor had approved the proposal and outline for *Katy Fox and the Wounded Fawn*, so I started framing it and doing the base research. It kept my mind where it belonged for the bulk of the day.

When Luce pulled in, I was feeling balanced again and was on top of the day's work. I tried to remember if she had ever known me in a balanced state and realized no, we had first overlapped when I'd started downward, and she had supported me, passively or directly, ever since.

For that I felt a glow of affection and gave her a one-armed squeeze and kiss on the cheek when I got into her car. She shot me a look of surprise but no other reaction, just shoved her chariot into Drive and zoomed us off to Mapleton.

It was nice to sit in the passenger seat and watch out the window while we chitchatted about unimportant things. She gave me space to warm up to an intimate elucidation I didn't want to give but admitted that she deserved.

I couldn't think of a smooth intro so just jumped into it. "So...how long have you known him?"

She didn't need to know who "him" was. She shrugged, keeping her eyes on the road. "Since we moved up here. Don't know him well, but we always seem to cross paths with him or his relatives. There's a lot of them."

"Rather."

"And as far as I know, not a loser among them. Salt of the earth. That's why we like Vermont. Many more of those kinds of folks."

I thought but didn't say, Are there really more, or are they just more visible in the smaller population that's lacking the urban go-getter type? Those tended to congregate where the money was.

The money, for sure, was not along the route to Mapleton. Normally I couldn't do more than glance at what I passed while driving alone, but even when I could, there wasn't a lot to see.

Like most of upper New England, this quadrant of Vermont had more trees than anything else. A century and a half ago, the region had been almost denuded by sheep farming, clear-cutting, and hilltown crop farming; all that had reversed over the generations, so forest covered most of the rocky landscape today. Logging and farming still remained as industries, but they had been condensed and now provided a tough and insecure living for few. A proliferation of ski areas had likewise shrunk back to a hardy dozen or so, keeping "gold towns" like Orton thriving while those around them decayed.

Beyond the ski towns, and the handful of larger communities that called themselves cities, settlements were just clusters of buildings separated by miles of trees, scrub, hills, and wetland, punctuated erratically by homes, farms, or camps, with general stores and post offices at intersections. Unlike the world I'd come from, where communities blurred together with only signs announcing their boundaries, here towns had no distinction outside their centers, and each building in between looked different, with most showing a shabbiness not present in wealthier parts of the country. Nicer places tended to be out of sight up long driveways, many owned by out-of-staters who visited a few times per year for vacation.

There weren't enough of those properties to offset the number that had been abandoned, or struggled on around collapsed outbuildings. One minor improvement over earlier eras was that solar farms were sprouting up where housing developments might once have taken over. I liked the idea but was saddened by how much arable acreage they consumed. Yet I couldn't blame farmers for selling off land. Small-scale family farms could hardly support themselves anymore, and most of the children decamped for better prospects, leaving no one to pass their parents' life work to. The communities, having little or no tax base from business, hit the homeowners and landowners hard.

I was lucky in being able to make a living through a fiberoptic cable instead of having to rely on dying or wildly up/down local industries. The company and readership who paid me were based out of state and, in some cases, around the world.

Once in Mapleton, Luce and I twirled through our shopping then headed back out of congestion to quaint and sleepy Allenburg. At the library she browsed through magazines in the reading room while I met with Helen to organize my author talk.

We were both crisp and businesslike, discussing how many copies of my books to order, what room to use with how many chairs, how long to schedule the event, whether or not to offer refreshments. In the course of this I noticed that Helen had acquired a tremor in her hands and bluish bags under her eyes.

"Are you okay?" I asked her after we completed our business.

"Just tired." She waved a limp hand and avoided my eye.

I wondered if she was ill, or under an emotional strain. That brought a flicker of an idea, which in turn kindled recklessness. Like with Detective Greene, like with Ned, there were things I needed to say—do—know—that I wasn't willing to wait for anymore.

So I asked Helen, "Do you know anything about Fiona Cobb?"

She looked up sharply. That answered my question, though she said only, "I've heard the name. Can I help you find something?"

Her tone was artificially even. I matched it with, "Yes. I'm looking for archive stories about her death last February."

Helen hesitated and looked away. "Oh yes, I remember. Such a tragedy. But that would be covered by the *Marble Valley Tribune*, and we don't have their records. I can give you a number to call, and you can probably find information online."

"I've only come up with one news report and an obituary. I need somebody to talk to, or microfiche or something to get more background."

"Why?" Helen blurted, holding her face still but looking white around the eyes.

An ugly idea rose in my mind but I pushed it aside. "Somebody mentioned her story and it struck me that the way she died could be converted to murder from accident. Maybe an idea to build my mystery novel around."

I'd brought with me the books I'd borrowed and read, and returned them now by sliding them across the counter toward her. All pertained to the conversations we'd had about unusual methods of homicide, and local history.

On seeing them Helen seemed to relax, although—because I was looking for it—I saw her hands quiver.

She put on her sweet and cheerful face and checked in my books.

"And for my latest Katy Fox," I said, "I need a copy of *The Yearling* and *Bambi*. Do you have those here?"

"Yes, the young-adult section."

She pointed. I nodded and walked around the corner to locate the volumes. *The Yearling* by Marjorie Kinnan Rawlings was on one side of the stack, and *Bambi* by Felix Salten was on the other. My own Susan Silver books were a few steps farther along that row. I checked them to see more copies missing than the time I had scoped out my publisher's complete series. A glow of gratification swelled inside—promptly canceled by a chill when, on my way back to the checkout desk, I passed a framed "K.I.S.S." sign on the wall.

I froze midstride as implications cascaded through my mind, connecting what had been random dots. Other patrons came and went around me, and Luce remained absorbed in a magazine, while Helen chatted with people at the desk.

When I stepped up to check out the deer books, she handed me a slip of paper with contact info for somebody who handled archives at the *Marble Valley Tribune*. As our hands connected during the paper exchange, we held gazes, long and unblinking. I broke it by chirping, "Thanks, see you next week!" then rounded up Luce. I didn't hear a thing she said or remember a word I responded as she drove me home, my knees rattling in my seat.

CHAPTER 18

Helen LaCroix? Really? Is it possible?

From checking the phone book and the Internet as soon as I got home, I learned that LaCroixs have lived in the area for generations. Helen is old enough to have been in the same little school with Jake Baldwin, although in different grades. As a lifelong resident and current property owner, she could have gotten into some sort of business dealing with Len Gustave. Where she might have connected with young Franklin Nye, I can't guess, but Fiona Cobb was also someone Helen might have known through school, or just small-town proximity.

But what—what!—could these people have done to make a sweet, generous, intelligent, well-educated, law-abiding woman take them out?

Her hands were shaking with no evident reason for that symptom to be an emotional reaction. Is she sick? How many diseases start with a simple tremor? Could she have some horrible diagnosis that pushed her into the option five I considered during my dark days—killing people because I had nothing to lose, owing to having a terminal illness? Or do her hands shake merely because she's in her sixties and a straining day gives her the wobbles?

That's the likeliest scenario, but I can't leave the idea alone. Helen as our serial killer is so far out as to feel possible. I scoured the Internet for clues and data, and updated my mystery file. If I'm wrong about Helen in real life, that doesn't matter. She's given me an excellent idea for my future book.

What if, what if…

Helen knows creative ways to kill people from her readings. She's so unlikely a suspect that nobody would think of her. If she adhered to keeping it simple, she could leave no incriminating evidence. She can overhear patrons talking when they come into her echoing workplace, and thus know things the rest of us don't, without having to involve herself in any conversations that might implicate her. If what I see parked outside the library is hers, then she drives a dark-colored, high-mileage Subaru hatchback (like half the state). Does anyone besides me consider her a suspect? Did Detective Greene look at her after I suggested a woman culprit? Can he legally get access to her medical records with no valid basis of suspicion?

People might consider me a suspect, too—a possibility I doubt but can't discount until solidly proven otherwise. I did, after all, give Detective Greene too much information. A difference between me and Helen—I think—is that I have books to write and a legacy to leave. Well, maybe she has her own obsessions that likewise rank above killing bad people. I'll have to get friendlier with her and find out. If she doesn't have something meaningful to do, however...if she's alone in the world and slated to die...killing evil people would be a hard temptation to resist. Oh yes.

Even if the police caught her, how much time would she spend in jail? A sick old white lady would probably be handled gently by the legal system. Put her in a hospital, likely a psychiatric one, where she would get three meals a day and medical treatment until she died from whatever ailed her. If families of her victims tried to sue her in the civic arena, they would get nothing. Helen is a librarian in rural Vermont. How much blood can you squeeze from that stone?

The scenario makes so much sense that even though it's all wild trajectory on my part, I'm afraid to see her again. That look we exchanged...what if she figures out that I've figured her out? Would she add me to her list of people to remove? Or maybe I'm just crazy, thinking this way. How can I live with that?

What on earth should I do?

* * *

I ended up doing the only thing one can do when powerless: I carried on. At least, I tried to. By evening my hormone overload had ebbed and my ankle was throbbing. Thinking about murder had pulled me back into the past, and unwanted emotions started to boil and bubble. I was too tired to resist them, and fell into moroseness. Ned had my phone message but he didn't call. I flayed myself for wishing for romance when I should know better. I needed to cook up a wholesome dinner and kick back with a good book but I couldn't whip up the motivation. The cats circled me, looking for food and play, but the best I could do was pet them a few times then ignore them.

I set up for bed, hating my body for craving the release it had enjoyed last night and the tight arms that had secured me for deep and restful sleep. The sheets still smelled like Ned; I could call him back for more. Would he come? Oh god, I remembered him coming sexually, twice, while I had orgasmed three times. The memory revved me up again. Asking him to drop whatever he was doing and hurry back for the night belied my insistence on keeping separate. I couldn't bear the humiliation if he refused.

The real question was, Could I have a sexual relationship with a man without romance?

Could I have either without revealing to him who I really was?

Could he take it if I did?

I doubted it. What man wanted to hear how much a woman hates his brethren?

I had come to despise men generically and collectively because of their betrayal of the human species, not to mention how they'd treated women through the ages. I didn't have enough fingers to enumerate the ways too many men had negatively countered the wonderful things too few men had brought into the world. A person only had to follow the news, and study history, to see that 2015 was the same as 1015 or millennia earlier, and the majority of problem-perpetrators and nest-soilers were male.

Violence, greed, stupidity, and arrogance existed within all genders, of course—male and female, hetero- or homosexual, or whatever in between—but these traits seemed to be most destructively attached to the Y chromosome of "normal" males. Why couldn't geneticists disconnect that thing as part of their research into curing disease? What the actor Alan Alda had dubbed "testosterone poisoning" was taking down the planet. If that wasn't an epidemic, what was?

I couldn't watch the news and read history anymore because every time I did, I wanted to load my guns and run out onto the streets shooting. It had almost come to that when dealing with certain men one on one. I'd always chosen my partners carefully, going for diversity; yet in the end, despite the origins and arrangements of our affairs, the cultures and activities involved, everything, ultimately, was about them.

When we had a priority conflict, their priority was more important. Their work was more important. Their friends and relatives were more important. Their sexual needs were more important. Their tastes were more meaningful, their wounds were more painful—on and on it went. None of them had been willing and/or able to be an equal partner, an equal opposite making a better whole. Which is why I'd told Ned what I'd already told him. He wasn't getting it because his pursuit of me was all about him being the white knight, not about my unique wonderfulness he couldn't live without. He might be burning with curiosity about my secrets, but I'd bet my house that once he knew them, I would become repellent, unreasonable, wrong.

Unless…

There was one chance…a minuscule chance…he was actually what he seemed to be, a well-balanced, happy, healthy, solvent person with a good sense of humor who wanted an equal partner.

Was I willing to bet on that chance?

Noooooo! screamed my decades of experience. *Yesssssss!* screamed my broken heart.

Torn thus in half, I neutralized myself and fell into restless sleep.

The next morning, I resumed carrying on. Ned never returned my call; instead, he resumed leaving mailbox messages. Today's was an object that set me back on my heels: a knife. No, I realized, turning the object over in my hands; it was a letter opener shaped like a sword, the hilt inset with a sparkly stone, and the blade wrapped in paper secured with a rubber band.

I made myself walk back indoors before unwrapping it. Tossed the bills and junk mail aside.

The paper wrap was a blurry photocopy of an old map from an old book, showing an ancient world where the continents were still unexplored and the seas beyond were labeled, in archaic script: "Here there be dragons."

He'd crossed out "dragons" and replaced it with "demons."

Then he'd scrawled in the corner: "This magic sword is effective in dispatching demons. Use it wisely."

After standing there for seconds resonating in astonishment, I dropped to my knees and wept.

Tears of shock, elation, fear. Once they burst the dam and started flooding, psychic pain from three decades joined the surge and wrenched out of me in physically painful honks and gasps, leaving me a sodden mass on the rug with distressed cats circling and poking at me, mewing.

Eventually I came to, at first embarrassed by how slaughtered I could be by kindness. Then irony crept in: *First he got the drop on me, now he's dropped me to the floor!*

I picked myself halfway up, grateful that only I and my furry children witnessed this breakdown. *Here's your head explosion, Ned; where's that mop and bucket now?*

Since the cats couldn't tell anyone about my weakness, and I most certainly wasn't going to, that added another secret to the list.

"Secrets, secrets…the curse of humankind, the origin of most miseries," I'd written in my journal. I was wiser than I'd known.

Get rid of those secrets, Jane!

I sagged back down and just lay limp and empty, with disconnected thoughts burping up in my mind, one at a time, many minutes apart.

Take care of the furry children.

Yes, priority one. A worthy thought. Yay, I could still have one. It stirred me into movement.

The cats had backed off when I'd calmed down but remained close by, waiting and watching. I'd already fed them but decided to reassure and reward them by dispensing treats. They followed my feet, tails up at a trot, when I dragged myself upright and headed to the kitchen calling them. I left them crunching in a little semicircle at their bowls and betook myself to the futon couch, where I flopped.

While I pieced myself back together, they dispersed to their customary spots to groom and then withdrew, Tessa to her cardboard box lined with a towel under a chair, Twinkie to her favorite windowsill, Tommy out the flap door into the kennel run. That signaled all was back to normal, so I worked on bringing myself to the same state.

Normal. *Whatever that is.*

After a while, another thought formed: *If I'm this empty, then there's room to fill with something new.*

Ned.

I have twenty-four hours.

A day in which to come up with some sort of response to his stab to my heart with his sword. I was pretty sure he would not arrive unannounced before I responded; his gesture felt like a gauntlet hurled down at my feet, and he would wait to see what he found in the mailbox tomorrow morning before he acted further. I had no idea what to do.

Which took me back to where I'd started the day. *Carry on, carry on.*

I had to meet a deadline. It seemed far away, but experience had proven that the longer it took to start a new book, the worse would be the crunch when delivery deadline loomed. I was in no shape to be creative, but there was still legwork needed to outline the story and define research points, which I could do at automaton level. That pushed me off the couch into my office chair, where I propped myself upright, started pushing keys and buttons, and resumed the job of building a story around Katy Fox and a wounded fawn.

That took me to midday meal break.

I wasn't remotely hungry. Or so I thought. I made a sandwich because I knew I needed nourishment, and was surprised when it disappeared in about thirty seconds. That was a good sign.

I couldn't pull my mind back to Katy so took a turn in the garden—out back, where nobody could see me from the road. Things were growing like crazy and I needed to weed and trim. That was beyond my ability this day, so I turned for the house, only to be struck by the idea I needed for replying to Ned.

I turned to my bookshelves, and then to still-unpacked boxes, until I unearthed a vintage illustrated copy of *The Sword in the Stone*. This was the tale of King Arthur as a boy, the only one able to withdraw an enchanted sword from its prison in an anvil embedded in stone, an act that designated him the rightful king of England. While my dynamic with Ned had nothing to do with the King Arthur legends, he had introduced sword symbology into our equation, and this story was the best I had to parry with. Besides, Luce had dubbed him a knight.

The illustrations didn't include exactly the image I wanted, which was just the sword sticking out of the stone without background or characters, so I dug out hardware and software I hadn't used in a long time and scanned the illustration, cropped and manipulated the image, then printed it out. After that I searched online until I found an illustration of Pandora's box with all the ills of the world pouring out of it, and printed that, too. The idea was to show what would happen if the hero succeeded in pulling the sword; in other words, what Ned Cavendish, White Knight, would get rushing up his nose if he uncorked Jane Brown, Neurotic Writer with Ugly Secrets.

If he was smart, he'd leave our relationship unexplored. If he was a hero, he would press on regardless. I really needed to know which he was.

These activities consumed most of the afternoon and left me stimulated. Normally at workday's end I retired with a drink and a pleasure book, but tonight I needed to make up for neglecting work so browsed *Bambi* and *The Yearling* and took notes until time for bed. Sleep didn't come easily, from aching to have Ned's body against mine and worrying about what would go on in his mind when he found my symbolic response.

Then I had to wait another twenty-four hours for him to respond to my message. All I got this day was a toot-toot from his horn after picking up what I'd put in the box.

Of course, I could call him. Nothing to stop me except the obvious reason that we were in the middle of a strange courtship headgame and I didn't feel confident enough to initiate a fresh move. Ball was in his court. Or, should I say, the sword was in his court.

So I carried on carrying on. In between sessions building *Katy Fox and the Wounded Fawn*, which held my attention for three whole hours, I caught up on correspondence, exercised my ankle without stressing it, and confirmed with Luce that I would help with river cleanup on Saturday.

None of that settled me. The weather was holding and I wanted to go out; I could have, should have, returned to the garden; instead, I decided to test whether my ankle was up to driving and go for a scenic toodle-about. I'd done a lot of exploring when house hunting, but that had been a different season in a different year when everything had been disconnected. I wanted to connect some of the dots I'd become familiar with, as well as see and inhale the spring without an agenda. As an ulterior motive, I wanted to see where Fiona Cobb had lived on Bear Pond Road, and scope out Ned's "leaning house and the remains of a hill farm" on Tamarack Hill.

His business card and Fiona's obituary provided addresses I could plot a course around. The Internet provided Google Earth for aerial views of both locations, taken two summers ago. Combined, they showed that Fiona's road was like mine, a dirt byway with a dead end, except that Bear Pond Road was twice the length of Rock Maple Road and invisible under the foliage canopy. Rock Maple opened up now and then for views and farm fields, but Bear Pond just burrowed through the woods. Off its terminus, a snowmobile trail extended up to the remote pond the road was named for. That trail was part of Vermont's state network—VAST in name (Vermont Association of Snow Travelers) and vast in scope (one could snowmobile border to border over a few thousand miles of trails). I already knew about the hiking and biking trails through the state, but a snowmobile network was new to me. It made sense, though, and surely contributed to the citizens' coffers in a meaningful way, like the ski industry did.

Ned's road, conversely, went up over the mountain that bulged between Allenburg and Parkerville, a struggling little town serving a struggling little ski area. Unlike the grand Fall Line Resort in Orton, this enterprise relied on natural snow and school ski clubs in season, and mountain biking and zip-lines the rest of the year. Tamarack Hill rose and fell two thousand feet between the communities, with Ned's place perched about halfway up the Allenburg side. The aerial view showed an open spread of farmhouse and outbuildings, including a single-wide mobile home, with the main house situated to enjoy what surely were splendid views of fields, forests, and ridges—and to not enjoy winter winds.

We could probably see each other's places if not for a lesser hump in between them. His place was only about two miles away on a straight line, probably double that by road. Likewise, Fiona's place was around eight miles by map, ten or more by twisty backroads.

As hers was the farthest-out point, I started there and backtracked. My plan was to end in Allenburg, at the dump ('scuse me—the transfer station, as its role was to transfer residents' garbage and recyclables to a processing facility somewhere else). No curbside pickup in these parts, so every community had its own transfer station, with inconvenient hours. This afternoon happened to coincide with the station being open, and I had amassed much to recycle and throw away. That destination made me feel virtuous in advance.

Once my ankle agreed to cooperate—no pain, just sore stiffness and occasional needlelike stabs—I set out for Bear Pond Road via the circuitous scenic route. It wasn't very scenic unless you like trees. The road eased lower instead of higher, and the landscape became moister and darker.

Bear Pond Road might have been twice the length of Rock Maple Road but had half the buildings and no population. I passed a burned-out house; two bar-gated driveways leading, presumably, to deer camps or vacation cabins; an abandoned trailer-home; and Fiona's scabby split-level exposed in front but backed up to forest. The house was unnumbered but I was sure it had once been hers, owing to the deck with steep, open-slat stairs down to the driveway, custom made for falling down in slippery conditions.

Though the middle of a spring afternoon, I saw no sign of life. The dooryard was strewn with evidence of life in the form of rusted vehicles, haphazard stacks of pallets and log butts, tattered tarpaulins, discarded tires, a dog house inside a pen, and more detritus than I could identify on a slow cruise past. The overall gloom and squalor moved me to accelerate, turn around, and get away.

My route brought me to Ned's homestead from the wrong direction. To see up his driveway required an acute look-back, whereas from the other way I could have gotten a nice view straight up his front slope. Like at Fiona's, I passed and turned around, and then could see his house occupying the crown of its hill-shoulder as if grown there with the maples and lilacs that framed it without blocking the view. The dwelling was indeed a little crooked, from standing for at least a century, and it indeed offered a heart-soaring view. No wonder he had no desire to shack up at my place.

To my delight/dismay and surprise/expectation, Ned was sitting on his wraparound porch in a rocking chair and could not fail to see me slow down and look up. Thus caught, I smothered a heartbeat spike with a sigh and lumbered into his driveway. The hammered-dirt track leveled at the top and arced around an ancient apple tree, delivering me to his front steps.

"Welcome," he said when I stood and thunked shut the driver's door.

"Hi. Uh, thanks."

He came to the porch railing, with an ancient dog shuffling behind him. "Come on up."

The dog sat beside him and affirmed the invitation with a "Whuf" and a few thumps of its grayed tail on the boards.

I mounted the step, trying not to blush. I didn't ordinarily impose myself on people, especially not men I was playing strange courtship games with, but lately I'd been a stranger to myself, evidenced by where I was standing.

He remained collected and said with twinkling eyes, "To what do I owe the pleasure?"

He pulled me into a one-armed hug with a kiss on the cheek. That surprised and relaxed me a notch. He released me before I could squeeze or peck back, then gestured toward a padded wicker chair beside his rocker. A round glass-topped table stood between them, with an almost empty beverage glass sweating a ring onto the surface.

I sat and confessed, "Spring fever," leaning back into the weathered cushion. "I got antsy. Wanted to go out. Needed to justify it somehow, so I decided to test my foot by driving around and doing research while at it."

"Research?" He resumed his seat. The dog creaked back to its position beside him.

"For my books. I mean, general reconnaissance for—well, I mean, I hardly know the area, I need to put some time into getting around—plus scoping out a setting for a book I'd like to write someday. Then, for the current Katy, I want to pick your brains about deer."

That earned me a pair of raised eyebrows. I elaborated, "It's called *Katy Fox and the Wounded Fawn.*"

"Ah. All right. But only if I can pick your brain, too."

My defenses shot up before I could have a reasonable chat with them. "About what?" came out in a suspicious tone.

He slid his gaze away and drained his glass. "Well, I was just sitting here wondering which of Pandora's troubles would get unleashed if I pulled that sword from your stone. Then, abracadabra, here you are. It would save a lot of time if you'd go the next step and just tell me."

"I…don't think that's a fair trade."

"I do. You need information; I need information. What's unfair about that?"

"Well, one's personal and the other is technical."

"Not necessarily. Some people's experience with deer is pretty personal. If you want to know about hunting, for example. Stalking and killing another being is about as personal as you can get."

I shuddered at the truth of that, then tried to squirm away from it. "I, uh, just want to know what other ways a deer can get hurt besides being shot or hit by a car, and when hunting season is, and what the rules are, and what time of year fawns are born, and when they leave their parents—stuff like that."

"And I just want to know what deep, dark secret you're keeping that gets in the way."

"It's not—"

"It's not a legal problem, I figured, 'cause you bought a house in your real name and, although antisocial, you're living openly; and the cops aren't interested in you, even though three murders happened right after you moved into town."

"It's n—"

"And since you've already claimed you don't have a rape or heartbreak issue with someone in particular, and proved it by accepting me into your bed despite your celibate intentions, I cross that one off the list. Stranger-violence is a possibility, given where you came from and your security measures, but you don't seem the right kind of jumpy for that. More like, you emanate fear and shame, and act like you're afraid somebody's going to find you out—outwardly organized and in control yet looking back over your shoulder. So I'm running down lists in my mind of what people consider shameful and what they might do if exposed."

He stopped and looked at me. "Am I on the right track?"

I gave him a cold, hard glare to cover my internal squirming, provoked by the pressure of holding on to rationality and neutrality and cordiality while burning to defend myself, biting and kicking—urges inflamed by bitter irony. Here I'd been hoping for some spontaneous "afternoon delight"—I'd actually bought into his bed-buddy thinking—and here he was pushing at major relationship edges. With a smile.

Not smiling back, I said through clenched teeth, "You have no idea what's inside my head."

He kept the maddening smile. "And you have no idea what's inside mine. What are you going to do about it?"

His challenge hit me like a slap. I had no idea how to respond, other than to suppress an excessive emotional reaction, such as clouting him in the chops.

He let me stew for a bit, both of us gazing out at the Green Mountains to the north and Taconics to the west.

Then he lifted his glass. "Care for some lemonade?"

I flattened my lips.

"The real thing," he tempted. "Made it myself."

I shook my head. "No, thank you."

He rose and passed me, swung open a screen door that hung loose on its hinges—which I expected to screech, but they didn't—then let it slap closed behind him. The kitchen must have been inside the wall my chair backed up against, for I heard muted thumpings close behind me.

I considered getting back into my car and departing from his life but that was the coward's way. I wasn't sure what to think, do, or say, but I stayed, putting more space between us by walking the length of the porch on a complaining ankle. The dog watched through clouded eyes but didn't follow.

I was surprised, given the sag of the house, that the porch underfoot felt stout and square despite scarring from bootheels, weather, and stacked firewood. The sunshine flooding the dooryard lit the surrounding lawns to lime green. They were bounded by perennials in bud or bloom and cross-tracked by flagstone and dirt paths that led out back to barns and sheds and equipment, also the vintage mobile home, which had a two-place UTV parked in front.

Beyond the outbuildings lay hayfields almost ready to cut, plus pastures with cows in one and horses in the other. Up close, chickens and guinea hens ran loose doing insect control. The only flat area hosted a vegetable garden with high fencing to prevent varmint access. Ned's truck and trailer, his mower still onboard, was parked next to the house so it wouldn't block the circular approach.

He caught up to me where the porch wrapped around the non-mountain-view side, and handed me a tall glass. I sipped, finding the beverage sweet and tart—and strongly alcoholic—at the same time.

"Do you want a tour?" he offered amiably.

I nodded and shook my head. Took another slug of the intoxicating drink.

"I'd expected," he said, "that your first time here would be for shooting lessons. We seem to have gotten ahead of ourselves again."

"That seems to be a recurring problem," I agreed.

"So let's sit back down and you ask me your questions. Do you need pad and pencil?"

"No, I've got stuff in the car."

He smiled. "You came prepared."

"Not quite. I brought them just in case. I didn't really think you'd be home this time of day."

I handed him my glass then descended to open the passenger door of the Subaru, where my purse and tote bag were on the seat heating up in the sun. The keys were still in the ignition and I looked at them for an extra second, recognizing my last chance to run away. Then I grabbed the tote and slammed the door, returning to where he waited, watching me keenly, back in his rocker on the porch. His fingers trailed against the dog's grizzled head as it dozed.

"What's his name?" I asked while taking out my notebook and recorder.

"Henry."

"He looks a little too old to be a guard dog."

"Seventeen. But if you'd driven up here while I was gone, he would have made a fine racket." He thumbed over his shoulder. "Hollis's dog, now, that's one you'd have to worry about."

I presumed he was gesturing toward the mobile home, which had a chain-link pen around the side but I'd seen no dog inside it.

"Who's Hollis?"

"One of my cousins. He gets free housing in exchange for helping me keep the place up, and feeding the animals when I'm not around."

"Doesn't look like he's here."

Ned shrugged. "Not sure where he went, but he takes the dog with him when he can, especially if I'm home. He's got a bunch of seasonal jobs at Fall Line—golf course, bar, ski lifts—plus buddies and a girlfriend, which would be my best guess right now."

I wanted to grill him for a complete life story but stayed on task. "Okay if I record our interview?"

He cocked a brow at "interview" but played along, looking curiously at the little voice-activated device I placed on the table between us. "I use it in the car," I explained. "I talk to myself, transcribe later. Used it for the first few days when I was down with my ankle, too. Sometimes I leave it on when I'm puttering around the house, 'cause ideas hit me at the weirdest times."

I also had voice-recognition software on my computer but I rarely used it, preferring to write by typing or in longhand. I hadn't bought any of the tablets or smartphones that did everything, since my uses were specific and I already owned satisfactory tools.

For this occasion, I'd organized and printed out my questions. I turned on the recorder, started at the top of the list, and scribbled his answers while we talked. Later, if those scribbles and my memory proved inadequate, I'd replay the recording.

He told me more than I needed for the story, which led to more questions, and kept us going until fading daylight, our earlier tension forgotten.

When we petered out, I switched off the recorder. "Thanks—that was really helpful."

"You're welcome." He stood and stretched, saying, "You have an interesting job."

"I think so." I smiled.

"When does this book have to be finished?"

I stated the deadline. He pursed his lips in a silent whistle. "Tight."

"Well, it's a job. I have to produce on time to get paid."

"I've read them, you know."

That heated me up with a combination of delight and anxiety. "Oh? Well...what do you think?"

He smiled. "Great job. Keep up the good work."

"Um, thank you." I silently thanked him a second time for not giving an "I like" or "I don't like" response.

"I've been wondering, though," he went on. "Do you ever get to write for yourself? Like, as an artist? Or are you just, um, a craftsman? Er, make that craftswoman. No, craftsperson."

This was easier to respond to. "I'm a working writer. No luxury of waiting for the muse, you just do it. Good days and bad days, hopefully it evens out in the end. We've got editors to help. The job is all about getting the ideas and writing them down coherently, and keeping readers engrossed and rooting for the heroine and happy at the end. It's art and craft at the same time."

"What gave you the idea for the fawn?"

I grimaced. "Lying in the grass with a wrenched ankle. Made me think about people who get more seriously hurt much farther away from home. And because the Katy books have to be about animals, and I'm programmed to seek story ideas anywhere, I started thinking right away how I could convert the experience into an animal story."

"Huh." He ruminated for a moment, then said casually, "You mentioned you were scoping out a setting for a book you'd like to write someday. Do you mean something different from a Katy story?"

I squinted at him, knowing what he was trying to do. On the surface, this was a nice, intellectual, get-to-know-you conversation like I'd had with his

Aunt Mary, but I sensed Ned was trying to lure me to safe ground where he could get at my secret sideways, even if he was genuinely interested in my work.

I preferred his usual direct approach but was willing to play his game this time. After all, I'd practiced with Detective Greene for what Ned wanted me to confess. I decided that if pushed I would go Detective-Greene far with him, but no further. Certain secrets I would keep for myself, and if that cost me relationships, so be it.

"Something different," I answered. "I've got a long-term idea for a murder mystery. Since circumstances here dropped a model into my lap, I'm looking at it from a writerly point of view. In fact, you're the one who aimed me in Fiona Cobb's direction. I looked up her place and went by it on the way over here."

"Fiona? You mean, you think she's part of our murder spree?"

"Maybe. Doesn't really matter." I paused. This would be a good moment to try out the Helen theory on him, but I couldn't bring myself to do it. "Fiona is either another victim of our serial killer or something completely different. I can build a story around her without getting in the cops' way." *Or the killer's.*

"So you think."

"Well, yes. But I recently had a conversation with Detective Greene, and he doesn't seem worried about me as long as I stick to fiction."

"I would encourage you to stick to your hermit habits and not look into anything having to do with murder while we've got an unsolved one dangling in our midst."

"I'm just gathering information."

"And possibly planting your foot into something dangerous completely unawares."

I sighed. "It's not like I'm doing investigative reporting."

"Doesn't matter how you see it. It matters how somebody else might see it."

I suppressed a shiver. "Hm, good point. At any rate, it couldn't hurt to drive by her house."

"Unless someone involved in her death or somebody else's happens to see you go by. Backroad people notice when a vehicle comes around, and pay attention if they don't recognize it."

I flashed back to my first morning when those passing vehicles had pressed themselves upon my attention, plus the older memory of Jake responding to my turnaround with his shotgun.

Ned continued, "I'm daily fare so they don't worry about me, but I'll tell you, I wish my route didn't go down certain roads. Some dangerous types live in the back corners, and one of them now owns the old Cobb place. Don't bring yourself to their attention."

"Jeez, you're making me nervous."

"That's my intent."

"You're awfully good at that," I retorted, feeling magma surge upward like gorge in my throat. The humiliation he'd engendered in me weeks ago with my guns in my house hadn't fully dissolved yet. I'd thought it had until this moment, and my claws sprang out in response. I really, really didn't like to be shown to be stupid, even if it was valid. Ned had the ability to make me feel special and idiotic at the same time.

I needed time and space to process that, but here I was right now in his space having to do and say the right thing or blow our chances for the future by saying/doing the wrong thing in an aggravated moment. The only way I could prevent a mistake was to clam up.

He must have seen my interior weather change happen in my face, for his eyes flickered suddenly and he muttered "Uh-oh" under his breath. Then he zoomed to me and wrapped me super-tight in his arms as if swaddling a fretting babe. I sagged in relief in the sudden cocoon, a reaction that made me wonder about aspects of my deep psychology I'd never considered, which might explain a few things.

He was saying into my hair, "Head explosion coming on?"

I moved my head to the extent possible inside his embrace, saying in a muffled voice, "Aftershocks."

His chest jiggled beneath me in a muted laugh. "Thought I saw steam coming out your ears. Sorry to have provoked you. Do I need to get the mop and bucket, or shall we just change the subject?"

"Change subject." I leaned back against his arms and he opened them. "Change of location might be better. I…just…need…"

"Probably exactly what I do." He paused to see if I would fill in the blank. When I didn't, he said, "Space."

I blinked at him in surprise.

He gave me that one-cornered smile I liked. "Some time, some space, to just mind my own business. That's why I postponed a few jobs today, and I'm real glad Hollis isn't around. I need to just be home and…chill."

I cocked my head, listening raptly. The dog had raised and cocked his head, too.

Ned went on to say, "There are too damn many people in my life, Jane, and they all want something, all the time. That takes up so much time, on top of multiple jobs, that I don't have any time left for myself. I really need a break now and then."

"I—I get it."

"I'm sure you do, which is why I'm telling you. What you may not get is the no-demons part. It's great to not be a haunted soul, but that makes me a magnet for everyone who is. I've got relatives and friends and associates and their attachments constantly leaning on me or interrupting me or wringing me dry. Which is why," he added hastily when I opened my mouth, "I appreciate your non-demands on me. In fact, I envy you your barriers when I'm not trying to bust them down."

I stood like a pillar, too amazed to respond.

"Maybe there's some perfect halfway point between your boundaries being too strong and mine too weak," he went on. "Maybe we can help each other with that. But not today. It was an exceptionally wringing wringer, and I just want a stiff drink, a good book, and a solid night's sleep."

"I can relate to that," I stated, still resonating from surprise.

"So go savor the same for yourself, and we can try again tomorrow."

"Uh, okay. Of course." When he slid an arm around my shoulders and steered me down the porch steps toward my car, I recovered enough to ask, "Your place or mine?"

We stopped beside my driver's door. "Come back here and I'll give you a full tour, or maybe that shooting lesson, then we can share a meal and some… liveliness. Or the other way around."

The pastel-tinted sky ripening behind him put his face into semi-silhouette, so that I saw both the man I knew and the man I didn't. The man I wanted to know better.

"That sounds great. What time?"

"Not sure yet. I'm subbing on the route tomorrow, so I'll leave you a note."

"All right." I reached for the car then turned back to him. "I'm sorry I intruded on you."

He pressed a forefinger against my lips. "Don't be. First, you couldn't know, and second, you made my day. I really enjoyed helping with your book, and hope I can do it again."

I smiled. "But not tonight."

He smiled back. "Definitely not."

I stepped forward and slid my arms around his back, drawing him into a kiss. He returned it gently, sweetly, wistfully, then stepped away, turned away, and withdrew to his sanctuary.

I got in the car and drove home to my own sanctuary, dazed by the fact my antisocial liability could be valued by someone who was social. Maybe he was right and there was some halfway point we could find together. I sure looked forward to finding out.

CHAPTER 19

What keeps bothering me is the dark side. For once, not my own darkness; rather, the dark side of other people and of every place, a quality built into the nature of things that seems heightened here, where we live closer to nature.

Outside my door, every day and every night, things are killing each other to survive. Where we humans differ from other life forms is that we kill independently of surviving. Or maybe we kill when it's sometimes physically necessary and other times when it's psychologically necessary to survive, whereas all other life forms kill for physical survival only. Then again, I once saw a TV program about chimpanzees killing monkeys for sport and malice. But hey, chimps are our closest relatives. Maybe I should say "Everything other than hominids kills for survival only."

Even in my most depressed and hostile days of the past, I didn't think as much about death as I've done since moving to rural Vermont. Here, people not only kill people but also kill animals. And animals kill animals. I've not yet heard about animals killing people but I'm sure that occurs, too, and I can't say I blame them.

On the people side, only laws keep things under control; but here in backwoods-and-backhoes land, where's the law? We don't have a patrolling police force likely to come upon a crime in progress. If something happens, you've got to call in the cops from afar. If you're careful and want to kill someone, or poach game off season, or otherwise do a dastardly deed, you can often get away with it because there are so few people around to witness and catch and punish you, and so many untracked square miles where you can hide, or dispose of evidence. We might as well be lawless, given how easy it is to commit crime in these parts.

In ironic contrast, Vermont has some of the most liberal gun laws in the country. Perfectly legal here to carry a weapon open or concealed. Yet we have one of the lowest, if not the lowest, murder rates in the union. What does that mean?

Granted, I don't get out much, but at the community activities and public environments and private homes I've passed through, I've not glimpsed a firearm. People talk about them, and I hear gunfire in the distance as people practice or hunt, and I've got a house full of guns myself, and so does Ned and I'm sure an alarming number of other folks, but they're not using their weapons where they're not supposed to. It only takes one to create a problem, of course, like in the murder of Jake Baldwin. That appears to have been premeditated, compared to some nutbag losing what's left of his mind and blowing off an innocent crowd like shooting fish in barrel. Had Jake's killer been more creative, he/she (Helen?) probably could have managed a backwoods or backhoe burial, and no one would be the wiser.

It's all very strange and complicated. And scary. And something I never expected to have to think about.

* * *

I spent the night wishing Ned would change his mind and drive over to sleep with me, but it didn't happen. No surprise, assuming he meant what he'd said. I did my best to emulate him and eventually slept, as I imagine he did, then got up to face the next day.

That contained leftover chores, like, the trash I forgot to take to the transfer station, which I further postponed in favor of typing up my notes from interviewing Ned. I could have postponed that, too, and worked from the recording later, but I wanted to connect my hands to the content while it was fresh in my mind.

Throughout, my ear was tuned to outside the house, waiting for his vehicle to stop by my mailbox. Wouldn't you know, that was the morning multiple cars came and went down Rock Maple Road. Wondering who they were distracted me—Jake Baldwin's family dealing with his "estate"? Prospective buyers of the ski house? Owners of the camp checking their property? The retirees going out for groceries? The town crew inspecting culverts between storms? Should I call Detective Greene and tell him there was unusual activity on the road?

I opted for uninvolved. Enough time—and murders—had passed that comings and goings here shouldn't be suspicious. I only cared about one vehicle, which eventually hove into view and stopped at my box. I peered at Ned's Jeep around the window frame, unwilling to expose myself as too eager. Once he drove out of sight, I dashed out to the box to find his note.

He did not disappoint. Among the bills he'd tucked a sheet of paper torn from a pocket notebook. It said, simply, "4:30. BYOG. Dinner's on me. Feed the cats before you leave."

Roger that.

I dove back into work to keep from jibbering. Since my imagination was focused on what might happen this evening, I didn't bother trying to write Katy Fox narrative. Instead I focused on the blood and guts of Ned's interview, building a notes file on how deer could be stalked, shot, trapped, lost, hit, starved, or otherwise wounded by two-legged and four-legged predators, not to mention Mother Nature. Once I decided on what beset the fawn, I would figure out how Katy found and saved it, and the book would take off. Not today, though. This exercise was part of the gruntwork behind creativity.

Nibbling at the back of my mind in weird contrast was the dilemma of what to wear for our next encounter. Specifically, what to put on for underwear, or whether to wear any at all. Many a year had passed since I'd gone out the door expecting to sleep in somebody else's bed, and I had long ago discarded my naughty lingerie. Was something like that even appropriate for this tryst, with Mr. Plain and Straightforward, Salt-of-the-Earth Cavendish?

Since puberty, I'd gathered the impression that all men liked women in sexy getup (whether they admitted it or not), but Mr. Cavendish defied my expectations at every turn. I was probably best off as Ms. Plain Jane Brown, and he could take me as he found me. That's how I was planning to take him. I hoped to find him clean and shaven and wearing fresh, easy-off clothing, so that's how I ended up presenting myself.

Before departing for his place, I fed the cats then gathered all my guns and stowed them in the back of the Subaru. That's what "BYOG" had meant in his note, I assumed. (Never assume. *It makes an ASS out of U and ME.*) I couldn't think of anything else "G" stood for. If he'd typed the note, I would have considered the "G" a typo, but he'd written the message by hand and we still had a "date" for a shooting lesson.

After a hesitation, I covered the guns with a blanket, even though they were in cases. Maybe long-term rural Vermont residents felt comfortable gadding about with firearms, but I'd never intentionally revealed my guns to anyone and felt as if a blinking red arrow hung in the sky pointing at my car. At least I didn't have to worry about police presence in the neighborhood or breaking any laws.

I ran out of excuses for delaying and drove off into the soft spring afternoon toward the possibility my life was going to change again. I was getting weary of the phenomenon but accepted that I had committed myself to jumping off a psychic cliff and had to wait to see where I landed (splatted?), and how.

This time Ned wasn't waiting on the porch but had left the windows and inner door open, so he heard me arrive and met me as I topped the stairs. "Hi, thanks for coming." He reiterated the welcome with a light kiss. I'd barely puckered to return it when he stepped away, back into the kitchen where he was already pouring drinks.

His kitchen would have been dubbed "retro" in the city. I couldn't do that here because it was the real thing: appliances, cabinets, floor, and counter hadn't been updated for a generation—at least. I gathered from that and what I'd glimpsed of the rest of the house that nothing was replaced unless it stopped working. Which might be why the standing-seam roof I'd noticed yesterday looked brand new.

I answered, "I'd love a stiff one"—at which inadvertent double entendre he lifted an eyebrow, making me smile—"but I don't want to mix guns and alcohol. Can we shoot first, or drink now and postpone shooting until later?"

"Up to you," he said, returning bottle and glass to the counter. "I'm perfectly content to drag you into my cave right now, if you'd prefer to skip preliminaries."

I rolled my eyes and, to my embarrassment, blushed. "I, um…"

He laughed. "I mean it. It's up to you, since you've set the tone by being reluctant and evasive. Do you need slow-motion seduction? Do you want to relax first with some distraction? I'm sorry I can't read your mind or your aura, Jane, so I have to be direct. The only thing I've got to work with is the fact you're here."

I stood like a pole as I'd done yesterday, not knowing what to do.

"I think," I said eventually, "that's as far as I'm able to get right now."

"In which case, I'll drive the bus. Let's relax first."

He finished pouring and handed me a tumbler of amber liquid. Although I routinely drank various whiskies, I hadn't developed a sophisticated palate. Even so, I recognized he was serving expensive good stuff. I couldn't see the label the way he placed the bottle back on the counter.

"C'mon, let me show you around." He started his slow seduction by placing a hand on the small of my back and steering me out of the kitchen.

Everything about the house shouted *history!*, from its low ceilings and cramped rooms designed for smaller people, to the near-threadbare braided rugs and weary furniture. All the floors and window and door frames were warped and uninsulated. Above it all, faded photographs almost completely covered the vintage wallpaper, which curled away from its seams.

I noticed these things despite an inner humming in response to his proximity, his casual touch, and the intimacy of seeing his home. Actually, I made a point to notice them to distract myself from that inner humming.

What genuinely distracted me in every room was books-books-books. Their weight bowed shelves, their stacks on the floor supported reading lamps, ashtrays repurposed to hold coins and screws and anything else that came out of pockets, plus stuff temporarily placed down, like gloves and work knives and flashlights. Books lined the stairs to the second floor, and filled the mantel over the fieldstone fireplace, which had a modern wood stove inserted into the hearth. They topped a TV so old I wondered if it still worked. I also wondered if the books trailed into his bedroom; but, as I'd done when he inspected my house, he didn't lead me into his private space.

About the time I was ready to ask, "Why did you come back here from Harvard?" he led me outside into the dooryard, keeping his arm around my shoulders while introducing me to the chickens, cows, and horses, and pointing out the track to his own back forty where his shooting range stood out of sight behind trees. "Ready to aim and fire?" he asked.

"No."

At that he gestured toward an open slope facing the mountains where just in view at the top lay the family cemetery, which, he said, dated back to the early 1700s. I couldn't imagine having such a long and known lineage, and said so. He didn't ask for my backstory, as I would have expected. Instead, he summarized his genealogy, affirming what I already knew: that his clan had settled here centuries ago and branched widely. Also that he was one of five siblings including a sister who had moved out of the area.

As he talked, his tone flattened and his gaze stayed away from mine, while his gestures lost their spontaneity. I started to sense disturbed wavelengths that made me wonder what percentage of people in his big, happy family weren't so healthy underneath. He might be deceiving himself in thinking he had no demons.

That thought moved me to slip my arm around his waist and turn us back toward the house. He stopped talking then and let me "drive the bus." I took us straight to the big, saggy couch in the living room, sat him down upon it, and straddled his lap. He took the hint and returned my kiss with hunger. We exercised that couch for a long time, strewing clothing at its feet. I never got a chance to fret about my underwear.

When we resurfaced in afterglow, we found ourselves tightly entangled and exchanging breaths. I felt liquidly, deliciously limp despite a numb leg where his weight compressed it. The sensation reminded me of the word *obdormition*: "numbness in a limb from pressure; 'falling asleep.'" I would have to leave that in the mailbox for him next time, sure he'd have to look it up.

Before my blurry thoughts could advance to full consciousness, he extracted an arm from where it was pinched beneath my weight on the couch. Instead of mumbling "obdormition," he whispered, "Hi."

I licked the tip of his nose. "Hi."

"Nice to meet you, Jane Brown."

"Back atcha."

"I think it's time for our shooting lesson."

"What?"

He propped himself up on one arm, leaving the other one draped across my breast. "Well, you didn't want to do booze and guns, which is highly sensible. Now you're totally relaxed, which is a good time to deal with shooting. Your aim will be good, and you won't have interfering anxieties. And we've still got light."

"I can't believe you're thinking about this. Sex and guns is as wrong an association as booze and guns."

"Unless"—he pushed himself fully upright, adjusting me around him—"you recognize that guns are tools, not symbols of human perversion. We've talked about hunting, and we've talked about murder, and I see that you have a defensive, almost paranoid attitude about weapons, like most people who didn't grow up with them. If you want to get over that, then you have to disassociate emotion from the equation. Ergo, this is as good a time as any for some practice. As I said, it might even be ideal, because you're relaxed."

"Jeezus." Nevertheless, I couldn't argue his rationale.

"So put your clothes on, Ms. Brown, and let's get off a few rounds. Then we can have dinner, and see what the evening brings."

Reluctantly I complied, though I had to admit a certain titillation at the prospect.

Once we had composed and garbed ourselves, we extracted my guns from the car, added a few of his, and piled them and us onto a shabbier UTV than the one parked outside Hollis's single-wide and scooted a quarter mile to Ned's range. He had previously set up targets and marked off distances. A clinical hour followed, during which we fired everything we owned, from standing, sitting, and prone positions, and discussed the differences. I hit more targets than I had when I'd practiced on my own range, and I came away feeling a fraction more competent, and confident, than I had any time previous.

By then dusk had closed in, so we returned to the house and he warmed a venison stew and tossed a salad. Now I hit the booze with enthusiasm and achieved a pleasant glow. He appeared to do same. Well before conventional bedtime we were in his room in his bed, and spent the night in a mix of love-making and drowsing. I never glanced at his decor or his books.

When his alarm went off at an annoyingly early hour, I hauled my drained body back home, fed the complaining cats, unloaded my guns from the car and returned them to their hidey-holes, then packed the gear I would need for the day before Luce arrived to ferry me off to the next adventure.

This was river cleanup day, which I'd promised her when I'd skipped Green Up Day. It involved convening with two dozen people from the Friends of the River nature group, which Luce and Peter supported with donations and labor, thirty miles from home at a river outfitter's shop. The staff shuttled us to a put-in and distributed us among a dozen canoes. We spent the day floating down a languid river picking up garbage that morons had thrown into it or had washed down its length during spring floods. The garbage started my magma a-boiling, but it never got a chance to consume me because I had no opportunity to indulge it.

I was paired with a stranger who hadn't been in a canoe before. My own experience was sketchy, and many years stale, but the outfitters had separated me from Luce to distribute anyone who had any experience among those who had zero. The challenges of maneuvering to snatch objects from branches against contrary currents, or beaching to scramble out and grab junk, kept my attention wholly and sometimes frantically in the moment. We gathered enough spoils to make our crafts sit low in the water, and everyone was grateful when we finally reached the takeout and got picked up. We were rewarded with a convivial picnic.

By the time Luce deposited me home, I felt so turned around and inside out and belonging yet alienated, I was incapable of thinking. The exuberant welcome from my furry children helped restore my equilibrium, as did the rituals of feeding them, cleaning their litter boxes, checking my e-mail, and putting my things away to clear the deck for tomorrow. I steamed myself clean in the shower, avoiding the bathroom mirror because I knew someone different would look back at me, and I wasn't ready to face her. Somehow I had to find my way back to the Jane who had deadlines to meet and didn't waver from them. But first, I had to seriously and deeply sleep.

CHAPTER 20

When I planned my new life, I didn't factor in things like friends, lovers, and activities. Nor did I anticipate murders or ideas for new books. These combined, in just two months, have thrown me out of the Katy Fox/Susan Silver head I used to be able to slip into like a comfortable bathrobe. Now my work pace and quality have been disrupted, and I'm feeling fresh anger because the whole purpose of moving away, into my cozy home, was to devote myself to writing. I need the income from the series to keep the lights on and roof over my head and food in my little family's bellies, and I need the privacy and unbroken time blocks to write well enough, on schedule, to sustain my readership, meet my contract, and enjoy the occupation I've chosen. How am I supposed to make room for all that and everything else? Nobody's yet figured out how to make a day longer.

According to our culture's social norms, nothing should be more important than people. I get that in principle, and embrace it by treasuring certain people more than material things, but life keeps bringing me back to the same conundrum: At what point do other people's needs and desires count more than mine?

This is a huge question when it comes to killing, but big in its own way during daily life. Other people can consume us if we don't have boundaries. The trick seems to be defining and holding those boundaries firm while not turning them into barriers. That's what Ned called mine, and I reluctantly admit he has a point. I didn't understand the distinction until he asked me to leave him alone the other day, and told me why. In that moment I recognized that asking people to respect my space is good, and slamming doors in their faces isn't. I think if one can master boundaries, one won't need barriers. Except solidly lockable, literal doors, of course.

* * *

My first task for the day, then, was to establish boundaries. That entailed e-mailing Luce and thanking her for a great day on the river and suggesting we get together in the next week for a meal, explaining that I needed to catch up on work and wouldn't be socializing for a while.

To communicate with computer-less Ned, however, I had to call him or drive back to his house, or else trust that he understood I needed a recovery day and leave him a note in the mailbox. Or wave him down on his way by.

I decided to call him, since we'd not talked on the phone before and if what had passed between us as lovers was real, I should acknowledge it with the warmth and sincerity I genuinely felt. By the time I committed to this, he was already out on his route, so I left him a straightforward note in my mailbox: *Hi, sorry I missed you on the phone. Just wanted to say thanks for your hospitality*—he would understand the unspecified underlayers—*and let you know the river run went well. Talk later. I'll have my head down for a while catching up on work.*

I wanted to add, "I love you" but figured it was the wrong time to say such a thing. Besides, I wasn't sure if what I felt qualified as love. I knew only that something hot and hard pressed my heart against my sternum from the inside, and made my brain spark and limbs tremble, and made me want to drop everything and wallow in memories and fantasies for the future. "Friends with benefits, indeed," I muttered to myself with a sarcastic cough. This guy was upending me and turning me inside out in a way my previous lovers combined hadn't achieved!

With relationship responsibilities thus attended to, I rolled up my sleeves and tackled the words, ideas, and facts that would ultimately result in Katy Fox rescuing a wounded fawn in a mature and emotionally satisfying manner. It would be a mental and emotional vacation to think about only that for unbroken hours. Too bad I looked at my calendar first.

All I meant to do was reorient myself to the timetable: How many weeks, exactly, did I have left to produce the draft?

The date that caught my eye first was my talk at the library. Yikes, I'd forgotten about that! Only two days away, and I hadn't even begun to organize and rehearse my presentation. I should postpone. *Boundaries.*

But short time wasn't the real reason my heart was thudding and skin felt hot. I was afraid to face Helen. Having mentally accused her of being a murderer, how could I look her in the eye? She'd been nothing but friendly and generous to me, and I had not the slightest evidence against her, even hearsay, yet I feared to go near her, lest I slip and trigger her awareness of my suspicions. As long as I had no contact, I could pretend she was what she appeared to be and never have to learn if I was wrong.

Since she wasn't standing in the room, I could get away with playing ostrich a little longer. Time to wrestle my attention back to the top priority, which was KatyFoxKatyFoxKatyFox.

Too twitchy to sit at my desk, I dug out my recorder and set it in voice-activate mode, then paced the house talking out loud. I asked myself "What if…?" with each scenario Ned had suggested, brainstorming ways the fawn could be wounded and Katy could find it and get involved, feeling out whether any of those ideas would fit into the story I'd already outlined. This spared me hours of typing material that would end up in the trash.

Unspoken were my thoughts about writing in the absence of a muse. I was pushing and probing without inspiration, persevering because I knew that labor would ultimately realign with creativity and set me back on path. For now it was just a big mush. I wished Ned could see me demonstrating what it meant to be a "working writer."

The most outrageous scenario I imagined, which I liked best, had to be abandoned because it rubbed against the grain of my readership's expectations. It was just too dark, violent, and sad for the girls who waited for each book to come out—like Ned's nieces. Just because my emotions and visions were running wild didn't mean I could visit those upon loyal readers. Maybe I should consult Alicia and Nicole about which idea was most appealing. No, wait: Should I consult Ned first? He was hardly my target reader, but he was involved with those girls who put a face to my audience. If I was to consult any adult, it should be the girls' parents, whose opinions I really didn't want.

At any rate, I couldn't consult the girls without talking to Ned for the simple reason I needed him to provide their contact information. I might as well wait until I saw all three of them at the library presentation, kill the proverbial two birds with one stone by not canceling. Ned had informed me that he intended to escort the girls to the talk, since it was scheduled for evening.

In that case, as long as I saw Helen with other people around, I should be okay to move forward and get my obligation out of the way.

Meanwhile, I flopped onto the futon couch with ice on my incompletely healed ankle. Between canoeing, driving, and frolicking in bed, I'd overexerted it back into puffy throbbing. That gave me an excuse to lie dormant for a bit and reminisce about one helluva fine night of lovemaking with someone I didn't feel sure about, nor whether that uncertainty was about him or me, which left a different sort of throbbing from that of my wounded foot.

The hiatus led to inspiration about what I could leave him in the mailbox in the morning. Keeping with the Pandora's box theme…

I levered myself upright and hobbled into the storage room. There I dug out a rosewood box about the size of a paperback, lined with purple velvet. Years ago somebody had given me a present in this box, and while I could no longer recall what the present was, I'd hung on to the box because it was lovely, and I'd thought I might re-gift it to another person someday, or else find a lovely thing to keep within it. That special objet d'art had never arrived, but now I had a recipient for the box.

I dug into another storage carton and found my old marble collection: pretty glass orbs with swirling colors inside. I was planning to put them into a big goblet on a windowsill when I reached the final layers of unpacking. That was supposed to have happened the day I got distracted and delayed by a murder—memories of which provoked a volcanic flare. Damping it down, I rummaged through the bag I kept the marbles in and extracted one swathed separately in pink tissue paper. Technically, it wasn't a marble, because it was shaped like a heart. I had bought it with allowance money when I was eleven or twelve and hanging out at malls with girlfriends. That had been a very short phase of my life but it had yielded treasures of this sort.

The heart's center was rose with sparkling gold stars. It fit inside the rosewood box. If you thought of the box as Pandora's, and knew the legend of how all the bad things of the world whooshed out when she opened it, leaving only Hope at the bottom when she managed to slam the lid shut, then my message should be clear. I expected Ned to be well read enough to understand it.

I inserted the latched box into a padded envelope to keep its finish protected in the mailbox, then left the package on the kitchen table for action in the morning. Completing this project took a weight off my mind, so that for the rest of the day and evening I was able to select which fawn scenario best suited Katy's story and make big headway into the draft.

CHAPTER 21

After last night's sack-out, this night I barely slept. Yeah, I miss having a warm man to snuggle with, but that's not what kept me awake and twitchy. My thoughts had turned back to murder, and I was tortured by the idea of our librarian playing the starring role.

How many news stories have we all read about unmasked killers whose neighbors and family shake their heads, saying, "But he's such a nice person"?

The counter to that is, How many of us go through life pretending to be nice while thinking bad thoughts, and, in some cases, doing very bad things?

I can't say I've done bad things yet, but I've spent way too long going through the motions of being a nice person while plotting to kill someone; or, in ordinary interactions, smiling while seething, pretending to listen and to care, superficially adhering to social mores, while resenting and rebelling with all my heart and soul.

If I can do it, why can't Helen? Or, if not her, whoever has taken out three men in the past two months. How many more are they planning?

Sweet, kind, gracious Helen as a killer is as incomprehensible as Luce. Or Ned. I can't wrap my head around any of those possibilities, but there's no reason why they can't be the one, any more than me, or anyone else. Real life and art have both shown, over and over again, just how possible the unthinkable is.

Helen makes sense if one considers the power of heartbreak. Because my own broken heart is suddenly, unexpectedly, starting to heal, I'm certain the killer is going for the people who have broken her heart. However many there were, whatever their relationship with her, they had in some way used their power to hurt her beyond forgiveness, taken something or someone away, devastated opportunity or hope. Or all of the above. It's more than rage. Yes, she killed them in revenge, but, more important, she needed to prevent them from hurting others. To destroy their wanton destruction. To stop the breaking of more hearts.

I can't help wondering, though: Would she have killed them if she had a Ned knocking at her door?

I know zip about Helen's personal life. Is something driving her because she's alone, or because she has loved ones to protect, or to avenge?

I can't fully walk in a killer's shoes anymore, because of Ned. Having him in my life has made me realize I've never truly given up hope for love and fulfillment. That buried hope is what has kept me from pulling the trigger on myself or anyone else during the worst of my despair.

But if I had abandoned hope? Really given up, down to my toes, down to my soul? Why, yes, I would seek and destroy those who had caused me to lose the inner light that counted. Especially if my body was also failing through disease, and there was no hope my life could have a happy ending.

By nature, if I dig down deep enough to see it, I'm heliotropic, turning toward the sun. Unlike my previous lovers, Ned has specifically offered goodness and light without wanting to take over my life or put me second to his. It's instinctive to rotate in his direction. Though he wants to know my secrets, he respects my limits. He even wants to help me protect myself rather than do the job for me. I can't ignore that.

What does Helen have to buffer herself against herself?

* * *

These thoughts transitioning into daylight led me to fretting about Detective Greene over coffee. Had my confessions pointed him in Helen's direction, or led him to someone else? Was the wrong person being investigated? Was the right one under surveillance, or being interrogated? Or had I been dismissed as a crazy writer lady, and no female was being investigated at all?

I regretted saying anything to him, at the same time wondering if I should honor his request to contact him if I came up with anyone who fit the profile I'd suggested. Ethically, I should. Morally, I shouldn't, as I could substantiate nothing.

Okay, then: By that standard, I should either keep my lip zipped or talk out my concerns with someone trustworthy and take advice. That meant Luce or Ned, neither of whom I felt comfortable voicing my suspicions to. They were too closely connected to the community to be neutral. I needed more information before I raised doubt. Asking either of them for referral to a criminal attorney would raise their curiosity, which I wasn't ready to field. What, then, could I learn on my own?

I could maybe find out who the police had interviewed, just by hanging out at the library and eavesdropping. Sooner or later gossip would resonate through those amplifying rooms. Or I could take my belated trip to the dump on the busiest day and linger, listening to the chitchat between residents who knew each other way better than I did as they trundled garbage and recyclables between their cars and receptacles. Better yet, I could nip into the post office for stamps on a slow day so the postmistress would talk too much. Unlikely that the cops would be hanging out in any of those places, so I might learn stuff without attracting their notice.

More likely, they would follow my hint about terminal illness and try to examine hospital records to learn if any of our residents had fatal diseases. Could they legally do that? It seemed to me that HIPAA privacy laws would nix the attempt, at least to the point of requiring that they have a solid case for suspicion and could produce warrants. Medical privacy laws were something I could look up, so I added the task to my to-do list.

Meanwhile, the news media had been silent for weeks about the police investigation. When open cases went quiet, it usually meant either the police were onto something and couldn't let it leak, or they were stumped and the investigation was stalled. In that case, maybe I could goose it into motion if I presented my suspicions. But really, what would be gained by that?

This was where my personal feelings interfered with the equation—which feelings, I suspected, other Allenburg residents shared. The invisible assassin was doing us all a favor. As long as we weren't among the people thwarting or hurting him/her, why should we try to stop them? How was that person hurting us by removing despicable citizens?

The question kept coming back to who was despicable. Some folks might think it was me, or some other innocent person, for whatever reason. Which cycled back to what innocent meant. Which cycled back in turn to, Was any of this my business?

Unable to resolve these questions, I yanked my attention back to my own business. Tuesday morning: What was I obliged to do for economic survival?

That answer was easy: Get back to work. Less black and white but nonetheless important was putting a message to Ned in the mailbox. I attended to that first, slipping my rose-and-gold heart into the mailbox and raising the flag for pickup. After that I played with the cats for a while, then poured a fresh coffee and settled myself at my desk.

And so another day passed. Ned tooted his horn when he picked up the mail, and I sweated through another interval wondering what his reaction would be to my gift. Luce e-mailed her reply to my boundary declaration by inviting me to lunch at one of the snootier restaurants in Orton soon after my library presentation so we could celebrate its presumed success. My editor loved my outline for *Katy Fox and the Wounded Fawn*, which goaded me into another few hours at the keyboard.

That ended when Ned arrived at my front door. I opened to him in surprise and delight although with a twinge of dismay. From his clean clothes and damp hair, I knew he'd gone home after the day's mowing, but his expression was stiff and eyes overbright. Something had changed, and I suspected what it might be.

He brandished the bottle of expensive whiskey we'd made a dent in the other night. "Thought you might like to finish this off with me. You done working for the day?"

"I am now. Just let me close up my files."

I'd already saved them but needed a moment to compose myself and reorient. Ned's tension jangled my nerves, signaling something important was brewing. I needed to give him full attention.

The kitties, meanwhile, greeted him with sniffing and mewing and twining around his ankles. He hadn't come equipped with treats for them, so I tossed him a baggy of catnip and let him distribute the wealth while I poured us stout drinks and conveyed them into the living room. There I sat in my usual place on the futon couch and he took position in the chair opposite. Then, after taking a belt from his glass, he transferred to the couch beside me and gathered me into his arms.

"I couldn't think of a way to respond to your missive today," he said. "You utterly flummoxed me."

Flummoxed! When was the last time I heard that in conversation?

"When somebody delivers their heart to me wrapped in velvet," he continued, "as Hope at the bottom of Pandora's box, well…I, uh—Jane, the only thing I can do is lay myself at your feet."

He underscored the sentiment with a long kiss that melted me. When we came up for air, he finished, "What I mean is, I've got to either learn your secret once and for all so we can move forward, or accept that we really can't put something together, and it was a nice affair while it lasted."

I disentangled and sat up. Fortified myself with my own belt of booze. "I didn't mean it as an ultimatum."

"But that's how I took it. You've got to come clean with me, babe, or I can't accept your gift."

Jeez. He'd surprised me yet again. Okay, I could cope. I'd known all along that this choice would come, and here it was. *Damn!*

I drained my glass and rose to refill it. "If you really want to know, then I need some Dutch courage."

He waited while I poured way too much booze and returned to the couch, sitting on the far end from him. He did not move to close the distance.

Then he waited with a calm I envied while I spastically gathered my thoughts and squashed my emotions so I could verbalize them.

"The secret…is…" I gulped. "Murder."

Ned's eyebrows jumped. After a long pause he said, "I hope you don't mean you're the one doing all these killings."

"Nope." I took a slug of my drink.

"That's…somewhat reassuring. But it could still mean you killed somebody, and that's why you're hiding out here. On the run, or fresh out of prison."

"No." I took another slug, then faced him. "But I came so close to killing someone I had to flush myself down the toilet and start over. That's indeed why I came here."

His face twitched, then he drained his drink before saying in a carefully neutral tone, "Please explain."

I put my glass down and felt suddenly calm. "I became overwhelmed with hatred. Still am. All I want to do is kill people to solve the world's problems. Everything else is a distraction from that."

"Okaaaayyyyy..."

He waited for me continue, his eyes intense. When I held silent, my own eyes blank on the ceiling as I thought, he rose and poured us both refills then resumed his seat at the other end of the couch.

Eventually I began again, and talked for a long time. I repeated everything I'd told Detective Greene about despair and options, added bits of my life story, and concluded with my desire to be an assassin in general and the specific plot to kill the guy down the hall in my old apartment.

"But you didn't," Ned said when I stopped. "You didn't kill him or anyone."

I shook my head. "There's not much room between the thought and the deed."

"That room is what matters. You did not commit the deed."

"Yet."

"Do you really think you would?" He leaned forward with elbows on his knees and hands between them clenched around his empty glass.

I hesitated many seconds. "Not anymore. But it was a near thing, and I can see a radical change of circumstances changing my mind."

He straightened to place his glass on the end table and said with a sardonic trace of his knightly demeanor, "Shall I relieve you of your guns?"

I released my breath at this acceptance, even though I could sense the control behind his response and knew he remained on guard. "I suppose you should," I conceded, "but I'd rather you didn't. Part of my test against myself is proving I won't use them the wrong way."

"Hm. I can see the point, but..."

He paled and blinked then brought his gaze sharply to meet mine. "How precarious are you, Jane? Do you struggle with it every day? Every hour? Or every now and then?"

I crossed my arms in a self-hug. "You don't have to worry about me shooting you, if that's what you mean."

"Not so much as worrying about you shooting yourself or someone else."

I stood and paced the room, aware of him watching me, aware of my limp, aware of how close he was between wanting to understand me and wanting to walk away.

I stopped pacing to face him. "I don't think about it much anymore. I've been deflected by, well, everything that's happened since moving here. Most of which is good. But: the killings. Jake. Len. And what's-his-name, the boy. If I'd lived here all my life, I'd be a good suspect for all three of them. Instead, they're faceless strangers to me, yet I'm pretty sure I know who did it, because in that person's place I would have done it myself."

Ned waited a few beats before asking, "Who?"

I shook my head. "I don't have an atom of evidence." *Just a look in the eye, a tremor in the hand.* "Entirely speculation. Probably fantasy."

"Who?" he repeated in a stronger voice.

"I—I just can't say yet."

Ned huffed. "Then you should talk to Detective Greene again. He asked specifically for a model."

I tilted my head side to side, then shook it. "Too easy to go foul. You've read enough history, you should know that horrors have been inflicted on innocent people because some idiot pointed a finger at them in the wrong context. Anybody can do it to me, too. I'm surprised it hasn't already. So I've got to cling to the Golden Rule, and not do to someone what I do not want done to me."

"Noble thought, but have you considered that you might be giving that person another chance to kill somebody?"

"Yes, and I don't want it to be me."

"Well, I don't, either. But you're playing with fire."

"And one way to get burned is look like I'm using my writer's imagination to push suspicion onto someone else. Or reveal myself as mentally ill."

"There you have a point." He paused to shake his head. "But…on one hand, you've confessed to murderous impulses. On the other hand, you're so morally virtuous, you don't want to implicate anyone else. You're right, that makes it hard to take you seriously."

I heaved a sigh and flopped back on the couch. Ned was already leaning back, but when I landed on the cushion he matched my sigh and leaned forward to state, "If you can't trust me enough to talk to me, Jane, then talk to a lawyer. I know someone you can call."

"Of course you do."

He glared at me under one eyebrow. "Sorry," I said hastily. "That was snippy. Unfair to take my frustration out on you."

He tilted the last droplet of whiskey into his mouth. "I asked for it, remember?"

I sighed. "I guess you did."

Silence sat between us for a few moments. I drained my own glass and marveled that I didn't feel a buzz after swiftly downing several ounces of alcohol. Then marveled that Ned was still in the room, although he was glowering into his glass.

Finally he plunked it down and said, "Is that it?"

"What?" I blinked.

"That's all of Pandora's ills? We're down to the nugget at the bottom of the box?"

"I—uh, yes, I guess so, unless you want to listen to me rant for hours about everything I loathe and all the people I want to erase from the planet."

"Let's save that for another day. I'm thinking about tomorrow night. Why don't I shuttle you to the library and back, since I'm going to your talk anyway?"

"Um, thanks, that would be great, but…will it work? I have to go earlier than you do, and you have to pick up the girls."

"They won't be a problem. In fact, they might like watching 'behind the scenes' while you set up. Famous author, and all that."

I wobbled a smile.

We sat in silence for minutes, not looking at each other, refilling and sipping our drinks. This silence lacked the electric tension of the previous one, now that we'd gotten over the worst of what had to be said.

Eventually, relaxed by the buzz I finally acquired, I confessed, "I am deeply relieved you haven't walked out."

His eyes slung around in a sharp glance. "I've been considering it. But not doing it, because the only real difference between you and a lot of other people is that you're aware of your feelings and being honest about them, trying to do something about them. Whether it's positive—changing yourself—or negative—preventing yourself—makes no difference. You've got awareness and self-control, and that rates."

Something inside me released. "Thank you," I sighed. The release was deep in my gut, however, and my mind wasn't ready to accept it. So I expressed my doubt. "Still…"

"Still, it's a normal part of human nature to want to kill the enemy. Peaceful civilization is built on control of that urge. Wars are the unleashing of it."

I thought for another interval, stuck between the rational need to accept the truth of his statement and a compulsion to be honest and a need for his acceptance. Best I could verbalize was, "I'm feeling guilty about feeling guilty for being human."

He smiled. "Better than being inflamed to violent action."

I gasped a laugh, feeling absolved. Then I sobered. "So…tit for tat. Have you ever wanted to kill someone?"

He hesitated then nodded.

"Really? Who?"

"Somebody you don't know. He's long gone. But I've also wished assholes like Jake Baldwin and Len Gustave would disappear from the planet. They never did anything to me so I wasn't motivated to take them out by any personal passion, but when somebody did, I didn't cry. Never knew the third guy, that kid, or anything about him. Same reaction as you, though, to them all: Good riddance to bad rubbish."

"Have actually you said that to anyone, or been a gentleman and kept such thoughts to yourself?"

"The latter."

"Well, I've been trying to do the same but it's burning my guts out. Why isn't that happening to you?"

He quirked a smile and winked. "How do you know it isn't? You're not the only one who can play fake."

I inhaled to retort but he spoke first, with a tone and expression that darkened fast. "I probably have a better handle on it than you because A, I'm a more live-and-let live person than you are, and B, I know what killing really means."

I waited in shocked muteness. He pressed, "Have you ever killed anything, Jane? Beyond squashing bugs?"

"No."

"Remember what I said the other day about hunting being very personal?"

"Yes."

"So, look at it this way. I have—many times—stalked, murdered, disembowled, cooked, and eaten other creatures. That's not the *idea* of killing, but the bloody, stinking *reality* of it."

I thought of Anna Rawson's marinated turkey breast in my freezer and gulped.

Leaning toward me, Ned asked, "Have you ever raised an adorable infant critter knowing you were going to kill and eat it when it grew up? That's what farmers do."

My gorge rose, and my hand rose with it to cover my mouth. My face must have changed color, too, for Ned suddenly laughed.

"Once you've gone through that, Jane, you get different ideas about life and death."

I looked away. He sat back. "Too bad it's not hunting season. You should go out with me and learn firsthand what killing is all about, see if it's something you honestly think you could do. Get some realism to go with your Katy Fox novel while you're at it."

When I remained wordless, still swallowing back nausea, he added, "But that's different from shooting people with a handgun on a dark night and walking away, or just bashing them over the head, or running them off the road and driving on. You don't have to clean up the mess. So yeah, that kind of killing is easy. Which is why some people don't have any problem doing it. Is that more your style?"

The jab replaced my boiling stomach with boiling mad. I managed to keep my voice flat and chilly. "You're making me feel like a fool."

"No, you're feeling that way all by yourself. I'm just giving you some hard facts of life—or, perhaps, anti-life—to process, hoping to convince you your only problem is an idea you've been torturing yourself with. Go ahead and hate all you want, Jane. It's as normal as love and fear and every other emotion in the book. Just find a better way to deal with it than internalizing it so bad it makes you sick. All those upbeat Katy Fox stories. Lord, I can't imagine the suppression you must go through to keep demons out of those. Try writing a crime novel or something."

I lost my breath for a moment, stunned by his matter-of-fact view of what had hamstrung me for years. Clawing back to what he actually said, I responded, "I've already done that. In fact, I'm outlining one now. But thinking about it just makes everything worse."

"Then next time we go shooting, let's make some man-targets and blow them to smithereens."

I smiled. *Smithereens.* Had I heard a human speak that word since childhood?

He was making me want to put a toe back into reality. I almost said so, but he'd gone off on a thought of his own.

"I suppose you're too old now, with all the wrong background, to join the CIA or some black-ops thing, where you can be covered for taking people out. Too bad." He returned his head to level then smiled. "Guess you're going to have to find some other way to battle those demons. In which case"—he stood and bowed deeply, sweeping an arm as if he'd just removed a plumed hat—"Sir Edward Cavendish at your service."

I squawked out something between a laugh and a sob. When he added, "Especially now that I've extracted the sword"—my sob won.

I swiped my eyes clear. "Your…service is welcome, kind sir."

He stood abruptly and pulled me to my feet into a swift, tight hug followed by a smacking kiss. "In that case, let us strategize for tomorrow. I am happy to escort milady to her assignation and make sure the Dark Knight has no chance to take a pot shot—or, should I say 'stab'—at her. Let's make it very clear to the community that you have a big, strong bodyguard. Better yet, flaunt that we are a couple and can be expected to be together at any time, even though you live alone. It's nobody's business what's actually between us behind closed doors."

"I...agree."

He shifted back to his somber persona. "In the meantime, I think you should start carrying your pistol until the situation is resolved. I can't be with you twenty-four/seven, as much as I wish to, including tonight. I believe what you've said, Jane, and trust you to not shoot yourself or me, but until you tell me—or Detective Greene, better yet—who you think is the killer, we must be prudent and assume you are a potential target."

"Yes, sir," I conceded in a little voice.

He kissed me like a hero a few more times, but I failed to respond like a lusty heroine. He didn't seem to expect it, recognizing correctly that he'd damn near drawn and quartered me with his magical sword. Finally he stepped away and grinned at me while pretend-sheathing that sword, then said, "See you tomorrow night" and swashbuckled away.

CHAPTER 22

What have I done to get so lucky?

Dear god, he has accepted me—warts and all!

I can't believe it. He's made what has ailed me for so long seem minor and human. Is that all it really is?

How different my life would have been if I'd met him years ago! But... really? I would have been living somewhere else, and unopen to what he's offering. Sometimes all the pieces have to come together at the right time and place. Maybe that's here and now, and we both had to be ready for anything to come of it.

Regardless, I still can't believe I have a hero to lean on when I'm afraid and don't know what to do. What kind of miracle is that?

Doesn't matter. Don't question it, Jane. Learn how to deal with good fortune whether you deserve it or not, and embrace it. You did that with your inheritance; do it again now.

* * *

Emotional exhaustion got me halfway through the night in hard sleep, but in the wee hours I was flung awake by images of blood and guts. Ned's descriptions about the reality of killing made me realize that my fantasies about it had always ended at pulling the trigger. Like a cartoon: point and "bang-bang," victim flops over out of the picture; or like a science fiction novel: point a ray gun and the victim bloodlessly dematerializes.

While consuming an entire pot coffee, I envisioned the three local crimes as if I'd been there myself and had to process the death scenes. Then, shuddering, I moved to my desk and wrote out violent scenes for my someday crime novel, after which I copied sections of the Katy Fox story into a new document and twisted them into gory outcomes. When done, I deleted the twisted Katy file but saved the pages of the crime story. I regretted putting myself a day behind in writing quota, but the exercise purged the foul emotions from my system and left me with a lighter heart, a clearer mind, and chunk of time before needing to prepare for the evening.

I used it to address the other dark item Ned had pressed me about: carrying my pistol. What, exactly, did that entail? Concealed, I presumed. Even if open, to carry the gun I needed some way to do so. That sent me to the storage room, where I rummaged around until I found my holsters.

The dig brought me back to my initial training, years ago. The instructor had emphasized that a gun wasn't just something you kept lying around and fired with successful outcome any old time. Acquiring guns, storing guns, transporting guns, purchasing ammunition for guns, and firing guns with anything resembling accuracy took time and effort, money and materials and knowledge. Carrying a gun openly or covertly complicated that by another factor.

Just getting used to the weight and feel of it, he'd said, and repeatedly drawing and dry-firing it, would not only improve one's marksmanship but also embed the vital reflex needed if one was ever forced to defend oneself. I'd never done this and didn't want to, which was why I'd always stowed my guns out of sight and never considered how to carry one outside the case it came in. Even when practicing with Ned, I'd kept the guns in their cases and took them out as needed, instead of using any of the holsters I'd been given years ago.

Jimmy had included three when he'd gifted me with the little revolver: one disguised as a purse, another a standard shoulder holster, and the third, a leather one mounted on a belt.

I tried on the belt holster and placed my revolver in it. The weight and bulk made me feel lopsided, reminding me of the police officers and utility workers I'd seen with their heavy equipment belts clunking at every step. Unlike them, I could cover my holster with an untucked shirt or tunic-length sweater—the latter of which I happened to be wearing, along with baggy pants with deep pockets. The gun was easily swallowed by one of those pockets, which felt more comfortable than the high, stiff belt. Even though it was a compact pistol designed for concealed carry, the gun formed a lump bumping against my thigh like the wallet/phone combo I occasionally walked around with when I didn't want to tote a purse. I could live with that, whereas the belt and the shoulder holster annoyed me so much I couldn't ignore their presence.

But for the evening presentation at the library, I put the gun in the purse holster along with my wallet. I didn't need anything more, since Ned would be driving.

Ah, Ned. Should I tell him what I was doing? Or just practice what he preached and mention it later? Did he need to be assured that I was following his advice?

I chose to solve a more girly problem: What to wear for the evening?

Professional, casual? Colorful, neutral? This plus a shower kept me occupied until Ned and the girls arrived. I half expected Ned to be dressed like one of the Three Musketeers, with plumed hat he would sweep off, or perhaps a knight in armor all set to pull the sword from the stone. Maybe even a mountaineer.

Nope. He wore dark khaki slacks and a polo shirt, and was shiny clean and scented with something spicy. The combination distracted me from gun thoughts until I picked up my purse on the way out the door and felt its weight. But I said nothing, and Ned worked to keep things lighthearted with his nieces. We united in faking it for the occasion.

The event played out as well as we could have wanted. Helen looked healthy (or was that an extra layer of expertly applied makeup?) and was gracious and bustling and organized. She didn't blink when Ned, Alicia, Nicole, and I showed up early (although she did blink upon seeing Ned holding my hand); and when attendees began arriving, she steered them to their seats by way of a refreshments table. We were set up in the library basement, which had a big square room normally used for children's activities. At a push, it would accommodate forty chairs. We prepared for twenty, based on normal community response to library programs on weekday evenings.

In the end, we needed every chair we could fit. Among the incomers, I knew Ned's Aunt Mary and Uncle Bill and other Cavendish relatives I recognized from the community dinner and the Memorial Day barbecue. Luce arrived with Bobbie and Nan; Peter sent his regrets, being at work downcountry for the week. Even Anna Rawson showed up, accompanied by her

Sasquatch-sized husband, followed shortly by Tammy with a slick-looking date. On their heels came the guy who'd installed my generator, with his wife and a teenage daughter.

I couldn't believe this many people were curious or cared about me, and felt tears tickle my eyes. They dried instantly when Detective Greene entered the room, hatless with slicked-back hair, wearing civvies. He didn't acknowledge me beyond a glance, nor did he acknowledge anyone else. But because I was facing outward while everyone else was sorting themselves out to face me, I was the first to see him. I could tell he'd been doing his job by the startled looks that most everyone in the room gave him, and their instinctive inching away of their chairs. They reminded me of Arlo Guthrie's classic song "Alice's Restaurant," the way they all moved away from him on the bench.

Helen greeted him with sugar on her lips and ice in her eyes. I caught the disparity only because I looked for her reaction at just the right instant. It confirmed my suspicions, but we both neutralized our expressions in an eyeblink. She continued cheerfully goading Ned and other males into rounding up more seating, while I stayed in place at the table where my books were stacked, smiling until my cheek muscles began to twitch. I hadn't used them so much since my first and only previous presentation, at a book-industry convention. That time I'd been under the aegis of my publisher and accompanied by famous writers. I had been introduced as the newest addition to our stable, then ignored.

Tonight I was the star, albeit on a smaller scale, less nervous about being the focus than I was about undercurrents. I'd expected to feel them bubbling, but aside from the collective reaction to Detective Greene, I could see no stress on anyone's face nor hear it in their voices. That meant either we all were accomplished actors, or my imagination had run amok and there were no undercurrents to be felt.

None of it mattered now. The audience had finally settled and their attention was facing forward. *Showtime, Jane.* I stood and smiled again, introduced myself, and commenced talking for my allotted hour.

Most non-writers were interested in where ideas came from and how a novelist got started and published, so I spoke of that then invited questions.

They came rapid-fire then petered out, and half the audience left while the rest lined up at my table. I sold and signed the whole stack of Katy Fox novels. Alicia and Nicole brought in their own copies for autographs and asked again when the next one would be coming out. I vowed to myself that they would each get their own signed copy as a holiday gift if Ned didn't beat me to it.

Even Detective Greene bought a book for someone in his family. He slid me an unreadable look as I handed back his signed copy, then he melted away through the crowd. Ned watched him go but said nothing, even as he drove us home afterward, because of the girls. After we dropped them off, he delivered me to my door at the very last vestige of June daylight.

"Come in for a nightcap?" I offered.

"Thought you'd never ask." He smiled and half-bowed then followed me inside.

As I poured us drinks, he sat at the kitchen table and asked, "So…what do you think?" then raised his glass to clink against mine.

"I think it went very well."

"That, yes, and kudos to you—but you know what I mean."

I nodded and swallowed. "Detective Greene."

"Who doesn't live in Allenburg, or anywhere near it as far as I can find out. His only possible reason for coming was to check out somebody. Or intimidate them."

"Or check us all out, and how we interact. Did you see anything odd between anybody? You know them a lot better than I do."

He shook his head then nailed me with a stare. "Who was he watching, Jane?"

I shook my head back at him, then conceded, "Who's the least likely suspect of everyone there?"

That silenced him for several moments while he stared into his glass. Abruptly he shook his head again then looked up at me. "Helen."

I kept my lips pressed together. He waited me out. When I looked away he said, "Like, the butler did it? In this case, the librarian did it?"

I held my tongue. After another silence, he said, "You've got to be kidding."

"I don't know for sure," I conceded. "As I said before, not an iota of evidence. It's all...gut feeling, from some shifty moments, glances, clues you can spin in any direction."

"God—tell Greene!"

"Since he was there, he's probably ahead of me."

"Or suspecting someone else who's innocent."

"Helen might be innocent."

"Tell me why you suspect her."

"I—I can't. I don't want to. Damn it—she's my friend!"

I shoved back my chair from standing so fast. Ned remained slouched in his chair but I could see the pose was forced to avoid reacting to me. At that moment I hated his ability to stay calm and felt a wild desire to provoke him.

But I bit it back as I had so many emotions so many times, and sat down. We regarded each other in stalemate.

"Okay..." he drawled. "I can understand that. But do you realize you're putting yourself in jeopardy?"

"Only if she suspects that I suspect her."

"Well, if all your *glances* and *shifty moments* go both ways, and you refuse to talk to the police—who you've already shared *ideas* with—then you could be in trouble, Jane. Don't mess with it."

"What do you suggest I do?" I said, almost crumbling in defeat.

"God, I don't know." He steamed through his nostrils and looked away. "Damn, I wasn't planning to stay here tonight. I've got to get up wicked early and help my brother-in-law bring in hay. Weather window is right and first cut is ready. And Jerry and his guys—he's a cousin-in-law—are doing your upper field tomorrow, too."

"Oh! Okay, but—" I bit off, *Why didn't anyone tell me?* then answered myself, Why should they? I'd signed papers giving them the right to work that land as they saw fit, on their own schedule, as long as the product remained hay. It hadn't meant anything to me at the time; indeed, I'd been grateful to leave the land in production rather than have it get overgrown from my neglect. Having the reality of it arrive unannounced in the context of our discussion jolted me further off balance.

Ned cocked his head when I stood up again. "But what?"

I sighed, again feeling the Great Cultural Divide, and shook my head. "It's not important. I was just surprised."

He smiled. "Well, now you know where the expression 'Make hay while the sun shines' comes from. It's going to be a-shining, and we're going to be a-haying. All hands on deck. But now it appears you need a bodyguard, so I have to refigure that."

"I don't need a bodyguard. What do you think my security system is for?"

"Not to mention six guns." His voice turned sharp. "Where are they all right now?"

I itemized the locations, including grabbing my purse holster and plunking it on the table in front of him. He flinched at the thump, but when the import got through, he gave his one-corner smile. I could hear him thinking, *Good girl!* but he had the grace to not say it.

Instead: "Okay, okay. Point taken. So if you'll bolt the house up tight like a good writer, not silhouette yourself in front of windows, and stay in all day tomorrow, I'll stick with my program."

"I'm okay."

He rose and gave me a light, stiff kiss. "In that case, I'll trundle off. But think seriously about calling Greene. Really. And I'll come by tomorrow when I can, and also call in if I can. Not sure where I'll have reception."

He headed for the door despite my non-reply.

Just as he put his hand on the knob, my mouth fell open and out came, "Please stay."

He backstepped at that, and looked me hard in the eye.

I looked away. "Sorry. Go ahead, do what you need to do. I don't mean to be needy. It's just…I've come to realize I truly do need you, as much as I want and like and love you, and, well, I don't know what to do about it except… please stay."

He stared, as surprised as me by the statement. Then he grinned. "By god, I really have conquered Everest!"

I smiled back, then sobered and shook my head. "Doesn't change the fact we live different lives. You really should go home and take care of your business, and I'll take care of mine. Come back as soon as you can."

"Heck with making hay while the sun shines. Better to make love while the moon shines!"

He kissed me with passion and duration. I clutched his shirt front, trying not to drag him to bed.

After a while, I pulled back enough to speak against his lips: "Will Hollis feed your animals if you don't show up, or do you have to arrange it?"

"He'll take care of it."

"So, if we retire now, we'll have a whole night's sleep behind us well before dawn."

"Yep." He didn't pause to do the math. We retired with cats to my bedroom, though they didn't join us on the bed until the mattress stopped moving.

CHAPTER 23

Happiness.

Not a word I expected to ever include in my vocabulary. But that alien internal glow, that sweet deep sleep, that awakening with enthusiasm for what the day might bring, that willingness to accept other people, that ability to flex without resentment, that sense of every day lasting more than twenty-four hours—that absence of angry burn in my gut—all are new and thrilling, and align with what I've always thought might compose the holy grail of happiness.

I'm...floating. A fragile bubble I know will burst, but today it's a lovely floating orb showing rainbow colors everywhere the light hits.

The glow comes not just from being loved. Ned hasn't spoken that word, nor have I said it to him beyond that matter-of-fact remark last night, but it's there, a calm equity between us, a balance I've only read about and never believed possible. On top of that, classic frosting on the cake: sudden success in my work: the writing itself going gracefully; the accolades I received last night; and, in my inbox this morning, a note from my editor that my proposal for the National Parks adventure series—Debbie Eagle, Park Ranger—has been accepted, ensuring years more income and growing readership.

I'm in! I've succeeded. And it came so fast, out of the blue!

Damn glad I didn't shoot myself two years ago.

Maybe I should volunteer on a suicide hotline. Would my rise from sewer to satisfaction inspire someone else to not pull the trigger or jump off the bridge? It's so hard to believe, when you're mired in despair, that anything will get better. You scoff at what role models are trying to persuade you of, because they haven't gone through your life and can't know your pain. When you're that deep into it, you can't believe you're walking a well-trodden path, just another person with a syndrome. Anyone trying to inspire you is as remote as Pluto.

But, by gum, the transition has happened to me. Suddenly I'm the poster child, proving that the teeth-grinding exercise of Carrying On can be worth the ordeal.

The hardest part, which nobody tells you about when you're in recovery, is moving on from the point of turnaround. The one-day-at-a-time program that takes you to the turnaround keeps going—on and on and on—you can never quit. So even though I'm happy now, I know I'll have to keep working to stay that way. It's a state of mind as well as a situation. You have to find it inside you to continue being happy when the situation changes, as it inevitably will.

I don't know if I can do it, having never been tested. But now that I know what happiness feels like, I'm finding the long-term prospect conceivable.

* * *

Being in a state of joy, I decided, was a great time to answer my brother's letter. I'd kept it on top of my desk pile all these weeks, feeling growing pressure to respond with growing anxiety about what to say and therefore procrastinating. I still didn't know what to say to him, but now I didn't have to pretend an upbeat tone. Jim had never understood who I was and what I was doing—which I reciprocated—so my story didn't really matter. The act of keeping in touch was what counted, which I spent an hour doing, focusing on the lighter side of leaving the city for rural Vermont.

I finished the letter before Ned's substitute picked up the mail, so I popped it into the box then returned to my desk and plunged into a writing session while my happy juice was coursing. The session was like the super-productive ones of my first week in residence, shorter but still a winner, resulting in a poignant scene about Katy finding the injured fawn that the whole book would revolve around. Scenes that came in a rush like that usually didn't need more than a few words of editing. I decided to quit while I was ahead and went outside and celebrated the season in my little pocket gardens.

The day was so perfect it inspired the poem title "What Is So Rare as a Day in June" to flute through my mind. The haying crews couldn't have a finer day. I considered going out to inspect my hayfield, watching the crews turn it from grass to fodder, but that would take time and involve interaction. I wanted to keep my floating bubble intact for a little longer, as well as keep the lowest possible profile. The world rewarded me with a breeze kissing my bare arms, the sun smiling upon my face, and plants growing so vigorously I could almost hear them. By the time Ned got here with his mower on Saturday, the grass would be halfway up my shins.

Communing with nature, safely in the confines of my dooryard, took me through the afternoon and got me wholesomely grubby. After showering, I wasn't ready to go back to desk work so took out vegetables for dinner while contemplating the chore I'd been putting off: more gun-toting practice. The best time to do that was when nobody was looking.

Having decided I didn't like the belt or shoulder holster, and the purse holster was impractical for puttering around the house, I tried on several pairs of pants with pockets. My favorite denims worked best, in terms of carrying the revolver's weight without sagging and giving clean hand access into the pocket to grab it. I drew and dry-fired at different objects around the house, scaring the cats into hiding from the unfamiliar snick and snap of the hammer, and my unfamiliar movements. Then I sorted through tops to find one that fell below and masked the bulge in my pocket. After examining myself in the full-length mirror on the closet door, I agreed with my image that I could walk around in public without anyone noticing I was carrying a firearm. Its legality made me wonder how many respectable folks passed by on a given day concealing lethal weapons. I hoped to never know.

But I had to take the exercise one more step. If I was going to tote a gun for self-protection, it had to be loaded. The thought of cooking dinner in my slouch clothes with the ability to blow my foot off stashed in my pocket gave me the willies. But…a revolver could not fire unless cocked, which had to be done manually. I was safe unless it snagged on my pants if I drew clumsily and fast. I'd eliminated most of that risk by my clothing choices. Okay, I would insert all five bullets into the cylinder and try to forget the whole thing as I prepped dinner.

Ned had said he had no idea when he'd get in from the fields so I shouldn't plan for dinner with him. I decided to make a one-pot meal that could sit, feeding me when I was hungry and him if he arrived before having his own meal. If he didn't, then I'd have leftovers for later in the week.

My creative juices hadn't fully wound down despite the distraction of gun practice, so I set my voice-activated recorder where it could hear me as

I moved between rooms, alternately chopping and tidying while I talked out my ideas.

Between my soliloquizing and the sizzling on the stove, I didn't hear any vehicles pass or pull into my driveway. So when the doorbell rang, I jumped and splattered myself while stirring the sautée. The visitor couldn't be Ned, because he always knocked with a cheerful tattoo. In fact, everyone who had visited had knocked. I didn't even know the doorbell worked.

I turned off the burner and peeked through the front window—to see Helen standing on the stoop. *Whoa.* My heart stopped a beat, then bucked.

I ducked back out of view before she noticed me, then tiptoed to the front door peephole, glancing at the wall clock as I passed. The library had just closed and Helen still wore her work clothes: a short-sleeve, square-neck linen sheath dress with neither pockets nor front opening. *Whew.* She couldn't be carrying a concealed weapon and expect to draw it. Her legs were visible from below the knee down to petite but sensible shoes, so no ankle holster. She carried no purse, presumably left in the car, the dark-blue Subaru wagon I'd seen at the library. Okay, I wouldn't be opening the door to a bullet.

I considered pretending I wasn't home since she hadn't seen me peek out, but I'd left windows open to screens with the front café curtains drawn. She would smell the food I had simmering on the stove and probably hear me moving around and nattering. So if I didn't let her in, the snub would be obvious. I could delay opening the door and call Detective Greene, or even 9-1-1 if he didn't answer, but what could I tell them? I had nothing more than ideas that made sense to me solely because I'd thought about killing people. No reason to accuse the librarian everyone in town knew and loved—who was about to prove my theories right or wrong.

Glad I was armed, I unbolted the door to my fate.

"Hi," Helen said with a twitchy smile.

"Hey, Helen. What a nice surprise. Come on in."

I figured that friendly innocence was my best defense. She appeared to accept it, and passed inside as I held open the door. She paused and looked around as if she'd never seen the place. Yet only weeks had passed since she'd visited while I was laid up with my ankle. That time she had knocked.

Up close she looked wan. Her makeup hadn't been put on as deftly as last night, though perhaps it had just worn thin after a long day and she'd not refreshed it since she was heading home.

Wanting to give her the benefit of the doubt, I offered, "I was about to sit on the back porch with a drink while dinner is cooking. Care to join me?"

"Yes, certainly—thank you."

"What can I get you?" I hoped my voice didn't sound as forced as my smile felt.

Her own smiled looked genuine, inflaming my doubts. "Do you have any white wine?"

"Sure." I gestured toward the exit onto the screened porch. "Have a seat out there and I'll get you something."

She turned in that direction but didn't leave the room, waiting for me to fulfill hostess duty and lead her there. I should have quizzed her on her wine preferences, but didn't feel up to the nicety and just poured a screw-top chardonnay from the fridge into a generous goblet. She probably wouldn't taste it if she had something on her mind. Why else would she be here? The wine would be more for something to hold in her hand than anything else.

For myself I poured a neat scotch then escorted her to the porch and gave her the chair to my left so I could reach my right side. My body blocked her view of the bulge in my pants. She genteelly sipped from the goblet, put it down on the wicker coffee table, and picked it up again. Her hand quiver wasn't obvious, but I could tell it was there.

"So, how were things at the library today?" I opened.

"Very good. I've had wonderful feedback on your talk last night. Thanks so much for doing it."

"You're welcome. I think it went great and am glad to hear the patrons think so, too."

"But what I…came to talk about…is Fiona Cobb."

That silenced me. Inside I went hollow with a subliminal hiss coming from my nerves.

"You were asking about her for the mystery you're writing?" Helen prompted.

I nodded. She continued, "I didn't want to talk about her with other patrons in earshot."

"Understood." Not really, but I hoped she would enlighten me on her own initiative rather than me having to draw her out. Then again, maybe I didn't want to know. Maybe I shouldn't know. I sure hoped Ned would call or arrive. I should've called him before letting her in. I should've called Detective Greene. I did have the presence of mind to carry my cordless phone onto the porch with us and place it on the coffee table, mentioning in passing I was expecting Ned to call so we might be interrupted. The point was to remind her we were not alone.

I remembered that my recorder was still on, and wondered if it could hear us outside, and how long its battery would last.

Helen looked at my phone long enough to calculate how fast either one of us could reach it. Her expression didn't change, and her voice was soft and calm.

"Well, it happens that I knew Fiona. In fact, once upon a time she was my best friend."

"Really!" I had to quell an unseemly excitement. *Here's the motive I've been looking for!* After privately slapping myself upside the head for being a ghoul, I zeroed in on what Helen had to say, denying the common sense warning me that things were going to change if I let her talk.

She sighed. "We grew up together. She was an angel, fun and funny and sweet, and we did everything together. And then…puberty hit."

She went quiet and looked away, her eyes unfocused.

In her pause I thought about what hormones could do to a person. Beyond my own fresh experience—dizzy, giddy, stupid—I knew that hormone-induced craziness was, for example, one of the explanations of poltergeists, attributed to teens. In general boys and girls often became different people when they crossed the chemical line between childhood and adolescence, driven by the changes in their bodies. Some for better, some for worse.

"That turned her mean," Helen continued. "There wasn't anything in her life to account for it. She just became…aggressive. And competitive and jealous, even if there was nothing to justify it. She created dramas for herself, and trouble for other people. She stopped paying attention in school, even became a truant. And…for no reason I could understand, she started acting like she hated me, as if she had to make up for all those years we'd been friends, to cancel out her goodness and replace it with badness."

I shuddered internally but kept mum. Helen still had her face angled away from me, but I saw a sparkle of moisture appear in the corner of her eye.

"Fiona enchanted my boyfriend, the only one I ever had, and seduced him away from me. Got pregnant, coerced him into marrying her. Drove him to drink until he broke down and his family moved him across the country to get away from her. By then she was pretty trashed out herself, drink and drugs. She married again, this time to a man who dragged her into poverty. But he died from his own abuses, and she got life insurance because he did have a job, and she inherited his house clear. Now her shiftless son has that house, though he rents it out to other lowlifes. I often wonder if he pushed her down those stairs and left her to die in the snow."

This last bit surprised me. I'd been chewing my tongue to not ask, *Did you kill her?* because it seemed inevitable. That someone else might be involved hadn't crossed my mind.

Whatever the truth was, she was giving me the driving force for my story.

To clarify the scenario, I asked, "Does the son have an alibi for the night she died?"

"Oh yes. He was up north ice fishing with his buddies. At least four people verified it. But that doesn't mean they were all telling the truth."

We sat silent for a moment, then I asked, "When was the last time you saw her?"

Helen emptied her goblet then placed it down again with a trembling hand. "Years ago, as far as direct contact goes. I'd occasionally see her around town." Her voice chilled. "She wasn't the type to come into a library.

"Sad," I said, for lack of anything better. My mind was churning, trying to get a measure of both women while extrapolating possibilities.

Helen straightened and put on her smiling librarian face. "It is. My heart still bleeds for her. But I thought you might want to hear about it, for your book. And that you might prefer to hear it from me, who lived it, rather than people who will just throw you dry facts. Either way, I'd rather you don't try to interview other people about her. Tragic pasts are best left buried."

"I, uh, don't really need the facts of this particular case, since I'm writing fiction, not journalism," I assured her.

Nonetheless, I wanted to know the facts, especially after she said, "The situation made me realize how easy it is to die alone and unloved."

That gave me a shiver. Her voice and face turned serious. "Take care of that nice young man you have so you don't end up in the same place."

"I'm hoping to avoid that. Do you have anyone?"

"No. My family is all gone, and I never married."

"No pets for companionship?"

She smiled again, though it twisted in wryness. "No, not since Jake Baldwin murdered my dog."

That struck me dumb. She'd held my eye as she said it, so she saw my sudden paralysis. Her expression didn't change, but I thought I saw a ghost of a gloat.

"Uh," I said after a long delay, "I'm not sure what to say. I'm sorry you had such a horrible experience, but at the same time you just dropped a twenty-pound ball on my foot. It might be better if you don't tell me the rest."

She sighed and looked away. After another long pause, she said in a meek voice, "Will you get me a refill?"

She held out her empty glass. I looked at her, suspecting a trick, but couldn't think of what she might do except escape out the back door while I was in the kitchen. Reluctantly I withdrew and poured her a very full goblet, hoping it would both relax her and open her up. On the way by, I slid my recorder out of sight line behind the toaster on the counter, and hoped anew it was listening. Its little green light still glowed.

She accepted the wine demurely. I returned to my chair, mind awhirl, and had to glance away for an instant to direct my rump into the seat and pick up my own glass. When I looked up at her again, she was pointing a two-barrel derringer pistol at me.

Oh SHIT! sliced through my mind.

"Sorry, Jane, to pay you back for your hospitality this way, and your kindly ear."

I was still thinking, *Thigh holster? Bra holster?*

While I gaped, she said, "I'm sure you understand that anything I tell you can't leave this room."

"I…hadn't planned on repeating it to anyone," I lied, my pulse almost flat-lined as I looked death in its round black eyes. "In fact, I'm intrigued, and would like to interview you for my novel so I know what facts I can use and what to avoid. But I can't think with you pointing that thing at me."

"Isn't it cute?" she said, her hands steady on the little gun.

Where did that tremor go?

"My grandfather gave it to my grandmother, and it passed down to me."

"That's nice, but would you please put it away."

She lifted a brow and looked at me askance. "I'm sorry, it's too late now. I would like to believe you would keep our conversation secret, but I'm sure you appreciate that I can't. I'm also sure you're curious, so I'm happy to tell you the rest. I think I need to. Be assured, however, that I'm going to walk out of here without your interference."

"I'm happy to let you."

"In that case—" She stood abruptly and snatched my phone off the coffee table. "We need to take care of this."

The phone was slim enough to fit it into her goblet, and she dunked it in. Then she looked at me sharply. "How many others?"

I grunted, feigning defeat while feeling heat rise within me as the old anger returned—*How fucking DARE you!*—along with awareness of the weight of the pistol against my thigh.

Dutifully I answered, "One in the kitchen, one in my office, and one on the wall you walked by." I sighed hard through both nostrils. "But Helen, why ruin my phones when you could've just cut the line outside?"

"Because I wasn't sure I'd need to, and you could see me out the window, not to mention anyone who drives by."

"Well. Still. Thanks a lot for not trusting me."

"But I do, Jane; I'm just making sure your conscience can't catch up with you faster than I can run."

I didn't dare react to that. Helen smiled grimly then settled back into her seat and kept the derringer pointed at me. Didn't matter how little it was; one bullet at this range was all she needed to shut me up.

"So," she said, "we'll take care of those other phones when we're done. What are your questions?"

I pulled my wits together. "Okay. Why are you doing this? You could have walked away and nobody the wiser."

"Because of you."

That gave me a flare. "What do I have to do with it?"

"You figured it out."

I couldn't deny that, but…"How do you know?"

"Well, I could tell by the look in your eye the other day, but also because Detective Greene showed up last night."

"I didn't tell him anything." Well, almost not. "Don't blame me for that."

"I don't. In fact, I know from that great echo chamber I work in that he could be suspecting three different people if he got onto the medical angle, and they were all present at your talk. Doesn't matter. It told me I'm out of time, so I had to switch to Plan B."

"What was Plan A?"

"To finish my list at leisure, then leave you a letter explaining it all, for your book, to arrive after I was long gone."

"You can still do that. Leave now and mail it."

She shook her head. "I want to have a final human interaction that isn't vile, and I once believed we could be friends."

"I did, too," I muttered, but she spoke over me.

"So I'm going to tell you my story, Jane. You can do with it what you wish. But I am not going to give you any chance to get heroic."

"I'm not going to," I insisted, itching to reach into my pocket. And desperately hoping Ned would not show up, whereas a moment ago I'd been hoping desperately he would. The last thing we needed was three armed people intersecting in close quarters where two of them would be surprised.

I would have to shoot Helen in the moment she was distracted by Ned's arrival in order to keep her from shooting him. Or holding both of us hostage because we were afraid to shoot her.

"So..." I continued. "Who's on your list?"

"You know about three of them."

"All right. What did Len Gustave do to you?"

She dropped her gaze for a moment then lifted it to meet mine, eyes blazing. "What didn't he do? He's been my lifelong enemy, Jane. As a youth, he poisoned my uncle's well at his father's command. Oh, he just loved helping his daddy do dirt. They slandered my own father enough that he lost his job—tried to frame him for a crime someone else committed—and we fell into poverty, living off my mother's inadequate wages. She was the woman Gustave Senior wanted, and he never stopped paying us back for losing that competition. Which of course he did because he treated women like scum. Taught his boy well there, too. Len Junior raped my cousin when she was fifteen, and she never got over it. Killed herself at twenty."

"Jesus!"

Had I been standing, I would have staggered backward. We stared until I recovered. "And the boy with the car?" I was too rattled to remember his name.

"Carrying on Len's legacy." She smiled thinly.

"What do you mean?" I asked her while asking myself, *How can I get out of this?*

"He was just like Len. Who was just like Jake, merely scum in a slicker package. Len knew how to hide behind civility and law while taking advantage of every chance to gain at other people's expense. On top of his youthful crimes, he cheated on his wife, terrified and twisted his children, was corrupt in business and politics, and never performed one honest act while in public office."

"He totally deserved to..." I couldn't say the rest, though I agreed.

Helen seemed gratified by this and leaned back into the chair cushion. Her gun stayed pointed at me.

"There are so many like him among us, believing they're untouchable. I wish I could get them all."

I suppressed a shudder, too familiar with that thought. She cast me a quick look then refocused her vision on what she saw in her mind.

"Len's weakness was ego—considering himself God's gift to women. That made it easy to entrap him. Once I figured out where he lived and learned something about his schedule, all I had to do was park and wait. The zoning commission meetings always adjourn at 8:30, so I knew when he would be coming along. A few minutes beforehand, I put up my car's hood and turned on the flashers. When I heard a car approaching, I stepped out and looked helpless. Incredible luck it snowed that night."

Jeesh—I was right! I had to work to keep the thought silent. Work harder to keep my body relaxed. By then I realized I was going to hear a full confession and didn't dare think what might happen after.

"I had only to simper to get him to look under my hood and turn his back to me. Once I'd bashed his head in and gotten home, I washed the sock and coins I'd used for the sap, then the next day took the coins to the bank and got rid of them through one of their automatic sorting machines. Took myself out to dinner with the bills I got in exchange. Then I reunited the sock with its mate and dropped the pair off at the Salvation Army in a bag of donated clothes. I went through the car wash on the way home to hose off any physical evidence. Nobody had a clue."

"Pretty slick," I said in reluctant admiration.

Helen nodded. "That left the boy, Franklin Nye. You're lucky you didn't cross his path. I wasn't sure what to do about him. Actually, it's the girl I was after, but Nye soon made it clear that he had nothing to offer society, either. His parents were decent sorts who didn't know what to do with the devil they had whelped, so they didn't do anything. He ran wild, developing a pathological ego. He was brutal, incapable of compassion, and with a gift like Len's to slip through loopholes and avoid punishment. Unlike Len and Jake, he was charming and handsome, a bad boy irresistible to bad girls. Fiona would have loved him."

Again she looked at me then away, her face seeming to melt. I said nothing this time, trying to decide whether she was sane or nuts. Feeling the weight of my pistol in my pocket.

"I learned about the boy and the girl through the library," she was saying. "Patrons have complained about them since they were children, whether directly to me or I overheard them from the other rooms. I even heard kids whispering and worrying about them. Neither Nye nor the girl ever did anything to me personally—I don't think they even knew who I am—but they hurt many good people in the community, with no apology, no consequence, no remorse. The girl was a bully, a liar, and a thief. Also stupid, which made her doubly dangerous. She let herself get knocked up by Nye to keep a hold on him. He had a job and connections, which was more than she could hope for in life."

"Sounds pathetic," I said into her pause.

Helen shook her head. "Their child would not only be a product of double bad blood, but also would be raised in an environment giving little chance it could become anything but another generation of predators and parasites. I guess she planned to use it to milk the welfare system or punish her parents or something other than a desire to bring new life into the world and raise it to be a well-loved, productive citizen. I'm sad that the car wreck didn't cause her to miscarry."

Nothing I could say to that.

"Nye had the extra trait of being an arsonist. Or so some people suspect. It wouldn't surprise me; he was capable of anything. But nobody could tie him to the several fires we had around the area, spread apart over years. Long before you got here. But all different in cause and effect, all seemingly random instead of an obvious firebug on a spree. If you could have seen him glorying in his invincibility, so cocky and contemptuous, so disrespectful to everyone he encountered, you'd have no trouble believing he would do anything he could get away with."

She waited for my reaction.

"I believe it," I stated.

Right response. She continued her story. "It was a cinch to take him out, like Len and Jake. I couldn't believe my luck when I learned, again by accident, where Nye and the girl would be that night. I had already researched where they lived, so once I knew where they were going, I knew what route they had to take. I'd seen his car and knew how to identify it at night. As with Gustave, all I had to do was position myself and wait."

Backwoods and backhoes, I wanted to say, but kept mum.

Helen's brow wrinkled. "I was worried that he might be crazy enough to play chicken and we'd crash head-on, but like all bullies he was a coward, and panicked and swerved before I was even close. The terrain did the rest. All it cost me was a little rubber squawked off my tires. I drove home by a circuitous route and was in bed at my usual time."

She paused again for my reaction. As I flailed mentally for something to say, she plucked the phone from her goblet and took a sip.

"So incredibly simple," I finally said, thinking, *K.I.S.S.*

"That's the thing. So easy, so simple, and so painless when you have nothing to lose. Jake was the simplest. I'm sure you've heard about him. He was a sadist to both people and animals. Where this affected me was back in childhood, when my beloved puppy Jingle escaped my arms and ran through the neighborhood in a frenzy of joy. Jake was passing through in his truck and hit the puppy. Jingle probably could have been saved by a fast trip to the veterinarian, but instead of stopping and getting out and apologizing and offering to help, Jake backed up and drove over the pup again and again until he was flattened paste. Right in front of me as I was screaming. Then he yelled at me to be more careful, calling me a little cunt, and drove away. There and then I vowed that someday I would make him pay."

I dropped my face into my hands. I was with her on that one.

Throughout her story, my magma had been boiling hotter and hotter. I had to fight to tamp it down, knowing that only icy calm would save me.

Helen started to lose her own icy calm. Her voice softened and cracked as she finished her tale. "My parents were afraid of him so didn't act against him despite my pleading. They tried to compensate by getting me another puppy, who I protected for all I was worth, but he died of distemper before he was a year old. We didn't know about, and couldn't afford, vaccines back then. I never got another pet even though I've wished for one every day since. But I just couldn't take the risk, endure the heartache." Her voice hardened and eyes cleared again. "Jake, meanwhile, went on to a lifetime of beating his wife and his own animals, using cruelty traps to catch furs, baiting and jacklighting deer. He lied and cheated and abused in every way he could, thinking he was smarter than everyone, while making himself more deserving of retaliation every day."

"I would have a hard time restraining myself," I admitted.

For the first time Helen's gun barrel faltered in its aim, dropping a bit as she fell into her dreadful memory. I wondered how much of a second I needed to distract her so I could pull my own weapon and turn the tables.

"It was ridiculously easy to kill him," she went on. "So many decades had passed, he'd forgotten I existed, and his crime against Jingle was lost in the blur of other animals he had brutalized. I wanted to do an eye for an eye and run him over myself, but that might leave enough evidence to catch me. I didn't want to be found out if I could avoid it, though I have no shame about doing him in. One day at the general store I heard someone say his guard dog had died. That told me I had a window of opportunity to approach his house. The weather soured soon after, and all the houses on your road were empty—except yours, I was startled to discover—which left me clear to just drive in and out. Even if you saw my car pass, you couldn't recognize me. So I caught him completely by surprise, just knocking on his door in a downpour. He could tell in the porch lights I was a woman, so he didn't feel threatened and chase me off with a shotgun."

Jeesh—I was right! I thought again. Did this make me clever or just like her?

"I made a point of looking female, wearing a skirt and a bright raincoat and a rain hat patterned with sunflowers. Last thing he expected was for me to pull a pistol from my pocket before saying hello. I used Daddy's old service revolver"—she waved the current gun, then aimed it back at me—"to avoid leaving casings. Then I simply tossed it into a garbage bag and took it to the dump with my weekly refuse. That meant I had to find a different way to get Len Gustave. I could have used this gun, but I didn't want to set a pattern, and I needed this one for me."

"You mean, you're planning to kill yourself when your spree is over?"

She shrugged. "Only if the cancer doesn't get me first."

I winced in sympathy, at the same time wishing she'd stop proving me right. Struggling to modulate my voice into a kindly tone, I asked, "What kind of cancer?"

"Pancreatic, caught too late. I don't have much time left before it takes me down."

I held her eye. "I'm really sorry, Helen. No one should have to go through that."

"Thank you, but my body isn't giving me the choice. And since the fates are cruel, and this sort of thing didn't happen to my enemies, I decided to take them out first, do some good before I got erased into nothingness."

I twisted my lips. "There are plenty of people who won't think you're doing good."

"And plenty who do. Remember how many people I see a day and how much I hear. There are a lot of folks actually thanking me without realizing it."

"Well, I would thank you to take that gun off me. I'm not going to do anything to you." That was true, I realized. I would let her go if she stopped threatening me. Law and order, or karma, would take care of the rest.

She shook her head. "I can't take the risk of believing you, much as I'd like to."

"Then why did you risk coming here? You could have never said a word and gotten away scot-free."

"Because I needed to tell someone, and I thought you might understand. In fact, I got the impression you might even carry on my work, until I realized you'd found a partner. He's about the best man around here, and I don't want to spoil that. I envy you him, Jane, and wish you well."

"So…does that mean you're not going to kill me?" I gestured at her gun.

"I don't want to hurt you, so you'll need to cooperate," Helen said.

Well, gee whiz—thanks for that. Masking my mental sneer, I said placidly, "Okay, what do you want me to do?"

"Show me those other phones. I can't have you contact anybody until I'm very far out of town."

"My promise isn't good enough?"

"Sorry, no. Now, get up." She waggled the gun.

I stood. "Which one first?"

She glanced around then jerked the gun barrel toward the kitchen. *Shit*—there were two phones thataway, but at least it was opposite direction from my computer. If she shot that up, I'd attack her with my bare hands and teeth.

I had to turn my back to precede her into the kitchen. Feeling her aim between my shoulder blades, I craved to reach into my pocket. I wished I hadn't listened to Ned and moved my other guns from where I'd first placed them. Much-shorter Helen might not have seen the one atop the refrigerator, and I'd have a better chance to surprise her as I walked by it. Where I'd repositioned all guns out of sight, I couldn't get to any of them without a dive and clamber that might spook her into shooting.

Except for the one in my pocket.

I've got the drop on you, Ned had said that day. My outrage surged; but never had I been more thankful for my lifetime of emotional suppression. I could get the drop on Helen if I held tight and chose my moment.

It came after she'd yanked the handset from my wall phone and pocketed the cord—keeping the phone alive but rendering it useless—and we turned the corner into the kitchen to get my other cordless in its cradle on the windowsill next to the table.

As we entered the room, I was able to extend my turn until I was sideways to her for the fraction of a second it took to slip my offside hand into my pocket, grab my revolver, and cock it with my thumb as I withdrew it. Before she registered the move, I had pivoted into a two-handed, leg-braced stance and thrust my gun at her face, not three feet away.

Her turn to freeze in surprise.

We held that tableau for seconds—her eyes popping, mine squinting through the gun sights—until she dropped her hand holding the derringer, threw back her head, and whinnied in laughter.

"Oh god, Jane, you're good!"

I kept my gun up in case she was trying a distraction tactic. The whole thing was pretty ludicrous, I had to agree, but no laugh came from me. My heart was fibrillating so hard I worried about fainting.

"Drop it," I ordered in the most menacing chest voice I could produce.

Her smile faded and she held my eye. My hands, bless them, held steady. But hers did not release the derringer.

"Drop it," I commanded. "Now."

Her fingers went flaccid and the gun clattered to the floor. I stepped forward like I'd seen in cop shows and kicked it away while keeping my gun pointed at her. If she made a move and I had to shoot, it would be a bloody mess at this range.

"Sit," I said, not caring where.

Now what?

To call the cops, I had to move toward the phone and look away from her to dial it, or dash into my office behind an unlockable door and hope she would run away.

Oh Ned, now would be a really good time to drop in!

Since she didn't move, I repeated "Sit" in a harsher tone. She smiled and shook her head.

"I don't think so. I'd rather leave you with this delicious dilemma. Are you going to shoot an unarmed woman in the back on her way out the door, Jane? I doubt you have it in you."

I growled, "You might be surprised."

I slitted my eyes to focus on her all the hatred I'd ever felt, which was tidal-waving from my gut through my arms and down the barrel toward her chest. What stopped me from pulling the trigger was the little voice of sanity peeping above the roar: *You'll have to clean up the blood, dispose of the body, and hide the crime for the rest of your life—or turn yourself in and seriously screw up your life, even if it's ruled self-defense.*

My finger wavered…but I didn't pull. Resisting the action grew more difficult as the seconds passed, because my arms were starting to tremble from the strain of holding them out so rigidly. Even though my gun weighed less than a pound, I hadn't developed the strength for a prolonged steady aim. Now adrenaline was coursing—or ebbing, I couldn't tell which—I knew only that a tempest was battering me inside, and I would soon run out of will to resist it.

"Then get going," I snarled. "Any funny business, you lose a kneecap."

She started inching past me, her eyes flared but cat-sly at the same time. I followed every movement through my sights. I couldn't miss killing her if she lunged at me, though if I lowered the barrel and tried for a moving leg, I would probably miss.

She didn't chance it, just affected nonchalance as she sidled beyond me to the door. For her parting remark, she pivoted to face my gun barrel.

"Do what you need to, Jane. I have no expectations of getting away with everything. My only regret is that I didn't kill Fiona—she did that to herself—nor live long enough to eliminate the other people on my list. But I got the ones who counted."

With a final twitch of her lips, she sprang out the door and slammed it behind her.

I didn't follow, remaining frozen in shooting stance until I heard her car start up. Then I dropped the revolver onto the side table and watched her drive away.

I should have run straight for the telephone and called 9-1-1. At that point, however, my legs gave out, and I barely made it to the couch.

CHAPTER 24

I was still lying there, shaking, when Ned's truck pulled in, unusually loud with my inner front door standing open. He recognized the abnormality of the door position and barged straight in.

"Jane?" He spotted me on the couch and strode across the living room, dropping to a hip on the edge of the cushion and grasping my forearms. "Jane? Are you all right?"

I nodded and groaned upright. Once we were sitting parallel, he tucked me under his arm. That clamping pressure broke my numbness and I began to sob.

"What happened?" he said softly, dropping a kiss atop my head then glancing around.

I gasped, "H—He—Hel—"

"Huh?"

"H—Hlln. The lib—libri—?"

"Helen LaCroix?" His voice shot up. "She was here?"

I nodded and shook my head in a wobble. "She came to confess. We had a…stand-off. She just left. I think. I—don't know how much time has passed."

Glancing out the window, I was surprised to see light. Couldn't see a clock from the couch.

"What you mean, stand-off?" Ned's voice sharpened.

I lifted my thumb and extended the index finger then flexed it twice in a classic "bang-bang." Then I re-aimed my finger at my pistol on the side table then Helen's on the floor.

"Jeezus! Did you shoot her?"

Before I could answer, he swiveled me in his arms to peer close. "She didn't shoot you, did she?"

"No, no, I'm okay, just—totally rattled."

"So she confessed to the killings? Have you called the cops?"

"Not yet."

"Christ! Why not?"

He sprang for the wall phone and saw it disabled. "What the hell happened here!"

I waved toward the kitchen. "It's all there, if we're lucky."

At his double blink, I directed him to where I'd concealed my recorder behind the toaster. It was still recording. When he handed it to me, I rewound to the start of the recording session, which played back me talking to myself then the doorbell ringing and all that happened after.

Ned listened intently, forearms on his thighs, hands clasped between his knees, frowning.

"Jesus Christ," he spat when the recorder paused after Helen had slammed the door. I clicked it off. He lifted his head and glared at me. "Call the cops. Now. She's got at least a half-hour lead!"

I flapped a hand, nauseated by the whole thing. It was over. I sighed and said, "It won't change the outcome. But go ahead. I've got Detective Greene's card in the other room."

He strode into my office when I thumbed in that direction. Greene apparently answered, for I heard bits of Ned's description, which stopped when Ned came out of the office with the phone still in hand and asked me, "Did you see which way she went?"

I shook my head and he retreated, voice still sharp-edged but lower-pitched. Presently he returned to me on the couch. "He'll be here as soon as possible. We're to stay put and not touch the guns or anything."

I nodded, hard pressed to remain sitting upright. My nerves were still shrieking and limbs felt like they weighed four hundred pounds from the down drag of exhaustion and grief. These let my mouth fall open and words tumble out that I shouldn't have spoken.

"If she hadn't pulled the gun, I'd've let her go and never told anyone. If she'd just spoken only of Fiona, or told me everything and promised not to do it again, we could have—"

"Don't even think it," Ned snapped. "Doesn't matter if she killed anyone. She came into your home and threatened you with a weapon. Period."

"Yeah, but—there is a but. She didn't intend to kill me. I'm sure. She just had to make a gesture, like I had to make one back, and ensure she had time to get away. We had a control dance; I don't think either one of us would have actually shot the other."

Bullshit, Jane: You'd have pulled the trigger if she'd forced it. I remembered one of my self-defense instructors saying, "Don't draw your weapon unless you're prepared to use it."

At that thought I straightened, realizing my near miss had two sides. Yeah, Helen could have killed me. She also could have tried the civilian version of suicide by cop, and rushed me so I'd kill her.

But she hadn't. "She wanted me to know, Ned. She needed someone to tell. She recognized she's done. She's as good as dead. I should have—"

"Don't take responsibility for her. There's nothing you should have done except what you did: defend yourself, and run her out. I'm proud of you. But don't make me lose that by defending her."

"I—"

Ned twisted to drill his gaze into mine. "Demons, Jane. This is all about your demons. She's done what you wish you could have. Don't say a word about that to anyone. Just keep patting yourself on the back that you didn't shoot her. Didn't shoot anyone. Didn't shoot yourself. You've triumphed. And Helen has, too, in her own sick way. Let her face her own fate. Meanwhile, you should be damn scared until they catch her in case she changes her mind and comes back for you after the shock you gave her wears off."

My own shock vaporized in a jolt of fear. I hadn't imagined an aftermath, assuming Helen would do what I expected after having been right about her in so many ways.

Ned stood to look out the window. "Let's just hope she's not running around on a final killing spree tonight."

I'd been wondering about that since she mentioned a list. Now that her timeframe had been truncated, was she going to go on a last hurrah?

Again I shook my head, then speculated aloud, "I think she came to me because she's done. She'd gotten my measure and knew I would either shut her down or waffle enough to buy her some escape time. I bet she went home after work, watered her plants, removed important papers, then packed her car for a long absence before stopping here."

"That's cold."

"Actually, it's hot. Takes a lot of emotion to decide this is the day you're going to die—literally or metaphorically. But she couldn't decide which way to do it, so she rolled the dice."

"Colder."

"She chose me because she sensed I'd be doing what she did if I had the guts and a good reason."

"Jeezus, Jane."

"Which is why I didn't drop her, and I'm not minding that the cops are taking so long to get here. I'm hoping they don't catch her at all. But if they do, I want her to eliminate as many more scumbags as she can before it's over."

He hesitated a long time, looking at me with one brow up, the other brow down, over squinty eyes and lips in a hard line.

"I can't decide which one of you is colder."

"Peas in a pod. Or maybe two cubes in an ice tray."

"Jeezus, Jane."

He shoved to his feet and started pacing. I sat hunched into myself, wondering when his steps would turn toward the door.

Instead he stopped and pivoted. "How much haven't you told me?"

"Fact-wise, all the truth."

"And what are you planning to tell the cops?"

"Not much, since they'll have the recording."

"Think carefully, since you're right on the borderline of aiding and abetting. Especially since you suspected her and didn't tell Greene. He's going to be ripping mad."

I shook my head. "All I did was stop her from threatening me, instead of shooting her to ensure it. Some people might call that good sense, or even compassion."

"We can also call it stupidity."

"Call it what you want. There's no law against stupidity, or sympathy for someone breaking the law."

He snorted, jamming his hands into his pockets.

I squiggled around on the couch, stood up, sat down, then said with all the coldness he believed in me, "Some people harm society through what they do to individuals, not just mass slaughter like war. Some people are so cruel—amoral—sociopathic, they need to be removed for the greater good."

Ned threw up his hands and resumed pacing. "That may be true on the large scale, but we're talking about here in Allenburg." He jabbed a finger downward. "You haven't been around long enough to know any of the victims, so you can't play God here."

"I'm not. I'm trying to explain what happened. Helen has lived here her whole life, and she knows them all. The ones she picked did plenty to her. They're just local versions of the too many evil people running around everywhere untouchable by the law. Either they don't break it by the letter, or they're smart enough to work around it, or they know the loopholes in the system, and they go on being evil with nothing to stop them except vigilantes."

I sat back and crossed my arms. "Helen might be selfishly indulging in revenge for something personal, but she's also stopping bad people from hurting anyone else. That may be illegal, but it's also altruistic."

Ned didn't quite spit, but the sound came out like *ptah*. Finally he said, "Okay, I'll acknowledge your good intentions, whether I agree with them or not. The illegal part is what matters. Despite what you think, the fact remains that in this country, in this time, homicide is a crime. Even if you're doing it for a personally justifiable cause. You'd be better off if you'd shot her in self-defense instead of letting her go because you sympathize. Her crimes were premeditated. So you're putting yourself in a bad position if you don't condemn her to the police and public. Your personal morality is beside the point."

I sat silent for a moment, then conceded, "You're right, but that doesn't stop me from being honest with you. Didn't you want that? Well, here it is. I'm sorry you don't like it. I didn't think you would. That's why I didn't want to tell you, or anyone. And definitely why I didn't tell anyone about Helen."

He just stared at me with a red face and iron eyes, both of us knowing I couldn't take back the words.

So I kept going. "She made her choice to kill them, but not me. I made my very not premeditated choice to not kill her. I admit it was close. I also didn't call the cops in thirty seconds because I needed to recover from the shock. I still feel sick. It's pure chance you walked in when you did. Had you been a little later, or not at all, I might have reacted 'appropriately.' But now I'll never know, because I didn't have the chance."

That silenced him for a long minute.

I took advantage of it by saying, "You lectured me before on my naivete about killing things, and how that changes your perspective. Well, answer me, this, Ned: What would you have done if I walked in and pulled a weapon on you while doing something mundane and relaxed, like cooking, after you'd trusted me to be under control? Has anything like that ever happened to you—did the deer ever shoot back? Do you know how *you* would react with a gun in your face, and if you got out of the situation alive, do you truly know how fast you'd get your shit together and do the right thing?"

He looked at me with a weird expression but kept to his point. "Sorry, Jane, but since you didn't join the a black-ops team, and you're stumbling around out here with the rest of us, you have obey the laws and do your killing with words. Otherwise way too many people will start killing each other, and too many people who don't *deserve* to will die."

We steamed at each other until I thumped against the back of the futon couch. Still expecting him to walk out, I fought the instinct to soothe away his outrage and make him like me again. No chance for that. All I could do was give him something to think about on his way out the door, hoping it would keep him up at night the same way it did me.

"Okay, let's talk about law, the foundation of which is presuming innocence. You're convinced from what I've said and this recording that Helen is guilty. I am, too. But—for all we know, her killings are a fantasy. She told me she's got a fatal cancer, but what if she was lying and it's Alzheimer's or something, and she's losing her mind? Or she's on a drug that gives her delusions? She may not have actually hurt anyone, and the real culprit is still on the loose."

"More reason to catch her, then."

"I agree. No matter what, she's done with freedom. It must have been very important to stop those people if she was willing to lose her life for it."

"She won't lose her life. There's no capital punishment in this state."

"I know. I mean life as free living, not life versus death. Hell, you can't even hang a serial torturer or terrorist who kills thousands anymore."

"Be glad, 'cause it means they can't hang little old ladies, either. Or middle-aged ones who think they're above the law."

"I'm not above the law, I'm expressing an opinion and a feeling. I believe in the law, which requires reasonable doubt before it condemns people. I wasn't sure about Helen until she pulled the pistol. Until then I tried to follow a moral law and give her benefit of the doubt. I wanted her for a friend. She wanted me for one. But her personal issues overrode that. Still, she chose to reveal herself to her friend-who-couldn't-be. I let her go for the same reason. What, did you want me to make a citizen's arrest? How was I supposed to restrain her and call the cops with a gun in my face? They'll get her in the end. Meanwhile, I didn't kill her, though from what you're saying I should have."

He turned his back to me, shoved his hands back into his pockets, rocked on his heels.

Ten, nine, eight...on zero, he would stride away.

He surprised me yet again by turning to face me, mouth open to either argue or say goodbye—but it was forestalled by arrival outside of a State Police unmarked car. My heart clunked to my feet. *Consequence time.* Bad enough in itself, but also anyone who drove by during the next while would know something was going on at Jane Brown's house.

Detective Greene was not alone this time. A carefully blank-faced woman in street clothes acknowledged us with a nod when he introduced her, but her name and title didn't stick in my mind.

Between them, they had us both repeat our stories twice, processed the evidence, listened to the recording, asked questions about who Helen might know and where she might go. All I could say to that was, "She told me she has no relatives" and "She's lived here all her life and probably knows everyone in town."

When they were done, the woman stepped outside with her phone, and Greene gave in to what had been making his face get redder the whole time.

"You shouldn't have opened the door to her, Ms. Brown. Your suspicions made it high enough risk that you should have bolted up as soon as you had them, and called us immediately."

"I didn't get what I needed to validate my suspicions until the conversation."

"You're lucky you lived through it."

"So is she," I growled back.

Ned shot me a warning glance. I clapped my mouth shut and turned away. After a stiff silence, Detective Greene shook his head with a hard sigh. "You could have saved us a lot of trouble if you'd spoken up sooner like I asked. Let us hope nobody else has to die because of it. Your choice now is whether to press charges for her threat to you in your home."

"No. I, uh, decline."

He gave me a few moments to change my mind. Ned stood stiffly silent, letting me hang or save myself.

In a firmer voice I finished, "No, why bother, because she's going to die anyway, whether by her own hand or someone else's or what's going on in her body."

Detective Greene had nothing to say to that. He ground his teeth as though he wanted to, as I could see from the flexing in his jaw. Finally he thanked me for my cooperation with a ferocious look. His parting shot was a wooden, "You'd be wise to find another place to stay until we've wrapped things up. And not talk to anyone about the situation even after we've wrapped things up, and to report any further developments that might occur before we've wrapped things up. And consider getting a lawyer."

I mumbled some sort of acceptance, then turned away as Ned followed him outside. They probably had a few man-to-man words together before the detective roared away into what finally had become sunset.

I was pulling curtains closed as Ned came back in and announced, "Time to pack up."

"What?"

He shook his head curtly. "You're not staying here or going anywhere else alone until this is over. You may have been right about Helen in general, but she blindsided you in the end, and she's still a rogue element who can surprise us again. We'll keep the police informed where you are, but other than that, you're invisible for the foreseeable future, Jane."

"No way!"

"Pack for a few nights. I'll stop by the house and feed the cats for as long as you're gone. It would be nice if you could stay at my place, but that's an obvious one if Helen decides to take a potshot at you while I'm on my route or something. Besides, no Internet. A motel in Mapleton is probably safe enough. Either that, or one of my relatives can put you up."

That command sent me over the edge. It made precautionary sense, but it also denied the validity of my judgment. Ned was already darting spastically around the room, looking for what to gather, planning what to do.

I set myself into a stone and declared, "No."

He froze, disbelieving.

"No," I repeated in a harsher tone. Then softened. "I'm sorry. I can't do it. You're right but you're also wrong. I'm not leaving."

"Goddamn it, Jane!"

"No." I stood, fists clenched, body shaking. "Yeah, I admit. My life was threatened at gunpoint today, and the culprit is AWOL with unclear purpose and unguessable plan. I should be grateful to what you're offering. But—"

He opened his mouth but I overrode him. "Listen. Just stop and listen, Ned. You've got to consider this. She said something we all heard but didn't pay attention to: 'I envy you him, Jane, and wish you well.' That means she's not going to hurt us. She thought she might pass her mission to me until she realized you and I had hooked up. That tells me she wouldn't have gone so far if she'd had somebody of her own to love, something worth losing. But she had no one—no husband or lover, no children or relatives, no real friends, no pets, no hope. It made her value everything I have and not want to take it from me; that would be counter to her plan, which was to destroy bad things for the sake of good. She might still hurt somebody else that suits her purpose, but most likely she's given up, maybe even killed herself by now. All we can do is make the rest of *our* lives worthwhile. That's its own sort of justice. And it might be the only thing she's accomplished."

He turned away and ruminated. Then he turned back, face somber. "The only way to guarantee we have the rest of our lives to make worthwhile is to stash you somewhere safe until we know what's become of her."

I shook my head. "Not going"—even though I understood he wouldn't be so keen on protecting me if he didn't want to live our worthwhile lives together. My heart crackled at the thought then shattered, because I knew if he couldn't accept my choice, we had no future together.

That choice shifted something deep inside me. Although I felt a familiar tide rising, hot and yearning for explosion, it lacked the livid red edge of rage. I couldn't call it magma anymore. It was more like a geyser, ready to gush hot watery things—grief, regret, and, unexpectedly, love—and I wasn't sure I could hold it in.

I managed by clamping my mouth shut and blinking rapidly. Ned blinked back at me, then turned away, then turned back again, himself caught in a similar trap he couldn't voice.

Finally he said, "Goddamn it, Jane."

I nodded, then jutted my chin toward the door. "Go if you must."

"Goddamn it, Jane!"

He too had his fists clenched and was shaking, as he looked back and forth between the door and me.

There was one more thing I could say. I delivered it a soft volume but hard tone: "Ned."

He flexed his fists, eyes blazing. "What."

"I've got to tell you."

He rolled his eyes. "Please don't say there's a whole nother side of this to come out."

"No. Something completely different."

He waited, rigid. I inhaled, holding his gaze, then released my gush, hoping it would come out coherently.

"I—just want you to know—how much I appreciate you. How much you've helped. How much I value your support. How much I love you."

He tipped his head back and laughed rawly at the ceiling. “It’s about damn time.”

I half laughed. “No, I’ve appreciated it all along. Truly. Thank you. I just—didn’t know how to…”

“You’re fucking welcome.”

He strode to the door, turned around, came back. Then sneered, “Dare I think this means you’ve purged your demons?”

“I don’t know. Maybe. I feel different now.”

“Different…better or worse?”

“Better.”

“So it took Helen to make you see?”

“No. Yes. It took both of you. I’m not sure what I’m ‘seeing’ yet, but something has changed. I can’t guess where anything will go from here.”

“Neither can I.”

Tears stung my eyes but I held them in. “Well, finally, we can agree on something.”

He frowned. “That’s as far as I can go at this point.”

A tear leaked. I refused to wipe it away. He noticed, though, but like me made no move. We were at impasse, with everything/nothing to be gained/lost.

CHAPTER 25

By the time we stopped staring at each other, the interior of the house had fallen dark enough to make us shadows. At last Ned said, "Greene told me that if I couldn't get you to leave, then I should park here and protect you."

He moved past me with such determination I had to step aside. Pausing to regard the wall phone, he grunted then said to himself, "I think there's a spare one of these at the house" and continued into the kitchen. I retreated to the futon couch, unsure what to do or say; unable, really, to think at all.

From his clanking and banging, I gathered he was scraping my incomplete dinner into containers, shoving them into the refrigerator, then yanking stuff out of the cabinets and drawers. Since the only light remaining in the room was red glow from the stove clock and battery indicator on my cordless phone, plus a wash from the refrigerator as he opened and closed, he fumbled as much as he accomplished, not knowing where everything was stashed. I didn't suggest turning on a light because that would make us targets for anyone outside.

Eventually he stomped back to me holding out a plate. Upon it was a peanut butter and jelly sandwich. "Eat," he ordered.

I obeyed, motivated by the glass of sharp-smelling liquor he followed with. He had poured one for himself, as well as provided his own sandwich. He thumped into the armchair and we ate and drank in sizzling silence, not looking at each other.

My mind untangled enough to notice no cats in evidence. Also to notice my hands were still shaking. A glop of jelly fell onto my chest, and the amber liquid sloshed in my glass.

But I got through the food and began to cohere. Arms and legs seemed to belong to me again. The prospect of walking entered the realm of possibility.

Ned, too, had regained some ease. He rose and snatched my plate, put the dishes in the sink. Then returned and again confronted me.

"Bed."

I shook my head. "Shower."

He hesitated then nodded, since the window in the bathroom was positioned so that an outside shooter could not see me and aim. I added, "I need to wash this nightmare off, and be alone for a while."

"Me too."

When he added no more, I wobbled off to the bath and steamed myself back into reality. Each time I tried to think of Helen, instinct pulled thoughts away. My body was protecting me from freaking out as much as Ned was protecting me from further harm from outside. I focused on hot water pummeling my skin, muscles unknotting, soap releasing scent, hair changing from seaweed to soft streams, letting my mind stay vacant and numb.

Normally I would have emerged in just a towel; with the windows closed, the house was so warm I didn't need even that. But tonight I pulled a terry robe off the door hook and wrapped up before switching off the light and stepping out.

Ned and I faced each other's shapes until I heard little muffled smacking noises in the kitchen. Recognizing the sound, I stepped around the corner to confirm. The red glow revealed three lumps on the floor intent on their dinner.

I turned back to Ned, who had taken over the futon couch. "As soon as you hit the shower," he said, "they came out from three directions and started yowling."

That's when I knew everything was going to be all right. At least for the night. Cats might not serve as warning devices like dogs, but they knew when something was wrong, inside or outside the house.

I declined to say this, not wanting to open the "You should get a dog" topic again. If Ned was holding that thought, he kept it to himself.

Despite relief, I could not bring myself to cross the room to him. He didn't move, either. So I just said, "Thank you" and "Good night" and retreated into my bedroom to pull the covers over my head. But I left the door ajar as invitation to man or animal. Meanwhile, the man took a shower.

I had expected to lie awake thrashing but was out cold in seconds. Thank you, body.

I awoke after dreamless sleep into predawn gloom, enough to vaguely see across the room with the curtains drawn. Just a few weeks from summer solstice, dawn was as early as it was going to get. Thus I saw Twinkie curled at the foot of the bed. The house was silent. I didn't want to wake up and face facts, but once I came conscious, I couldn't slide back into oblivion. Besides, my bladder was full and I needed to deal with that.

Because of the house's vintage, the bedroom was not en suite with a bathroom. I had to get up and walk down a hall. Problem with that was, I knew Ned was armed—if he hadn't been carrying his own weapon when he arrived, then he knew where mine were and would have grabbed one and be keeping it near in case of a midnight disturbance—so if I skulked around trying to avoid waking him, he might in fact jerk alert at the slightest sound and go off half-cocked in defense.

Couldn't risk that, as unlikely as I thought it was.

So I threw on the hallway light and walked naked to the bathroom. Flushed the toilet, a gushing roar he couldn't miss. Returned to my room, cut the light, and left my door open. Nothing stirred in the living room dark.

I sensed him awake, though, listening for my next step, while I stretched out to consider it. No chance I'd return to sleep for what was left of the night. Stupid to lie there berating myself with doubts, fears, worries, and regrets. That was a normal waking condition anyway, which I'd taught myself to manage through my recovery journal. Which I wrote in every morning over coffee, save for when a certain man was around.

Said man was surely wondering what he should do next, too.

Said man might not be in my home ever again after this morning. I had to walk past him to retrieve my journal from the kitchen. Unless…

I clicked on the little bedside lamp and dug out pad and pen from the side-table drawer, where my confiscated revolver normally rested. Even with the lamp on, I was below window line if I propped up on an elbow to write, so nobody could shoot at me.

There: a perfect compromise. I rustled into a comfortable position. Twinkie tucked into the crook behind my knees. .Barely had I headed the page with the date when my bedroom door creaked wider open.

"Jane?"

I looked up at him. This time I could see his face. It seemed more sad than angry, his eyes glittering with something different and a little scary. Most compelling, he wasn't wearing any clothes.

I snapped off the lamp, placed writing tools on the stand, and flung the top sheet aside. Twinkie skedaddled as Ned reached forward into my arms. We rolled our lengths together across the bed, kissing hard, not talking. This conversation was to be in body language. We both needed to know what still lay under last night's words, what truth remained uncovered. To be clear in our hearts and consciences which way to go once full morning brought the next new reality into play.

Answers came fast. Each kiss and stroke declared yes, yes, and yes. I melted into knowing we loved each other as much as we lusted; loved more than lusted, since we could satisfy our bodies anywhere but would never have the same kind of frankness and trust with anyone else. Somehow we would work out the rough stuff, if only so we could stay together. Somehow.

Awakening within his arms sure made it easier to accept the return to consciousness. Even better, he had wakened first and was waiting for me to rouse before shifting around. I thanked him with a kiss, then we both wriggled into more comfortable position. Movement was made more difficult by two cats pinning down the sheets from diagonally opposite corners.

"Since it appears we survived the night," Ned opened, "I must do one of two things very soon."

I assumed he meant using the bathroom as one of them, but before I could query the other, he explained. "Either call in to work and cancel, which has consequences I can live with but would rather avoid, or call Detective Greene and inform him where I will be today. If running the mail route, I've got"—he peered past me to the beside clock—"exactly 27 minutes to get to the post office."

"Well..." I sat up and stretched. "I understand the need to make paycheck hay whether the sun is shining or not, being two days behind quota and doubtful I'll get anything done today besides waiting for news. So I vote you go to work."

"If you'll make coffee and then do your vault thing for the rest of the day, I'll take my chances on the road. You've convinced me that Helen isn't going to come for either of us, but I still consider it an outside chance."

"Then you hit the phone. I'll put together coffee and toast."

"I need another shower, too," he said, sniffing under his arm.

We rose and went in opposite directions. The summer morning and closed windows made the house warm enough to caper around naked. Nevertheless, I donned my terry bathrobe and took out an old frayed flannel one for him. I'd acquired the man-sized robe for a former boyfriend—couldn't remember just then which one—and kept it in case another man ever entered my life. Well, one now had, but we'd not graduated to the point he kept spare clothes in my closet. He would have to go to work in yesterday's garb again. Not a big deal for someone who sat in a vehicle all day, but it was something to start thinking about.

By the time I'd microwaved leftover coffee and fed the mewing cats, Ned was in the office making somber noises into the telephone. "I see…yes, I'll tell her…no, she'll be here all day, I'll be back by midafternoon…okay, thank you."

He returned the phone to the cradle so softly I didn't hear it click into place.

I waited in the doorframe for him to turn around. He wore a hangdog look as he approached me. "They found her."

I stiffened. "Dead or alive?"

He dropped his chin and shook his head. "Dead. In one of the marble quarries. She threw herself in and weighted her pockets with rocks."

Had I been holding a coffee mug, my suddenly limp fingers would have dropped it. "Rocks."

We stood in silence until he embraced me. I felt queerly numb from surprise, not surprise, anticlimax, relief, regret.

Then I leaned away and said, "That's how Virginia Woolf died. The writer. Rocks in her pockets. She walked into a lake."

Ned looked up at the ceiling and exhaled a sardonic laugh. "Trust a librarian to make a literary exit."

"When did they find her?"

"Dunno. Sometime in the night. Greene said watch the news, it's breaking this morning."

I stepped past him to boot up my computer and went straight to the *Marble Valley Tribune*'s website. The story was featured top and center:

Woman Drowns Self in Quarry!

An elderly woman was found dead last night in the Westfold Quarry outside Mapleton. Identification is being withheld pending notification of next of kin.

The death is being considered suicide. A car registered to the deceased was found at the base of the pedestrian walkway around the quarry, its door open so the dome light was on but nobody around. A local man out walking his dog before bed thought this looked wrong and approached the vehicle, finding an envelope on the driver's seat addressed "To Whom It May Concern." Inside was a single sentence—"Please tell Dr. [name withheld] that I've decided to opt out of treatment."

The citizen promptly called the police.

Within two hours they found the woman's body in the quarry. Long out of service, the quarry has filled with water up to fifty feet deep. There are ledges around the perimeter at different depths, and the body had landed on one of them and was easily retrieved. The woman was wearing a coat with multiple pockets filled with rocks.

I sat back and exhaled obscenities with tears trickling down my cheeks. Ned, standing behind me, placed a hand on my shoulder. We held that tableau, chests concave, until he reached past me to the phone, punched numbers, asked for his boss, and announced, "I'll be in a little late today."

Then he turned to me. "Maybe call Luce, if you need the company…"

I swiveled my chair. "She went to Connecticut yesterday to spend the weekend with Pete. Besides, once she finds out, she'll be over here in a flash and wanting to know everything. I'd rather wait alone, and I hope you get back before Greene follows up. If he does. I don't know why he would have to, I've already told him everything."

"He's got to untangle a suicide from a triple murder, needs to pick your brain until he's sure he's got every little bit. We still don't know if she killed anyone else, or mailed you that target list, stuff like that."

I nodded grim understanding, and he headed for the shower.

It seemed too hard to move from my chair, so I kept rotating between news sites for more information. They all repeated the same story, promising updates later in the day, but some refreshed my memory about quarries in the region. They were relics of the marble industry that had built the area then waned to nearly nothing, like the steel industry and others around the country—but I had yet to see a quarry myself. That was on my get-around-to-it list, if I ever settled and sought recreation time. Many historic sites and natural wonders were also on that list. All of which seemed trivial right now.

Ned caught up to me in the kitchen, all fresh inside his stale clothes. He tossed down cold coffee, didn't wait for toast, kissed me, and put on his shoes. "Gonna set a land speed record on the route today. See you soon. And Jane—" He waited until I looked him in the eye. "I'm sorry for your loss. All of our loss. This was a really bad thing to happen. But we'll get through."

He punctuated that with a final peck on my lips and departed.

I sat at the kitchen table listening to him drive away. How different from that dreary first morning when I listened to him drive in. Not even two full months ago. A lifetime of change in less than a season. Yet despite it all, I felt unchanged within.

That was because rage still lived within me. Not magma any longer, but its remnant cooled into stone. I had to appreciate that I likely wouldn't have met Ned without Helen's murderous handiwork, but the fact she'd been driven to it showed how hopeless the world remained.

I pulled out my journal and wrote.

How, oh how, do we stop it from happening? Helen's story is just a drop in the historical bucket. Humanity keeps producing people who are cruel, greedy, immoral, hurting others to the point they must act in self-defense or revenge. There's a nebulous distinction between those who are born unredeemable and those who are set on the wrong path for whatever reason and potentially can be saved. How can we distinguish between them early enough to do something about it? What can be done to prevent them in the first place, or redirect them once identified? Why, over millennia, has nobody figured it out?

Any society that has tried to control human breeding—for quantity or quality—has ultimately been condemned. It seems universal that punishing or eliminating problem people after the fact is the lesser evil. But unless we become proactive about them, we'll always have to be reactive to them.

I don't think it's fair that humans control all other species: managing their numbers through hunting and habitat manipulation, managing their genes by breeding out undesirable traits. Why can't we do unto ourselves as we do unto others?

There has to be some morally acceptable means to cull the human herd. Nature's way is too broad: a weather cataclysm, a plague, a societal crisis leading to war—all of these are unselective. We need to isolate and manage individuals who intentionally do harm. No system of identification or punishment has yet made a difference.

Is there any new idea left to be discovered, which might, maybe, ever work? Or must we resign ourselves to the fact the problem is unsolvable?

* * *

I put down my pen, sat back, and shifted thinking from global back to local. Helen had done a mix of my options five and one: knocking off evildoers who instigated pain and destruction, not just for her own satisfaction but also other people's benefit; then she abandoned hope and killed herself. Ned had pointed out that the national and international version of option five—working in dark ops to assassinate key players who operated on the mass scale—was unviable for anyone like me or Helen because of age, background, and skills.

I had tried option six: withdrawal and immersion. That hadn't worked, either, since no matter what I did, reality intruded.

That left my options two, three, and four: continue ignoring reality and fumble through the days pretending there would always be a better tomorrow and other people would solve all the problems; or become a superwoman, diving into politics and devoting one's life to preventing escalation and injustice; or surrender to what could not be changed and savor each day as if it were the last regardless of consequence, indulging in every pleasure, because life was too short even without pending doom, and it's the only life any of us would ever have.

Maybe…those could be combined into a new option seven: doing whatever positive thing one could, however small, one person at a time to another person, and hope it would catalyze a domino chain and spread the positive thing around, gaining mass and momentum.

I had already started in that direction with Katy Fox. Could I take it further?

Or even break out with an adult novel? I'd once had an idea about how to manage killing, in that science fiction story I'd outlined then stuffed in the drawer. I'd stopped reading science and speculative fiction altogether because they offered so many ideas and hopes proven impossible by reality.

Then again, some of that fiction had proven prescient over decades. Perhaps more would.

Perhaps I should stop reading crime novels and history and revisit science fiction and fantasy. My storage boxes still held some classics; perhaps I should dig them out and restock my shelves, put the crime novels back into the boxes. I wouldn't be visiting any libraries for a while, but I owned enough visionary fiction to reread for months.

What if I went looking for ideas, instead of waiting for them to come to me?

What if I imbued some into my stories and let the next generation ruminate on them and explore them?

What if I started with Ned's suggestion, and went hunting with him, and learned some of the gory truth about killing? I'd already touched on death involving animals in the Katy Fox books, but I'd always skirted the ugly parts. My editorial directive required that, but the series was successful now and perhaps I could slide some words and sentences under the radar. And now, with Debbie Eagle, well, she would surely encounter situations where reality and idealism conflicted. Being an older heroine, she would give me more leeway to touch upon them directly.

And what if, instead of breaking out later as a crime novelist, I wowed the world with a science fiction novel instead?

A line from George Bernard Shaw I'd read twenty years ago leaped out of memory: "You see things; and you say 'Why?' But I dream things that never were; and I say 'Why not?'"

The line had resonated with me back then but I'd ignored it. Now it filled me with a new energy—enough to reopen my journal, write it down, then return to my desk. I tugged open drawers until I found my folder of notes for story concepts. I placed the science fiction one on the desk, then emptied every file pertaining to murder onto the floor, and deleted all the electronic versions and associated files.

I took the papers outside to the fire pit in the backyard. It was overgrown so I hacked at it for a while, wanting to enjoy the mild air and burgeoning growth and morning birdsong but actually resenting it all. Life had no business going on when one was mourning.

Once I had a mound of brush and papers, I returned inside for a fire starter. Finally found one in the back of a kitchen drawer. In no time I had a nice blaze going in the fire pit.

Not sure how long I sat in a tattered folding chair feeding papers into the flames. Cars passed now and then, leaves and grass stirred in the breeze. I hoped the smoke wouldn't inspire someone to call the fire department. Ned noticed the plume, however, when he finally went by with the mail. I heard his Jeep pull in and its door thunk shut. Moments later, he came around the back of the house.

I acknowledged him with a nod but couldn't find the words to explain myself. He waited then jutted his chin at the fire. "Guess you're not going to write about it, eh?"

I shook my head. Then the right word bubbled to the surface: "Too much metanoia."

He cocked his head. After a pause I said with a sardonic smile, "Gotcha."

He grinned. I quoted from the dictionary: "'A profound transformation in one's outlook.'"

"Ah."

We watched the fire for a few moments before Ned said, "You all right?"

"Yes."

"I've still got that mop and bucket if you expect a head explosion."

"It's already passed."

"Okay…then I'll be back in a few hours. Just don't burn the house down."

He smiled when I looked up at him. I smiled back.

Then I resumed scowling at the flames, waiting to feel something I could identify and grab from the emotions swirling through like phantoms and bad dreams. But nothing stuck. I reached inside for the familiar magma in my belly, to keep rage alive; as with last night, though, it failed to glow red-hot and bubbling. Even this morning's glacial stone was gone. What, had my hatreds died with Helen?

That thought ran uncomfortably close to a religious saying I'd grown up with, and rejected—*Christ died for your sins*—but I began to sense what it might mean, now that other people's deaths had released me from my toxic prison.

I touched my chest in wonderment. This was what it must mean to pass through a crucible. Maybe I couldn't feel what I should be feeling because I had been scorched clean and was starting anew.

As the fire shriveled at my feet, I promised Helen silently that I would not travel her road. I thanked her for making that freedom possible.

Still, I wondered how many others like us were out there. Was it only good health and emotional support that stopped us from giving in to our killer hearts?

I considered Luce and Ned. *Yes, it's that simple.*

My friend and lover determined to live in the light and drag me along, kicking and screaming if necessary. They had proven it so many times, sticking with me despite the multiple opportunities and good reasons to wash their hands of me. I'd never been able to do the same for anyone and felt lucky and blessed that I'd been given the chance to try. People not so lucky traveled a different road usually to a darker end.

My road to redemption had started with Katy Fox. Now I had better reason and experience to imbue her stories with more than a happy ending. Especially now that I had Debbie Eagle, Park Ranger, to expand my scope.

The new stories would give my readers their chaste adventures, but also something to extra think about: life and death, and meaning of same. Everything would still come out right in the end, but Katy and Debbie were going to have to work harder and suffer more for it, so when life kicked my young readers in the teeth, and when their spirits were at their lowest, and their identities were mush, and they needed something to cling to and a model to follow, they would find their answers in my pages.

The other pages, about death and darkness and defeat, were wafting in ashes into the sky.

About the Author

Carolyn Haley lives and breathes books as a writer, editor, reviewer, and contest judge. Along with novels, she writes a mix of articles and commercial copy for magazines, corporations, and blogs. She also helps other authors with fiction and nonfiction projects through her editorial services business, DocuMania.

She lives in rural Vermont and when not writing enjoys outdoor pursuits—gardening, paddling, walking, riding, birdwatching—along with autosports and aviation.

Learn more at Carolyn's website:

https://carolynhaley.wordpress.com/

www.ingramcontent.com/pod-product-compliance
Lightning Source LLC
LaVergne TN
LVHW091030080826
845145LV00002B/436